HIGH ACCLAIM FOR

the forest house

"*The Forest House*, prelude to Bradley's masterpiece *The Mists of Avalon*, is a fine historical novel in its own right. . . . A vivid picture of an era and those who gave it life. . . . A magical evocation of a lost age."   —*Starlog*

"The setting evokes a fascinating time of change. . . . The mythic elements grow to hint satisfactorily at the Arthurian wonder to come. . . . The stuff of legend."   —*Locus*

"An historical novel with a mythic undertone. . . distinctive enough to achieve success in its own right [and] likely to appeal to a wide audience."   —*Science Fiction Chronicle*

"A seamless weave of history and myth."   —*Library Journal*

"The sure touch of one at ease in sketching out mystic travels."   —*Kirkus Reviews*

Marion Zimmer Bradley is the bestselling author of the classic *The Mists of Avalon*, *The Firebrand*, and the popular *Darkover* series. She lives in Berkeley, California.

MARION ZIMMER BRADLEY

the forest house

A ROC BOOK

ROC
Published by the Penguin Group
Penguin Books USA Inc., 375 Hudson Street, New York, New York 10014, U.S.A.
Penguin Books Ltd, 27 Wrights Lane, London W8 5TZ, England
Penguin Books Australia Ltd, Ringwood, Victoria, Australia
Penguin Books Canada Ltd, 10 Alcorn Avenue, Toronto, Ontario, Canada M4V 3B2
Penguin Books (N.Z.) Ltd, 182–190 Wairau Road, Auckland 10, New Zealand

Penguin Books Ltd, Registered Offices: Harmondsworth, Middlesex, England

Published by Roc, an imprint of Dutton Signet,
a division of Penguin Books USA Inc.
First published in the United States by Viking.

First Roc Printing, April, 1995
20 19 18 17 16 15 14 13 12 11

The Library of Congress has cataloged the Viking edition as follows:
Bradley, Marion Zimmer.
    The forest house / Marion Zimmer Bradley.
        p.   cm.
    ISBN 0-670-84454-3 (hc.)
    ISBN 0-451-45424-3 (pbk.)
    1. Great Britain—History—Roman period, 55 B.C.–449 A.D.—Fiction.
2. Man-woman relationships—Great Britain—Fiction.   3. Druids and
Druidism—Fiction.   I. Title.
PS3552.R228F67   1994
813'.54—dc20   93–33686

Printed in the United States of America

BOOKS ARE AVAILABLE AT QUANTITY DISCOUNTS WHEN USED TO PROMOTE PRODUCTS
OR SERVICES. FOR INFORMATION PLEASE WRITE TO PREMIUM MARKETING DIVISION,
PENGUIN BOOKS USA INC., 375 HUDSON STREET, NEW YORK, NEW YORK 10014.

For my mother, Evelyn Conklin Zimmer, who
has borne with my working on the book for
most of my adult life

To Diana Paxson, my sister and friend, who anchored
this book firmly in time and space and added Tacitus
to the cast of characters

AUTHOR'S NOTE

Those who are familiar with Bellini's opera *Norma* will recognize the origins of this story. In homage to Bellini, the hymns in Chapters Five and Twenty-two are adapted from the libretto of Act I Scene i, and those in Chapter Thirty from Act II Scene ii. The hymns to the moon in Chapters Seventeen and Twenty-four are taken from the *Carmina Gadelica*, a collection of traditional Highland prayers collected in the late nineteenth century by the Reverend Alexander Carmichael.

PEOPLE IN THE STORY

* = historical figure
( ) = dead before story begins

ROMANS

Gaius Macellius Severus Siluricus (called Gaius, native name, Gawen), a
    young officer, born of a British mother

Gaius Macellius Severus, senior (called Macellius), father of Gaius,
    Prefectus Castrorum of the II Adiutrix Legion at Deva, Equestrian rank

(Moruadh, Royal Woman of the Silures, mother of Gaius)

    Manlius, physician at Deva

    Capellus, Macellius's orderly

    Philo, Gaius's Greek slave

    Valerius, secretary to Macellius

    Valeria (later called Senara), half-Briton niece of Valerius

Martius Julius Licinius, Procurator (financial officer) of Britannia

Julia Licinia, his daughter

    Charis, her Greek maid

    Lydia, nurse to her children

Licinius Corax, the Procurator's cousin in Rome

Marcellus Clodius Malleus, senator, Gaius's patron

Lucius Domitius Brutus, Commander of the XX Valeria Victrix Legion
    after its move to Deva

Father Petros, a Christian hermit

    Flavius Macro ⎫
    Longus   ⎬ two legionaries who try to raid the Forest House

* (Gaius Julius Caesar, "the deified Julius", who began the conquest of
    Britannia)

* (Suetonius Paulinus, Governor of Britain during Boudicca's rebellion)

* (Vespasian, Emperor AD 69–79)

* (Quintus Petilius Cerealis, Governor of Britain AD 71–4)

* (Sextus Julius Frontinus, Governor of Britain AD 74–7)

* Gnaeus Julius Agricola, Governor of Britain AD 78–84

* Gaius Cornelius Tacitus, his son-in-law and aide, a historian

* Sallustius Lucullus, Governor of Britain after Agricola

* Titus Flavius Vespasianus, Emperor Titus AD 79–81

* Titus Flavius Domitianus, Emperor Domitian AD 81–96

* Herennius Senecio, a senator

* Flavius Clemens, a cousin of Domitian

BRITONS
Bendeigid, a Druid living near Vernemeton
Rheis, daughter of Ardanos and wife of Bendeigid
   Mairi, their eldest daughter, wife of Rhodri
   Vran, her young son
Eilan, their middle daughter
   Senara, their youngest daughter
Gawen, Eilan's son by Gaius
Cynric, foster son of Bendeigid
Ardanos, Arch-Druid of Britannia
Dieda, his younger daughter
Clotinus Albus (Caradac), a Romanized Briton
   Gwenna, his daughter
Red Rian, an Irish raider
Hadron, one of the Ravens, father of Valeria (later called Senara)
* (Boudicca, "The Killer Queen", queen of the Iceni, leader of the revolt in AD61)
* (Caractacus, a leader of the rebellion)
* (Cartimandua, queen of the Brigantes who betrayed Caractacus to Rome)
* Calgacus, Caledonian chieftain who led the tribes at Mons Graupius

PEOPLE OF THE FOREST HOUSE
Lhiannon, Priestess of the Oracle, High Priestess of Vernemeton (the Forest House)
   Huw, her bodyguard
   (Helve, High Priestess before Lhiannon)
Caillean, a senior priestess assisting Lhiannon
   Latis, the herb mistress
   Celimon, instructor in ritual
Eilidh ⎱ Eilan's friends
Miellyn ⎰
   Tanais ⎱ entered Vernemeton after Eilan became High Priestess
   Rhian ⎰
   Annis, an old deaf woman who serves Eilan during her pregnancy
   Lia, nurse to Eilan's son Gawen

DEITIES
Tanarus, British thunder god, equated with Jupiter
The Horned (or Antlered) One, archetypal god of beasts and woodlands with many local variations
Don, mythic mother of the gods, and by extension, the British people
Cathubodva, Lady of Ravens, a war goddess similar to the Morrigan
Arianhrod, Lady of the Silver Wheel, maiden goddess associated with magic, the sea, and the moon

Ceres, Roman goddess of grain, agriculture
Venus, Roman goddess of love
Mars, Roman war god
Bona Dea, the Good Goddess
Vesta, goddess of the sacred hearthfire of Rome, served by virgins
Mithras, a Persian hero-god worshipped by soldiers
Jupiter, king of the gods
Juno, queen of the gods, his wife, patroness of marriage
Isis, an Egyptian goddess worshipped in Rome as protectress of commerce
on the sea

PLACES

Britannia Superior – southern England
Mona – the island of Anglesey
Segontium – a fort near Caernarvon
Vernemeton (most holy grove) – the Forest House
Hill of the Maidens – Maiden Castle, Bickerton
Deva – Chester
Glevum – Gloucester
Viroconium Cornoviiarum – Wroxeter
Venta Silurum – Caerwent
Isca Silurum – Caerleon
Aquae Sulis – Bath
The Tor – Glastonbury
The Summer Country – Somerset
Isca Dumnoniorum – Exeter
Lindum – Lincoln
Londinium – London

Britannia Inferior – northern England
Eburacum – York
Luguvalium – Carlisle

Caledonia – Scotland
Bodotria estuary – Firth of Forth
Firth of the Tava – River Tay
Sabrina Firth – Solway
Trimontium – Newstead
Pinnata Castra – Inchtuthil
Mons Graupius – location uncertain, perhaps near Inverness

Hibernia – Ireland
Temair – Tara
Druim Cliadh – Kildare

Germania Inferior – upper western Germany
  Colonia Agrippensis – Cologne
  the Rhenus – the Rhine

The BRITISH ISLES ~
1st Century A.D.

OCEANUS HYPERBOREUS

OCEANUS GERMANICUS

OCEANUS OCCIDENTALIS

Caledonii

CALEDONIA

Mons Graupius

Pinnata Castra

Firth of the Tava

Bodotria Estuary

Selgovæ

Trimontium

Votadini

Novantæ

Sabrina Firth

Luguvalium

BRITANNIA INFERIOR

Brigantes

Eburacum

Ulaid

Connachta

HIBERNIA

Midhe

Mona

Deva

Lindum

Temair

Druim Cliadh

Segontium

ORDO

Vernemeton

Hill of the Maidens

Viroconium Cornoviiarum

BRITANNIA SUPERIOR

Bendeigid's Dwelling

DEMETÆ

CORNOVII

Mumu

Laigin

Silures

Venta Silurum

Glevum

Londinium

ICENI

OCEANUS VERGIONIUS

The Summer Country

Isca Silurum

Aquæ Sulis

Cantiaci

The Tor

Atrebates

Dumnonii

Isca Dumnoniorum

OCEANUS BRITANNICUS

Peter McClure 1993

PROLOGUE

———～～———

A cold wind was whipping the torches into fiery tails. Angry light glittered on the dark waters of the strait and the shields of the legionaries waiting on the other side. The priestess coughed at the reek of smoke and sea fog and listened to the clangor of camp Latin echoing across the waters as the Roman commander harangued his men. The Druids sang out in answer, calling down the wrath of the skies, and thunder shook the air.

Women's voices rose in a shrill ululation that sent a chill through her body, or perhaps it was fear. She swayed with the other priestesses, arms raised in imprecation; their dark cloaks flaring out like raven wings.

But the Romans were howling too, and now the first rank surged into the water. The Druid war harp throbbed with a dreadful music, and her throat was scraped raw with shrieking, but still the enemy came on.

The first red-cloaked soldier set foot on the shore of the Holy Isle and the gods did not strike him. Now the singing faltered. A priest pushed the priestess behind him as Roman steel caught the torchlight; the sword fell and blood sprayed across her dark robe.

The rhythm of the chant was lost. Now there was only screaming and she ran for the trees. Behind her the Romans were scything the Druids down like grain. Too quickly, they finished, and the red tide swept inland.

The priestess stumbled through the trees, seeking the sacred circles. An orange glow filled the sky above the House of Women. The stones loomed up ahead, but from behind her came shouting. She turned at bay, clinging to the central altar stone. Now, surely, they would kill her ... She called out to the Goddess and straightened, waiting for the blow.

But it was not weapons of steel they meant to use against her.

She struggled as hard hands grabbed at her body, tearing off her robes. They forced her down upon the stone, and then the first man battered against her. There was no escape; she could only use the sacred disciplines to withdraw her mind from this body until they were done. But as awareness winged away, she cried out: "Lady of Ravens, avenge me! Avenge!"

"Avenge . . ." My own shout woke me, and I sat up, staring. As always, it took a few moments for me to realize that it was only a dream, and not even my own, for I was still a child in the year when the Legions murdered the priests and raped the women of the Holy Isle; an unwanted girl-child called Caillean, safe in Hibernia across the sea. But since first I heard the story, soon after the Priestess of the Oracle brought me to this land, the spirits of those women have haunted me.

The curtain at my door fluttered and one of the maidens who served me looked in. "My Lady, are you well? May I help you to robe? It is almost time to greet the dawn."

I nodded, feeling the cold sweat dry on my brow, and allowed her to help me into a clean gown and arrange the ornaments of a High Priestess on my breast and brow. Then I followed her out on to the summit of another isle, a green Tor that rose from the mingling of marsh and meadow that men call the Summer Sea. From below came the singing of the maidens who watch over the sacred well, and from the vale beyond it the bell that calls the hermits to prayer in the little beehive church beside the white thorn tree.

They were not the first folk to seek sanctuary on this island at the end of the world beyond the narrow seas, nor do I suppose they will be the last. So many years have passed since the death of the Holy Isle, and though in my dreams ancient voices still cry out for revenge, a hard-won wisdom tells me that the mixing of blood strengthens a breed, so long as the ancient knowledge is not lost.

But to this day I have never found any good in the Romans or their ways. This is why even for Eilan, who was dearer than a daughter to me, I could never trust in any Roman, not even Gaius, whom she loved.

But no tramping of iron-shod legionary sandals on stone-paved roads disturbs us here, for I have cast a veil of mist and mystery to keep out the straight-edged Roman world.

Today, perhaps, I will tell the maidens the story of how we came here, for between the destruction of the House of Women on the Isle of Mona and the return of the priestesses to the Isle of Apples, the women of the Druids dwelt at Vernemeton, the Forest House, and that story must not be forgotten.

It was there that I learned the Mysteries of the Goddess and taught them in turn to Eilan daughter of Rheis, who became the greatest High Priestess and, some would say, the greatest traitor to her people of all. But through Eilan the blood of the Dragon and the Eagle have mingled with the blood of the Wise, and in the hour of greatest need that line will always come to Britain's aid.

In the marketplace men say that Eilan was the Romans' victim, but I know better. In its time the Forest House preserved the Mysteries, and the gods do not require that we all be conquerors, or even that we all be wise, but only that we serve the truth that we are given until we can pass it on.

My priestesses are gathering around me, singing. I lift my hands, and as the sun strikes through the mists I bless the land.

one

S hafts of golden light shone through the trees as the setting sun dropped below the clouds, outlining each new-washed leaf in gold. The hair of the two girls who were making their way along the forest path glowed with the same pale fire. Earlier in the day there had been rain. The thick, uncleared forest that still covered much of the south of Britain lay damp and quiet, and a few low boughs still shook scattered drops like a blessing across the path.

Eilan breathed deeply of the moist air, heavy with all the living scents of the woods and sweet as incense after the smoky atmosphere of her father's hall. In the Forest House, she had been told, they used sacred herbs to purify the air. Instinctively she straightened, trying to walk like one of the priestesses who dwelt there, lifting the basket of offerings in her best imitation of their balanced grace. For a moment, then, her body moved with a rhythm both unfamiliar and completely natural, as if she had been trained to do this in some ancient past.

Only since her moonblood began had she been allowed to bring the offerings to the spring. As her monthly cycle made her a woman, said her mother, so the waters of the sacred spring were the fertility of the land. But the rituals of the Forest House served its spirit, bringing down the Goddess herself at the full of the moon. The moon had been full the night before and before her mother called her in, Eilan had stood for a long time staring up at it, filled with an expectancy she could not define.

Perhaps the Priestess of the Oracle will claim me for the Goddess at the Beltane festival. Closing her eyes, Eilan tried to imagine the blue robes of a priestess trailing behind her, and the veil shadowing her features with mystery.

"Eilan, what are you doing?" Dieda's voice startled her back to awareness, she stumbled over a tree root and nearly dropped the basket. "You are lagging like a lame cow! It will be dark before we get back to the hall if we do not finish soon."

Recovering, Eilan hurried after the other girl, blushing furiously. But already she could hear the gentle murmur of the spring. In another moment the path dropped downward, and she followed Dieda to the cleft where the waters trickled out from between two rocks and fell into the pool. In some time long past men had set stones around it; over the years the water had worn their spiraled carvings smooth. But the hazel to whose branches folk tied their wishing ribbons was young, the descendant of many trees that had grown there.

They settled themselves beside the pool and spread a cloth for the offerings, exquisitely prepared cakes, a flask of mead, and some silver coins. It was only a small pool, after all, where the minor goddess of this forest had her dwelling, not one of the holy lakes where whole armies sacrificed the treasures they had won, but for many years the women of her line had brought her their offerings every month after their moon-times, that their link to the Goddess might be renewed.

Shivering a little in the cool air, they pulled off their gowns and bent over the pool.

"Sacred spring, you are the womb of the Goddess. As your waters cradle all life, may I bear new life into the world . . ." Eilan scooped up water and let it trickle over her belly and between her thighs.

"Sacred spring, your waters are the milk of the Goddess. As you feed the world, let me nourish those I love . . ." Her nipples tingled as the cool water touched them.

"Sacred spring, you are the spirit of the Goddess. As your waters well for ever from the depths, give me the power to renew the world . . ." She trembled as the water bathed her brow.

Eilan stared into the shadowed surface, seeing the pale glimmer of her reflection take shape as the waters stilled once more. But as she stared into the water, the face that stared back at her changed. She saw an older woman with even paler skin, and dusky curls in which red highlights glinted like sparks of flame, though the eyes were the same.

"Eilan!"

As Dieda spoke, Eilan blinked, and the face looking back at her from the water was her own once more. Her kinswoman was

5

shivering, and suddenly Eilan felt cold as well. Hastily, they pulled on their clothes. Then Dieda reached for the basket of cakes, and her voice soared, rich and true, in the song.

> *"Lady of the sacred spring,*
> *To thee these offerings I bring;*
> *For life and luck and love I pray,*
> *Goddess, accept these gifts today."*

In the Forest House, thought Eilan, there would be a chorus of priestesses to sing the song. Her own voice, thin and a little wavering, blended with Dieda's in an oddly pleasing harmony.

> *"Bless now the forest and the field,*
> *That they their bounty to us yield;*
> *May kin and kine be hale and whole,*
> *Safeguard the body and the soul!"*

Eilan poured mead from the flask into the water while Dieda crumbled the cakes and cast them into the pool. The current swirled them away, and for a moment it seemed to Eilan that its sound had grown louder. The two girls leaned over the water, letting drop the coins they had brought.

As the ripples stilled, Eilan saw their two faces, so alike, mirrored together. She stiffened, fearing to see the stranger there once more, but as her sight darkened, this time there was only one face, with eyes that shone in the water like stars in the dark sea of heaven.

"Lady, are you the spirit of the pool? What do you want from me?" her heart asked. And it seemed to her that words came in reply:

"My life flows through all waters, as it flows through your veins. I am the River of Time and the Sea of Space. Through many lives you have been mine. Adsartha, my daughter, when will you fulfill your vows to Me?"

It seemed to her then that from the Lady's eyes flashed brightness that illuminated her soul, or perhaps it was sunlight, for when she came to herself she was blinking into the radiance that flared through the trees.

"Eilan!" Dieda said in the tone of one who is repeating a summons for the second time. "What is wrong with you today?"

"Dieda!" Eilan exclaimed. "Didn't you see Her? Didn't you see the Lady in the pool?"

Dieda shook her head. "You sound like one of those holy bitches at Vernemeton, babbling of visions!"

6

"How can you say that? You're the Arch-Druid's daughter – at the Forest House you could be trained as a bard!"

Dieda frowned. "A female bard? Ardanos would never allow it, nor would I want to spend my life mewed up with a gaggle of women. I'd rather join the Ravens with your foster brother Cynric and fight Rome!"

"Hush!" Eilan looked around her as if the trees had ears. "Don't you know better than to speak of that, even here? Besides, it's not fighting you want to do at Cynric's side, but to lie there – I've seen how you look at him!" She grinned.

Now Dieda was blushing. "You know nothing about it!" she exclaimed. "But your time will come, and when you grow foolish over some man it will be my turn to laugh." She began to fold up the cloth.

"I never will," said Eilan. "I want to serve the Goddess!" And for a moment then her sight darkened and the murmur of the water seemed to grow louder, as if the Lady had heard. Then Dieda was thrusting the basket into her hands.

"Let's go home." She started up the path. But Eilan hesitated, for it seemed to her that she had heard something that was not the sound of the spring.

"Wait! Do you hear that? From over by the old boar pit –"

Dieda stopped, her head turning, and they heard it again, fainter now, like an animal in pain.

"We'd best go and see," she said finally, "though it will make us late getting home. But if something has fallen in, the men will have to come and put it out of its misery."

The boy lay shaken and bleeding at the bottom of the boar pit, his hopes of rescue fading with the ebbing light.

The pit where he lay was dank and foul, smelling of the dung of animals trapped there in the past. Sharp stakes were set into the bottom and sides of the pit; one of these stakes had pierced his shoulder – not a dangerous wound, he judged, nor even particularly painful as yet, for the arm was still numb with the force of his fall. But still, slight though it was, it was likely to kill him.

Not that he was afraid to die; Gaius Macellius Severus Siluricus was nineteen years old and had sworn his oaths to the Emperor Titus as a Roman officer. He had fought his first battle before the down was thick on his face. But to die because he had blundered like a silly hare into a deadfall made him angry. It was his own

7

fault, Gaius thought bitterly. If he had listened to Clotinus Albus, he would now be sitting by a warm fire, drinking the beer of the South Country and flirting with his host's daughter, Gwenna – who had put off the chaste ways of the up-country Britons and adopted the bolder manners and bearing of girls in Roman towns like Londinium as easily as her father had adopted the Latin tongue and toga.

And yet it was for his own knowledge of the British dialects that he had been sent on this journey, Gaius remembered now, and his mouth curled grimly. The elder Severus, his father, was Prefect of the Camp of the Second Adiutrix Legion at Deva, and had married the dark-haired daughter of a chieftain of the Silures in the early days of the conquest, when Rome still hoped to win the tribes by alliance. Gaius had spoken their dialect before he could lisp a word of nursery Latin.

There had been a time, of course, when an officer of an Imperial Legion, stationed in the fort of Deva, would not have troubled himself to phrase his demands in the language of a conquered country. Even now, Flavius Rufus, tribune of the second cohort, cared nothing for such niceties. But Macellius Severus senior, Prefectus Castrorum, was responsible only to Agricola, Governor of the Province of Britain, and it was the responsibility of Macellius Severus to keep peace and harmony between the people of the Province and the Legion that occupied, guarded and governed them.

Still licking their wounds a generation after the Killer Queen Boudicca had attempted her fruitless rebellion – and had been fiercely punished by the Legions – the people of Britannia were peaceful enough beneath the heavy impositions of tax and tribute. Levies of manpower they bore with less meekness, and here, on the outskirts of the Empire, resentment still smoldered, fostered adroitly by a few petty chiefs and malcontents. Into this hotbed of trouble, Flavius Rufus was sending a party of legionaries to supervise a levy of men being sent to work in the Imperial lead mines in the hills.

Imperial policy did not admit of a young officer being stationed in the Legion where his father held a post as important as Prefect. So Gaius now held the post of a military tribune in the Valeria Victrix legion at Glevum, and, despite his British half-blood, from his childhood he had undergone the severe discipline of a Roman soldier's son.

The elder Macellius had sought no favors for his only son as yet. But Gaius had taken a slight wound in the leg during a border skirmish; before he had quite recovered, a fever had sent him home to Deva, with permission to convalesce there before returning to his post. Recovered, he was restless in his father's house; the chance to go with the levy to the mines had seemed nothing but a pleasant holiday.

The trip had been largely uneventful; after the sullen levies had been marched away, Gaius, with a fortnight of his leave yet to run, had accepted the invitation of Clotinus Albus, seconded by the daughter's immodest glances, to stay for a few days and enjoy some hunting. Clotinus was adept at this too and – Gaius knew – had been pleased at the thought of offering hospitality to the son of a Roman official. Gaius had shrugged, enjoyed the hunting, which was excellent, and told Clotinus's daughter quite a number of pleasant lies, which was excellent too. Just the day before, he had killed a deer in these same woods, proving himself as adept with the light spear as these Britons with their own weapons; but now . . .

Sprawled in the filth of the pit, Gaius had poured out despairing curses on the timorous slave who had offered to show him a short cut from Clotinus's home to the Roman road that led straight, or so he said, to Deva; on his own folly in letting the simpleton drive the chariot; on the hare, or whatever it was that had dashed in front of him and frightened the horses; on the ill-trained animals themselves, and on the fool who had let them bolt; and on the off-guard moment in which he had lost his balance and been thrown, half-stunned, to the ground.

Stunned, yes, but if he had not been half out of his mind from the fall, he'd have had sense enough to stay where he'd fallen; even such a fool as the driver must sooner or later have regained control of his horses and come back for him. Even more than this he cursed his own folly in trying to find his own way through the forest and for leaving the path. He must have wandered a long way.

He must have been still dazed from the earlier fall, but he remembered with sickening clarity the sudden slip, the slither of the leaves and branches as the deadfall gave way, and then the fall, driving the stake through his arm with a force that had deprived him of consciousness for some minutes. The afternoon was getting on before he had recovered enough to take stock of his injuries. A second stake had torn the calf of his leg, ripping open his old wound; not a serious injury, but he had struck his ankle so hard that it had swollen to the size of his thigh; it was broken – or felt like it at least. Gaius, unwounded, was as agile as a cat and would have been out in moments; but now he was too weak and dazed to move.

He knew that if he didn't bleed to death before nightfall, the smell of blood would certainly attract wild beasts who would finish him off. He tried to stave off memories of his nurse's tales of worse things that scent might bring.

The damp chill was seeping through his whole body; he had shouted himself hoarse. Now, if he had to die he'd do it with Roman dignity. He huddled a fold of his blood-soaked cloak around his face, then, his heart pounding wildly, dragged himself upright; for he had heard voices.

Gaius put all his failing strength into a cry – half shriek, half howl; he was ashamed of the inhuman sound moments after it left his throat, and he struggled to add some more human plea, but nothing would come. He clutched at one of the stakes, but managed only to pull himself to his knee and lean against the dirt wall.

For a moment a last ray of sunlight blinded him. He blinked, and saw a girl's head framed in light above him.

"Great Mother!" she cried out in a clear voice. "How in the name of any god did you manage to fall down there? Did you not see the warning marks they put on the trees?"

Gaius could not manage a word; the young woman had addressed him in an exceptionally pure dialect that was not altogether familiar. Of course, they would be Ordovici tribesmen here. He had to think a moment to turn it into the Silure patois of his mother.

Before he could answer, a second feminine voice, this one richer and somehow stronger, exclaimed, "Lack-wit, we ought to leave him there for wolf bait!" Another face appeared beside the first one, so like it that for a moment he wondered if his vision was playing tricks on him.

"Here, grab my hand and I think, between the two of us, we can get you out," she said. "Eilan, help me!" A woman's hand, slender and white, reached down to him; Gaius put up his serviceable hand, but could not close it. "What's the matter? Are you hurt?" the girl asked more gently.

Before Gaius could answer, the other – Gaius could see nothing about her except that she was young – bent over to see for herself.

"Oh, I see now – Dieda, he is bleeding! Run and bring Cynric to pull him out of there."

Relief washed over Gaius so powerfully that consciousness nearly left him, and he slumped back down, whimpering as the movement jarred his wounds.

"You must not faint," came the clear voice above him. "Let my words be a rope to bind you to life, do you hear?"

"I hear you," he whispered. "Keep talking to me."

Perhaps it was because rescue was coming that he could allow himself to feel, but his wounds were beginning to hurt very badly. Gaius could hear the girl's voice above him, though the words no longer made sense to him. They rippled like the murmur of a stream, bearing his mind beyond the pain. The world darkened; Gaius realized that it was daylight and not his sight that had failed him only when he saw the flicker of torchlight on the trees.

The girl's face disappeared and he heard her call, "Father, there's a man caught in the old boar pit."

"We'll get him out then," a deeper voice replied. "Hmm ..." Gaius sensed movement above him. "This seems a job for a stretcher. Cynric, you had better go down and see."

The next moment a young man had scrambled down the sides of the pit. He looked Gaius over and asked pleasantly, "What were you thinking about? It must take real wit to fall in there when everyone around knows it's been there thirty years!"

Mustering the scraps of his pride, Gaius started to say that if the fellow got him out he would be fitly rewarded, then was glad he had not spoken. As his eyes gradually adjusted to the torchlight, the young Roman realized that his rescuer was about his own age, not much over eighteen, but he was a young giant of a man. His fair hair curled loosely about his shoulders, and his face, still beardless, looked as gay and calm as if rescuing half-dead strangers was all in a day's work. He wore a tunic of checked cloth and trews of finely dyed leather; his embroidered wool cloak was fastened with a gold pin bearing a stylized raven done in red enamel. These were the clothes of a man of noble house, but not one of those who welcomed their conquerors and aped the manners of Rome.

Gaius said simply, "I'm a stranger here; I don't know your markings," in the language of the tribes.

"Well, don't worry about it; let's get you out and then we can talk about how you came to fall in." The young man slid his arm beneath Gaius's waist, supporting the young Roman as easily as if he were a child.

"We dug that pit for boars and bears and Romans," he remarked tranquilly. "Just bad luck you got caught in it." He looked up at the pit top and said, "Let down your mantle, Dieda; it will be easier than finding something for a stretcher. His own cloak's all stiff with blood."

When the mantle had been let down, the boy knotted it around Gaius's waist, then, fastening the other end about his own, he set his foot on the lowest of the stakes, and said, "Yell if I hurt you; I've hauled out bears like this, but they were dead and couldn't complain."

Gaius set his teeth and hung on, almost fainting with the pain when his swollen ankle struck a projecting root. Someone at the top leaned over and grabbed his hands and at last he struggled over the edge, then lay there just breathing for a moment before he had strength to open his eyes.

An older man was leaning over him. Gently he pulled away Gaius's fouled and blood-smeared cloak and whistled.

"Some god must love you, stranger; a few inches lower and that stake would have gone into your lungs. Cynric, girls, look at that," he went on. "Where the shoulder is still bleeding, the blood is dark and slow, so it is returning to the heart; if it were coming from the heart it would be bright red and spurting forth; and he would probably have bled to death before we found him."

The blond boy and the two girls bent over, one after the other, to see. Gaius lay silent. A dreadful suspicion had begun to steal over him. He had already abandoned all thought of identifying himself and asking them to take him to the house of Clotinus Albus in return for a substantial reward. Now he knew that only the old British tunic he had put on that morning for traveling had saved him. The offhand medical expertise of that speech told him that he was in the presence of a Druid. Then someone lifted him, and the world darkened and disappeared.

Gaius awakened to firelight and the face of a girl looking down at him. For a moment her features seemed to swim in a fiery halo. She was young and her face was fair, but the eyes were an odd shade between hazel and grey; wide-spaced under pale lashes. Her mouth was dimpled, but so grave that it looked older than the rest of her; her hair was as light as her lashes, almost colorless except where the firelight lay red across it. One of her hands moved across his face and he felt it cool; she had been bathing his face in water.

He looked for what seemed a long time, until her features were drawn for ever on his memory. Then someone said, "That's enough, Eilan, I think he's awake," and the girl withdrew.

Eilan . . . He had heard the name before. Had it been in some dream? She was lovely.

Gaius struggled to see, and realized that he was lying in a bench bed built into the wall. He looked about him, trying to understand where he was. Cynric, the young man who had drawn him out of the pit, and the old Druid whose name he did not know, were standing beside him. He was lying in a wood-framed roundhouse built in the old Celtic style, with smoothed logs radiating out from the high peak of the roof to the low wall. He had not been in such a house since he was a little child, when his mother had taken him to visit her kin.

The floor was thickly strewn with rushes; the wall of woven hazel withies was chinked and plastered with whitewashed clay, and the partitions between the bed boxes were made of wicker as well. A great flap of leather curtained the entrance instead of a door. To lie in this place made him feel very young, as if all the intervening years of Roman training had been stripped away.

His gaze moved slowly around the house and back to the girl. Her dress was of red-brown linen and she held a copper basin in her hand; she was tall, but younger than he had thought, her body still straight as a child's beneath the folds of her gown. Light from the central hearth behind her glowed in her fair hair.

The firelight also showed him the older man, the Druid. Gaius shifted his head a little and looked at him from beneath his lashes. The Druids were learned men among the Britons, but he had been told all his life that they were fanatics. To find himself in a Druid's house was like waking up in a wolf's lair, and Gaius did not mind admitting that he was afraid.

At least when he had heard the old man calmly discoursing on the circulation of the blood, a thing he had heard from his father's Greek physician was a teaching of the healer-priests of the highest rank, he had the sense to conceal his Roman identity.

Not that these folk made any secret of who *they* were. "*We dug that pit for boars and bears and Romans,*" the young man had said quite casually. This should have told him at once that he was a good long way outside the little protected circle of Roman domination. Yet he was no more than a day's ride from the Legion post at Deva!

But if he was in the hands of the enemy, at least they were treating him well. The clothes the girl wore were well made; the copper basin she carried was beautifully worked – no doubt it had come from one of the southern markets.

Rushlights of reed dipped in tallow burned in hanging bowls; the couch where he lay was covered with linen, the straw mattress smelled of sweet herbs. It was heavenly warm after the chill of the pit. Then the old man who had directed his rescue came and sat down beside him, and for the first time Gaius got a good look at his rescuer.

He was a big and powerful man, with shoulders strong enough to throw down a bull. His face was rough-cast on his skull, as if carelessly chiseled out of stone, and his eyes were light grey and cold. His hair was liberally sprinkled with grey; Gaius thought he was around the age of his own father, about fifty.

"You had a remarkably narrow escape, young man," the Druid said. Gaius had the impression that lecturing came very naturally to him. "Next time keep your eyes open. I'll have a look at that shoulder in a minute. Eilan –" He beckoned to the girl and gave her instructions in a low voice.

She went away and Gaius asked, "To whom do I owe my life, Honored One?" He had never thought to show respect to a Druid. Gaius, like everyone else, had been brought up on Caesar's old horror stories of human sacrifice, and tales of the wars which had been fought to subdue the Druidic cult in Britain and in Gaul. Nowadays those who remained were pretty well controlled by Roman edicts, but they could be as much trouble as the Christians. The difference was that while the Christians spread dissension in the cities and refused to worship the Emperor, the Druids could incite even conquered peoples to bloody war.

Still, there was something about this man that commanded respect.

"My name is Bendeigid," the Druid said, but he did not question Gaius, and the young Roman remembered hearing his mother's people say that among the Celts a guest was still sacred, at least outside Roman lands. A man's worst enemy might claim food and shelter and depart unquestioned if he chose. Gaius breathed a little freer at the reprieve; this was one place it might be safer – and wiser – to claim hospitality as a guest than to exact it as the right of a conqueror.

The girl Eilan came into the alcove again, carrying a small chest of oakwood bound with iron, and a drinking horn. She said timidly, "I hope this is the right one."

Her father nodded to her brusquely, took the chest, and gestured to her to give the horn to Gaius. He reached for it and found to his surprise that his fingers had not the strength to close.

The Druid said, "Drink that," with the unmistakable manner of a man who is accustomed to giving orders and to having them obeyed. He added after a minute, "You'll need it by the time we get through with you." He sounded pleasant enough; but Gaius had begun to be frightened.

Bendeigid gestured to the girl and she came back to Gaius's bedside.

She smiled, tasted a few drops in the traditional gesture of hospitality, then held the horn to his lips. Gaius tried to raise himself a little but his muscles would not obey him. With a compassionate cry, Eilan lifted his head in the curve of her arm so that he could drink.

The young Roman sipped at the cup; it was strong mead, to which some bitter, obviously medicinal spice had been added.

"You had almost won through to the Land of Youth, stranger, but you will not die," she murmured. "I saw you in a dream, but you were older – and with a little boy by your side."

He looked up at her, already too deliciously drowsy to find that disturbing. Young as she was, lying against her breast was like being back in his mother's arms. Now, when he was in pain, he could almost remember her, and his eyes stung with tears. He was vaguely aware when the old Druid cut away his tunic and the old Druid and the young man Cynric washed his wounds with something that stung – but not any worse than the stuff old Manlius had put on his leg when he hurt it before. They smeared his leg with something sticky and stinging, and bound it tightly with strips of linen. Then they moved the swollen ankle, and he watched without much interest as somebody said, "Nothing much wrong here – not even broken."

But he snapped out of the dreamy daze when Cynric said, "Brace yourself, youngster; that stake was filthy, but I think we can save the arm, if we burn it out."

"Eilan," the old man commanded curtly, "get out of here; this is nothing for a young girl to see."

"I'll hold him, Eilan," Cynric said. "You can go."

"I will stay, Father. Maybe I can help." Her hand closed over Gaius's, and the old man growled, "Do as you like, then, but don't scream or faint."

The next minute Gaius felt strong hands – Cynric's? – holding him flat and hard. Eilan's hand was still twined in his, but he felt it quiver a little; he turned his head away, closing his eyes and grinding his teeth lest some shameful cry should escape him. He smelled the approach of the heated iron, and then a frightful agony ripped through his whole body.

A scream contorted his lips, he felt it escape as a gagging grunt; then the rough touch released him and he felt only the girl's soft hands. When he could open his eyes, he saw the Druid looking down at him, a bleak smile tight around the greying beard. Cynric, who was still bent over him, was very white; Gaius had seen that look on youngsters in his own command after their first battle.

"Well, you're certainly no coward, lad," the youth said in a choked voice.

"Thanks," Gaius said absurdly. And fainted.

two

When Gaius came to himself again, feeling as if he had been unconscious for a long time, the rushlights had burned down. Only a little light came from the coals on the hearth, and by it he could just make out the girl Eilan seated beside him nearly asleep. He felt tired, and his arm throbbed and he was thirsty. He could hear women's voices not far away. His shoulder was done up in thick wrappings of linen – he felt as if he had been swaddled like a newborn babe. The injured shoulder was slick with some greasy salve and the linen smelled of fat and balsam.

The girl sat silent beside him on a little three-legged stool, as pale and slender as a young birch, her hair combed away from her temples, waving a little; it was too fine in texture to lie perfectly flat. She had a gilt chain around her neck with some sort of amulet. These Briton girls matured late, Gaius knew; she might be as old as fifteen. She was hardly a woman, but just as certainly not a child.

There was a clatter as if someone had dropped a pail and a young voice yelled, "Then you can go and milk them yourself if you've a mind!"

"And what's to do with the byre-woman?" a woman's voice asked sharply.

"Oh, wailing and weeping like the banshee because those Roman butchers came and marched her man off with the levies, and she left with three babes," said the first voice, "and now my Rhodri has gone off after them."

"The curse of Tanarus on all Romans –" began a voice Gaius recognized as Cynric's, but the older woman's voice cut him short.

"Hush now. Mairi, put the dishes on the table, don't stand here shouting at the boys. I'll go and speak with the poor woman – tell her she can bring the little ones here to the house – but someone

17

must milk the cows this night, even if the Romans carry off every man in Britain."

"You are good, Foster Mother," Cynric said, and the voices subsided into a hum again. The girl looked toward Gaius and rose from her stool.

"Oh, you are awake," she said. "Are you hungry?"

"I could devour a horse and chariot and chase the driver halfway to Venta," Gaius said gravely, and she stared a moment before her eyes widened and she giggled.

"I'll go and see if there is a horse and chariot in the cookhouse," she said, laughing, and then the light behind her broadened and a lady stood in the doorway. For a moment he was astonished at the brightness; for there was sunlight in the room.

"What is it, the next day?" he blurted without thinking, and the lady laughed, turned aside and drew the horsehide curtain wide, catching it on a hook and extinguishing the guttering rushlight in one easy motion.

"Eilan would not let us disturb you even to eat," she said. "She insisted that rest would do you more good than food. I suppose she was right; but you must be very hungry now. I am sorry I was not here to welcome you to our house; I was out attending to a sick woman in one of our clanholds. I hope Eilan has been looking after you properly."

"Oh, very," said Gaius. He blinked, for something in her manner had reminded him painfully of his mother.

The lady looked down at him. She was beautiful, this Briton woman, and so like the girl that the relationship was obvious, even before the girl said, "Mother –" and stopped, too shy to continue. The woman, like the girl, had fair hair and dark, hazel-grey eyes. She looked as if she had been working with her maids, for there was a smear of flour on her fine woolen tunic, but the shift that showed beneath it was white, finer linen than he had yet seen in Britain, edged with embroidery. Her shoes were a good dyed leather, and fine fibulae of spiraled gold fastened the gown.

"I hope that you are feeling better," she said graciously.

Gaius raised himself on his good arm. "Much better, lady," he said, "and eternally grateful to you and yours."

She made a little gesture of dismissal. "Do you come from Deva?"

"I have been visiting near there," he answered. The Latin flavor of his speech would be explained if she thought he came from a Roman town.

"Since you are awake, I'll send Cynric to help you bathe and dress."

"It will be good to wash," said Gaius, pulling up the blanket as he realized that he was naked except for his bandaging.

The woman followed his gaze and said, "He'll find you some clothes; they may be too large for you, but they'll do for the moment. If you'd rather lie here and rest, you can; but you're welcome to join us if you feel able."

Gaius thought for a moment. Every muscle in his body felt as if he had been beaten with cudgels; on the other hand, he could not help feeling curious about this household, and he must not appear to scorn their society. He had believed that the Britons who had not allied with Rome were mostly savages, but there was nothing primitive about this establishment.

"I will join you with pleasure," he said, and rubbed a hand across his face, dismayed at the untidy stubble. "But I would like to wash – and perhaps shave."

"I don't think you should put yourself to the trouble of shaving – certainly not for us," she said, "But Cynric will help you to wash. Eilan, find your brother and tell him he's needed."

The girl slipped away. The lady turned to follow, then looked at him, seeing him more clearly in the light of the recessed cubicle. Her eyes softened from a smile of courtesy to one that reminded him of the way his own mother had looked at him, long ago. "Why," she said, "you're nothing but a boy."

For a moment Gaius felt stung by the words – he had done a man's work for three years – but before he could frame any courteous answer, a mocking young voice said, "Yes, and if he is a boy, Stepmother, I am a babe in long clothes. Well, stumble-foot, are you ready to go tumbling in some more bear pits?"

Cynric came through the door. Once more Gaius was struck by how tall he was, but except for his great height he too was still a youth; though he would have made two of Gaius. He laughed. "Well," he said, "you look a little less ready to be carted away by the old man who kills off fools and drunks. Let me look at your leg and we'll see if you're fit to set your foot to the ground." For all his size, his hands were gentle as he examined the hurt leg, and when he was finished he laughed again.

"We should all have legs so fit to walk! It's mostly a bad bump; what did you do, knock it on a stake? I thought so. Anyone less lucky would have broken it in three places and gone limping for life; but I think you'll be all right. The shoulder's another thing; you won't be fit to travel for seven days or so."

Gaius struggled upright. "I must," he said. "I must be in Deva in four days." His leave would be ended . . .

"I tell you, if you're in Deva in four days, your friends will bury you there," said Cynric. "Even I know that much. Oh, by the way" – he took on a deliberate stance and repeated as if reciting a lesson – "Bendeigid sends his greetings to the guest in his house, and bids him recover as best he may; he regrets that necessity keeps him absent this day and night, but he will rejoice to see you on his return." He added, "It would take a braver man than I am to face him and tell him you wouldn't accept his hospitality."

"Your father is most kind," Gaius replied.

He might as well rest. There was nothing he could do. He could hardly mention Clotinus. What happened next all depended on that fool who drove the chariot; if he went back and dutifully reported that the Prefect's son had been thrown and maybe killed, they'd already be combing the woods for his body. On the other hand, if the halfwit lied, or took this opportunity to run away to some village not under Roman rule – and there were plenty of them, even this close to Deva – well, it was anyone's guess. He might not be missed until Macellius Severus began asking questions about his son.

Cynric was bending over a chest at the foot of the bed; he drew out a shirt and surveyed it with a mixture of amusement and dismay. "Those rags you were wearing are only fit to scare crows," he said. "I'll set the girls to clean and mend them, if it can be done; they haven't much else to do in this weather. But you'd look like a maid in a long gown in this." He flung it down. "I'll go and borrow something nearer your size."

He went away, and Gaius fumbled in the remnants of clothing that lay folded beside the bed for the purse on the leather belt they had cut off him. Everything was untouched as far as he could make out. A few of the tin squares that still passed current for coin outside the Roman towns, a clasp, a folding knife, one or two small rings and a few other trinkets he had not wanted to wear hunting – ah yes, here it was. Much good it had done him! He glanced briefly at the scrap of parchment with the Prefect's seal; his safe-conduct would be no good to him here, if it did not in fact endanger him; but when he left here, he would need it to travel.

Swiftly he fumbled it back into the pouch. Had they seen the signet ring? He started to slip it off his finger and put it into the purse; but then Cynric, some clothes over his arm, came back into the room. Gaius felt almost guilty; it looked as if he was examining his possessions to see if anything had been stolen.

He said, "I think the seal of the ring became loosened when I fell," and worked the green stone back and forth a little. "I was afraid it might come out if I wore it."

"Roman work," said Cynric, looking at it. "What does it say?"

It bore only his initials and the arms of the Legion but he was proud of the ring, for Macellius had sent to Londinium and ordered it from a seal-cutter when he took up his commission; but Gaius said, "I don't know; it was a gift."

"The design is Roman," said Cynric, scowling. "The Romans have strewn their rubbish from here to Caledonia." He added scornfully, "There's no telling whence it came."

Something in Cynric's manner told Gaius he stood in more deadly danger now than in the pit. The Druid himself, Bendeigid, would never violate hospitality; he knew that from tales his mother and his nurse had told him. But there was no telling what this young hothead would do.

On an impulse, he took one of the smaller rings from his pouch.

"My life I owe to you and to your father," he said. "Will you accept this as a gift from me? It is not costly, but it may serve to remind you of a good deed done."

Cynric took the ring from his hand; it was too small for any but his smallest finger. "Cynric, son of Bendeigid the Druid, thanks you, stranger," he said. "I know no name by which I may return thanks . . ."

It was about as broad a hint as good manners permitted, and Gaius could not in courtesy ignore it. He would have given the name of his mother's brother; but the name of the Silure chieftain who had given his sister to a Roman might have made its way into even this corner of Britain. A small breach of truth was better than a major one of manners.

"My mother called me Gawen," he said finally. This much at least was true, for Gaius, his Roman name, had been foreign to her tongue. "I was born in Venta Silurum, to the south, of no lineage you would know."

Cynric thought about this for a moment, twisting the ring on his little finger. Then a curious light of comprehension dawned in his face. He said, gazing intently at Gaius, "Do ravens fly at midnight?"

Gaius was no less astonished by the question than by Cynric's manner. For a moment he wondered if the young man were simple; then he answered carelessly, "I'm afraid you have the better of me in woodcraft; I never knew any that did."

He glanced down at Cynric's hands, saw the fingers were enlaced in a peculiar manner, and began to understand. This must be the sign of one of the many secret societies, mostly religious like the cults of Mithras or the Nazarene. Were these people Christians? No, their sign was a fish or some such, not a raven.

Well, nothing could interest him less, and his expression must have showed it. The young Briton's face changed slightly, and he said hastily, "I see I have made a mistake –" and turned away. "Here, I think these will fit you; I borrowed them from my sister Mairi, they're her husband's. Come, I'll help you to the bathhouse and get father's razor for you if you want to shave – though you're old enough, I would think, to grow a beard. Careful – don't put all your weight on that foot or you'll fall on the floor."

Bathed, shaved and, with Cynric's help, dressed in a clean tunic and the loose breeches the Britons wore, Gaius felt able to get up and hobble. His arm throbbed and burned, and his leg ached in several places, but he could have been much worse, and he knew that his muscles would stiffen if he remained in bed. Even so, he leaned gratefully on Cynric's arm as the taller boy guided his steps across the yard to the long feasting hall.

A table of hewn boards ran down the center, with heavy benches to either side. Warmth was provided by a hearth at either end of the hall. Near these a mixed number of men and women and even a few children were assembling. Heavily bearded men in roughly woven smocks talked to one another in a dialect so crude Gaius could not understand a word.

Although his tutor had taught him that the Latin *familia* originally meant all who shared living quarters: master, children, freedmen, and slaves, the Romans now kept their serving folk apart from the family. Cynric mistook his look of mild distaste for weakness, and hastened to lead him to a cushioned seat at the upper end of the long room.

Here, a little apart from the mixed crew at the lower end of the table, the lady of the house was seated on a wide chair. Near by, another seat, covered with a bearskin, was evidently reserved for the master. Other wide settles and benches were occupied by several young men and women whose finer garments and well-bred manners proclaimed them children or fosterlings of the household, or perhaps upper servants. The lady of the house nodded at the boys but did not interrupt her conversation with an old man seated near the hearth, tall and gaunt as an elderly ghost, with grey hair curled and cut in almost foppish fashion. His beard was grey, too, and elaborately curled. Green eyes twinkled in the old man's face; his long tunic was of snowy white, embroidered lavishly, and the small wire-strung harp by his side was trimmed and ornamented with gold.

A bard! But that was not so surprising in a Druid's hall. It needed only a soothsayer to have all of the three classes of Druid that Caesar had described represented here. But a diviner might have seen through the young Roman's disguise. As it was, the old bard favored Gaius with a long glance that made the skin prickle along his backbone before the old man turned to his hostess again.

Cynric said in an undertone, "You know my stepmother Rheis; this is the bard Ardanos, I call him grandfather, for he is my foster mother's father; I am an orphan."

This silenced Gaius completely, for he had heard of Ardanos in the headquarters of the Legion. He was believed to be a powerful Druid, perhaps the chief of those who remained in the British Isles. Although at first glance Ardanos looked like any other harper about to play, his every gesture compelled the eye. Not for the first time, Gaius wondered how he would escape with a whole skin.

He was glad to drop on to a bench near the hearth and be ignored. Although it was still bright outside, he felt a chill, and welcomed the heat of the fire. It had been a long time since he had needed to remember the ways of his mother's kin. He hoped he would not make a mistake that would betray him.

Cynric went on, "My sister Eilan you know; beside her is my mother's sister Dieda." Eilan was sitting near Rheis. Cynric laughed at Gaius's astonishment as next to Eilan he saw another girl in green linen, leaning against the back of her chair and listening to the old bard. For just a moment she seemed as like to Eilan as one oak leaf to another; then he saw that the girl Cynric had named Dieda was a little older, and that she had blue eyes, where Eilan's were almost grey. Vaguely he remembered seeing two faces looking down at him from the edge of the boar pit, but he had thought that delirium.

"There are really two of them; they are more alike than twins, are they not?"

It was true, but Gaius was suddenly certain that the sureness with which he had recognized Eilan would always remain with him. All his life he would be one of the few who could tell the two women apart as if by instinct. A fragment of memory bound up with pain and fire came to him – Eilan had dreamed about him.

And now that he considered them, he could see that they were unlike in many small ways too; Dieda was a little taller, and her hair lay flat and smooth against her forehead while Eilan's escaped from its binding in a tiny halo of curls. Dieda's face was smooth and pale and perfect, she looked solemn; Eilan looked rosy, as if her face had caught the sunlight and held it there.

They seemed very different to him, and their voices were altogether so. Dieda said something carelessly courteous; her voice was rich and musical, without Eilan's shyness or her laughter.

"So you are the simpleton who goes about tumbling into boar pits?" Dieda said, gravely. "From what Cynric told me I expected to see some moon-struck lout, but you seem reasonably civilized."

Gaius nodded noncommittally; it was strange to see so young a girl with so much cool reserve. He had warmed at once to Eilan, but somehow, though there seemed no reason she should care, he fancied that this one did not like him.

Cynric nodded and turned to a young woman who had passed by with a jug of milk. "Mairi, our guest is named Gawen, if you have not turned dairy woman in such earnest that you cannot even greet him." The older woman bowed her head in polite acknowledgment, but did not reply. As she turned he could see that she was not plump, but exceedingly pregnant. She looked as if she had been crying.

"And that's all of us, except for my baby sister Senara," Cynric said. This was a little girl of six or seven, with fair hair like Eilan's. She looked out shyly from behind Mairi's skirt and then grew bolder, saying, "Eilan did not come to bed with me at all; Mother said she sat by you all night long."

"Then I am honored by her kindness," Gaius said, laughing, "but I have little success with women if the prettiest of them pays me no heed. Why were you not anxious to watch by me, little one?"

She was a round-faced, rosy little thing, and reminded him of his own sister, who had not long survived his mother's death three years ago. He drew the child to him with his good arm and she crept up on the seat beside him where she rested contentedly. Later she insisted on sharing his plate when the older girls, Mairi and Dieda, brought them food, and Gaius laughed and humored her.

Cynric and Dieda were talking together in low tones. Gaius tried to deal with his food, but his bandaged arm made it difficult. Eilan saw the trouble he was having and came and sat on his other side. With a little sharp knife she wore at her belt, she unobtrusively cut up his food into morsels that he could manage, and told the child, in a quiet voice that did not carry beyond their own ears, not to bother their guest. That done, Eilan's shyness returned. She went to the fireplace without speaking, and Gaius was content to watch her.

One of the servants brought a child about a year old to Mairi, and the young woman, without the slightest self-consciousness, unfastened her dress and sat nursing it, chatting with Cynric. She glanced at Gaius with innocent curiosity, saying, "Now I can see why you sent to borrow my husband's other tunic and breeches. He has gone off to –" She broke off, frowning. "I did not think he would mind loaning his gear to a guest, though he may have a word to say to me if he finds I gave his dry clothes away while he was shivering in the forest. Tell me, Gawen, are all the Silures as short as you, like one of the little people, or did some Roman creep into your grandmother's bed one night?"

Any answer Gaius might have made was drowned in laughter all along the table. Gaius remembered that the Britons were given to grosser jesting than a Roman of good breeding would think tasteful. It was true that the Silures were small for Britons, dark and fine-boned compared to the big, fair-skinned men of the Belgic tribes. Cynric and Eilan and Dieda and Rheis were of that type. But Gaius's few memories of his uncle who ruled the Silures were of a man of power despite his lack of height, a man quick to fury or laughter, with tattooed dragons coiling up his arms.

An answer came to him which he would not have dared to make in Roman company, but which might serve here. "As to that, I cannot say, Mistress Mairi, but they fit me well enough – and you were not unwilling I should fill them."

Cynric threw back his head with a great bass roar of laughter, taken up by all the others. Even the quiet Rheis smiled a little, but quickly sobered, as if she knew something Mairi did not. For a moment it seemed as if she were forcing herself to congeniality. She turned to Ardanos.

"Father, shall we have some music?"

Ardanos picked up the harp and looked sharply at Gaius. The younger man had a sudden conviction that the old Druid knew perfectly well what — and perhaps who — he was. But how could he? Gaius was dark-haired like his father, but the Silures, like some of the other races of the West and South, were also known for their dark and curly hair. He was almost sure he had never set eyes on the old man before. He told himself he was imagining things — probably that stare of supposed recognition had been only short-sightedness.

The old Druid picked up the harp, struck a chord or two, then put it aside. "I'm in no mood for singing," he said, looking at one of the fair-haired girls. "Dieda, my child, will you sing for us?"

Eilan dimpled and said, "I am always at your service, Grand-father, but you don't really want to hear me sing, do you?"

Ardanos laughed in chagrin. "Ah, I've done it again, Eilan, it is you? I swear you and Dieda always try to confuse me. As if anyone could tell you apart until you open your mouths!"

Rheis said gently, "I cannot see they are as much alike as that, Father. Of course, one is my sister and one my daughter, but to me they seem hardly alike at all. Are you sure it is not the failing of your eyesight?"

"No, I always confuse them until one of them begins to sing," protested the Druid. "No one could mistake one for the other then."

Eilan said, "You need not make a face like a sour crab apple, Grandfather, I have not been apprenticed as a bard!" Then they fell silent as, unaccompanied, Dieda began to sing:

> *"A bird in the air told a riddle to me;*
> *A fish is a bird that swims in the sea,*
> *A bird is a fish that swims in the air."*

Under cover of the song, Rheis beckoned Mairi to her, and said, "Have the Romans taken anyone but the byre-woman's man?"

"Not that I know of, Mother, but Rhodri went off after them before I could ask." Mairi said, shaking her head. "He said that most of the other levies were made to the north."

"That fat hog Caradac! Or I should say Clotinus, as the Romans call him!" Cynric burst out. "If Old Bedbugs would stand with us the Romans would never dare send their Legions into this part of the country — but as long as everyone goes either over to the Romans or to the Caledonians —"

"Be still!" Dieda said sharply, breaking off her song. "You'll wind up having to go north yourself –"

Rheis said gently, "Hush, children, these family matters will not interest our guest." But Gaius could tell that what she meant was, "It isn't safe to talk like this with a stranger in the house."

Ardanos said calmly, "This part of the country is quieter than it has been for years. The Romans think us tamed, fit only to be milked for taxes. But the best of their troops are off trying to conquer the Novantae – and as a result there is less order here."

"Such order as that we could well spare," Cynric said sharply, but Ardanos glared at him and he subsided.

Gaius leaned a little forward into the firelight. He suspected that he would almost certainly do better to remain silent, but he was curious.

"I was in Deva lately," he said slowly. "There was talk there that the Emperor may call Agricola back from Alba despite his victories. They say there is no profit in spending men and supplies to hold such a barren land."

"We could hardly be so lucky," Dieda said, and laughed in contempt. "The Romans may indeed vomit up what they have eaten to make room in their bellies for more; but no Roman ever ceded an inch of conquered land!"

Gaius opened his mouth; then thought better of it. Rheis said, "Is Agricola so formidable? Could he really conquer Britannia all the way to the northern sea?"

Ardanos grimaced. "The gossip in Deva may have some truth in it; between the wolves and the wild men I doubt that even Roman tax farmers could squeeze out much profit there."

Dieda looked at Gaius with a sudden malice. "You who have lived among Romans," she said, "perhaps you can tell us why they are carrying off our men and what will happen to them?"

"The provincial senators pay their taxes with the men of the levy. I suppose they will take them to the lead mines in the Mendip hills," he said reluctantly, "and I know not what will befall them there."

But he did know. The whip and poor feeding would be used to break their spirit, and the gelder's knife to unman any who continued to resist. Those who survived the march would be set to work in the mines as long as they lived. A flicker of triumph in Dieda's eyes told him she had guessed he knew more than he would say. He winced as Mairi began to weep. He had never met – or ever thought he would – anyone who could be subject to the levies.

"Can't something be done?" she cried.

"Not this year," the old man answered.

"Not much anyone can do about it," Gaius said defensively, "but you can't deny that the mines have enriched all Britain —"

"We can live without such enrichment," Cynric said wrathfully. "Rome enriches at the top, and enslaves at the bottom."

"It is not only Romans who have become wealthy —" Gaius began.

"You mean traitors like Clotinus?"

Rheis leaned forward as if to terminate a conversation that had become awkward, but Cynric would not be stopped.

"You who have lived among Romans," Cynric said angrily, "do you know how Clotinus the White-Washed made his fortune? He guided the Legions to Mona, or are you too much a Roman to remember that once there was a holy place there — the Isle of Women — the holiest place in Britain perhaps before Paulinus came?"

"I knew only that there was a sanctuary," Gaius said neutrally, his neck prickling again with that sense of danger. For the Romans, the destruction of Mona had been overshadowed by the catastrophe of the Iceni rebellion, but he knew better than to discuss Mona in the house of a Druid, especially since Agricola had mopped up whatever resistance might have been left there only last year.

"Here sits a bard at our own fireside," said Cynric, "who can sing of the women of Mona so that your heart will crack!"

Almost simultaneously the Druid said, "Not tonight, lad," and the lady of the house leaned forward. "Not at my table; it is not a story to be told while guests are trying to eat their dinner," she said emphatically.

The suggestion, thought Gaius, was unpopular — or sufficiently political to make unsafe conversation. But he agreed with the bard's sentiments; he had no wish to hear any story of Roman atrocities right now.

Cynric looked sullen for a moment, then said to Gaius in an undertone, "I will tell you later then. My foster mother may well be right; it is not a tale to be told at the dinner table, nor before children."

"We would do better," said Rheis, "to talk about our preparations for the feast of Beltane," and Mairi and the girls, as if at a signal, rose from the table. Cynric offered his arm to Gaius, and helped him back to his bed. The young Roman was a good deal more weary than he had realized; every muscle in his body ached, and though he was resolved not to sleep before he had thoroughly thought all this through, he soon found himself drifting off.

In the next few days, Gaius's injured shoulder swelled, which kept him abed in considerable pain – but Eilan, who nursed him devotedly, said that this discomfort was nothing to the illness that could have come from such a dirty stake.

The only part of the day that was tolerable was when, two or three times a day, Eilan – who seemed to have appointed herself his nurse – brought him his meals and fed him, since he could hardly hold a spoon, let alone cut up meat. He had not been so close to any woman since his mother had died, and had never quite realized how much he had missed that closeness. Whether it was because she was female or because she was of his mother's people, or perhaps from some sympathy of spirit that went beyond either, he found himself truly able to relax with her. In the long hours between her appearances, he had nothing else to think about, and each day, it seemed, he looked forward to seeing her more.

One morning Cynric and Rheis suggested that it would do him good to get out into the sunshine for a little and try to walk. He hobbled painfully out into the courtyard, where little Senara found him, prattling that she and Eilan were going to the meadow to pick flowers and make garlands for the Beltane festival the next day.

Under normal circumstances the idea of going along with a couple of girls would not have attracted Gaius very much; but after his last few days in bed, he would have welcomed a trip to the cowshed to watch Mairi – or even the byre-woman – milk the cows. In fact it seemed more like a picnic; for Cynric and Dieda joined them. The younger girls bullied Cynric as if he were truly their brother, and gave him their shawls and the lunch basket to carry.

Senara escorted Gaius; he leaned harder on her than he really wanted to, and told himself that he was humoring the child. Cynric seemed to hover over Dieda in something other than a brotherly way, talking in low tones. Watching them, Gaius wondered if they were pledged to each other; he did not know enough of this tribe's customs to tell, but he knew better than to bother them.

They laid the contents of the lunch basket out on the grass; there was fresh baked bread and cold sliced roast meat, and apples –

rather withered and brown – the last, the girls said, of the winter store.

"Let me go find some berries." Senara jumped to her feet, looking around her, and Eilan laughed.

"Silly, it's springtime. Do you think our guest is a goat you can feed on flowers?"

Gaius did not care what they ate; he was exhausted.

There was a flask of pressed fruit juice and another of fresh brewed country beer. The younger girls would not drink it, saying it was too sour; but Gaius found it refreshing. There were sweet cakes too, which Dieda had made herself. She and Cynric shared a drinking horn and left Gaius to the company of the other girls.

When they had all eaten as much as they could hold, Senara filled a bowl with clear water from a spring in the corner of the meadow and told Eilan to see if she could see the face of her sweetheart in it.

"That is an old superstition," Eilan said, "and I have no sweetheart."

"I have," Cynric said, seizing the bowl and staring into it. "Will the water show me your face, Dieda?" She came and looked over his shoulder. "It is all nonsense," she said. Gaius thought she looked prettier when she blushed.

"Did you look in the water, Eilan?" asked Senara, tugging at her sleeve.

Eilan said, "I think it is blasphemous to try to compel the Goddess to speak that way! What would Lhiannon say?"

"Does anyone here care?" Dieda asked with a strange hard little smile. "We all know she says nothing unless it is given her by the priests."

"Your father cares," Cynric said soberly.

"True, he does," Dieda said, "and so I suppose you must care too."

Senara turned to her. "Tell me what you saw in the water, Dieda," she demanded shrilly.

"Me," said Cynric, "or at least I hope so."

"You would really be our brother, then," Senara smiled at him.

"Why do you think I want to marry her?" Cynric grinned. "But we have yet to speak to your father."

"Do you think he will oppose it?" Dieda seemed suddenly anxious, and it occurred to Gaius that being the Arch-Druid's daughter might be even more constricting than being a Prefect's son. "Surely if he had pledged me elsewhere, he would have told me of it before now!"

"And who will you marry, Eilan?" Senara asked. Gaius leaned forward, his attention abruptly focusing.

"I had not thought of it," Eilan said, coloring. "Sometimes it seems to me that I hear the Goddess – perhaps I should enter the Forest House as one of the maidens of the Oracle."

"Rather you than me," Dieda said. "I would never grudge you that life."

"Ugh!" Senara shook her head. "Would you really want to live all alone?"

"That would be a shameful waste." Gaius said. "Is there no man you wish to marry?"

Eilan looked up at him and was silent a moment before speaking, then she said slowly, "None to whom my parents would be likely to give me. And life in the Forest House can be very rewarding. The holy women learn all manner of wisdom and the healing arts."

So, Gaius thought, *she would like to be a healer-priestess*. As he had said to Senara, he thought that would be a great waste of one who brought such beauty to the world. Eilan was quite different from everything he had heard of British girls, whom he had thought were like Clotinus's daughter. His father had sometimes spoken of pledging him in marriage to the daughter of an old friend, a high official in Londinium, but he had never seen the girl.

Now it occurred to him that it might be more useful for him to marry someone like Eilan. After all, his own mother had been a British tribeswoman. He looked at Eilan so long that she grew uneasy.

"Is there a spot on my face?" she asked. "We should get started on our festival garlands." Suddenly she jumped up and started across the meadow, which was liberally starred with blue, purple and yellow flowers. "No, not the bluebells," she said to Senara, who had followed her. "They will fade far too soon."

"Show me which ones I should use, then," Senara demanded. "I like these purple orchids – last year I saw the priestesses wearing them."

"I think their stems are too stiff to braid, but I will try," Eilan said, taking the handful of flowers from Senara. "No. I cannot do it; no doubt Lhiannon's maidens know some skill I do not," Eilan declared. "Let's try the primroses."

"They are as common as weeds," Senara complained, and Eilan frowned.

"What happens at the festival?" Gaius asked to distract her.

"They drive the cattle between the fires, and Lhiannon calls down the Goddess to deliver the Oracles," Eilan declared, her hands full of flowers.

"And lovers meet at the fires," said Cynric, looking at Dieda, "And pledged couples make known their vows. Here, Senara, try these."

"They are the ones I was trying to weave," Eilan complained, "but their stems are too stiff. Dieda, will those blossoms work?"

The older girl was kneeling before a hawthorn bush in full, starry bloom. At the question she turned and pricked her finger on a thorn. Cynric came over to her and kissed it, and she blushed and asked quickly, "Shall I make you a wreath, Cynric?"

"As you wish." Then a raven cawed from somewhere in the trees and his face changed. "What am I saying? I should not be thinking of garlands now."

Gaius saw her open her mouth as if to to ask Cynric why not, then stop, and wondered if it was because he was a stranger. She cast the blossoms away, and began to pick up the platters from which they had eaten. Eilan and Senara had finished their garlands.

"Rheis will be very cross if we forget to carry back any of these plates," Dieda pointed out. "And you girls had better finish these cakes."

Senara took one of the cakes and broke it in half, handing the remainder to Gaius.

"Now we have shared a single cake, you are my hearth-guest," she said. "Almost my brother."

"Don't be so silly, Senara," Eilan said reprovingly. "Gawen, don't let her pester you."

"Oh, let her alone," Gaius said, "she isn't bothering me." He thought again of his own dead sister, and wondered what his life would have been like had she lived. As he rose to his feet, he stumbled a little and Eilan came to take his arm, handing her garlands to Dieda.

"I'm afraid we have tired you, Gawen," she said. "Here, lean on me. Careful, don't knock your arm on anything," she warned, guiding him away from a tree.

"Why, Eilan, you are a healer-priestess already," Cynric said. "Gawen, you can lean on me if you like. Of course, Eilan's much prettier than I am, so perhaps I should help Dieda," he said, his face brightening, and he took Dieda's arm as they started back along the path. "I think you had better go straight back to bed instead of getting up for supper, Gawen. Eilan will bring it to you. I worked too hard on that arm to have you undo all my labor."

three

‾‾‾‾~~‾‾‾‾

he dwelling of the Priestess of the Oracle was square, like a shrine, surrounded by a roofed portico and set a little apart from the other buildings within Vernemeton's walls. Although folk referred to the whole enclosure as the Forest House, in truth it was an entire community whose clustered buildings were connected by covered walkways. Gardens and courtyards lay between them so that the whole was like a maze. Only the dwelling of the High Priestess was set apart from the others, just as only she was surrounded by the kind of absolute simplicity that is harder to maintain than the most rigid ritual.

When the Arch-Druid Ardanos arrived, he was ushered into her presence at once by her attendant priestess, a tall dark-haired women called Caillean. She was clothed much like the High Priestess in a robe of dark blue linen, but Lhiannon's arm rings and the torque at her throat were of pure gold, while those of her attendant were of silver.

"You may go, child," Lhiannon told Caillean.

Ardanos waited until the striped door-curtain had closed behind her, then smiled. "She is no longer a child, Lhiannon. Many winters have passed since you came here with her to the Forest House."

"True, I lose track of the years," Lhiannon replied.

She was, the Druid Ardanos reflected dispassionately, an exceptionally beautiful woman still. He had known her for many years and was probably the nearest thing to a friend of her own generation yet living. When he had been younger, this had cost him many sleepless nights; he was now elderly and seldom even remembered how she had disturbed his peace.

All the priestesses of the Forest House at Vernemeton, the Most Sacred Grove, were chosen as much for their beauty as for any other attribute. It always surprised him. He could understand that a god might wish to be served by beautiful women, especially if he were some worthless Roman deity, but it did not accord with what he knew of women that a goddess should wish her servitors to be too beautiful.

His silence was not in the least constrained by the presence of the great churl Huw, who bore a cudgel and was stationed at the door, and who would immediately dash out the brains of any man – even the Arch-Druid himself – who made an offensive move or spoke a disrespectful word to the Priestess. Ardanos, of course, had no such intention; Huw's presence simply assured Lhiannon's safety and allowed her a freedom in entertaining visitors not permitted to others.

Ardanos knew that he did not look sufficiently venerable to grace the office of Arch-Druid, nor was he the Merlin of Britain reborn. But he consoled himself with the thought that Lhiannon no longer looked much like the living incarnation and prophetess of the Holy Goddess of Wisdom and Inspiration either. She was gracious and gentle and her face was refined by austerity, but for the rest she was just an aging woman, though her hair was so fair it was all but impossible to detect the graying strands he knew must be there. Her dark blue sacramental gown fell in stiff and unbecoming folds. The straight shoulders had begun to droop a little with fatigue. Ardanos felt his own age the more in beholding such clear signs of hers.

In recent years, in deference to her age, Lhiannon had begun to wear a headcloth, as most matrons and older women did, except when her hair was unbound for ritual. And yet, Ardanos reflected, for twenty years – and he had known her for most of them – this woman's face and form had been central to their faith, and through her lips had come, if not the literal word of the gods, then that word as it was interpreted by the priests of the Oracle.

And so perhaps there was something of divinity in the aging woman's face after all, a divinity that clung like a fragrance. Perhaps it was something invested there by the multitudes for whom this woman appeared as the Goddess herself; not, for them, a mere symbol of their faith, but in their literal child-minds, the Goddess-self – the great Virgin Mother of the Tribes, Lady of the Land in living form.

Lhiannon raised her head. "Ardanos, you have been staring at me for long enough to milk a cow! Did you come here to tell me

35

something, or to ask? Out with it, man! The worst I can do is to refuse. And when have I ever been able to say no to you?"

And these were the words of divinity, thought Ardanos, glad to pull a mantle of cynicism over a mood that was becoming oppressive.

"Forgive me, Lady of Holiness," he said mildly. "My thoughts were elsewhere."

He saw her surprise as he rose again, paced restlessly a few steps, then said abruptly, "Lhiannon, I'm worried; I heard a rumor in Deva, and it was repeated by no less a person than the son of the Prefect: Rome may withdraw the Legions. It's the third time that I have heard it spoken, and granted there is always a faction howling, 'Down with Rome', but –"

"And too many of those who pass rumors on and howl, are expecting – or at least hoping – that we will get up and howl along with them. I do not believe your rumor," said Lhiannon bluntly. "But if it should be so, I am sure we could live without them. Is that not what we have been praying for since Caractacus walked the streets of Rome in chains?"

"Have you any idea what chaos that would create?" Ardanos asked. "The very same faction howling, 'Down with Rome' –" He was still pleased with the metaphor . . .

"– certainly do not understand what will happen if they get their wish," said Lhiannon.

Ardanos thought, *She knows me very well; even now, we finish one another's thoughts.* But he did not wish to finish that train of thought.

"Granted that there has been such a faction since Caesar won the fame he needed to rule Rome by invading Britannia! Even now, they will expect those of us from the Sacred Grove to join in their cries," Ardanos said, "and will not understand when we are silent. Just now I am worried that it will erupt into rioting at Beltane –"

"No, I think Beltane is safe enough," Lhiannon said. "People come for the games, the fires and feasting, and all the rest. If it were Samaine, now –"

"These last levies have made things worse," said Ardanos. "They took thirty of Bendeigid's men, all the slaves set free when he was proscribed, and his own sworn man. Proscribed!" He laughed mirthlessly. "He doesn't know how lucky he was; only forbidden to live within twenty miles of Deva! And even so he hasn't found out about all the levies yet, but when he does – well, he's called me worse things than traitor before; his name-calling doesn't bother me.

"I have permission to hold the Beltane gathering – I went to Macellius Severus himself and asked him for leave to hold a peaceful festival – as it's been this last seven or eight years – in the name of Ceres, and it's because he knows and trusts me that they didn't send along a few legionaries to make sure they don't get out of order and – shall we say – decide to worship Mars instead."

Lhiannon sighed, and he knew that she was remembering those days of blood and fire when Boudicca had sacrificed men to the Goddess in return for victory. They had all been so young in those days, so sure they could bring back the days of glory with a little courage and a sharp sword.

"If there's any disturbance," said Ardanos, "any demonstration even, you know as well as I do that this part of the country will be cut to pieces. But how could I know their Legions had just marched through and levied thirty good men to rot in those filthy Mendip mines?"

But he should have known; he was supposed to know what the Romans were up to almost before they knew it themselves. He had to be ready for the next outrage, whatever it might be.

She said, "Canceling the rites at this late date would probably create unrest even where there was none. Do you want me to try it? Have there been any incidents, reaction to the levies, perhaps?"

"I'm not sure," Ardanos said. "Someone seems to have tried to arrange for the Prefect's son to . . . disappear –"

"The Prefect's son?" Lhiannon raised one thin eyebrow as if wondering why anyone should care. "To protest, or to make trouble for our people? Wouldn't it be more like Bendeigid to murder the men who came to take away the levies?"

"He found the lad trapped in a boar pit and saved his life, and now the boy is a guest in his home."

Lhiannon stared at him for a moment and began to laugh. "And your son-in-law Bendeigid does not know?"

"The lad looks enough like his Silure mother to pass for one of ours, and he's self-possessed enough not to give himself away. But he'll need to do some healing before he can be moved. If anything happens to the youngster, who's never, as far as I know, done anything much either good or ill, you know as well as I do that we'll be blamed for it. We get blamed for everything else, all the way back to and including the sack of Troy, and the very fact that the Legions are here and not back in Gaul where they belong. There are all the old atrocity stories that go back to the deified Julius – may he rest in peace," Ardanos added with a fierce grin that meant, she was certain, the exact opposite.

"Still, there is an element of rebellion," he said. "You don't see it, placed as you are; I don't see it much, living among Romans as I've done for so long. But it's my business to watch the winds. To see signs and omens. For instance – where ravens fly at midnight; I speak of the secret society that worships the Lady of Battles."

This made her laugh. "Oh, Ardanos! Those half-crazy old men who sacrifice to Cathubodva, telling fortunes and looking for omens in dead birds' guts – as bad as the Legions with their sacred chicken-coops – no one has ever paid the slightest attention to them –"

"That's what they were," Ardanos said. He told himself that he welcomed being able to tell Lhiannon something she did not know. In the old days, the priestesses had been equal with the Druids in their councils, but since the fall of Mona they had learned to be secret in order to survive. On occasion, the Arch-Druid even had to act on his own. Ardanos wondered sometimes if they might not be carrying it too far – if the priestesses might carry out the decisions of the Council better if they had a voice in making them. Then he would not have felt so alone with the problem.

"That is surely what they were, not three years ago. Now suddenly, instead of old priests and sacrificers, they're a group of young men, not one of whom is over twenty-one and most of whom were born in the Holy Island, who think they are reincarnations of the Sacred Band –"

"*Those* children! Born as they were, it would not surprise me." Her smooth brow wrinkled as she began to understand.

"Exactly so," he continued. "That boy Cynric whom Bendeigid is fostering is one of them, and my son-in-law, who always did have a touch of the fanatic, has lost no opportunity to share his politics with the boy!"

Lhiannon turned white. "How, may I ask, did that happen?"

"I never knew it would make any difference; it was before my daughter Rheis married Bendeigid, and I did not know him so well. By the time I realized how much trouble either of them could make, it was too late. Cynric's all set to begin where his foster father leaves off. He and Bendeigid between them managed to find most of the other boys – and there were the Ravens, with a name and an organization ready to hand . . .

"If anything should happen to me, or to you –" He shook his head, grimacing. "Who could stop them from trying to avenge their mothers' shame on Rome? Already folk from here to the lakes are going about telling one another that these men are reincarnated heroes."

"And so they might be," Lhiannon said,

Ardanos grunted. "The worst of it is, they look it."

"I recommended that they should all be drowned, remember, not just the girls," said Lhiannon, recovering her composure. "Cruel as it sounds, it would have saved trouble now. But there were some who had other ideas; they were tender-hearted or, like Bendeigid, they wanted to raise the boys to take revenge for the priestesses. And so they are still alive and it is more than twenty years too late to deny their existence. I cannot now say that they have no right to avenge."

Never that, Ardanos thought. He must never suggest that the word of Lhiannon was her own word, or the word of the priests, and not the word of the Goddess. He must not remind her that the word of Lhiannon had never differed in any essential way from the agreed will of the Council of Druids, or that the Goddess – if she existed at all, he thought cynically, had long since ceased to care or to intervene in what became of her worshipers, or of anybody else, except – or maybe including – her priestess.

He said carefully, "I was implying nothing. I merely remind you – will you not be seated? Your guard is eyeing me most disquietingly – I said only that if the Goddess answers your prayers for peace, She also hears, and ignores, the prayers of most of the population for open rebellion or war. How long will She continue to hear your prayers and ignore theirs? Or to put it even more bluntly" – *but not bluntly enough*, he thought – "forgive me for this, but you are not a young woman – what of the day when you no longer serve the shrine?"

If I could only speak the truth to her. A passion he thought he had forgotten tightened his throat. *She and I grow weak with the years, but Rome is still strong. Who will teach the young ones how to preserve our ancient ways until Rome in her turn grows old, and our land is our own once more?*

After a moment she dropped into a chair and shielded her eyes with her hands. She said, "Do you think I have not considered that?"

"I know you have thought of it," he said. "And I know the result of your thoughts. Vernemeton might one day be served by one who, let us say, answered the cries of the many for war, rather than the prayers of her Priestess. And then there *would* be war. And you know what will become of us then."

"I can only serve the shrine while I live," said Lhiannon bitterly. "Even you cannot ask more of me than that."

"While you live," echoed the old Druid. "It is of that we must speak now." Lhiannon passed her hand across her eyes. More gently, he asked, "Do you not choose your own successor?"

"In a sense." She drew a deep breath. "They say I will know when I am to die and thus pass on my powers and such wisdom as is mine. You know who makes the real choice. I was not Helve's chosen. She loved me, yes, but I was not her choice. That one – her name does not matter; she was but nineteen, and disturbed in her wits. It was she on whom Helve's choice fell; she gave that girl the kiss of farewell, and yet she was not even considered nor given any trial at the hands of the gods. Why not? No doubt you know better than I. The priests make the final choice. What I say about my successor will have little weight – unless I am careful to name someone acceptable to them."

"Yet," said Ardanos, "It could be arranged – that your choice would be theirs."

She said, "Your choice, you mean."

"If you will." He sighed. She was simply too quick to see through him, he could hardly resent that – certainly not now.

"I tried that once," said Lhiannon wearily, "with Caillean; and you know how that experiment turned out."

"Do I?" he asked.

Lhiannon looked at him oddly. "You should pay more attention to what is happening in the Forest House. I suspect you would find it hard to trust her; she has the extremely awkward habit of thinking, usually at precisely the wrong time."

"But she is the senior priestess. If you were to die tomorrow you know Caillean would be chosen – unless," he added with emphasis, "she were to die in the hour of trial." Lhiannon paled, and he went on, "You know best if she would be acceptable to the gods . . ."

She was silent this time, and he added persuasively, "But if there were someone else, less well known, whom you could train. If the Council . . . never suspected prearrangement –"

"If the girl was suitable and intelligent I cannot see why it should be thought a crime or a blasphemy to prepare her for the choice of the gods . . . or even for the ordeal at their hands," the old High Priestess said thoughtfully.

Ardanos was silent; he knew he could drive her only so far. Outside he could hear wind soughing in the trees, but there was no sound but their breathing within the room.

"Whom have you chosen for me to choose?" Lhiannon asked.

For the three days preceding one of the festivals at which she was to serve as the Voice of the Goddess, the High Priestess lived in seclusion, attended only by her chosen priestess, resting, meditating, and purifying herself. Caillean, who almost always stayed with her, welcomed this time of separation. The shelter of the Forest House could be constricting, and whenever so many women, however holy, lived together, there were bound to be conflicts from time to time.

But now she found it hard to put memories of the outside world behind her. She spooned oat porridge – made more nourishing by the addition of nutmeats, since the High Priestess might have no animal flesh during her time of purification – into a carved wooden bowl and offered it to Lhiannon.

"What did Ardanos want of you?" Caillean heard the bitterness in her own voice, but could not stop the words. "I did not expect to see him here until the day of the festival."

"You must not speak so of the Arch-Druid, child," Lhiannon shook her head, frowning. "He has a heavy load to bear."

"So have you," Caillean said tartly. "And he makes it no lighter with his demands on you."

Lhiannon shrugged, and Caillean thought once more how fragile those shoulders were to bear the weight of so many hopes and fears.

"He does the best he can," the High Priestess said as if she had not heard. "He worries about what will happen when I am gone."

Caillean looked at her in alarm. It was said that a priestess, especially one of high degree, would know her time. "Have you seen some omen – has he?"

Lhiannon shook her head fretfully. "He spoke in general, but someone must take thought for these things. No one is immortal, and whoever is to succeed me will have to begin her training soon."

For a moment Caillean looked at her. Then she laughed.

"By that am I to understand that none of us who are already trained is acceptable – especially me? Do not bother to answer," she said then. "I know that you will only defend him, and in truth I do not mind. The title of High Priestess is not enough to justify what I have seen you suffer all these years." Especially, she thought, since the honor of it was empty so long as Lhiannon did not choose to exercise her power.

Lhiannon made a movement of discomfort, and Caillean realized that she was treading too near forbidden ground. She had been closer to the older woman than a daughter since before her moonblood began to flow, and that was more than twenty years ago, so she knew how Lhiannon depended on the illusions that cushioned her reality.

Another woman might have asked Caillean what she wanted instead. Caillean's lips twisted wryly as she cleared away the half-eaten porridge for, indeed, she herself did not know. But her heart told her that there must be more to serving the Goddess than these formal rituals with their tantalizing hints of power.

The secret teachings of the Druids included tales of a time long ago when priests from a lost land now sunk beneath the sea had come to Britannia. They had been masters of magic, and as they married into the ruling lines of the people they found here and later into the families of each new group of conquerors, the old blood, and the old knowledge had been preserved. But those most learned in that lore had died on Mona, and their knowledge with them.

Sometimes it seemed to Caillean that what they retained at the Forest House was only the dregs of greatness. Most of the other women were content with their small magic, but from time to time Caillean would feel an odd conviction that there must be more. She had spoken truth to Lhiannon – she did not want to be Priestess of the Oracle. And yet if not that, what was it that she wanted to do?

"It is time for our morning devotions," Lhiannon's voice pierced her distraction. The older woman gripped the table and pushed herself upright.

And Goddess forbid that we should fail to perform even the slightest step in the ritual! thought Caillean as she helped the High Priestess to move out to the garden and settle herself before the plain stone altar there. But as Caillean lit the lamp set on its top and brought the flowers to lay before it, she found a measure of peace returning to her soul.

"Behold, Thou art come with the dawning adorned with flowers," Lhiannon said softly, lifting her hands in salutation.

"Thy radiance blazes in the strengthening sun and in the holy fire," Caillean replied.

"In the east arising, Thou art come to bring new life to the world." The voice of the High Priestess seemed to grow younger, purer, and Caillean knew that if she looked, she would have seen the lines of age fading from Lhiannon's face, until the beauty of the Maiden Goddess shone from her eyes.

But by then, the same power was filling her own heart.

"The flowers spring up in Thy footsteps; the earth grows green where Thou dost pass . . ." As she had so many times before, she allowed the rhythm of the rite to carry her to a place where there was only the Lady's harmony.

On the morning of the Beltane festival, Eilan woke before dawn in the women's house where she slept with her sisters. Eilan's bed, a wooden frame strung with rawhide and covered with skins and fine woolen blankets, was built up against the sloping thatched roof, so close that she could reach up and touch it. Over the years she had widened a crack in the mud plastering to a chink through which she could peer. Outside, the light of an early summer dawn was just beginning to break.

With a sigh she lay back again, trying to remember her dreams. There had been something about the festival, and then the scene had changed. There had been an eagle there, she knew, and she had been a swan, and then, it seemed to her, the eagle had become a swan as well, and they had both flown away.

Little Senara still slumbered; she slept closest to the wall for she was still small enough to fall out of bed. Her sharp bent knees poked into Eilan's side. Across the room Mairi, who had temporarily moved back in with her sisters until they learned what had happened to Rhodri, slept with her child; and on the outside Dieda, her loose pale hair scattered across her face, and her shift undone so that Eilan could see about her neck the chain that held Cynric's ring.

Rheis and Bendeigid did not know yet that the two had plighted themselves to one another. The secrecy made Eilan uneasy. But they meant to announce it at this festival, and ask the family to begin the complex negotiations regarding dowry and settlements so that they could be wed. At least Cynric had no living kin, which would make it simpler.

The only other furniture in the room was a bench fixed against the wall and the oaken chest in which the girls kept their extra shifts and holiday garments. It had belonged to Rheis before she married, and she had always said that when Dieda was wed it would be a part of her dower. Eilan did not grudge her this, for another, equally fine one intended for Eilan was already taking shape at the hands of old Vab the joiner. And in due time there would be one for Senara. She had seen the oak planks rubbed until they shone, and the wooden pegs stained till they did not show.

The baby whimpered sleepily and then began to squall, and Mairi sat up with a sigh, her curly hair an aureole around her face. She got up to change his breech-clout, then came back and laid him across the bed. He gurgled and she patted him.

Eilan put her feet into clogs and said, "Listen; I hear Mother outside. I suppose we had better get up." She pulled on her gown, and Dieda opened her eyes and said, "I'll be dressed in a minute."

Mairi laughed. "I'll help Rheis as soon as I've fed the babe. You and Eilan can stay here and make yourselves beautiful for the festival. If any of the young men have caught your fancy, you'd best be prepared to shine." She smiled kindly at her young kinswoman. Dieda, with two younger brothers at home, was not accustomed to being pampered, and they all connived to spoil her a little whenever she was here.

When Mairi and her child had gone, Dieda smiled and said sleepily, "Is it truly festival day? I thought that was tomorrow."

"It is today," teased Eilan, "when you and Cynric will plight your troth."

"Will Bendeigid approve, do you think?" Dieda asked. "He is Cynric's foster father after all."

"Oh, if *your* father gives his consent, it does not much matter what mine thinks," observed Eilan shrewdly. "And if he did disapprove of the two of you being together, I suppose he would have said so before now. Besides, I dreamed last night about you and Cynric at the festival."

"Did you? Tell me!" Dieda sat up, wrapping the bedclothes around her, for the air was still cool.

"I don't remember much about it. But your father was happy. Are you sure you want to marry that brother of mine?"

"I do, indeed," said Dieda with a small smile, and Eilan knew she would say no more.

Eilan said, "Maybe I should ask Cynric – he might have more to say!" and laughed.

"And maybe he would not," said Dieda. "He does not talk that much either. You do not want to marry him yourself, do you?"

Eilan shook her head emphatically. "He is my brother!" If she had to marry, surely the great hulking lout who used to put frogs in her bed and pull her hair was the last boy she would choose!

"That's not really so, you know," Dieda said.

"He is my foster brother, and that is like kin," Eilan corrected. "If Father wished us to marry, he would not have fostered him." She reached for a comb of carved horn and began to unbraid the glistening strands of her hair.

Dieda lay back with a sigh. I suppose Lhiannon will be at the festival . . ." she said after a time.

"Of course she will. The Forest House lies by the spring at the foot of the hillfort after all. Why?"

"Oh, I don't know. Now that I'm thinking about getting married it makes me shiver to imagine spending one's life that way," said Dieda.

"No one has asked it of you," said Eilan.

"Not in so many words," said Dieda. "But Father did ask me once if I had ever thought of giving myself to the gods."

"He asked you that?" Eilan's eyes grew wide.

"I said I had not," said Dieda, "but for weeks after I had nightmares that we had quarreled and he had imprisoned me in a hollow tree. And I do love Cynric. Anyway, I could not bear to live my whole life within the Forest House – or confined in any other house whatever. Would you?"

"I do not know – Eilan said. "Perhaps if I were asked I would agree –" She remembered how the priestesses moved through the festival, so serene in their dark blue gowns. They were honored like queens. Wouldn't that be a better life than being at some man's beck and call? And the priestesses were taught all the hidden lore.

"And yet I saw you looking at the young stranger," Dieda teased; "the one Cynric rescued. I think you would make a worse priestess than I!"

"Maybe you are right," Eilan turned away so that the other girl would not see the color that was heating her brow. She was concerned about Gawen because she had spent so much time tending him, that was all. "I have never thought much about it. But now I remember," she said thoughtfully, "Lhiannon was also in my dream."

four

Later that morning the family set out for the festival. It was a fair May day, with a freshness in the air from the rain the night before, but the wind had driven the last of the clouds eastward and overhead the sky was clear. On such a morning, all the world's colors seemed newly created to honor the day.

Gaius was still limping, but Cynric had taken the bandage from his ankle, saying it would do him good to walk on it. He walked carefully, breathing deeply of the cool air, doubly inebriating after so long spent lying down indoors. Two weeks ago it had seemed he would never walk under the open sky again. For the moment it was enough to be alive, watching the sunlight on the green leaves and the spring flowers and the bright clothing of the folk around him.

Eilan had put on a long loose gown woven in crossed squares of pale golds and browns and a color like budding leaves over an undertunic of pale green. Her hair lay in a shining cape across her shoulders, brighter than the gold of her brooches and bracelets. It seemed to him that in all that glowing world she was the fairest thing of all.

He paid little attention to their chatter about the festival. He had seen a few celebrations among his mother's people when he was a child, and he supposed this one would be much the same. He heard the noise of the festival before they got there, for the great Celtic festivals were generally combined with a market fair. The festivities had actually begun some days before, and would go on for some time after, but this – the eve of Beltane – was the focus of the festival. It was at dusk that the Priestess of the Oracle would appear.

The woods had blossomed with tents and bothies of woven branches, for the festival had attracted folk from many days' journey away. Most of the people here were Cornovii, but Gaius recognized the tribal tattooing of Dobunni and Ordovices and even some Deceangli from up near Deva. After two weeks in the house of Bendeigid, the British speech of his birth came easily to his tongue, and Deva and the Legion were beginning to seem dim and far away.

Around the base of the old hillfort were clustered stalls selling dishes and small wares, some looking as if they had been made by local peasantry, and some which could have been sold in Rome itself. Perhaps they were of Roman make, for there was a growing trade between Britain and Rome, and the Greek and Gaulish traders went everywhere. There were stalls of apples and sweets, markets where people were trading horses, and a hiring fair where you could find anything, so Cynric said, from a swineherd to a wet nurse.

But when Gaius reached the flattened top of the hill that lifted like an island above the sea of forest, his eyes widened. The fair occupied the grounds of a great cleared earthwork, too full of booths and folk for the perimeter to be visible. But at the far end of the main aisle rose a great earthen barrow, whose entrance was of stone. Cynric made a sign of reverence as they crossed the road.

Gaius asked, "Is that your temple, then?"

Cynric gave him a curious look, but said only, "It is the burial place of a great chief among our forefathers. Unless some of the older bards know who he was, his name is lost, and if there was ever a song about him I have forgotten it, or never learned."

Another, longer avenue led to a building like a small square tower surrounded by a thatched portico, and Gaius gave it a curious glance. Eilan whispered, "That is the shrine where they keep the holy things."

"It looks like a temple," he said in a low voice, and she stared at him.

"Surely you know that the gods cannot be worshiped in any house made with human hands, but only under the open sky?" She added after a moment, "On some of the western islands, where no trees grow, they hold the rites in forests of stone; but my father says that the secrets of the great ancient rings of stone here in the South were lost with the senior Druids who were killed when the Romans came."

A booth where they were selling bangles of Greek glass caught her eye and she stopped talking. Gaius sighed. Better not ask any more questions, he thought, lest he betray himself further. There were some things they would certainly expect even a Silure tribesman to know.

There were stalls of brooms and mops, and pretty girls selling garlands – almost everyone wore a garland – flowers and a good many other things, some too alien for Gaius to recognize. The young people wandered among the booths, casually looking at their wares. Cynric inquired for a swineherd but said that they all demanded too much for their labor.

"The accursed Romans have taken so many men in their levies that we must hire men to tend our beasts and till our fields," he said. "But so many folk have been driven from their lands that we can sometimes find men who will come for shelter and food alone. I suppose if I were a farmer I would be glad of that. But may the gods save me from tilling the land!"

At noon Rheis gathered her family together beneath a spreading oak tree at the base of the hill for some cold meat and bread. The old hillfort was the focus for many pathways. From here they could see a broad and well-tended way that ran westward, lined with stately oak trees. At its very end the thatched roofs of the Forest House and its outbuildings showed pale against the deep green of the Sacred Grove.

Cynric and Gaius had gone off to look at horses, and Rheis had drifted away to speak to an acquaintance. The girls were packing up the food, when Eilan froze and whispered, "Look, there is Lhiannon."

The High Priestess, with a few of her attendants, was coming along the Sacred Way between the long line of trees. Her slight figure glimmered in the dappling of sunlight that sifted through the branches, and she moved with the gliding pace of a trained priestess, so that she did not seem quite like a human being at all as she drew near. Lhiannon stopped as if to wish them a joyous festival, and her eyes fell on the girls. "You are the kinswomen of Bendeigid," she said. Her gaze fixed on Dieda. "How old are you, my child?"

"Fifteen," whispered the girl.

"Are you yet married?" Lhiannon asked. Eilan felt her heart begin to thud heavily in her breast. This was the face of the High Priestess as she had seen it in her dream.

"I am not," Dieda said in a still voice. She was staring at the Priestess as if entranced by that clear gaze.

"Nor pledged in marriage?"

"Not . . . yet, although I have thought . . ." her voice faltered.

Tell her, thought Eilan. *You are pledged to Cynric! You have to tell her now!* But though her lips worked, Dieda stood frozen, like a young hare when the falcon's shadow falls.

Lhiannon unfastened the heavy blue cloak that hung from her shoulders. "Then I claim you for the Goddess; henceforth you shall serve Her whom I serve and no other . . ." The cloak opened like a dark wing as the priestess swung it round, and light flared as the branches moved in a sudden wind.

Eilan blinked. Surely it was only sunlight – but in the dazzle, for a moment she thought that the opening of the cloak had revealed a radiant figure. She closed her eyes, but imprinted upon her inner sight she saw still a Face with a mother's tender smile and a bird of prey's fierce eyes, and it seemed to her that it was she, not Dieda, who was fixed by that gaze. But Lhiannon had not spoken to her, nor seemed to see her at all.

"From henceforward, you shall dwell with us in the Forest House, my child. Come to us there – well, tomorrow will be time enough." Lhiannon's voice seemed to come from a great distance. "So be it."

Eilan opened her eyes once more and saw the shadow fall as the cloak settled across Dieda's slim shoulders.

The women who followed Lhiannon intoned, "She is the beloved of the Goddess; Her choice has fallen. So be it."

Lhiannon took the cloak from the girl's shoulders and her attendants helped her to fasten it again. Then she moved away from them, towards the festival.

Eilan's eyes were still fixed on her. "The choice of the Goddess . . . you are to be one of them . . . What is the matter with you?" She came back to herself and saw that Dieda's face was deathly white, her hands locked together.

Dieda shook her head, shivering, "Why couldn't I speak? Why couldn't I tell her? I cannot go to the Forest House – I am pledged to Cynric!"

"But you aren't not yet, not formally," said Eilan, still dazzled by what she had seen. "Private promises aren't binding, and nothing has gone so far that it cannot be undone. I should think that anyone would rather be a priestess than marry my brother –"

"You should think –" said Dieda furiously. "Yes, you really should think, sometime – it would be a new experience for you, I dare say –" She broke off in something like despair. "You're such a child, Eilan!"

Eilan stared at her, realizing that the other girl did not share her excitement. "Dieda, are you saying that you don't want to be a priestess?"

"What a pity her choice did not fall upon you," said Dieda helplessly. "Maybe we should say it was you. Maybe, like Father, she mistook us. Maybe it was really you she meant –"

"But that would be impiety, if the Goddess has chosen you," Eilan protested.

"What am I going to say to Cynric? What is there that I can say to him?" Her control broke and she began to laugh helplessly.

"Dieda," Eilan put her arm around the other girl, "can't you speak to your father? Tell him that you don't want this? If it were me, I should be happy, but if you hate the idea –"

Numbly, choked with misery, Dieda said, "I dare not. Father would never understand, nor cross the High Priestess. There is something –" In a voice which hardly reached her kinswoman's ears, she said, "Father is so much Lhiannon's friend – it's almost as if he were her lover –"

Scandalized, Eilan turned her eyes upon the other girl. "How can you say that? She is a priestess!"

"I don't mean they've done anything wrong, but he has known her so long. He seems at times to care more about her than anyone alive – surely more than any of us girls!"

"Take care how you say such things," Eilan warned, her face flushing. "Someone else might hear who would understand you no better than I did."

Dieda said dismally, "Oh, what does it matter? I wish I were dead!"

Eilan did not know what to say to comfort her. She was silent, clinging to the other girl's hand. She could not understand how Dieda might wish to refuse this honor. And how happy it would make Rheis, that her youngest sister should be chosen.

Bendeigid too would be pleased; Dieda was like another daughter to him and he had always been fond of his wife's little sister. Eilan tried to forget her own disappointment.

Gaius and Cynric moved through the holiday crowd, pausing from time to time to comment on the points of some pony, then moving on. After a time Cynric asked, "Is it true then, friend, that you know nothing of what befell on the Isle of Mona? I had thought – if you lived near Deva –"

"I have never heard the story," Gaius said. "I'm from the country of the Silures, remember, away to the south." *And knowing that my mother was married to a Roman officer*, he thought then, *it would have taken a braver man than most to tell me*. "Is it some well-known tale?" he said aloud. "You said that the Druid Ardanos could sing it."

"Hear it then, and wonder no more why I have little that is good to say of the Romans," said Cynric angrily. "There was – in the days before the Romans came – a sacred enclosure of women where now is nothing but a polluted pool. One day the Legions came – and did what they always do; cut down the grove and plundered its treasures, murdered such Druids as contested with them, and raped all the women – from the oldest priestess to the youngest novice. Some were near to grandmothers in age, some no more than little girls of nine or ten, but that did not matter to them!"

Gaius gasped. He had never heard that part of the story. The Romans spoke only of the Druids with their tossing torches and the dark-clad women who had shrieked imprecations, and said that the legionaries had been afraid to cross the boiling waters of the Menai strait until their commander shamed them into attacking. Mona had been the final stronghold of the Druid priesthood. Until meeting Bendeigid and Ardanos, he had thought most of them had been wiped out. Military logic made it obvious that Mona must be destroyed. But a good commander, he thought angrily, kept his men in line. Had the soldiers reacted so violently because the women made them afraid?

"What happened to the women? You may well ask," said Cynric. As a matter of fact, Gaius had not asked; but he knew that Cynric was telling the tale as he had been taught, and would sooner or later get around to that.

"The Romans left most of the women pregnant," Cynric went on. "When the babies were born, the girls were drowned in the sacred pool the Romans had already desecrated, and the boys were fostered with the families of Druids. When they came to manhood they were told of their background, and they were given training at arms. And one day they are to avenge their mothers and their gods; and, believe me, they will! They will – I swear it by the Lady of Ravens who hears me!" he added vehemently. He fell silent, and Gaius waited uneasily for him to go on. Cynric had spoken of an underground movement called the Ravens. Was the other boy, then, one of them?

After a moment Cynric continued, "That was when all the women of the Druids on this isle were brought here to the Forest House where they could be guarded."

Gaius listened, wondering if the tale had been told him for a reason. But Cynric did not know he was Roman, and Gaius was very glad. At the moment he was not sure he wanted to be a Roman himself, although it had been the wellspring of his pride.

As dusk began to fall young men in white robes with golden torques about their necks began piling up two great heaps of wood in the open space before the barrow, making sure – as Cynric informed him in a whisper – that each included the wood of the nine sacred trees. Gaius had no idea what those were, but was afraid to admit it, so he simply nodded. Between them a plank of oak had been placed with a piece set upright like an axle. Nine Druids, old, imposing men in spotless white robes, took turns to spin the axle to the beat of a drum. As the sky darkened, people gathered around them, watching, and silence spread through the crowd.

And then, just as the sun slipped beyond the trees, Gaius glimpsed a spark of red. Others had seen it as well. A murmur rippled through the crowd, and in the same moment one of the Druids cast something powdery at the base of the axle and it seemed to explode into flame.

"The fires will burn till dawning, while folk dance around them," said Cynric. "And some of the lads will keep watch over the Beltane tree." He gestured towards a tall pole that stood at the other end of the hilltop. "The rest will be out until dawn with their sweethearts gathering greenery, or at least that is what they say" – he grinned suggestively – "and will bring it back in the morning to crown the pole and dance in the day."

The need-fire had been carried to the woodpiles, which were now beginning to crackle merrily. It was growing dark; Gaius stepped back as the first blast of heat tingled on his skin.

A line of dancers formed and began to circle the bonfires. Someone set a wine flask to Gaius's lips. Already the crowd was getting rowdier, dipping freely into the vats of ale and mead. He had seen rites like this before and knew what to expect. He noticed now that the smaller children had been taken away; the young priestesses in the blue robes and fillets and veils of the Forest House were no longer among the crowd.

Gaius and Cynric wandered together through the laughing throng until, near the fires, they encountered Eilan and Dieda.

"There you are!" exclaimed Cynric, hurrying forward. "Dieda, come dance with me."

All the color left Dieda's face and she held on to Eilan's hand.

"You have not heard?" asked Eilan brightly.

"Heard what, Sister?" Cynric began to frown.

"She has been chosen for the Forest House – by Lhiannon herself, this very afternoon!"

Cynric reached out to Dieda, and then, slowly, let his hands fall. "The Goddess has spoken?"

"How can you accept this?" Dieda's spirit seemed to come back to her. "You know I cannot marry you if I must take vows."

"And you know what vows already bind me," he said somberly. "I have been torn to pieces trying to decide. I love you but I cannot encumber myself with a wife and children for years, if ever. Perhaps the gods have chosen this way for us."

He drew a shaken breath and this time when he reached out she came to him. Dieda was a tall girl, but she seemed fragile, encircled by his strong arms.

"Listen, beloved, there is still a way," he said softly, taking her aside. "Three years you can give the Goddess – you need not pledge yourself lifelong. There is a battle college in the northern islands, and it is there that I am bound to go. But you are no battle-maiden; even if we were publicly pledged you could not come to me there. Perhaps it is as well you are to serve in the sanctuary for a time – you will be safer there. And if war should come . . ."

Dieda gave a little sob and buried her face against his shoulder. Gaius saw Cynric's big hands close on her arms.

"For three years other vows will bind us," he whispered, "but tonight is ours. Eilan, stay here with Gawen," he added, his voice muffled by Dieda's hair.

Eilan hesitated. "Mother said that Dieda and I were to stay together – it is Beltane –"

Dieda lifted her head, and her eyes were wild. "Have some pity! Rheis dares not cross your father – and my father –" She swallowed. "If they knew, they would not let us have even this little time!"

Her eyes wide and grave, Eilan nodded.

"Was I wrong to leave Eilan alone with the stranger?" Dieda whispered as Cynric led her away. "After all, he has lived among the Romans and may have their ways with women."

"He is a guest in our house; even if he were the son of the Procurator himself . . ."

"He can't be," Dieda giggled suddenly. "My father says that the Procurator has only a single daughter."

"– if he were, surely, he would respect the daughter of his host. And Eilan is only a child," Cynric replied.

"She and I were born in the same year," Dieda said. "You think her a child because she is your sister."

"What were you expecting?" Cynric asked irritably. "That I should tell you how much I love you before them both?"

"What is there left to say? Certainly not enough –" And she stopped, for his arms were around her, and he stooped to cut off her words with a kiss.

She clung to him for a moment, then broke uneasily away. "That doesn't help," she said. "And if we should be seen . . ."

He laughed mirthlessly. "They haven't put you under vows yet, have they? And I could always say it was Eilan I kissed." He put his hands under her elbows, lifting her on tiptoe, and bent to kiss her once more. After a moment all her resistance melted, and she let him mold her against him, kissing her again and again. When he broke away, his voice cracked, "How sane I sounded, a few moments ago! But I was wrong. I can't let you do this thing!"

"What do you mean?"

"I can't let you be walled up with all those women."

"What else can I do?" Now she had to be the sensible one. "Cynric, you're Druid-bred, you know the laws as well as I. Lhiannon has chosen. Where the hand of the Goddess has fallen . . ."

"You are right, I know it, but still . . ." He pulled her to him roughly, but his voice was very gentle as he said, "It's Beltane. Lie with me tonight, and your family will be glad enough to let us marry."

Her mouth was too young to be so bitter. "Perhaps you would like to explain nicely to my father how it happened? Or to yours."

He said, "Bendeigid is not my father."

"Yes, I know," she said. "Not that it makes any difference. But whether he is your father or not, Ardanos is mine, and he would strangle me and take a bullwhip to you. It is done, whether I like it or not. I am now a pledged virgin of the Sacred Grove and you are a Druid's son – well, at least you have been raised as one – and you are the son of a priestess in any case," she added quickly. "Cynric, you said it yourself. I can ask to be released at the end of three years. And then –"

"And then," he promised, "I will take you away to the other end of the earth if that is what I have to do."

"But you said you ought not to encumber yourself with wife or children," she protested, for the sake of hearing him say, "I don't care what I said; I want you."

Then he added, "Sit here beside me, then; let us watch the fires. It may be for the last time. Or for three years, which," he added despondently, "is almost the same thing."

The Arch-Druid of Britain stood at the gateway to the Forest House, watching the last light fade from the sky. From the hilltop he could hear the sounds of many voices, their clamor faded by distance to a music like a lake full of migrating birds, and beneath the other sounds, the deep heartbeat of the drums. Soon they would be lighting the Beltane fires.

Though time was passing, Ardanos felt curiously unwilling to move. That morning he had been in Deva, listening to the Roman Prefect. Tonight he would have to hear the complaints of the people the Romans ruled. There was no way he could satisfy all of them. The best he could hope for was to maintain an uneasy balance until – what, really, was he waiting for? – for all the old wounds to heal?

You will be dead before that happens, old man! he told himself. *And Lhiannon too*. He sighed, and saw that the first star had pricked through the darkening sky.

"The Lady is ready," said a soft voice behind him. Ardanos turned and saw one of the maidens, Miellyn, he thought, holding open the door.

Lhiannon's chamber was lit by hanging lamps of bronze. In their flickering light he saw her already slumped in her chair, Caillean standing watchfully by her side. For a moment the younger priestess met his gaze defiantly, then she stepped aside.

"She has taken the sacred herbs," Caillean said in a neutral tone.

Ardanos nodded. He was well aware of the girl's hostility, but as long as Caillean observed the forms of respect, he cared little what she thought of him. It was enough that she was devoted to Lhiannon.

Still frowning, Caillean left them alone. At such a time, when the High Priestess was already beneath the shadow of the Goddess she served, even her bodyguard might not be present here.

"Lhiannon," he said softly, and saw a tremor run through her thin frame. "Can you hear me?" There was a long silence.

"I always hear you . . ." the High Priestess said at last.

"You know that I would not be doing this, my dear," he said, almost to himself, "if there were any other way. But I have learned that there is more trouble over the levies. Bendeigid's son-in-law Rhodri went after the men they took from the Druid's clan and attacked the soldiers who were guarding them. There was a fight and Rhodri was captured.

"Macellius has managed to keep his identity a secret, but there is no way he can save him. The fool was taken in arms against Rome. If that word gets out there surely will be a rebellion. You must counsel peace, my dear." His voice dropped to a croon. "Let there be peace in the land – the Goddess wills it. Rome's time will come, but not yet, and not through war. The people must help one another and be patient – tell them, Lady. Let them pray for peace to the gods."

As he spoke, he saw her begin to sway, and knew that his words were reaching that deep place beyond conscious memory through which the words of the Oracle came. Despite what Caillean might believe, Ardanos had never doubted that *something* spoke through the High Priestess when she was thus tranced. But the Druids knew well that the ability of a spirit to speak through a human oracle was directly related to the content and sophistication of the mind that was its vehicle. An ignorant girl, no matter how sensitive, could only speak in simple, homely, terms. It was one reason why the Druid priestesses were so carefully selected and trained.

Some might have accused him of manipulation, but to the Arch-Druid it seemed that he was only adding his own particular knowledge of the country's needs to the resources at the Oracle's command. Though he did his best to impress certain information on the Oracle's memory, the Goddess, if it were truly She who was speaking, was surely at liberty to decide what to say.

"Peace and patience . . ." he repeated slowly. "Rome will fall when the gods will it, but not by our hands . . ."

fIVE

━━━∿∿∿━━━

Gaius watched Dieda and Cynric disappear into the crowd, fighting a desire to call them back again. Eilan, grown suddenly shy, was staring at her feet. He wondered what he could say to her. Hearing the story of the priestesses of Mona had left him feeling oddly diffident, not at all the lord of the world, as a Roman ought to be. Thank the gods Cynric did not suspect his real identity. He had the uneasy feeling that old Ardanos had guessed, but if so, the Druid had kept his secret, which in its way was even more disturbing.

He cast about for some harmless topic of conversation, and said at last, "Tell me more about how your tribe keeps this festival. The Silure customs are somewhat different, and I do not wish to offend against your ways." A safe way, he thought, of covering the fact that he had only been to one native Beltane celebration, when he was six years old.

She colored. "Are they?" Now she was genuinely embarrassed. "It is a very ancient festival. Perhaps once all the tribes kept it the same way. Ardanos says our people brought it with them when they came to these islands. And he should know."

"Yes indeed," Gaius said. "He is so old – your grandfather – do you suppose he came over with those first ships from Gaul?" She giggled, and Gaius sighed with relief, feeling the tension between them ease.

"You have seen how they made the sacred flame," she said then. "Tonight when the Priestess comes out to bless the fires we will hail her as the Goddess. I do not know how it is with the southern tribes, but in the North, in the olden times, women were more free than now. Before the Romans came, the Queen sometimes ruled the tribe in her own right. Now it is the Priestess and the Druids. That is why Cartimandua could command the Brigantes, and the Iceni followed Boudicca."

Gaius stiffened. Among the Romans, Boudicca, the Killer Queen, was still a name to frighten children. In Londinium you could see the marks where the basilica had burned, and workmen digging foundations as the city grew sometimes found the bones of those who had tried to flee the bloodlust of the Iceni hordes. Eilan, oblivious, was still talking.

"Only in wartime did she appoint a duke of war to lead the armies; sometimes he was her brother, and sometimes her consort, but whatever he was, it gave him small power in the tribe. The Queen ruled of her own right, and whatever you may say, women know more of ruling, because each woman runs her own household. Isn't she better qualified to rule over a tribe than a man who can only do what his war chief says?"

"Over a tribe, perhaps," said Gaius. "Absurd it would be indeed, for a woman to command a Legion – or to rule a great empire like that of the Caesars."

"I cannot see why that should be so," Eilan said. "Surely a woman who can govern a large household is as fit to rule an empire as any man. Have there been no mighty queens among the Romans?"

Gaius grimaced, remembering the history that his Greek tutor had insisted he learn. "In the days of the Claudian Emperors," he said carefully, "I have heard there was an evil old woman named Livia, the mother of the deified Tiberius. She poisoned all her kinfolk. Perhaps that is why the Romans are not fond of female rulers."

Their walking had brought them to the far side of the fires, where the barrow mound sloped down to the festival ground.

"Gawen, do you think women are evil?" Eilan asked.

"*You* are not evil, certainly," he said, meeting her clear gaze. Her eyes were like a well of pure water into which he could sink for ever. A well of truth – at that moment it seemed to him monstrous that he should have to live this lie. Though it made no sense, he felt that he could trust her with his life; and if he entrusted her with his true identity, he might be doing just that.

There was a stir behind them. The shouts and singing grew closer. Gaius turned, and saw men bringing up images made out of wicker or straw. Some were human in shape, some, figures out of nightmare. One was even clad in a recognizable simulation of a legionary's helm.

The hair lifted on his neck. Earlier he had told Eilan he

remembered nothing of the Beltane rites, but now, whether because of the drumming or the flickering light or the scent of sweet herbs they had cast on the fire, he suddenly knew that he had seen something like this before. He closed his eyes, seeing in memory tattooed dragons coiling up strong arms, hearing a young man's laughter. For a moment the drumming deafened him; blood filled his vision, and a grief so long suppressed that even now he could not give it a name.

His grip tightened on Eilan's arm.

"Silly!" Eilan laughed at his expression. "They are only effigies. Even in the old days it was only every seven years that the Summer King or his substitute was offered to renew the land."

"You are a Druid's daughter," he said, easing down upon the grass. "I suppose that you would know."

She smiled and sat down beside him at the edge of the circle. "I have not the lore they teach them in the Forest House, but I have heard that tale. They say that the Chosen One would be treated like a king for the year before his doom. It was a great honor for his family. His every wish was fulfilled, he had the best of food and wine, and the most beautiful young women were brought to him. It was an honor to bear a child to the god; even the women of the sanctuary were not forbidden to him; though it is death for any other to lie with one of the priestesses. And at the end of his time . . ." She hesitated. "He was given to the fire."

Eilan was sitting very close to him. He could smell the fresh, wild-flower scent of her hair.

"I have heard that there is a new cult in Rome called the followers of the Nazarene who believe that their prophet was the son of their god and died for their sins," said Gaius. Personally, he favored Mithras, the soldiers' god.

"They are not only in Rome," she said. "My father says that some of them fled to Britannia when the Emperor was killing them. And the Druids allowed them to build a sanctuary at the Isle of Apples far to the south in the Summer Country. But here we have only the consort of the Goddess – or his substitute, who gives his blood to the land."

Shouting, teams of young men swung the effigies on to the bonfires, cheering as the flames surged against the sky. Eilan flinched as another group ran past, and Gaius put his arm around her protectively.

"Now they are burning all the evil spirits, and presently they will drive the cattle between the fires to keep them safe throughout the summer when they pasture them in the hills. The fires are very powerful . . ." She went red suddenly with something more than the heat of the flames.

"What else happens around the fires?" he asked gently, trembling a little with the effort it took not to draw her closer. Even through the gown he could feel the slender softness of her body. When he first met Eilan, he had thought her a child, but now, slender though she was, he realized that she was a woman, and knew that he wanted her.

"Well," she began hesitantly, looking fixedly into the flames, "on this night, while the fires of the Goddess burn, couples who are pledged leap over them, hand in hand, to honor the Goddess and to plead with her for children. And then they go into the forest together. Perhaps in the old days it was not known how children were made; but Ardanos says that they observed that children were born after they so honored the Lady — and folk still honor her by following that old custom . . ."

"I see," said Gaius gently, and felt his pulsebeat quickening.

"Of course," Eilan went on quickly, "it is not a thing that the daughters of chieftains or Druids do —"

"Of course not," said Gaius, very softly. His body was telling him that this was something the son of a Prefect could do very well, but he hoped he could keep it from Eilan. As the daughter of his host she should be as sacred to him as his own sister. "And yet, it would be lovely if . . ." he took a deep breath, "if we might honor the Goddess thus together . . ."

He could sense the heat and color in her cheeks, though it was now almost too dark to see. She stilled within the circle of his arm.

"I never thought . . ." She said softly, and stopped, beginning to tremble a little in turn. But she did not pull away.

"That is how I would show you what I feel for you," he said even more softly, as if he feared to frighten a wild bird that had alighted on his hand. She had told her tale with such innocence! Clotinus's daughter had made it clear that she would welcome his advances; and Gaius had only been disgusted by her boldness, but it seemed to him that he had never before felt for any maiden what he now felt for Eilan, sitting so trustingly by his side. She was so close to him that he could feel the warmth of her body. And every breath filled him with the flower scent of her fair hair.

As the shouting died down he heard the faint small sounds of the night: small animals rustling in the grass where the hill fell away behind the barrow; the rustle and snap of the fires, the cry somewhere of a bird. And now, excited by her story, he could hear other sounds in the spring night. On the slope behind them, men and women were making love.

He touched Eilan's cheek, and it was like the petal of a flower. Gently he turned her face towards him. Her eyes were wide and wondering, her lips a little parted. He felt her start of surprise as he kissed her, but she did not pull away. Her lips were sweet, so sweet that he held her against him and kissed her again, and after a moment of resistance felt her mouth opening beneath his like a flower.

Gaius fell into her sweetness. Dazed, every pulse pounding, it took him a moment to understand what had happened when she pushed him away.

"We must not!" she whispered. "My father would kill us both!"

Gaius forced his hands to open, to let her go. To lay hands on the daughter of his host was an impiety of the worst kind. Eilan should be as sacred to him as his own sister. Sacred ... he understood abruptly that what he felt for her was a holy thing. He realized that when he let her go he had plunged his fingers instead into the grass, and sat up, wiping his hands.

"It is true." He was surprised that he could speak so steadily. His senses were still awhirl, but he felt the warmth of certainty within him. Since that first moment when he saw her looking down into the pit where he had fallen, haloed in light, it seemed to him that this moment had been preordained.

"It would shame us both, and there is no dishonor at all in what I feel for you. I love you, Eilan, as a man loves the woman he would make his wife."

"How can you?" she whispered, staring at the fire. "You are a stranger. You never even saw me until two weeks ago. Have you dreamed of me, too?"

"I am more of a stranger than you know," he said grimly. "But I will prove my love to you —" He gathered his courage. "Now I will put my life in your hands. I am a Roman, Eilan. I did not entirely lie," he added quickly as she pulled away. "Gawen was the name by which my mother called me; but my true name is Gaius Macellius Severus Siluricus, and I am not ashamed of my lineage. My mother was a royal daughter of the Silures, and my father is Camp Prefect of the Second Adiutrix Legion. If that makes you hate me, summon the guards and let them take my life."

She flushed and then went pale again. "I would never betray you."

He stared at her. *My mother did* . . . Suddenly he realized what an odd thought that was, for surely his mother had not wanted to die and leave him alone. Only now, back in her warm and colorful world, was he realizing how painful the shock of being wrenched away from it to the chill discipline of an army camp had been. Was that why he had never been able to reveal himself to any Roman girl as he was doing with Eilan now?

"Tomorrow I must go back to my people, but I give you my pledge that if I leave here unscathed, and if it does not displease you, I shall ask your father honorably for your hand!"

He could feel his heartbeat shaking his chest, but he could think of nothing else to say.

"It would not be displeasing to me, Gawen – Gaius," she said at last. Her voice was very soft, but her gaze never flinched from his own. "But I do not think my father would consent to give me to a Roman, especially to one born of the Legions. And even if he should agree, my grandsire would not; and Cynric –" The words came in a rush. "Cynric would kill you if he knew!"

"That might not be so easy," Gaius said, his pride wakening, though the same thought had occurred to him. "But is it really so impossible? Since we came to this island, a number of our officers have married British women of good family to cement alliances. I am half a Briton myself, after all."

"Perhaps," she said doubtfully, "but not in our family!"

"Well, my blood on both sides is surely as good as yours!"

She gave him an odd look, and he realized that his Roman pride was speaking. She did not seem to dislike it, but she was not convinced, either, and her stern father would be even harder to persuade.

"I have never met anyone I liked so well as you," she said helplessly, "and in so little time. I do not understand it, either," she admitted, "but somehow it seems as if I had known you from the beginning of the world."

"Maybe you have," Gaius said, almost in a whisper. For a moment he felt as innocent as the girl in his arms.

He said, "Some of the Greek philosophers believe that each soul comes back again and again to complete its mission on earth, and knows again those it has loved and hated in other lives. It may be that some fate from another life has guided us together, Eilan."

Even as he said it, he wondered at himself. How could he, Gaius Macellius Severus, speak so to any woman? But Eilan, he defended himself, was not "any woman"; never in his life had he felt so close to anyone. For the first time in his life, his feeling for a girl was almost mystical, something he did not know how to explain.

"The Druids teach this also," she said quietly. "The greatest of our priests have been many lifetimes upon this earth, living as stags and salmon and boars so that they may understand all that lives; and heroes whose lives are cut short are often born again. But as for me and you . . ." She frowned, and he found it hard to meet her clear gaze.

"I looked in a pool once and saw myself with a different face, and yet it was me. I think that then I was a priestess. Now I look at you, and I do not see a Roman or a Briton either. My heart tells me that you were a great man among your people – like a king."

Gaius flushed. This kind of talk always made him uncomfortable. "I am not a king now," he said gruffly, "and you are not a priestess. I want you in this life, Eilan!" He took her hand. "I want to see you in the morning when I wake and sleep with you in my arms. I feel as if all my life something has been missing and you make me whole! Can you understand?" It seemed impossible that tomorrow he would be going back to the Legions, impossible that he might not see her again.

For a time she gazed into the fire, then she turned back to him. "Before I met you I dreamed of you," she said softly. "Many of my family are second-sighted, and I see true things sometimes in my dreams. But this I have told no one. You are in the center of my heart already. I do not know what power is drawing us together, but I think that I have loved you before."

He bent to kiss the palm of her hand and she gave a tremulous sigh.

"I love you, Gaius. There is a bond between us. But how we can be together, that I cannot see . . ."

I should take her now, thought Gaius, *then they would have to let us marry!* He was about to pull her closer when a shape passed between them and the light. The space around the bonfires was filling with people. A glance at the stars told him that it was near midnight, and the moon was high. Where had the hours gone? Eilan exclaimed softly and started to get to her feet.

"What is it?" he asked. "What is going on?" In the distance he could hear rowdy shouts and laughter, but the mood of the people here was both subdued and joyous. The sense of expectation around him set his skin prickling.

"Hush!" Eilan whispered as he stood up beside her. "The Goddess comes . . ."

Somewhere beyond the circle of firelight flutes twittered, and Eilan went still. In the sudden silence, the hiss of the fire came clearly. The flames had burned down to brands that lit the space with a steady glow, cooled by the moonlight to a pale golden radiance like no light he had ever known.

Something glimmered beyond the circle of light. Druids in white robes were coming; men with flowing beards crowned with oak leaves, and with golden torques about their throats. Sunwise they circled the fires and halted, waiting. Their circle was as evenly spaced as guards around a camp perimeter, but their movement had none of the military precision which Gaius had learned. They simply came to rest where they ought to be, like the stars.

Silver bells shivered sweetly and the tension in the circle grew. Gaius blinked, but he could see nothing, and yet there was something moving, a mass of shadow that swept towards them. Abruptly he realized that he was seeing women's shapes swathed in draperies of a blue like midnight. They flowed into the circle and around it, silver ornaments jingling faintly, faces a pale blur beneath the veils.

Suddenly he understood. These were the priestesses of the Forest House, the sacred women who had escaped the rape of Mona. To see so many Druids together raised his hackles, and when he looked upon the shadow shapes of the priestesses he felt terror, and a sudden sense of destiny. Was his fate somehow entangled with that of the priestesses of the Forest House? The thought made his blood run cold and his grip tightened on Eilan's hand.

The last three priestesses moved towards the long-legged stool that had been set between the fires. The foremost was slender, a little bowed beneath her robes, flanked by a tall woman and another who was sturdier. Both had dark hair and silver ornaments. Both were unveiled, and he could see the woad-blue crescents tattooed between their brows. Gaius's first thought was that the tall girl would be a worthy opponent in a fight, while he sensed discontent in her companion's eyes.

The group paused, and there was some ritual with a golden basin that he could not understand. Then they helped the priestess to sit down on the three-legged stool and carried it to the top of the mound between the fires. The shimmer of sound from the bells reached a climax, then stopped.

"Children of Don, why have you come here?" The tall woman asked, calling them by the name of the mythic ancestress of the tribes.

"We seek the blessing of the Goddess," one of the Druids replied.

"Then call Her!"

Two of the women cast handfuls of herbs on the coals. Gaius's nostrils flared as the sweet-smelling smoke puffed and swirled outward, filling the space with a glowing haze. He was accustomed to incense, but he had never felt this odd sense of pressure before. He would have said the weather was changing, but the sky was clear.

Around him the whisper was becoming a murmur of many voices, a soft mutter of invocation and appeal. Beneath it all he heard the Druids humming, and it seemed to him that the earth beneath his feet throbbed in answer. Once more he was afraid. He glanced over at Eilan and saw her gaze, rapt and exalted, fixed upon the three figures between the fires.

From the veiled woman came a little whimper and he saw her sway.

She is like the Sibyl, thought Gaius, *or the Pythia of Delphi that my tutor told me about.* But he had never expected to see such a thing himself. The humming grew in intensity, and suddenly the veiled woman stilled and the other two backed away. He caught his breath, for somehow she seemed to have grown taller. She straightened, turning as if she was looking around her. Then she laughed softly and put back her veil.

Gaius had heard that the High Priestess of Vernemeton was old, but this woman blazed with beauty, and she gestured with a restless energy that had nothing to do with age. His Roman cynicism fled and his mother's blood rose up in him. *It is true – all the tales are true – the Goddess is here . . .*

"I am the green earth that cradles you and the womb of the waters . . ." she said in a voice whose soft resonance made it seem as if she spoke in his ear. "I am the white moon and the sea of stars. I am the night from which the first light was born. I am the mother of the gods; I am the virgin; I am the dark serpent that swallows all. Do you see me? Do you desire me? Do you accept me now?"

"We see . . ." came the murmured answer. "We see you and adore . . ."

"Rejoice then, that life may continue. Sing, dance, feast and make love and you will have my blessing; the cattle will bear and the corn will grow."

"Lady!" a woman's voice rang out suddenly. "They have taken my man to the mines and my children are hungry. What will I do?"

"They took my son!" a man cried, and others echoed him. "When will you deliver us from the Romans? When will the war arrow fly?" A babble of protest rose and Gaius tensed, feeling the tension in the air. Eilan had only to say the word and they would tear him in pieces. But when he looked at her he saw her eyes bright with tears.

"Are you my children, that hear your sister's cry and do not provide for her?" Dark draperies swirled as the Goddess turned. "Care for one another! In the arcane volumes of the heavens, I have read the name of Rome, and on that scroll I say their name reads *Death*! Indeed, Rome will fall, but her fate is not yours to declare! So I have said, heed now my word!

"Remember the circle of life. All that you lose you will one day find, and that which has been taken from you will be restored. Behold, I bring down the power of heaven, that the world may be renewed!"

She lifted her hands to the moonlight, and it seemed to Gaius that the radiance grew brighter, so that her figure was obscured. The priestesses grouped around her began to sing:

> *"Upon these holy ancient trees,*
> *Now cast your lovely silver light;*
> *Uncloud your face that we may see*
> *Unveiled its shining in the night –"*

Gaius shivered. He had never known that women's voices could be so beautiful. For a moment the whole world seemed spelled to silence; then the arms of the High Priestess swept outward. Her two priestesses whirled to either side, and in the same moment the bonfires blazed up furiously. Had they cast something on to the flames? He could not see – he could hardly think, for everyone was shouting.

"Dance!" The voice of the Goddess rose above them all. "Rejoice, receive my ecstasy!" For a moment she arched upward, arms extending as if to embrace the world. Then she slumped into the arms of the tall priestess.

But Gaius could not see what happened afterwards, for someone bumped into him. His grip tightened on Eilan's hand and he felt his other hand seized by a stranger. Drums sounded and suddenly they were moving, the whole circle was moving, and there was nothing in the world but the beat of the drum. As the beat whirled him outward, he glimpsed Cynric and Dieda across the circle, and it seemed to him that Dieda's face shone with tears.

A long time later, it seemed, the dance came to an end and Cynric and Dieda found them, but once the ecstasy had faded, their own despair kept them from wondering what Gaius and Eilan had found to talk about on that Beltane Eve. It was very late by the time they reached the home of Bendeigid, and no one appeared to suspect that the two couples had not spent the whole time together. Gaius was happy to have it so – far better to seek Eilan's hand from Deva with his father's force behind him than to let the Druid suspect that his guest had compromised his child while Gaius was in the older man's power.

But if he had been Eilan's acknowledged suitor, they might at least have allowed him to see her to say goodbye. Rheis had decreed a cleaning day, and all the women were hard at work. As it was, he had only Rheis's promise to convey his carefully edited farewell and a glimpse of Eilan's bright hair to sustain him as he took the road for Deva and the world of Rome.

SIX

━━━〜〜〜━━━

acellius Severus senior, Prefectus Castrorum of the Second
Adiutrix Legion at Deva, was a man just entering middle
age, of a tall and commanding presence, who could
conceal a formidable anger beneath an outward surface of calm.
His mildness was deceptive. Big as he was, he never blustered or
bellowed; he was soft-spoken, almost scholarly, and from time to
time those who did not know him well were deceived into thinking
him ineffectual.

This apparent mildness was a valuable asset in the position he
now held: Camp Prefect, Prefectus Castrorum of Deva. In addition
to remaining permanently in charge of the camp, he served as a sort
of liaison between Legion and populace; he was not responsible to
the Commander of the Legion, but only to the Governor of the
Province, and the newly instituted *Legatus Juridicus*; but since the
Governor was in the field in Caledonia, and the Juridicus was
stationed in Londinium, that meant, in this distant outpost, that his
word was effective civilian law. Fortunately he worked well with
the legionary Commander, under whom he had served in several
campaigns long ago, and who had encouraged his efforts to fulfill
the financial requirements necessary to rise to the rank of
equestrian, the middle classes who were the backbone of the
Roman government.

Macellius Severus secured supplies and rations for the entire
Legion, directed quartering, and acted as general liaison officer
between the populace – both Briton and Roman – and the army. In
theory, he also represented the interests of the civilian population.
In requisitioning supplies for the Legions, he was required to see
that the people who provided them were left with adequate food
and manpower to avoid driving them to revolt. Hence the actual
management of the Ordovia lands around Deva lay more in his

hands, except in time of war, than in those of the legionary Commander.

His office, small and austere, and constructed with a rigid economy of space, somehow accommodated a daily overflow of civilians and military personnel, with a long string of complaints, requests and petitions. Sometimes Macellius, who was not a small man, seemed as if physically forced into a corner.

He had almost finished with this morning's accumulation. Seated on a kind of folding chair and frowning at a roll of parchment in his lap, he was pretending to listen patiently to a plump and effeminate townsman in the toga of a Roman citizen who had been talking uninterruptedly for about twelve minutes. Macellius could have stopped him at any time, but as a matter of fact he had not heard one word in twenty; he was reading the supply list. It would have been rude to turn away a petitioner simply to study a list; it cost nothing to let the man talk while he read it. In any case, he had heard enough to know that Lucius Varullus was simply saying one thing over and over with a number of oratorical variations.

"Surely you don't wish me to go to the Legate, Macellius," the falsetto voice continued querulously. Macellius rolled up the list and put it aside, deciding he had listened long enough.

"You can if you like, of course," he protested mildly, "but I doubt if he'd give you even this much of a hearing, if he had time for you at all." He knew his Commander well. "You must remember that these are restless times. A certain amount of sacrifice . . ."

The plump underlip of the man across the table went out in protest. "No, no, of course not," he said, waving his hand in a delicate gesture. "My dear fellow, no one, absolutely no one is readier than I to realize that, but how can I work my farms and my gardens if all the men in the area have been levied? Surely the peace and comfort of Roman citizens must be the first consideration? Why, I've had to put my landscape gardeners to work in the turnip patches! You should see my flower gardens!" he concluded mournfully.

"Now really," Macellius said offhandedly. "I'm not responsible for arranging native conscriptions." Silently, he cursed the shade of the Emperor who had extended Roman citizenship to fools like this. "I'm sorry, Lucius," he said – he was lying, and wasn't sorry at all – "I can't do anything for you now."

"Oh, but my dear fellow, you simply must."

"Look," said Macellius briefly, "you're chasing the wrong horse.

69

Go to the Legate if you like, and see what kind of answer he gives you; I doubt he'll be anywhere near as patient as I have been. Bring over slaves from Gaul, or offer better wages." *Or*, he added silently, *get out there with a pitchfork yourself and work off some of that fat.* "Now, if you please, I'm very busy this morning." He let his gaze fall on the scroll again and coughed discreetly

Varullus started to protest, but Severus had already turned to his secretary, a skinny sad-looking youngster. "Who's next, Valerius?"

After Varullus had grumbled his way out, the secretary showed in a drover who had sold cattle to the Legions. Bonnet in hand, he begged the Excellency's pardon in stumbling market-Latin for troubling him, but the roads were so beset with bandits . . .

Macellius addressed the man fluently in his own Silurian dialect. "Speak up, man. What's troubling you?"

When the countryman poured out his story, it appeared that he had been hired to drive his cattle overland to the coast, and there were thieves and robbers, and the cattle already belonged to the Legion, and he was a poor man who could not support the loss of them to outlaws . . .

Macellius held up a hand. "All right," he said, not unkindly, "you want a military escort. I'll give you a note to one of the centurions. Take care of it, Valerius." He nodded to the secretary, "Give him a note to Paulus Appius and tell him to take care of escorting this army beef. No, man, don't apologize, that's what I'm here for."

When the drover had gone out, he added testily, "What's Paulus thinking of? Why in heaven's name did this come all the way up to me? Any decurion down the line could have handled it!" He drew breath, striving for his customary calm. "Well, send in the next one."

Next was a Briton named Tascio who had come about selling some rye. Macellius scowled. "I won't see him; that last lot he sold us was rotten. But we need it; grain's in short supply. Listen. Offer this gouger half of what he asks; and before you sign for the treasurer to give him his pay, get half a dozen of the cooks from the messes to come and look it over. If it's rotten or moldy, dump and burn it; rotten rye will give the men the burning sickness. If it's good, pay him the half agreed on, and if he gives you any trouble, threaten to have him flogged for cheating the Legion. Sextillus told me five men were poisoned by the damned stuff last time. If he still kicks up a fuss, turn him over to Appius," he went on, "and I'll put in a complaint to the Druid Curia, and what they'll do to him won't be half so kind. And by the way, if this lot is rotten put him on the blacklist and tell him not to come around here again. Is that clear?"

Valerius, looking sadder than ever, complied. For all his skinny poverty of appearance, he was extremely efficient at this sort of thing. As he started to leave, Macellius heard his incongruously husky bass rise in surprise.

"Hullo, young Severus. You're back again?" Macellius heard a familiar voice reply, "Salve, Valerius. Hey, take it easy, that arm's still sore! Is my father in?"

Macellius arose so precipitately that he upset his chair. "Gaius! My dear boy, I was beginning to worry about you!" He came round the desk and briefly clasped his son in his arms. "What kept you so long?"

"I came as soon as I could," Gaius apologized.

He felt the boy flinch as his grip tightened and abruptly let go. "What's wrong? Are you hurt?"

"Not really, it's nearly healed. Are you busy, Father?"

Macellius looked around the small office. "Nothing here that Valerius can't handle perfectly well." He regarded his son's dusty garments with disapproval, and said with some sternness, "Must you go about the camp dressed like a freedman or a native?"

Gaius's lips tightened briefly, as if "native" had stung. But his voice was matter of fact and without apology when he replied. "It's safer to travel this way."

"Humph!" But Macellius knew it was true. "Well then, couldn't you at least bathe and dress decently before coming into my presence?"

"I thought you might be anxious about me, Father," Gaius said "seeing that I'd overstayed my leave by a couple of days. With your permission I will go and bathe and dress. The only bath I've had this week was in the river."

"Don't be in a hurry.," Macellius said grumpily. "I'll come with you." He let his hand rest on the younger man's forearm, gripping it without words. For some absurd reason he always worried whenever Gaius was away that the boy would not return; he did not know why, for the youngster had always been very self-sufficient. Seeing the bandaged arm had frightened him. "Tell me what happened now; why the bandages?"

"I fell in a trap dug for boars," Gaius said. "One of the stakes went through my shoulder." His father paled, and Gaius added reassuringly, "It's all but healed now; doesn't even hurt unless I knock it against something. I'll be carrying a sword again in six weeks."

"How – ?"

"How did I get out?" The boy grimaced. "Some Britons found me and doctored me till I was on my feet again."

Macellius's face betrayed what he could not express. "I hope you rewarded them suitably." But Gaius appeared to understand the solicitude hidden behind the indirection.

"On the contrary, Father, hospitality was offered in a noble manner and I accepted it in kind."

"I see." Macellius did not press the matter. Gaius tended to be touchy about his British blood.

At the military baths just outside the stockade, Macellius chose a low chair while Gaius was stripped and scrubbed by the army attendants. Once his personal slave had been despatched to their house for clean garments, Macellius lay back in his chair wondering what the boy had been up to now. There was a difference in him, something more than could be explained by the injury. For a moment he wished himself back in his office dealing with questions that could be quickly dismissed.

Presently Gaius emerged from the bath looking young and very clean in his short wool tunic, his damp hair curling down his back. He sent for a barber-slave and as the man clipped the unruly hair to proper military shortness and scraped away the nascent beard, he recounted his adventure. Clearly he was leaving some things out, thought Macellius. Why had Clotinus Albinus not reported the accident? He felt a moment of gratitude at being spared the kind of unpleasantness any irregularity would involve.

"You should have a regular army doctor look at that arm," he said simply when the tale was done.

Gaius protested irritably, "It's doing well enough." But Macellius insisted, and after a certain amount of delay old Manlius came and unbound Cynric's careful bandages, and probed and poked and pressed until Gaius was white-faced and sweating. Then he solemnly pronounced that the arm was healed as well as if he had had the care of it from the beginning.

"I could have told you that –" muttered the boy, refusing to meet his father's eyes. *Good*, thought the older man, *he knows better than to argue with me . . .*

Gaius lay back limply, his good hand falling away from a fumbling attempt to repin his tunic, yet he grinned as Macellius reached out and refastened it, reaching up to take his father's hand in his own.

"I told you I was all right, Dad, you old Stoic," he said roughly. Macellius thought again, *He's a handsome boy; I wonder what sort of devilry he's been up to? Well, he has a right to a certain amount of folly. Better not let him know that, though . . .*" He cleared his throat, glad that no one else was using the bathhouse at this time of day.

"So, what excuse can you offer for overstaying your leave, Son?"

Gaius nodded at his arm.

"I understand; of course you couldn't travel with that injury, and I'll speak to Sextillus. Another time, allow for accidents. But you're not some patrician puppy who can slack. Your grandfather was a farmer outside Tarentum, and I've had to work hard to get this far. Gaius, what would you say to not going back to Glevum?"

"Do you mean they would courtmartial me for overstaying leave because of an accident —?" He looked so upset that Macellius hastened to reassure him.

"No, no, I didn't mean it that way. I mean, would you care to be transferred to my staff? I need someone to help me here, and when I spoke to the Governor on his way north he agreed to make an exception and let you serve with me. It's time I started introducing you to my connections here. The Province is growing, Gaius. Intelligence and energy will carry a man far. If I could rise to the rank of Equestrian, only one rung below the nobility, who knows how far you might go?"

He saw the trouble in Gaius's eyes, and wondered if his son was in pain. It seemed a long time before the boy replied. "I've never understood why you stayed here in Britain, Father. Couldn't you have risen more quickly if you had been willing to go elsewhere? It's a big empire."

"Britain isn't the whole world," said Macellius, "but I like it." His face grew grave. "They offered me a Juridicus post once in Hispania. I should have taken it, if only for your sake."

"Why Hispania, Father? Why not of Britain?" As soon as the question left his lips, Gaius seemed aware that it had been a mistake. Macellius felt his own face stiffening.

"The Emperor Claudius was so busy trying to reform things at home, from the Senate and the coinage to the state religion, that he never got around to reforming the military laws," Macellius explained, "and the emperors who came after him seemed to think that he, as the official conqueror of Britain, knew what he was doing."

"I don't understand what you mean, Father."

"I visited Rome just once," Macellius said. "And Londinium is more like the Rome I was brought up to honor than Rome is now. The Empire is in the devil of a mess, Gaius; that shouldn't come as any surprise to you." He frowned, then with sudden irritability turned on the slave who stood by their chairs and demanded, "Get us something to eat, don't stand there gawking."

When they were alone he turned back to Gaius, "What I'm going to say now comes under the official heading of treason; when I finish speaking, forget you heard it won't you? But as an officer of the Legion I have a certain responsibility. If there's ever going to be any reform, it may have to come from the Provinces, like Britain. Titus . . . this is dangerous talk . . . Titus is well meaning, but he seems to care more about increasing his popularity than governing the Empire. Domitian, his brother, is at least efficient, but I've heard rumors that his ambition may outrun his patience. If he falls heir to the purple and becomes Emperor, then what little power is left to the Senate and People of Rome may disappear.

"I would advance my family in the old way, by service and solid achievement, one generation following another," Macellius continued very deliberately. "You asked me why I stayed in Britain. Julius Classicus tried to create a Gallic empire not ten years ago. After Vespasian crushed him, he decreed that auxiliaries could not be used in the country of their birth, and the Legions must be drawn from a mix of men from all over the Empire. That's why I had such a hard time gaining permission for you to serve in Britain, and why, it might have been wiser for us to seek our fortunes in Hispania, or somewhere like that. Rome's deepest fear is that the subject nations may rise again . . ."

"But you raised me to revere the old virtues of Rome. What do you want, Father — since we are speaking frankly — and what do you fear?"

Macellius looked at the smooth face of the boy before him, searching for some trace of his own father's rugged strength. There was a resemblance, perhaps, in the strong line of the jaw, but the boy's nose was Celtic, short, almost snubbed, like his mother's. No wonder he had looked like a Briton when he walked through the door. *Is he weak*, he wondered, *or only young?* And then, *Where do his loyalties really lie?*

"Chaos . . ." he said soberly. "The world upside down. The time of the four Emperors, or the Killer Queen again. You wouldn't remember, but it seemed to us that the world was ending the year that you were born . . ."

"You think Roman and British rebellion are equally dangerous?" Gaius asked curiously.

"Have you read Valerius Maximus?" his father said suddenly. "If not, read him sometime; there used to be a couple of copies in the legionary library here. It's a scandalous book; he never should have written it. He damn near lost his head in Nero's day, and I'm not surprised. He started writing in the days of the deified Tiberius, but he makes some good points about some of the Emperors that followed him – to say some of them were as fallible as G—, well, as gods always are, isn't treason – not now, anyway. The point is, even a bad Emperor is better than civil war."

"But you said that reform might have to come from the Provinces –"

Macellius grimaced. At least there was nothing wrong with the boy's memory.

"Reform, not rebellion . . . You may remember that I also said that these days Londinium is like Rome used to be. The old Roman virtues can survive in the Provinces, away from the corruption that surrounds the Emperor. In a lot of ways, the tribes here are like the country people where I was born. Give them the best of Roman culture, and maybe Britain can become what Rome was supposed to be."

"Is that why you married my mother?" Gaius said into the silence.

Macellius looked at him and blinked, seeing once more a girl's fine-boned face and dusky hair, remembering how she used to sing as she pulled the horn comb through her heavy curls, sparkling with red glints as they caught the light of the fire. *Moruadh . . . Moruadh . . . why did you leave me alone?*

"Perhaps it was one reason," he replied at last. "But perhaps it justifies it. We had hopes then of joining our two peoples. But that was before Classicus . . . and Boudicca. Perhaps it can still happen, but it will take longer, and you will have to be more Roman than the Romans to survive."

"What have you heard?" asked Gaius, frowning.

"The Emperor, Titus, has been ill. I don't like it. He's still a young man. He might die in bed, but after him, who knows? I don't trust Domitian. A piece of advice, Son: try to live without ever coming to the attention of a prince. Are you ambitious?"

"All gods forbid," said Gaius.

But Macellius had seen the flash of pride in his eyes. Well, ambition was no bad thing in a young man, if well directed. He gave a short laugh. "In any case, it's time we took the next step to advance the family. Nothing that will upset the Emperor ... but you are, what, nineteen now? It's time you were married."

"I'll be twenty in a few weeks, Father," said Gaius suspiciously. "Do you have someone in mind for me?"

"I suppose you know that Clotinus – yes, old Bedbugs – has a daughter ..." Macellius began, and stopped when his son started laughing.

"All gods forbid. I practically had to kick her out of my bed when I guested there."

"Clotinus is going to be one of the big men in the Province, even if he is British. If you'd set your heart on his daughter, I would be willing enough to go along, but not if she is so immodest. My father may have been only a plebeian, but he could name all his ancestors. The honor of the family requires that your sons be of your own fathering."

He looked up as the slave appeared in the doorway with a tray of hard biscuits and some wine. He poured, handed a goblet to Gaius, and drank deeply before speaking again.

"Here's an idea you may like better. You may not remember this, but when you were a child a tentative betrothal was arranged between you and the daughter of an old friend. He's now the Procurator, Licinius."

"Father," Gaius said quickly, "have you spoken to him lately? – I hope you haven't settled things too far –"

Macellius stared at him narrowly. "Why? Is there some other young girl you're lusting after? It won't do, you know. A marriage is a social and economic alliance. Be guided by me, Son; these romantic attractions don't last." He could see the dull flush that darkened his son's fair skin.

Very carefully, Gaius took another sip of wine. "There is a girl, but it is not lust I feel for her. I have offered her marriage," he said evenly.

"What? Who is she?" Macellius barked, turning to stare at his son.

"The daughter of Bendeigid."

The wine cup clicked loudly as Macellius set it down.

"Impossible. He's a proscribed man, and, if I mistake not, a Druid. Of good family, so I'll say nothing against the girl if she's his kin, but that only makes it worse. Those sorts of marriages –"

"You made one," Gaius interrupted.

"And it nearly destroyed my career! Your girl may be as fine a woman as your mother, but one misalliance of that kind is enough for any family," Macellius exclaimed. *Moruadh, forgive me*, his heart cried. *I loved you, but I have to save our boy.*

"Things were different then," he continued more temperately. "Since Boudicca's rebellion, a connection with any but the most loyal of British families would be a disaster. And you especially must be careful, *because* you are your mother's son. Do you think I have endured thirty years in the Legions just to see you throw it all away?" He splashed more wine into his cup and drank it down.

"There's no limit to what you could do if you have the right connections, and the Procurator's daughter is a prize. The family is related to the Julians after all. Meanwhile, if you have a taste for romantic adventure, there are plenty of slaves and freedwomen; keep your thoughts off these British girls." He glared at his son.

"Eilan is different – I love her."

"Your Eilan is the daughter of a Druid!" Macellius replied. "He was charged once with inciting the Auxilia to revolt. They couldn't prove it, so they banished him; he was lucky not to have been hanged or crucified. But for all that you don't want to get yourself entangled in any way with his family. She's not pregnant or anything?"

"Eilan is as innocent as any Vestal," Gaius said stiffly.

"Humph; I wouldn't bet on it; they don't view these things as we should," Macellius observed. Seeing Gaius's gaze darken, he added, "Don't look at me so – I'm not doubting you. But if the girl is virtuous, it is all the more ruinous for you to set your heart on her. Accept it, lad, she's not for you."

"That's for her father to decide," Gaius said hotly, "not you!"

Macellius grunted. "Mark me, her father will view such an alliance much as I do, as a major catastrophe for both of you. Forget her, and turn your thoughts to some good Roman girl. I've won enough status here to ally you to whomever you choose."

"So long as she's named Julia Licinia ..." Gaius answered bitterly. "What if Licinius's daughter doesn't want a husband with British blood?"

Macellius shrugged. "I'll write to Licinius tomorrow. If she's a proper Roman girl, she'll think of her marriage as part of her duty to her family and to the State. But married you shall be, before you disgrace us all."

Gaius shook his head stubbornly. "We shall see. If Bendeigid is willing to give me his daughter, I will marry Eilan. My honor is pledged to her."

"No; impossible," Macellius said. "And what's more, if I know anything about Bendeigid, he'll react pretty much the same way." *Damn it*, he thought, *the problem is that he's too much like me. Does he think I'll let it drop?* The boy might believe his father did not understand – young people always thought that they were the only ones who had ever loved – but the truth was that Macellius understood only too well. Moruadh had been fire in his blood, but she had never been happy, prisoned by square stone walls. The Roman women had laughed at her and her own people had cursed her. He would not let his son live with the pain of knowing that he, too, had brought only sorrow to the woman he adored.

Macellius's campaign bonuses had been well invested, and he had enough wealth to be comfortable when he retired, but not enough for his son unless Gaius also had a career. He would do Moruadh no honor by allowing her son to throw his future away.

"Father," Gaius continued, in a tone his father had never heard before, "I love Eilan; she is the only woman I will ever marry. And if her father will not give her to me, Rome is not the whole world, you know."

Macellius glared. "You had no right to make such a commitment. Marriage is a matter for families; if I send to request her hand for you, it will be against my own better judgment."

"But you will do it?" Gaius persisted, and against his will Macellius softened.

"There is no parting a fool and his folly; I can send to Bendeigid. But when he refuses you we will hear no more of this. I will write to Licinius then, and have you married before the new year."

There was something to be said, he thought, for the old days when fathers had held the power of life and death even over grown sons. The law was still on the books – for all the good it did anyone; no father in hundreds of years had formally invoked it, and he knew himself too well to think he would be the first. But he would not have to. Eilan's father could deliver that blow far more effectively than he.

seven

~~~~~~~

In the days following Gaius's departure the bright sun of Beltane hid behind weeping skies, as if the season had decided not to turn into summer after all. Eilan crept around the house like a ghost. Days passed and Gaius sent no word. Just before leaving for the Forest House Dieda had said that she should have given herself to Gaius. Would he be more or less likely to forget her if she had done so?

After all, the high festivals existed in a time of their own. That night when they sat together watching the fires was like some dream of the Otherworld. In that time when the doors opened between the worlds, anything seemed possible – even the marriage of the daughter of a Druid to a Roman officer. But now, surrounded by the familiar sights and sounds of her home, she began to doubt herself, her love, and Gawen – or Gaius, as she supposed she ought to call him – most of all.

And the worst of it was that no one seemed to notice her pain. Mairi had insisted on returning to her own dwelling to await the return of her husband, and Rheis was busy with all the tasks that summer brought. She might have confided in Dieda, but her kinswoman was in the Forest House, where she must be dealing with her own heartaches and regrets. The skies wept, Eilan's heart wept with them, and no one seemed to care at all.

At last a day came when her father sent for her. He was sitting beside the hearth in the feasting hall – only ashes now, for though the sky was grey and clouded, it was warm enough not to need a fire. An odd mix of anger and amusement softened his usual sternness. "Eilan," he said gently, "I feel I should let you know this; an offer has been made for your hand."

Gaius, she thought. *My doubts wronged him!*

"But of course it was one I could not entertain. How much do you know about the young man who called himself Gawen?"

"What do you mean?" Surely he could hear the rapid beating of her heart.

"Did he tell you his true name? Did he tell you that his father is Macellius Severus, Prefect of the camp at Deva?"

She saw the anger now beneath Bendeigid's gentleness, and fought to still her trembling; but she nodded.

"Then at least he did not deceive you." Her father sighed, "But you must put him far from your thoughts, Daughter. You are not yet of full age to marry —"

She raised her head to protest. Why had she not considered that her own father was far more likely to refuse permission than Gaius to deny his love?

"I can wait," she whispered, not daring to raise her eyes.

Her father went on, "I am not used to being a tyrant to my children, Eilan; if the truth be told I have been all too gentle with you. If you feared me, you would not speak this way. But this thing cannot be, Daughter — no, hold you still," he commanded, "I still have something to say to you."

"What else is there?" Eilan exclaimed, flinching at his grip on her wrist. "You have refused him, haven't you?"

"I want you to understand why." His tone softened. "I bear no grudge against the lad, and if he were one of our own, I would gladly give you to him. But oil mixes not with water, nor lead with silver, nor Roman with Briton."

"He is only half Roman," she protested. "His mother was a tribeswoman of the Silures. He seemed Briton enough when he guested here."

Her father shook his head. "That makes it all the worse. He is the bastard son of a marriage — an unlawful marriage I call it — into a race of traitors, for traitors were the Silures before ever the Romans came over the sea, stealing our cattle and poaching in our hunting runs. It would be to compound folly upon folly to marry you to a child of our ancient enemies. I have even spoken to Ardanos of this and though he talks of peace to come of it, as if you were child to one of our queens and he son to a Caesar, I know it cannot be."

Her eyes widened at the thought that the Arch-Druid, of all people, might stand her friend. But her father was still talking.

"From the tone of the letter, my guess is that Macellius Severus likes it no better than I. Nothing could come of such a marriage but torn loyalties for you both. If Gaius is willing to forsake Rome for you, then I want him not among our kin. And if he cleaves to his own, then would you be outcast among our people, and I would not have that for you."

Eilan did not look up. "For him I would bear it," she said, her voice just audible.

"Yes, in your madness, I believe you would," her father said harshly. "Youth is ever ready to defy the world. But our blood is not traitor blood, Eilan. For every moment you betrayed your kin with him, the ravens would peck at your heart in secret. His voice softened, "What is more, it is not you alone but all our kindred who would be forced to break one bond after another.

"Eilan, this you must understand; I bear no grudge against Gawen; he was a guest in my house, and it were to chop logic to say he lied to me when none had asked his true name. If grudge there might be, it would only be that he worked in secret to set you against your kin."

Eilan's words were all but inaudible. "He dealt honorably and uprightly with both me and you."

"Have I questioned that?" responded Bendeigid. "But he who asks pledges himself to abide the answer. They asked me fairly and honorably for your hand; fairly and straightforwardly I answered. And there's an end of it."

She said in a strangled voice, "Another man less honorable might have so dealt with me that you would have been grateful to be rid of me."

Black anger suffused her father's face and for the first time in memory she feared him. He jerked her towards him, and struck her – though not hard – across the mouth.

"No more –" he said. *"No more!* Had I slapped you more often when you were a child, I should not now need to strike you for that shameless speech."

Eilan sank down on the bench as he released her; ten days ago she would have wept if her father spoke so to her; now she felt that nothing would ever make her shed another tear.

He said emphatically, "You will marry no Roman while I am above ground; no, nor after it either if I have my way. And if you should tell me that things had so gone with you that you must marry this son of half-Roman traitors, or give me a bastard to call me grandsire, no man in all the length and breadth of Britain would blame me if I drowned you with my own hands. Spare me that blush of modesty, Daughter, you had none a moment ago!"

Eilan would have preferred to face her father on her feet, but her knees were trembling so that she could not rise. "Can you really think such shame of me?"

"It was not I who first named it," her father retorted. Then his voice softened. "Child, child," he admitted, "I spoke in anger. You are a good girl, and my true daughter, I ask your forgiveness. Now, enough of this kind of talk. You ride north tomorrow; your sister Mairi will have need of a kinswoman, for her child will be born soon, and at this season your mother cannot be spared. It seems all too likely now that her husband, Rhodri, was captured by Romans when he went off after the levies. So even if all had gone otherwise, this would be no season to be offering me a Roman son-in-law."

Eilan nodded dumbly. Bendeigid put his arm around her, and said gently, "Wiser I am and older than you, Eilan. The young see for themselves alone. Do you think I have not seen you pining? I thought it was only that you missed Dieda, but my main anger at this half-Roman bastard is that he has given you such pain."

She nodded, standing stiffly in his embrace, feeling a world away. He had said that a raven would peck at her heart if she married Gaius, and she had thought it only a poetic way of speaking. But now she realized that he had spoken sober truth, for the pain in her heart was as sharp, as if indeed a raven's beak were stabbing her.

Feeling her resistance, her father said irritably, "Your mother spoke truth when she said you were too long unmarried. This winter I will seek out a husband for you, one of our own."

Eilan tore herself from his arms, her eyes blazing. "I have no choice but to obey you," she said bitterly, "but if I am not to marry at my own will, I will marry no man upon the face of this earth."

"As you will," he said bitterly. "I will never seek to force you. But Senara I will pledge before she binds on her maiden's girdle. I will not have this sort of struggle with a daughter again!"

The rain continued to fall for many days, swelling rivers and streams and drowning fields, roads and paths. It was very near the time when Mairi should be delivered, and still her husband's fate was unknown. She had admitted that she would perhaps have done better to remain under her father's roof until her child was delivered, but in such weather it would have been more risky for her to travel than to stay at home. It was Eilan, therefore, who traveled to her sister's steading, escorted by two of her father's men.

Although she still wept at night when she thought of Gaius, Eilan found herself glad that she had come. She was useful here; her sister needed someone to talk to, and her little nephew was fretful and confused because his mother had ceased to suckle him and his father had disappeared. Mairi was too clumsy now to pay him much heed; but Eilan had the patience to sit for hours feeding him with a horn spoon, and he recovered some of his laughter when she played with him.

As the rain continued to fall, there were times when Eilan wondered if she would be left alone to deliver her sister's second child. But Mairi had arranged for a priestess to come. "All the women of the Forest House are trained in such matters, Sister," Mairi told her, rubbing her back which ached constantly now. "You've no need to fear." It was the evening of her fourth day with her sister, and Eilan was beginning to feel at home.

"Wouldn't it be wonderful if they were to send Dieda to us?"

"She is new come to the Forest House and may not go outside during her first year. They have promised to send one of Lhiannon's attendants, a woman of Hibernia called Caillean." She spoke so dryly that Eilan wondered if Mairi disliked the woman, but thought it better not to ask.

Three days later, Caillean herself arrived: a tall woman, bundled in shawls and scarves that left only her eyes and heavy dark hair visible. Against the blackness of her hair and brows her skin looked milk-pale, but her eyes were blue. As she unwrapped herself, a shift in the wind brought gusts of smoke from the hearth, and the priestess began to cough. Eilan hurried to fill a mug of ale and offered it to her silently.

The priestess said in a low voice, "I thank you, child, but I am not allowed; if I might have some water . . ."

"Of course," Eilan murmured, blushing, and hastened to fill a drinking cup at the cask by the door. "Or I could draw it freshly from the well –"

"No, this will do very well," the priestess said, taking the cup from her hand and draining it. "I thank you. But who is the woman with child? You are not much more than a child yourself."

"It is Mairi who is having the baby," Eilan murmured. "I am Eilan, Bendeigid's middle daughter. And there is another, Senara, who is only nine."

"My name is Caillean."

"I saw you at Beltane, but I did not know your name. I thought surely that Lhiannon's assistant would be –" She stopped bashfully.

Caillean completed the sentence. "Older? More dignified? I have been with Lhiannon since she brought me from the western shores of Eriu. I was four-and-ten or thereabouts when we came to the Forest House, and I have been there now for sixteen years."

"Do you know my kinswoman Dieda?"

"Certainly I do, but she dwells with the maidens; there are many of us, and we are not all of one order. Now that I see you, I understand – but that is for later. Let me speak now to your sister."

Eilan led her to Mairi, now so pregnant that she moved with difficulty, and withdrew a little to give them some privacy. She could hardly hear the low murmur as Caillean questioned Mairi at length. There was something soothing in the quiet lilt of the priestess's voice.

Eilan could see the tension leaving Mairi's face, and realized for the first time that her sister had been afraid. She did not flinch as Caillean pressed her belly with her long hands. When she had done, Mairi lay back with a sigh.

"I think the babe will not be born today, and perhaps not tomorrow. Rest now, lass, for you will need all your strength when the time comes," Caillean said soothingly.

When Mairi was settled again, Caillean rejoined Eilan near the fire. "Is it true that her husband has disappeared?" she asked in an undertone.

"We fear he was taken by the Romans," Eilan replied. "My father warned me not to mention it to Mairi."

For a moment Caillean's gaze went inward. "Do not, for I fear she will not see him again."

Eilan looked at her in horror. "You have heard something?"

"I have seen the omens, and they bode not well."

"Poor Mairi, poor love. How shall we tell her?"

"Say nothing now," Caillean counseled. "I will tell her myself after the birthing, when she will have reason to live for her child."

Eilan shuddered, for she was fond of Mairi and it seemed to her that the priestess had spoken of death just as she spoke of life, without feeling or regret for either. But she supposed that to a priestess, life and death must mean something quite other than what they meant to Eilan.

"I hope she has menfolk to care for her children's inheritance," Caillean went on.

"My father has no sons," Eilan said. "But Cynric will do a brother's duty to Mairi if there is need."

"Is he not the son of Bendeigid?"

"A foster son only; we were brought up together; he has always been very fond of Mairi. He is away in the North now."

"I have heard of this Cynric," Caillean said, and Eilan wondered just how much the priestess did know. "And indeed your sister will be in need of kin."

That night a new storm came whirling in from the west, and Eilan, waking in the night, heard it beating around the house like a wild thing; when morning came, the trees were still blowing and tossing before the blast. But though a few handfuls of thatch were plucked from the roof, the roundhouse only groaned and shuddered before each new gust of wind, where a more rigid structure might have given way. The rain still fell relentlessly, but Caillean, staring out into the downpour, looked pleased.

"There are rumors of raiders from the coast," she said when Eilan questioned her. "If all the ways are flooded, they will not come this far inland."

"Raiders?" Mairi echoed, looking frightened. But Caillean would not repeat herself, saying only that to name an evil was often to draw it near. By early evening the worst of the wind had blown itself out, and the weather settled to hard, insistent rain, leaving all the world awash with the sound of water, and of springs and cisterns overflowing. Fortunately there was a good supply of wood cut and stacked in a shed near the main house, so they built up a cheery blaze and Caillean unwrapped the small musical instrument she carried swaddled like a child. Eilan had never known a woman to play a harp; she herself had been beaten as a child for touching her grandfather's.

"Oh, it's true, there are woman bards among us," Caillean said, "though I play only for my own pleasure. I think that Dieda will become one."

"I am not surprised," said Eilan a little wistfully. "She sings beautifully."

"Are you envious, child? There are other gifts than music, you know." The priestess frowned at Eilan thoughtfully, then appeared to come to a decision. "Did you not know she was chosen by mistake for you?"

Eilan stared, remembering all those times during her childhood when she had played at priestess, and the vision that had come to her when Lhiannon's cloak enfolded the other girl.

"Have you never thought of it, little one?"

Eilan did not reply. Of course, she had dreamed of such a thing for a long time, but then she had met Gaius. How could she be meant for a priestess if she was capable of such love for a man?

"Well, there is no need to make a decision now," Caillean said, smiling. "We will talk of this another time."

Eilan stared at her, and suddenly with doubled vision she saw the two of them together, lifting their arms in homage to the moon. But though recognition was total, she realized in surprise that Caillean's hair was not dark, but red, their features alike as those of sisters, and her own face was the one she had seen once before in the forest pool. *Sisters . . . and more than sisters. Women, and more than women . . .* The words came to her from some place beyond memory.

Then, with a little shock she remembered that she had never spoken with Caillean until yesterday. But as it had been with Gaius, it suddenly seemed to her that she had known the priestess from the beginning of the world.

Caillean had been playing for a long time when Mairi stood up suddenly and cried out, staring down at the dark stain that was spreading across her gown. The other two looked up in surprise.

"Have your waters broken already?" the priestess asked. "Well, love, babes come when they wish and not at our convenience; we'd better have you to bed. Eilan, go find the shepherd and have him bring in more wood for the fire. Then build up the fire and fill the cauldron and bring water to a boil. Mairi will be wanting hot tea before this is over, and so will we."

As Caillean had no doubt expected, having something to do calmed the younger girl. "Are you better now?" the priestess asked when Eilan returned. "I have often found it a mistake to allow any woman who has not herself borne a child to be in the room at a birth; it only frightens. But if you are to join us in the Forest House, sooner or later you will have to learn."

Eilan swallowed and nodded, determined to justify the older woman's faith in her. For the first hour or two Mairi dozed between pains, rousing only a few times an hour to cry out, almost as if in her sleep. Eilan dozed on the bench near the fire; it was the darkest part of the night and the rain had settled down to a soft insistent pounding when Caillean bent and wakened her.

"Come, now, I shall need you; stir up the fire, and make

Mairi a cup of berry-leaf tea. I don't know how long this will take, and I will want your help."

When the tea was ready, Caillean bent over Mairi, who was moving restlessly, and held the cup to her lips. "There, sip this now. It will make you feel stronger."

But in a few moments Mairi shook her head, her face growing red and contorted.

"It will not be long, my dear," said Caillean encouragingly. "Do not try to sit upright now."

As Mairi slumped, gasping, after the contraction, Caillean said, low and quick, "Eilan, sponge her face, while I make all ready." She moved to the fire, and spoke to Mairi once more. "See, I have a fine swaddling ready for the little one, and it will not be long now till you hold her. Or do you think it will be another fine son like the one you have already?"

"I do not care," Mairi groaned, breathing hard. "I only want – it over – ahh – will it be long now – ?"

"Of course not. Just a little while, Mairi, and you will have your child in your arms . . . ah, that's right, just a little more . . . One begins just as another ends; I know it's hard, but it means your babe will be here all the sooner –"

Eilan felt almost rigid with fright. Mairi did not even look like herself any more. Her face was red and swollen, she cried out and seemed not even to know she was doing it. Then she gasped, arching her back and bracing her feet against the end of the bed.

"I can't – oh, I can't," came the hoarse cry, but Caillean was still crooning encouragement. It seemed to Eilan that the birthing had lasted a lifetime, but the sun was barely set.

Then Caillean's voice changed. "Now I think we are ready. Let her hold your hands, Eilan; no, not like that – at the wrists. Now, Mairi, push just once more. I know you are tired, child, but this will soon be over. Breathe – that's right, breathe hard, just let it come. There, there, now look!" Mairi's body heaved, and the priestess straightened, holding something, unbelievably red and tiny, that jerked in her hands with a thin cry. "Look, Mairi, you have a fine little daughter."

Mairi's red face relaxed in a blissful smile as Caillean laid the newborn child upon her belly.

"Ah, Lady," breathed the priestess, looking down at them. "More times than I can remember I have seen this, and always it is a miracle!" The thin mewing became a shrill and demanding cry, and Mairi laughed.

"Oh, Caillean, she's so beautiful, so beautiful . . ."

With swift efficiency the priestess tied off the birthcord and cleansed the child. When Mairi began to deliver the afterbirth, Caillean handed the baby to Eilan.

It seemed impossible that anything so fragile should be a human child; its fingers and feet were thin and spidery, its head covered with a downy dark fuzz. As Mairi fell into an exhausted sleep, Caillean hung a small metal amulet around the infant's neck, and began to cocoon it in swaddling bands.

"Now she cannot be stolen by the elf-kind, and we have watched her every moment since she was born, so we know she is no changeling," Caillean said. "But not even the Good Folk would be likely to come out into this rain. So you see, even from such a flood some good can come."

Caillean straightened her weary back, realizing that a red watery sun was beginning to peer through the heavy low-lying clouds for the first time in many days.

The baby was long and frail. Her hair turned to a downy reddish fuzz as it dried.

"She looks so delicate – will she live?" Eilan asked.

"I see no reason she should not," Caillean replied. "It is a mercy of the gods we did not leave here last night. I thought it might be safer to take refuge in the Forest House after all; and then this babe would have been born beneath some tree or in an open field, and we might well have lost both mother and child. My foresight is not always true."

The priestess sat down heavily on a bench before the fire. "Why, it is day again; no wonder I am weary. And no doubt before long, the boy will wake and we can show him his little sister."

Eilan was still holding the baby, but as Caillean looked up at her a veil seemed to fall between them, like a breath of cold mist from the Otherworld. As it swirled, a dreadful sorrow chilled Caillean's bones; suddenly she was seeing an Eilan who was older, in the blue robe of the Forest House, with the blue tattooed crescent of a sworn priestess between her brows. In her arms she held a young child; and in her eyes Caillean saw a grief so great it tore her heart.

Caillean shuddered, shaken by that flood of sorrow, and tried to blink the tears away. When she looked again, the young girl was staring at her in amazement. Involuntarily the priestess took a step forward and snatched Mairi's child, who mewed softly and fell asleep again.

"What is the matter?" Eilan asked. "Why were you looking at me like that?"

"A draught," Caillean murmured. "It chilled us both." But they could both see that the rushlights burned unstirringly. *My foresight is not always true*, she told herself. *Not always . . .*

She shook her head. "Let us hope the streams are still impass-able," she said. Even the thought of raiders was a welcome distrac-tion after that vision.

"Why do you say that, Caillean? My father will certainly want to come as soon as he can, and my mother too, to see their new grandchild. And all the more so if, as you say, Mairi is widowed –"

Caillean started. "Did I say that? Well, surely the weather will do as it will; never did I hear that even for the will of the High Druid we had more either of sun or rain. But I cannot help thinking that your kinsmen are not the only ones who can ride the roads. Come," she added, "The babe must go back to her mother's breast. She moved toward the box bed, the swaddled child in her arms.

eight

━━━〰〰〰━━━

Over the Roman camp at Deva rain continued to fall with maddening insistence. The men stayed in their barracks, dicing or repairing worn gear, or made their way to the wine shop to drink the afternoon away. In the midst of the all-encompassing wetness, Macellius Severus sent for his son.

"You are familiar with the country to the west," he began. "Do you think you could guide a party along the roads to Bendeigid Vran's household?"

Gaius stiffened, letting his oiled leather cape drip on to the tiled floor. "Yes, but, Father —"

Macellius guessed his meaning. "I am not suggesting that you should spy on a friend's household, my boy, but Hibernian raiders have been sighted off Segontium. Every British housestead in the region will be at risk if they slip by. It's for their own good, though I don't suppose they will see it that way. But if I must send a troop in to see what's happening, is it not better that it be led by a friend than by a Celt-hater, or some idiot fresh from Rome who thinks the Britons still go about painted blue?"

Gaius felt himself coloring. He hated the way his father could suddenly make him feel like a child.

"I am at your service, Father — and at Rome's," he added stiffly after a moment, feeling so cynical about the polite formula that he half-expected a sneer in response. *How corrupt I am becoming, but at least I know when I am being a hypocrite. Will I be so accustomed to putting on that air of benign superiority by the time I am my father's age that I believe it?*

"Or do you fear that your temper will run away with you because Bendeigid refused you his daughter's hand?" his father went on. "I told you how it would be."

Gaius felt his fists clench and bit his lip hard. He had never bested his father in a confrontation and knew he would have no chance now. Still, those words had been like salt on a raw wound.

"You told me, and you were right," Gaius said through his teeth. "Trot out whatever heifer you will – any girl with broad hips and good bloodlines, this Julia if you like – and I will do my duty."

"You are a Roman and I expect you to behave like one," Macellius said more gently. "You acted honorably, and you will continue to do so. In Juno's name, boy, the girl you loved may be in danger. Even though you can't marry her, don't you want to make sure she is safe and well?"

And to that, of course, he could make no answer at all, but he felt his stomach curdling with a dread that owed nothing to physical fear as he saluted and went out of the door.

Perhaps I am simply afraid to face them all, Gaius thought as his little troop of horsemen detached from the Auxilia trotted through the gate of the fortress and splashed down the hill. *In a way I did betray their trust, and they were all kind to me.* During the confusion of detailing the men and packing he had been able to suppress his feelings, but now the sick apprehension washed over him once more.

He had only seen Cynric once after leaving the house of Bendeigid . . . One day in the market town of Deva he had turned and recognized the blond young giant bartering for a sword at a smith's stall. Cynric was so deeply engaged in conversation with the weapons seller that he had not seen Gaius, and, in spite of his upbringing, Gaius had turned on his heel and fled. It was just after he had received his reply from Bendeigid. If the household knew of the offer Gaius would be shamed, and if not, what could Cynric, seeing the lad he had befriended wearing the uniform of a Roman tribune, presume but that they had been betrayed?

He wondered who had written the Druid's Latin response for him. Gaius had burned the wax tablets on which they were written, but the words remained engraved on his memory. They were simple enough. The Druid did not feel he could give his daughter in marriage, because of her youth and Gaius's Roman heritage.

Gaius had resolved to put the whole thing completely out of mind. After all, he was a Roman, trained to discipline both mind and body. But it was proving harder than he had expected. He could control his thoughts during the daytime, but last night he had dreamed once more that he and Eilan were sailing westward together on a white ship. Yet even if there were any land to the west where they might flee, he did not have the faintest idea how one would go about abducting even a willing girl, nor whether Eilan would be willing to run away. He had no intention of facing down all his kinsmen, to say nothing of hers. Nothing could come of that except misery for them both.

Perhaps Eilan was betrothed to somebody else by now, despite what her father had said about her youth. Certainly most Roman girls were married by that age. His father could go ahead, if he wished, and pledge him to whomever he willed. Licinius's daughter was young too, so perhaps he need not face it for a while. Better, Gaius thought, to stop thinking about women entirely. The gods knew he had tried. But now and again, seeing – perhaps in some Gaulish slave – a flash of fair hair and grey eyes, her image would return to him so vividly he wanted to cry.

He would have liked to learn from Cynric how the family fared. But by the time he had got up his courage again the young giant had vanished. And all things considered, it was probably just as well.

Eilan woke suddenly, blinking as she tried to remember where she was. Had the baby cried? Had she dreamed? But Mairi and the babe lay quiet in the bed box on the other side of the fire. As she moved, her nephew, Vran, turned in his sleep and nestled closer against her. The priestess, Caillean, lay still against the wall. Eilan, at the edge of the bed nearest the fire, had slept badly, restless. If she had been dreaming, she could not remember it; she knew only that she was awake and staring at the red coals where the fire had burned to embers.

In the dark Caillean said softly, "I heard it too. There is someone outside the house."

"At this hour?" She listened, but there was only the dripping of water from the eaves and the hiss of the fire.

But Caillean said with peremptory haste, "Be still." She slipped from the bed and silently tested the bar across the door. It was secure in its slot, but after a moment Eilan heard again the sound that had wakened her and saw it bow slightly as the door was pressed inward.

Eilan shivered. She had been weaned on tales of raiders, but had always lived in the great house of Bendeigid, protected by her father's armed men. The two serving men who helped with the farm work slept in the other roundhouse, and the homes of the other men oathed to Rhodri were scattered through the hills.

"Get up – quietly – and dress as swiftly as you can," whispered Caillean. The door shook again, and Eilan obeyed, trembling.

"My father always said to hide in the woods if raiders came –"

"That is no good to us now, with this rain, and Mairi still weak from childbirth," Caillean murmured. "Wait."

The door groaned as someone thrust more strongly, and Mairi woke, muttering. But Caillean, fully dressed now, had her hand over her lips. "Be silent, as you value your life and your child's," she whispered. Mairi subsided with a gasp, and the baby, luckily, slept on.

"Shall we hide in the storage pit?" Eilan whispered as the door shook again. Whoever was outside was determined to force his way in.

Caillean said softly, "Stay here, and whatever happens do not scream," and went to the door. Mairi cried out as Caillean began to lift the bar. The priestess said fiercely, "Do you want to put this door back together after they break it down? I do not."

As she drew back the bar, the door banged open. A dozen men burst through it as if blown by the wind and stopped short as Caillean cried out a single word that sounded like a command. They were big men with wild and untrimmed hair streaming over their shoulders, swathed in skins and hairy cloaks of heavy wool over tunics even more brightly checked than those the Britons wore. Caillean seemed slender as a willow wand before them. Her dark hair flowed to her waist over her ungirt blue robe, lifting a little as the wind blew through the door. It was the only thing about her that moved.

Mairi dived beneath the covers, clutching her child. One of the men laughed and said something just audible, and Eilan shuddered. She felt like following Mairi, but was too paralyzed to move.

Caillean cried out again in a ringing voice and took a step backwards to the hearth. The men seemed mesmerized by her gaze. They stood, staring, as she knelt and plunged her hands into the embers. Then suddenly she was rising, casting the coals at the intruders with both hands. She shouted again and the strange warriors gasped and recoiled; then they were gone, surging back over the doorsill, cursing in an odd sort of British and another tongue she did not know, knocking each other off their feet as they struggled to get away.

The priestess followed them to the door, laughing, and cried out something in a high voice, like the cry of a falcon. Then she slammed out the surging wind and all was still once more.

When they had gone, Caillean sank down on the settle by the hearth and Eilan, who was shaking to her very toenails, went to her. "Who were they?"

"Raiders, a mixed band, I think, from the North and from my country," Caillean said. "More shame to me, for I am a woman of Eriu, brought here by Lhiannon." She stood up and began to mop up the rain water that had come in.

Eilan quavered, "And what did you say?"

"I told them I was a *bean-drui*, a she-Druid, and if they laid a hand on me or on either of my sisters I would curse them by fire and water; and I showed them that I had that power." Caillean stretched out her hands. The slim fingers that Eilan had seen her thrust into the coals were white and unharmed. Was this all a dream?

Eilan, remembering what Caillean had cried out after them, said hesitatingly, "Sisters?"

"By the vows I have taken, all women are my sisters." Her lips twisted. "And I said if they went away and left us in peace I would lay a blessing on them —"

"And did you bless them then?"

"I did not; they are wild wolves of the forest, or worse," Caillean said defiantly. "Bless them? As soon bless a wolf and his teeth in my throat."

Eilan's gaze returned to Caillean's fingers. "How did you do that? Was that a Druid's illusion, or did you really take fire in your hands." Already she was beginning to wonder if her eyes had deceived her.

"Oh, that was real enough." Caillean gave a short laugh. "Anyone with my training could have done it."

Eilan stared at her. "Could I?"

"If you were taught, certainly," said Caillean with a trace of impatience. "If you had the trust, and the will. But I cannot show you now. Perhaps in the Forest House, if you come there."

The reality of what they had escaped burst over Eilan then and she dropped down upon the seat next to the priestess, shuddering. "They would . . . they would have —" Eilan swallowed. "We all owe you our lives."

"Oh, I think not," said Caillean. "A woman in childbed is small temptation even to such as these. And I might well have been able to frighten them from me; but you, yes; rape is the least you could have expected from them. They do not kill fair young girls; but you might well have ended a captive wife, if you so call it, on the shores of wild Eriu. If that is a fate that would have pleased you, I am sorry to have interfered."

Eilan shuddered, remembering the feral faces of the men. "I think not. Are the men all like that in your land?"

"I do not know. When I left it I was still very young." After a moment's silence Caillean went on. "I do not remember either my mother or my father, only that in the hut where we lived – all of us – there were seven children smaller than I. One day we went to the market and Lhiannon was there. I had never seen anyone so beautiful.

"And something – I know not what – reached out to her, for she cast her cloak over me, thus claiming me in the oldest of rites for the gods. Years later, I asked her why she had chosen me from all the others there. She said that she had seen that the others there were cleanly dressed and that their parents clung to them. There was no one to cling to me," she added somewhat bitterly. "In the home of my parents I was only another mouth to feed. Nor was my name Caillean; my mother – I do not really remember her – she called me *Lon-dubh*, Blackbird."

"Is Caillean a priestess name then?"

Caillean smiled. "It is not," she said. "Caillean, in our tongue, means only 'my child, my girl'. So Lhiannon called me whenever she spoke to me; I think of myself now by no other name."

"Should I call you that then?"

"You should, though I do have another name given me by the priestesses. I am sworn never to speak it aloud or even whisper it, save to another priestess."

"I see." Eilan stared at her, then blinked, because for a moment a name had echoed in her awareness as loudly as if it had been spoken. *Isarma . . . when you were my sister, Isarma was your name . . .*

Caillean sighed, "Well, dawn is still far off. See, your sister has already fallen back into slumber. Poor lass, the birth exhausted her. You should sleep as well –"

Eilan shook her head, trying to bring the world back into focus. "After such a disturbance, I do not think I could sleep even if I tried."

Caillean looked at her and suddenly laughed. "Well, to be truthful, neither can I! Those men terrified me so that I could scarce speak. I thought I had forgotten their dialect – the last time I heard it was so long ago."

"You did not look terrified," said Eilan. "You looked like a goddess standing there." She heard once more the other woman's bitter laugh.

"Things are not always as they seem, my little one. You must learn not to put all your trust in how folk look, or in what they say."

Eilan stared into the fire, whose embers, stirred back to life by Caillean's raking, snapped and sparkled on the hearth. The man she had learned to care for as Gawen had been an illusion, but even as Gaius the Roman, the thing that made her love him was the same. And he had spoken truth to her. *I would know him*, she thought then, *if he came to me as a leper or a wild man*. For a moment she grasped at something that lay beyond face or form or name. Then a coal snapped, and it was gone.

"Tell me what is true, then," Eilan said to fill the silence. "How did that cotter's child you say you were become a priestess who could hold fire in her hands?"

Tell me what is true ... Caillean stared at the girl, who had lowered her fair lashes over those changeable eyes as if frightened by her own boldness. What other truths might come back to haunt her, as her mother tongue had returned on the lips of those monstrous men? She was twice Eilan's age – old enough to be her mother if she had married young, and yet at this moment the younger woman was like a sister, a twin soul.

"Did you come at once then to the Forest House with Lhiannon?" persisted Eilan.

"I did not; I think that Vernemeton was not yet built then," Caillean pulled herself together enough to answer her. "Lhiannon had come to Eriu to study with the *bean-drui*, the priestesses at the shrine of Brigid at Druim Cliadh. When she returned to Britain, we dwelt at first in a round tower on the shore far, far to the north of here. I remember that there was a ring of white stones laid around the tower, and it was death for any man, save only the Arch-Druid – not Ardanos, but the one who was before – to come within this ring of stones. Always, she treated me as her foster daughter; once she said, when someone asked, that she had found me abandoned on the seashore. It might as well have been true; I never saw any member of my family again."

"Didn't you miss your mother?"

Caillean hesitated, shaken by the flood of memories. "I suppose you had a good and a loving mother. Mine was otherwise. It is not that she was evil, but I cared little for her nor she for me." She stopped herself, eyeing the younger woman warily. *What power is in you, girl*, she thought, *that you can conjure such memories from me?* She sighed, trying to find the right words.

"For her, I was only an extra mouth to feed. Once, years later in the market at Deva, I saw an old woman who reminded me of my mother. She was not, of course, but I did not even feel regret when I realized it. It was then that I knew I had no kinfolk but Lhiannon and, later, the other priestesses of the Forest House . . ."

There was a long silence. She could see Eilan trying to imagine what it would be like to grow up without a family. Caillean could see that Mairi's bossiness had held affection, and, from what Dieda had told her, she had been like Eilan's twin. And yet, she realized suddenly, just as she herself had never unburdened her heart to her fellow priestesses, never could Eilan have talked to any of her family as she was speaking with Caillean now.

It is like talking to myself, to say these things to her, Caillean thought ruefully, *or perhaps it is like talking to the self I should have been, forever innocent and pure.*

"The darkness and the fire glow here remind me of my earliest years," the priestess said at last, and as she spoke the dull light captured her vision and she was falling down the tunnel of the years, the words pouring out of her as if she were under some spell.

"All I truly recall of the hut is that it was dark and always smoky. It hurt my throat, so I was always running alone down to the seashore. Mostly I remember the crying of the seagulls; they were about the tower too, so that when I came here to the Forest House many seasons ago, for more than a year I could hardly sleep for being out of the sound of the sea. I loved the ocean. My memories of my . . . home . . ." she continued hesitantly, "are all of children, always a baby at my mother's breast, always the whimpering and squalling, and tugging at her skirts and at mine when I could not escape them. But even beatings could not keep me within the house to pound barley, or to be pulled around by the whimpering naked brats. It is surprising I can endure babes," she added, "but I have no dislike for such as Mairi's who come where they are much longed for and are well cared for once they are born.

"I must have had a father, but even when I was very small, I knew he did nothing for my mother except to make sure that there was always a new baby at the breast." She hesitated. "I dare say Lhiannon pitied me as a starveling."

Caillean heard her own words, surprised that they held no bitterness; as if she had accepted all this too long ago.

"So I do not even know how old I am, not really. It was about a year or so after Lhiannon took me away before my body showed the first signs of womanhood. I think I was about twelve then." She broke off suddenly, and Eilan looked at her in amazement.

I am a woman, a priestess, Caillean told herself, *a sorceress who can frighten armed men!* But the fire trance had taken her too far into memory, and she felt like a terrified child. Which was the truth? Or was the deception only in the flickering of the fire?

"I must be more shaken than I knew," she said in a stifled voice, "or perhaps it is the hour, and the darkness, as if we had stepped outside time." She looked at Eilan, forcing herself to honesty, "Or it may be because I am talking to you . . ."

Eilan swallowed, and steeled herself to meet the other woman's gaze. *Truth . . . tell me the truth* – Caillean heard the thought as if it had been her own, and could not tell which of them had a greater need for it.

"I never told Lhiannon, and the Goddess has not struck me down . . ." She felt the words dragged out of her. "But after all these years it seems to me that perhaps someone should know."

Eilan reached out to her, and Caillean's fingers closed hard on her hand.

"It was the sight and sound of those raiders that made me remember. In my old home there was a man I sometimes saw on the shore. He was, I suspect, one who lived there apart from other men, an outlaw driven from his clan. I would not wonder at that," she added bitterly. "At first I trusted him; he gave me small gifts, pretty things he had found on the shore, shells, bright feathers." She hesitated. "More fool I for thinking him harmless; but how would I have known better? Who had there ever been to teach me?"

She stared blindly towards the fire, but there had been no light in the hut, and no light could reach her now in this place of memory. "I suspected nothing, I never knew what he wanted when he dragged me into his hut one day –" She shuddered, racked by memories for which, even now, she had no words.

"What did you do?" Eilan's voice came from a great way off, like a distant star.

"What could I do?" Caillean said harshly, clinging to that little light. "I – I ran away, crying – crying till I thought I would melt, and filled with such horror and disgust – I can't speak of that. It seemed there was no one I could tell, no one who would have cared." She was silent for a long time. "To this day I remember the smell in his hut – filth, bracken, seaweed, and being pushed down on it while I whimpered – I was too young to imagine what he wanted. The smell of the sea and of bracken still makes me ill," she added.

"Didn't anyone ever know? Didn't they do anything?" asked Eilan. "I think my father would kill anyone who had touched me so."

Caillean had said it at last, and breathing was a little easier now. She let out some of the pain in a long, shuddering, sigh. "Wild as our tribe was, women could not be molested, nor a child so young. Had I accused my attacker, he would have come to the wicker cage and roasted in a slow fire. He knew it, when he threatened me. But I did not know it then." She spoke with a strange detachment now, as if it had all happened to someone else.

"It was about a year afterward that Lhiannon came. She would never have suspected that a girl so young could already be impure – and by the time I came to trust her and believe in her goodness, it was too late; I feared I should be sent away. So, after all, that divinity you thought you saw in me is all a lie," she said harshly. "If Lhiannon had known, I should never have been made priestess – but I made sure she never knew." She turned her face away. For a moment that seemed far too long, there was silence.

"Look at me –"

Caillean found her gaze drawn back to the child and saw Eilan's face, one side Goddess-bright and the other in shadow.

"I believe in you," said the girl gravely.

Caillean drew a shaken breath and Eilan's image was blurred by her tears.

"I live only because I believe that the Goddess forgives me as well," the priestess said. "I had already received my first initiation before I understood the enormity of my deception. But there were no evil omens. When they made me priestess I waited for a thunderbolt, but none came. I wondered then if perhaps there are no gods, or if there are, they care nothing for the doings of humankind."

"Or perhaps they are more merciful than men," said Eilan, then blinked as if amazed at her own temerity. It had never occurred to her to question the wisdom of men like her father and grandfather before. "Why did you leave your tower by the sea?" Eilan prompted after a time.

Caillean, lost in memory, started and said, "Because of the destruction of the shrine on Mona – you know that story?"

"My grandfather – he is a bard – has sung it. But surely that was before you were born –"

"Not quite," Caillean laughed. "But I was still a child. If Lhiannon had not been in Eriu, which you call Hibernia, at the time, she too would have died. For some years after that disaster the remaining Druids of Britain were too busy licking their wounds to take much thought for their priestesses. Then the Arch-Druid made some kind of treaty with the Romans that ensured sanctuary for the surviving sacred women within Roman lands."

"With the Romans!" Eilan exclaimed. "But it was the Romans who killed the others!"

"No, they only despoiled them," said Caillean bitterly. "The priestesses of Mona lived long enough to bear the bastards the Romans had begotten on them, then killed themselves. The children were fostered out to loyal families like your own."

"Cynric!" exclaimed Eilan with a look of sudden comprehension. "That is why he is so bitter about the Romans, and always wants to hear the story of Mona, though it happened so long ago. They always hushed me when I asked about it before!"

"Your Cynric the Roman-hater has exactly as much Roman blood as that boy your father refused to let you marry," said Caillean, laughing. But Eilan hugged her arms and stared into the fire.

"Don't you believe me?" asked the priestess. "It is all too true. Well, perhaps the Romans feel some guilt for what was done, but your grandfather is as wily a political animal as any Roman senator, and he bargained with Cerealis, who was Governor before Frontinus. At any rate the Forest House was built at Vernemeton to shelter women and priestesses from the whole of Britain. And at last Lhiannon became High Priestess and a place was made for me among them, mostly because they did not know what else to do with me. I have attended Lhiannon since I was a little child, but I am not to succeed her. That has been made clear to me."

"Why not?"

"At first I thought it was the will of the Goddess . . . because of what I told you. But now I believe that it is because the priests cannot trust me to obey. I love Lhiannon, but I see her clearly, and I know that she will bend with the wind. Perhaps the only time she ever defied the Council was when she insisted on keeping me. But I see through their plots and speak my mind, though not," she shook her head ruefully, "as I have spoken to you!"

Eilan returned her smile. "That must be true, for I cannot imagine saying even half the things I have heard this night in my father's hall."

"They would not dare let me speak with the voice of the Goddess – they would always be wondering what I was going to say!" Caillean found herself laughing again. "They will want someone more loyal. I thought for a time it was to be Dieda; but I overheard a bit of what Ardanos said when she was chosen. I believe that they had planned it should be you."

"You said something like this before, but I think my father means to arrange a marriage for me."

"Truly?" Caillean raised one eyebrow. "Well, perhaps I am wrong. I knew only that the son of the Prefect of the camp at Deva had asked for you."

"My father was so angry . . ." Eilan blushed, remembering the things he had said to her. "He said he would have Senara married off before she could cause him any trouble. I thought he meant the same for me. But he said nothing of sending me to Vernemeton. If I cannot be with Gaius," she added dully, "I do not suppose it matters what I do."

Caillean looked at her thoughtfully. "I have never been tempted to marry; I have been pledged to the Goddess for so long. Perhaps because of what happened to me when I was a child I never felt I wished to belong to any man. I suppose if I had been unhappy in the temple, Lhiannon would have tried to find a way to give me in marriage; she has always wanted to make me happy. I do love her," she added. "She has been more to me than a mother."

She hesitated. "It galls me to think of giving way to Ardanos's plans, but the Goddess may have had a hand in this as well. Would you like to come with me to Vernemeton when I return?"

"I believe that I would," Eilan replied, and a flicker of interest leaped in those odd, changeable eyes that sometimes looked dark hazel, and sometimes gray replacing the pain. "I cannot think anything else would please me so well. I never really believed they would let me and Gaius be together. Long ago, before I met Gaius, I used to dream of being a priestess. This way, at least, I will have an honorable life and interesting things to learn."

"I think that could be arranged," Caillean said dryly. "No doubt Bendeigid will be delighted, and Ardanos as well. But Lhiannon is the one who must agree to it. Shall I speak to her?"

Eilan nodded, and this time it was the older woman who took her hand. At the touch of the girl's smooth skin Caillean felt the familiar dizziness of shifting vision, and saw Eilan grown older and even more beautiful, swathed in the Oracle's veils. *"Sisters, and more than sisters . . ."* Like an echo she heard the words.

"Don't be afraid, child. I think it may be . . ." she paused and finally said, "fated that you come among us." Her heart lifted suddenly. "And I need hardly say that I would welcome you there." She sighed as the vision left her, and heard, like an echo, a lark outside, giving greeting to the dawn. "Dawn is breaking." With an effort, Caillean made stiff muscles obey her and stumbled towards the door. "We have been talking all the night. I have not done that since I was younger than you." She opened the door, letting the rising sun flood into the room. "Well, at least the rain has stopped; we had better go and see if the byre survived the night – at least those wretches could hardly burn it in this rain – and if they have left us any cows, and anyone to milk them."

For the next four days Gaius slogged along at the head of the troop of Dacian auxiliaries whose sick decurion he was replacing, with Priscus, their optio, all of them cursing the mud and the damp that seemed to creep through every opening despite the capes of oiled leather, rusting armor and chafing wherever wet leather touched skin. The woodlands dripped steadily and the fields lay sodden to either side, pools of standing water rotting the roots of the young corn. Summer's end would bring a poor harvest, he thought grimly. They would need to bring in grain from parts of the Empire where the gods had been kinder. It was no wonder the raiders were roaming if the weather had been the same in Hibernia.

Despite the slow going, by the middle of the fifth day they were well into the country of his adventure. They spent that night at the home of Clotinus. The next day they passed the very boar pit into which he had fallen and turned down the track that led to the household of Bendeigid. The rain was letting up at last, and westward between the banks of breaking clouds the sky glowed gold.

Gaius felt his pulse quicken as he recognized the home pasture and the wood in which he had hunted for primroses with Eilan. Soon she would see him, clothed in the majesty, however mud-spattered, of Rome. He would say nothing; she could judge the depth of his suffering from his silence. And then, perhaps, she would seek him out, and –

"Gods below! Are those more stormclouds?" It was the optio, Priscus, behind him. "I hoped we'd have a day at least to get dry!"

Gaius focused on the outside world and saw that though the sky to the south was clearing, the clouds ahead were an ominous dark gray. His horse tossed its head nervously and a little prickle of apprehension roughened his skin.

"Not rainclouds," said one of the Dacians. "Smoke . . ."

At that moment the rising wind brought him the reek of smoldering timbers. All the horses were snorting now, but they had smelled fire before, and the men kept them under control.

"Priscus, dismount and take two scouts through the woods to see," said Gaius, a little amazed at the cold precision of his tone. Was it training that kept him from spurring his horse forward, or was he simply numbed into inaction by the thought of what he might see? It seemed only a few moments before the scouts returned.

"Raiders, sir," said the optio, his seamed face set like stone. "The Hibernians we heard about, I would guess. But they're gone now."

"Any survivors?"

Priscus shrugged and Gaius felt his throat close.

"Warm welcome here, but no place to sleep, eh? Guess we ride on," said one of the men, and the others laughed. Then Gaius turned, and his face silenced them. He dug his heels into his mount's sides and in silence the troop followed him.

It was true. Even as they came around the edge of the wood to the rise on which Bendeigid's steading had been, Gaius had been hoping that Priscus was mistaken somehow. But it was all gone – only a few blackened timbers at the ends of what had been the feasting hall still stood in mute memorial. No sign of the building where he had convalesced, and no sign of life. Thatched buildings burned fast.

"Fierce indeed must have been the fire, to burn when the straw was wet with rain," said Priscus.

"No doubt," Gaius numbly agreed, picturing little Senara, Eilan, all the family, prisoners in the hands of the wild raiders from the coasts of Hibernia, or worse still, heaps of charred bones among the tangle of burnt timbers that had once been a home. He must not let the men see how much this was affecting him; he pulled his hood over his face, coughing as if from the smoke that still drifted from the outbuildings. Priscus had been right. Nothing could have survived this blaze.

He said fiercely, "Let's get the men going then. We've no time to stand about staring at foundation stones if we're to have shelter before night falls!" His voice cracked and he turned it to another cough, wondering what, if anything, Priscus had deduced from his tone. But the optio, an old soldier, was familiar enough with the effects on the young of seeing pillage and slaughter.

Priscus gave him a kindly glance and looked away. "We promised these people peace when we conquered them – least we could do, you'd think, would be to protect them. But we'll catch up with the bastards that did it, never fear, and teach them not to meddle with Rome. What a pity the gods never invented any other way to civilize the world. Oh well, we could have been turnip farmers; but one way or the other, we picked soldiering for our job, and that's part of it. Friends of yours, were they?"

"I guested here," Gaius replied stiffly. "Last spring." At least his voice was back under control.

"Well, that's the way the world goes," Priscus replied. "Here one day and gone the next. But I reckon the gods must have known what they were doing."

"Yes," Gaius replied, as much to cut off the man's homely philosophy as anything else. "Give the order to march; let's get the men out of the rain as soon as we can reach the next town."

"Right, sir. Column, form up!" he bawled. "Who knows, maybe the family were all away visiting friends. That's the way it goes sometimes."

As they moved on through a gathering mist that was once more turning to rain, Gaius recalled seeing Cynric in the marketplace shortly before leaving Deva; there had been some talk of sending the young man to some college of weapons in the North, so he might very well have survived. The death of a Druid as important as Bendeigid would make some stir. Gaius suspected that his father had sources of information he kept secret. Surely he would know. He had only to wait and see.

Gaius tried to summon up some hope. Priscus was right. The

burning of the house did not necessarily mean the death or imprison-
ment of the people who had lived there. Mairi might well have
returned to her home; Dieda was not even a member of Bendeigid's
household, at least not any more. But Eilan . . . probably it was too
much to hope that Eilan, or little Senara, or the gentle Rheis, had
survived. At that moment he would not have given the smallest of
copper coins for his own career or for the whole of the empire.

He thought, *If I had taken Eilan away she would still be living –
if I had stood up to my father, even stolen her away . . .*

A sudden memory made his throat ache – the vision of his
mother lying cold and white in her sleeping place, and the women
wailing over her body. He had wailed with them, but then his
father had taken him away and taught him that a Roman does not
cry. But he wept for her now, as he wept for these women who had
for a little while, made him feel part of a family.

He could not let the soldiers see him cry. He put his cloak over
his head and tried to pretend that the tears that rolled down his
cheeks were rain.

nine

———〰〰———

"I want my husband." At mid-morning, the day after the birth of her child, Mairi had awakened, fretful and demanding. "Where is Rhodri? He would have protected us from those men —"

The roundhouse was warm after the cold outside. Eilan, who was beginning to feel the effects of her own interrupted night, looked at her sister in exasperation and sat down by the fire. It was bad enough that the raiders had driven off all their milk cows, and she had had to slog several miles through the wet woods to borrow a beast so that Mairi, whose own milk had not yet come in, could feed the child. At least the main herds were off in the summer pastures, so her sister was not without dowry if she married again, although Eilan was not heartless enough to speak of that yet.

"The cows would not have been taken if Rhodri had been here!"

"More likely he would have tried to fight the raiders, and you would still —" Eilan bit her lip, appalled at what she had been saying. She had forgotten that Mairi did not know. "Caillean —" She looked at the priestess in appeal.

"You would still be a widow —" Caillean said brutally, bringing the pannikin of warm milk from the hearth and setting it down.

Mairi's eyes widened. "What are you saying —" She looked up into the face of the priestess and her own grew pale at what she read there.

"I would have waited, but we no longer have that luxury. Rhodri was caught by the Romans when he tried to rescue the levies. They executed him, Mairi."

"It is not true . . . you are lying to me. He could not be dead and I not know! Better that the raiders had killed me — why didn't you let them, Caillean? Oh, I ought to be dead — I wish I were!" Mairi sank back into the feather bed, sobbing, and the baby began to cry.

Caillean handed the child to Eilan, bent over the other woman, murmuring softly.

"There, now, it's no use weeping. You have two fine children with their lives ahead of them. You must gather your strength, Mairi, to get them to safety before the Scotti come again!"

Mairi's eyes flew open and she reached out wildly. Eilan, shaken between tears and laughter, set the baby in her arms. Caillean had been right. Once Mairi was done weeping, she would go on living for her children. Caillean had experience of women's hearts.

A little while later, while Mairi still slept, exhausted with weeping, Eilan heard a horse's hoofs sloshing in the mud left by the storm. They came to a halt outside. *The raiders!* Eilan thought wildly. But no attacker would strike so slowly and heavily upon the door. Her heart beating like a war drum, Eilan drew the bar. When she peered out, she saw her father there.

At the moment she could think only of Rhodri. Had her father come to bring Mairi the news? The young man had been one of their best warriors, living like a son of the house and treating her like a sister even before she was one. Now that Mairi knew about her loss, Eilan too could grieve.

She pulled open the door. Bendeigid stumbled as he entered, as if the ride had wearied him or he had suddenly become old. Then she felt the hardness of his hands closing on her shoulders. For a long moment he stood looking at her.

"Caillean has just told Mairi about Rhodri," she said in a low voice. "Did you know?"

"I knew," her father said with great bitterness. "I hoped that the word that had come to me was not true. A curse will certainly light on all Romans for that deed. Now do you see, Eilan, why I would not allow you to marry into that accursed people?" He let go of her and dropped down upon the settle by the fire.

Gaius's people might be guilty of such evil, but she did not believe that Gaius himself would have done it. But looking into her father's harsh face, she held her tongue.

"But that is not the worst evil we have to mourn." Bendeigid's face contorted suddenly, and Eilan felt the first twinge of real fear. "I do not know how to say it, Eilan."

"It may be that I already know," Caillean spoke behind them. "I am sometimes foresighted, and the night before I left the Forest House I dreamed I saw a house lying in ashes, and knew it for yours. But then I found Eilan here and thought I must have been mistaken. Last night we had a visit from a band of raiders. I know the size of pack such wolves run in – and I feared. Did the main body turn south, then, to you?"

"A band came here?" he croaked, turning to stare at her.

"Only a few of them, and I managed to frighten them off."

"Then I have you to thank that I have children yet alive!"

Eilan needed no foresight to understand his words, but what she was hearing was too horrible to believe. She felt the color draining from her face. "Father –"

"Child, child, how can I tell you? Word came that a mixed band of raiders were attacking Conmor's steading. I took my men to go to his aid. But there were more of them than we dreamed could come in such weather. While we were gone –"

"Are Mother and Senara dead then?" Her voice cracked, and Mairi, rousing, pushed back the bedcurtains and stood unsteadily, staring. Caillean went to her and the Druid continued.

"I dare to hope so." His face contorted with pain. "For the alternative, to be carried off as slaves beyond the sea, is worse still. To think that either might live in such dishonor –"

"Would you rather see them dead than alive in slavery?" Caillean asked in a low, tense voice.

"I would that," Bendeigid exclaimed fiercely. "Better a quick death, even in the flames, and a welcome in the Otherworld, than life with the memory of all our people's deaths to haunt them, as I must live now. The gods know those monsters would have paid in blood for their deaths, and mine, if I had only been there!"

He broke off and stared fiercely from Eilan to Mairi, who took a tottering step towards him. Groaning, he gathered both of his daughters into his arms. Sobbing, Eilan held on to her sister. Once she would have found comfort in her father's arms, but these were griefs from which he could not protect her.

"Senara's body was not found in the ashes," he said brokenly, "and she was not yet ten years old . . ."

Eilan thought, *Then it may well be that she still lives* . . . but she did not say it aloud.

"I had meant to bring Mairi home when the news about Rhodri was confirmed, but now I have no home to offer her. I can give no protection to anyone now . . ."

"Lord Druid, perhaps you cannot," said Caillean quietly, "but your Order can. The Forest House will shelter Mairi and the little ones for as long as they have need. And I want to ask if you would permit Eilan to enter as a novice priestess of the shrine."

Bendeigid sat up and looked sharply at Eilan. "Is that what you want, child?"

"It is," she said simply. "If I may not marry where I love, then let me give my love to the Lady. It would please me indeed, for I used to dream about such a life before I was old enough to think of marriage at all."

For the first time, her father smiled, albeit shakily. "It will please your grandsire, at any rate. I had not intended this life for you, Eilan, but if it is truly what you want, then I am pleased too."

"But what –" Eilan bit back the words. How could she have forgotten? Her mother would never say anything more to her at all. But her father seemed to have sensed what she could not say. He sank down again by the hearth, his face buried in his hands. She had never guessed that her father could weep. But when he looked up again she saw his cheeks streaked with tears.

Eilan was likewise bereft, but she had no tears. *Will Gaius think me dead when he hears? Will he weep for me?* Better, perhaps, that he should think her dead than faithless to his memory. But it did not matter; she would be a priestess of the Forest House. Beyond that she could not make her mind go.

"They shall be avenged!" exclaimed the Druid, gazing into the flames. "In all of Britain shall those wild devils find no lives so costly as these! Even the Romans have never dared so far, and I tell you I would accept help even from them to get revenge! This will mean war! For it is not only rapine and murder, Eilan; it is sacrilege. To attack the home of a Druid, kill the wife and daughter and granddaughter of Druids; and destroy the sacred things – how could they do it? The Northerners are our kinsfolk, and I have studied with the Druids of Eriu."

"It has ever been the way of our people to fight each other when there was no common enemy," Caillean quietly observed.

"But we do have such an enemy," exclaimed Bendeigid. "Do not we all hate Rome?"

"Perhaps the wild tribes think of us as Romans now . . ."

The Druid shook his head. "The gods will surely punish them; and if they do not, our people will. Cynric has been as a son to me, and I tell you, he will curse when he hears of this day! But he is away in the islands to the north. You and Mairi are all that are left to me, Eilan."

Indeed, she thought, remembering. *I have so few kin left and Dieda too has lost a sister. Will she welcome me to the Forest House?*

Well, whatever came of it, a priestess she would be. Of her father's blood remained Mairi, and her newborn daughter, and her son; she wished that these children might be a comfort to her father. He was not yet old; he might marry again and have others of his own or, more likely, Mairi would find a new husband and have more. But if Eilan went to the Forest House, he would get no grandchildren from her.

Bendeigid rose, looking at Caillean beneath bent brows. "I am in need now of your skills, priestess; Cynric must be recalled. Can you summon him for me? And will you do so?"

"With Lhiannon's help, I can," Caillean replied. "In any case she would need to know –"

"I also need your skills to seek out these men," Bendeigid interrupted.

"That is easily done; I saw them when they burst in here, and if they were not among those who burned your home yet they must be under the same command. Some of them were Caledonians, and the others Scotti from Eriu."

"If they came here last night, the Scotti would have been on their way back to the coast and the Caledonians on their way north again." Bendeigid had risen to pace restlessly; now he resumed his seat by the fire. Caillean brought him a mug of ale and he sank his beard in it for a long draught, then repeated, "We need Cynric home, faster than even a mounted man can ride. Send the message, Caillean, with your magic –"

"I will," said the priestess. "I will stay here with your daughters while you ride to tell Lhiannon. Then go to Deva, for the Arch-Druid must know as well."

"You are right; my wife Rheis was his daughter," Bendeigid said, rubbing his brow distractedly. "Perhaps he will have some counsel for us as well."

News of the raid spread quickly through the countryside. On the lips of wandering peddlers it travelled, and with couriers of the Legions; it seemed that the birds of the air themselves bore the news on their wings.

Three days after the raid, Ardanos, the Arch-Druid, coming out of his house in Deva in the morning, heard a raven croak on his left and recognized an omen of disaster. But he had earned his rank by the kind of worldly wisdom that enabled him to out-think the Romans and undermine opposition among his own people. Not for the first time he regretted the worldly limit of his powers. Then he saw the mud-spattered man coming up the street and knew that he would not have to wait for the raven to tell him, for grief was written plainly in his son-in-law's burning eyes.

When Ardanos had recovered a little from the shock of Bendeigid's news, he went to Macellius Severus, who demanded a hearing from the Commander of the Adiutrix Legion.

"These raiders from over the sea grow too bold," Macellius said angrily. "These Britons too are our people, wards of Rome. No one shall oppress them while I live. The family of one of the Druids who lives near by, Bendeigid —"

"A proscribed man," interrupted the Commander of the Legion, frowning. "He should not be here at all!"

"That makes no difference! Do you not understand that Rome is here to protect all the men of this country — our citizens and the natives as well," Macellius insisted, still haunted by the memory of Ardanos's grief. Over the years he had come to respect the old man, and he had never known the Arch-Druid to be other than perfectly collected before. "How can we persuade them to lay down their arms if we cannot then protect them? With two Legions we could conquer Hibernia —"

"You may well be right, but it will have to wait until Agricola is finished with the Novantae. It has always been that way — with each province we settle we must pacify a new frontier. In the days of the Governor Paulinus, the Druids of Mona were broken so that they could not set the West Country afire. Now it is the Caledonians who must be taught they cannot raid the Brigantae. I suppose that when the Empire stretches to Ultima Thule we will have a peaceful border, but I doubt it will happen before.

"In the meantime all we can do is to hurry the construction of the new coastal fortresses," said the Legion's commander cynically, "and ready a troop or two of cavalry to go out if they should be sighted again. Your son is out there now with some troops, isn't he? Detail him to this duty when he reports in." The Commander grunted. "The people of Britannia are ours to oppress, and no one else shall do it."

But building fortresses and planning campaigns took time. Long before the log walls were finished or the grain that had survived the rains had been harvested, Bendeigid returned to escort his daughters to the Forest House. He brought gently paced mules for Mairi and the children to ride. Eilan rode with Mairi's older child before her, warmly wrapped against the light rain. She was not used to riding and it took all her concentration to balance behind the excited child. The distance was not great, but the unaccustomed journey seemed long.

Darkness was just falling as they came within the palisaded walls. Within the compound were half a dozen large buildings; Caillean took Mairi and her children to a guest house, lifting the little boy down from his perch before Eilan, and pointed out a large building of stout timbers, thatched almost down to the ground.

"There is the House of Maidens," she said. "The chief of the younger priestesses, Eilidh, has been told of your coming, and she will welcome you there. I will come later when I can; but first I must go and see if Lhiannon needs me."

The new moon – the first of Mairi's newborn's life – rode low on the western horizon. As the serving woman led her into the building and across an inner enclosure, Eilan was surprised to find that already she missed her sister.

Then a gate opened and the woman led her into the inner court. Ahead of her was a long building something like her father's feasting hall. As she passed through the door a sea of strange faces surrounded her. She looked around, feeling abandoned. The serving woman had left her alone at the door. The hall seemed very large and there was a faint scent of sweet herbs in the air. Then one of the priestesses came forward.

"I am Eilidh," she said.

"Where is my kinswoman, Dieda?" asked Eilan nervously. "I had hoped to see her here –"

"Dieda attends on Lhiannon and is secluded with her in preparation for the rites of Lughnasad," said the priestess. "She is your cousin? I would have thought you even more closely akin; even twins.

"Caillean has asked me to take you in charge, for now that she is back she will have to attend Lhiannon. You are almost as beautiful as she told me."

Eilan colored shyly and lowered her eyes. The priestess was herself quite beautiful; fair-haired, with curly short hair that circled her face in the lamplight, like a delicate halo. She was dressed like the other junior priestesses, not in the dark robes they wore outside the walls but in a dress of undyed linen of an extremely old-fashioned cut, girdled with a woven belt of green.

"You must be half dead with fatigue," Eilidh said kindly. "Come to the fire, child, and get warm."

Eilan obeyed, feeling a little stunned by all the strange faces. She had not thought what might confront her here. Now she wondered what she would find, and whether she had made a decision she would regret all her life.

"Don't be afraid of us," said a grave voice behind her. The new speaker was tall and sturdy, with reddish hair. "There aren't half as many of us as there seem to be. You should have seen me when I first came here, staring about me and sobbing like a wild thing. My name is Miellyn. I have been here five or six years, and now I cannot imagine any other life. All my friends are here, and one day you will have friends here too. For all that we must seem so strange to you now." She took Eilan's cloak from her, and laid it aside.

"I think Lhiannon wishes to speak with you before anything else," said Eilidh, "so come with me." So saying, she led Eilan across a blustery courtyard to a separate dwelling and rapped on the door. After a moment they heard footsteps and Caillean peered out.

"Eilan? Come in, child," she said, gesturing to someone behind her. "Dieda, you see, I have brought Eilan to you at last."

"So you have," said Dieda, emerging from the shadows behind her. "My father, the Arch-Druid, is here too; and Bendeigid, so we shall be a regular family party, I suppose." She laughed, and Eilan thought she had never heard so cynical a sound. "And if he has his way Cynric will be brought here as well. I have heard they want to use your Sight, Caillean."

"Or yours, perhaps," said Caillean, and Dieda laughed a little. Eilan sensed hostility between the two and wondered why.

"I think they know what I would say to that," Dieda said. "If it is to seek out Cynric, yes; but to make an oracle for Lhiannon to deliver obediently as if she were no more than a puppet for the will of Rome—"

"In the name of the Goddess, any goddess, be silent, child," Caillean ordered, listening to a gate slamming somewhere near by. "What is it? Who is here?"

"Only his holiness, my father," Dieda muttered, "and the greatest priestess of all the Forest House, who will obediently deliver such oracles as he shall desire."

"Be silent, you wretched creature," hissed Caillean. "You well know that what you say is sacrilege."

"Or perhaps there is a greater sacrilege here, in which I have no part," Dieda replied. "Perhaps, with Sight, they want to make certain they send the Romans against the right party. If so, what will you do, Caillean?"

"I will do whatever Lhiannon commands," said Caillean, her voice sharpening. "As we all do."

Caillean was trying to speak reasonably to soften Dieda's wrath; but the other girl seemed angrier than ever. Dieda had always been sharp-tongued, but Eilan had never heard her so bitter before.

"I know what you would have us think —" Dieda began, but Caillean's face flushed with anger. Still she spoke calmly.

"You know perfectly well that it is not what you think, or what I think, that matters," she began, "but what the High Priestess wills; and that is what I will do."

"If it is her will," Dieda answered more quietly, "but under present conditions, how can Lhiannon's will be done — even if her will could somehow be determined or if she even has one any more."

"Dieda, I have heard this all before," Caillean said wearily. "But is it such an evil thing to summon our kinsman Cynric so that he may fittingly mourn his foster mother?"

"We could have done that weeks ago," Dieda began.

"Perhaps, but that is all that you — or I — are being asked to do," Caillean repeated. "Why have you set yourself so stubbornly against it now?"

"Because I know, if you do not," Dieda said, "that this use of power is to trick Cynric into doing what his whole life has been spent in learning to oppose; what Bendeigid himself would rather die than do, and that is to clasp hands with Rome. Know you not that for his sake it was that Bendeigid allowed himself to be proscribed?"

"Oh, in the name of the Goddess, girl! I know something of Cynric too, and of Bendeigid," said Caillean crossly. "And, believe it or not, even something of the Romans; at least I have lived under their rule longer than you. And I say that there shall be no violence done to your precious ethical precepts, nor to Cynric's. Do you think, perhaps, that you are the only person in all of Britannia who knows what Cynric wishes to do?"

"I know enough —" Dieda began, but Caillean said harshly

"Hush; they will hear us. And Eilan must be thoroughly confused by now –"

Dieda's face softened. "I suppose so, and it is an ill welcome for her to hear us disputing so." She came and embraced Eilan, who knew enough not to protest lest she start the argument again.

At this moment the inner door opened and Lhiannon stood before them.

"Children, are you quarreling?"

"Of course not, my mother," said Caillean quickly. And after a moment Dieda added, "No, certainly not, Holy Mother; we were only welcoming the new novice."

"Ah, yes; I heard that Eilan was to come," said Lhiannon, and turned her gaze on the young girl who stood quietly between them. Eilan felt her heart thump loudly as she looked at the woman she had last seen standing like a goddess beside the Beltane fire.

"So you are Eilan?" Lhiannon's voice was sweet but a little thin, as if being the mouthpiece of the Goddess for so many years had worn its strength away. "It is true; you are very like Dieda; I suppose you are weary of being told that. But we must devise some way to tell you apart here at the shrine." She smiled, and Eilan felt an odd surge of protectiveness.

Lhiannon reached out one hand to Eilan, who was still standing nervously by the door. "Come in, child. Your father and grandfather are here with us, you know." Eilan wondered why she should be surprised, since her father had escorted her here. Was he then living among the priests?

Lhiannon took Eilan's arm gently and drew the girl into the inner room, adding to the two older priestesses, in her sweet voice, "Come in too. Both of you will be needed here."

The inner room seemed small, or perhaps it was only that too many people had crowded into it. Smoke curled thickly from herbs burning in a brazier in the center of the room; their smell made Eilan's head swim. Between the smoke and the crowd, for a moment she found it hard to breathe.

After a moment her focus steadied and she saw her father, his face made gaunt by the past moon's grief until he looked almost as old as Ardanos.

Her grandfather, who was adding something to the fire, looked up at the women and said, "So we are all here. And once again I am confused; which of you is which?"

Eilan stood silent, waiting for someone older to answer, but

Dieda said boldly, "It is easy to tell, Father. Eilan has not yet been given the dress of a priestess."

"So that is how you expect me to tell my daughter from my granddaughter! Well, perhaps it is only the smoke in here. But I still find them too much alike for my comfort," said the older Druid briskly. "So, Eilan, you have arrived here at a sad time; we must summon Cynric to our Councils, and as he has been brought up with you as a foster brother your assistance will be helpful. Are you ready, Caillean?"

Caillean said quietly "If Lhiannon wills it."

"I do," Lhiannon answered. "Whatever comes of this, Cynric must know of the death of his foster mother and of these new outrages. The Romans are not our only enemies –"

Dieda said quietly through her teeth, "How would you like to say that to Mairi at this moment, Father?"

"Peace, child," Ardanos said. "Whatever you may think, Macellius Severus is a good man; he was as angry when I told him as if his own house had been burnt."

"I doubt that," Dieda murmured, but low enough so that only Caillean and Eilan could hear.

The old Druid frowned at her; then he said, "Caillean, my child –"

Caillean, with a glance at Lhiannon, went to a cupboard and took out a small silver bowl, simple but for an elaborate chasing of patterns on the outside. She filled it with water from a ewer and set it on the table. Ardanos pulled up a three-legged stool so that she could sit down before it, while Lhiannon took her place in a carved chair near by.

Ardanos waved Caillean aside. "Wait," he said; "Dieda, it was you who were closest to him; it is you who must look into the water and summon him."

Dieda flushed and for a moment Eilan wondered if she would refuse outright. Dieda had always had more courage than she – or had her grandfather mistaken them again? He was looking at her; then he turned aside and his eyes sought out Dieda. "You were pledged," he said. "I ask it of you, child –" and his voice was more tender than Eilan had ever heard it. "For your sister's sake I ask it; she was his foster mother before you were born."

Eilan thought, *He plays on us all as if we were his harps.* But Dieda could not ignore the tenderness in his voice either. She murmured, "As you will, Father," and took her place before the bowl.

Ardanos began, "So then, we are gathered here in this place that is already protected and purified to summon Cynric, the foster son of Bendeigid. All of you, who are of all the living the nearest he has to kindred, must hold his image in memory, and add the calling of your hearts to mine." He struck the floor with his staff, and Eilan heard the sweet jangle of silver bells.

"Cynric, Cynric, now do we call you!" his strong, bard-trained voice rang out suddenly, and Eilan blinked, for suddenly the room seemed to have become darker, and Ardanos – his whole body, not just his white robes – seemed to glow. "Strong son, beloved boy, your kindred call you . . . Warrior, Raven-son, we summon you by the powers of earth and oak and fire!"

As the echoes of his calling faded, Dieda's breathing, growing harsher as she drew in great lungfuls of scented smoke, was the only sound in the room. Eilan stifled a cough. Even the small amount of the smoke she had breathed in had made her dizzy; she could imagine what it was doing to Dieda, who gazed into the water unmoving.

Only now did Eilan notice Dieda's long hair hanging loosely to either side so that it framed the bowl. They had all moved into a loose circle. From where she stood Eilan could see the surface of the water. Her skin prickled a little as Dieda swayed, or was it she herself? Perhaps it was the world that was moving; she blinked as the shapes around her dimmed and flowed until the only thing on which she could focus was the surface of the bowl.

As she stared, it slowly clouded over, and after a moment there was a gray swirling that first darkened; then cleared. Eilan gasped; a face, a well-known face – that face of her foster brother Cynric – peered from the water.

Dieda stifled a cry; then said quietly but clearly, as if she spoke to someone a long way off, "Cynric, you must come. This time it is not a Roman outrage but the people of the North who have burned your house and have killed your mother and sister. Return to the Ordovici lands. Your foster father is alive and has need of you."

After a time the face disappeared, the water swirled darkly in the bowl, and Dieda stood up, clutching a little dizzily at the edge of the table. "He will come," she said. "The keeper of the college of priestesses there will give him supplies. With good roads and good weather he should be here in a few days."

Bendeigid said, "But what of the barbarians who burnt our house? If you are not too wearied, child, we must see them and know whence we go to punish them –"

"I will not," said Dieda. Her hair was still hanging about her face. "Always you can bend me to your will, but let Caillean do this; it is her will that we work with the Romans in this, not mine. I will find it hard to forgive you."

"My child —"

"Oh, I well know the necessity; but to use me to draw Cynric here, how could you?"

Caillean took the bowl and flung the water out through the door, letting in a welcome blast of fresh air. Yet in spite of the warmth of the summer night after a few moments Eilan began to feel cold. Caillean refilled the bowl and bent over it, motionless.

This time it seemed that the picture took longer to form, and the swirling clouds in the water lasted longer. Caillean's intent face grew paler, pale as death; then she spoke, softly still, and with a deathly weariness in her voice: "Behold, if you will."

Eilan never knew what the others saw, but as the surface of the water cleared, before her eyes a small picture formed: the raiders as they had been when they burst into Mairi's house, arrested, frozen on the doorstep; men clad in multicolored and ragged fabric. Some bore swords, which she had not seen at the time, and some bore spears. The picture was so clear that she could see the raindrops glittering on their ragged blond or reddish beards and long streaming hair. The men crowded around the bowl, blocking the image that Eilan saw still in memory and knew she would be able to call up at will until the day she died.

In her memory she saw Caillean rush forward, scooping up handfuls of live coals and scattering them towards the strange men. She supposed that her father and grandfather must have seen something like this, for her father's face was clenched and drawn tight. "Red Rian," he said between his teeth. "A curse on his sword and his shadow! And they are on the seashore still —"

"So be it, and I add my curse to yours for what that is worth," Lhiannon said, stirring in her chair. "I declare to you that your people and the Romans together shall work to punish them."

Bendeigid began to speak but Lhiannon silenced him with a gesture. "Enough; I have said it. Now go; let it be as Caillean has seen and I have declared. You can take Red Rian on the seashore."

"Lady, how know you this?"

"Have you forgotten that I and mine can rule the winds when we choose?" Lhiannon said. "He will not find a breeze to bear him hence till you have caught up with him. Will all this content you?"

"For the sake of vengeance against those devils – if it must be so," Bendeigid declared. "But I swore to ally even with Romans if they would help me to vengeance, though it goes against the grain – and we will need their help to drive these raiders and murderers forever from our shores!"

Dieda drew a long breath. "Will you await the coming of Cynric?"

"That will be at least partly for Macellius to say," Bendeigid said grudgingly after a moment. Lhiannon's gaze fell on Eilan.

"But look you, our newest novice is quite perished with cold," she said. "Where is your cloak, child?"

"I left it in the other hall with the priestesses," Eilan murmured, unsuccessfully trying to control her shivering.

"You must go to bed soon. But the herbs have burned off now, come to the brazier and warm yourself, child. In a little, Caillean shall see to taking you to the novices' dormitory and give you nightclothes and the dress of a priestess."

"Well said," put in Ardanos, "and it is time we were going as well."

Lhiannon drew Eilan to the fire, and gradually the girl's shivering subsided. But still she trembled within. Caillean put an arm around her.

"It will pass, child, I know . . . It can be very cold between the worlds; I felt you riding with me, though it was not intended. We shall have to guard against that another time."

Bendeigid wrapped his cloak around him, but before he followed Ardanos out he paused before Eilan. "Daughter." He coughed as Eilan looked up to meet his gaze. "I do not know when we will meet again. But I leave you in safety, and that is a comfort to me. May the Goddess bless you here." He embraced her.

"I will pray to Her for your safety, Father," she said softly, her throat tightening.

Bendeigid reached out and touched the tendrils that had escaped from the braid coiled upon her brow. "Your mother's hair grew just this way," he whispered, and quickly, then, kissed her on the brow. She was blinking back tears when the door closed behind him.

"Well, that is done, and it is late indeed," Caillean said with a touch of relief. "Eilan, is there anything you want to ask me?" She came and took the girl into a hearty embrace. "If you are warm now, come along and I will get you settled into the novices' dormitory."

This time with Caillean at her side, Eilan crossed the windy courtyard which separated Lhiannon's dwelling from the hall where she had first been welcomed among the priestesses. Years later, when she knew every inch of these dwellings as well as the house in which she had been born, she was to remember her first sight of the Forest House and wonder that on this night it had seemed so enormous.

Eilidh and some of the other women were still gathered in the hall where Eilan had been first welcomed. They all looked at Eilan with curiosity, but a gesture from Caillean kept them still.

"We cannot ask you yet to take vows," Caillean said to Eilan, "But for your first year among us you must make promises." She stood upright and her face changed. Eilan watched her warily, wondering what was coming now.

"First of all – you have come among us of your free will? You have not been forced or threatened into seeking admission here?"

Eilan looked at her, astonished. "You know I have not been."

"Hush – it is routine. You must answer in your own words."

"Very well," Eilan said. "I came here at my own wish." This seemed very silly to her. She wondered if they had asked Dieda this, and what the other girl had answered.

"Do you promise that you will treat every woman in this dwelling as your sister, mother and daughter, as your own kin?"

"I will." She now had no mother living, and if she took permanent vows, she would have no daughter either.

"Do you promise that you will obey every lawful command given you by an older priestess here, and that you will lie with no man –" Caillean stopped and made a face, amending, "Saving only that you may lie with the Summer King, if his choice should fall on you."

Eilan smiled. "I will obey, and it is no hardship to promise to give myself to no man." *Since the one man I could have loved is forbidden to me.*

Caillean nodded. "So be it," she said. "In the name of the Goddess, who, though She has many names, is one, I accept you."

She embraced Eilan, and, one by one, the other priestesses did the same. By the time they were done, Eilan found herself weeping, as if in some odd way she had regained the kindred she had lost.

The older priestess put Eilan's cloak over her shoulders and led her through a thatched passageway to a roundhouse with about a dozen beds – not box beds such as she was accustomed to, but narrow cots – set round the wall. Some of them were already occupied. One or two girls sat up, blinking sleepily, as Caillean pulled back the curtain of the bed nearest the door, then lay back again.

"A place has been made for you here," whispered Caillean. She put Eilan into a coarse white shift which seemed a little too big. "Someone will wake you for the sunrise services in the grove. Do not expect to see me – I will be attending upon Lhiannon in preparation for the ceremonies of the full moon. Here is the dress you are to wear tomorrow." She took from a nearby chest a bundle of clothing.

Eilan got into the narrow bed and Caillean tucked her under the thick blanket. Then she bent down to embrace her, and Eilan sat up to hug her back.

"Whatever you may think, remember that you are welcome among us," Caillean said. "Even to Dieda; she is very unhappy now, but a day will come when she is glad you are here too."

She kissed Eilan on the forehead. "Tomorrow one of the girls will help you to dress in the robes of a priestess; most likely Eilidh. And for a day or two she will go everywhere with you and show you what to do."

Eilan lay back. The sheets were rough against her skin, and smelled of scented herbs. She asked, wanting to prolong the moment, "What scent is that on the sheet?"

"Lavender; we lay it among our linens when we wash them."

Eilan told herself not to be surprised. The priestesses were women, if not exactly like any others she had known; of course they took thought to the plucking of herbs and the washing of linens like anyone else. She too would learn all these things.

Caillean said quietly, "Sleep now, and don't worry. It is well that you have come here. I think you have a very special destiny among us."

Neither of them could have guessed how that prophecy was to be fulfilled.

ten

"Why do we keep secret from the common folk the names of those herbs that are most powerful for healing?" Old Latis, the most senior of their herbalists, turned to the girls who were sitting beneath the oak tree, holding a stalk of foxglove bells in her hand.

"So they will have to come to us and respect the priestesses?" asked one of the younger girls.

"Their respect must be earned, child," Latis said sternly. "Unlearned they may be, but they are not stupid. The reason for secrecy lies deeper – that which is most powerful for good is also powerful for evil, handled wrongly. Foxglove can stimulate an ailing heart, but give too much and it will gallop like a frightened horse until it breaks down. For the healer, judgment is all."

Eilan frowned, for she had never thought of it quite that way. Later, looking back on her years in the Forest House, she wondered what she had expected. Peace, perhaps, or mystery, and even a little boredom. She had not expected that days spent studying with a group of other women would be simply so *interesting*.

Her nights were harder, for in the first months she often dreamed of Gaius. At times she saw him riding with his men, or practicing with the sword. He swore sometimes as the blade bit into the man-shaped wooden post – *This for Senara, and this for Rheis. This, for Eilan!* When he finished his brow would be damp with sweat, but the moisture on his cheeks was tears.

Eilan would wake, then, weeping for his sorrow. She understood now how the grief of the living could torment the departed. She thought of sending a message to let him know she still lived, but there was no way to do it, and presently she began to realize that she was indeed dead to him, and the sooner he accepted that, the better for both of them.

In these early months, she was only one of a group of potential priestesses. She spent much of her time beginning to memorize the whole body of Druidic lore. Just as the gods might not be worshipped in a temple made with human hands, none of the divine lore might be entrusted to writing. Sometimes she thought this strange, for the human memory was itself so fragile. But she had seen her teachers perform amazing feats of memorization. Much of the old knowledge had been lost when Mona was destroyed, but much remained. Ardanos, for instance, could recite the whole of the Law from memory.

She was happy enough with her fellow priestesses. The ones she knew best were the two who had welcomed her to the House of Maidens that first night: Eilidh and Miellyn.

Eilidh was older than she looked and had been in the Forest House since early childhood. Miellyn was closer to her own age. Apart from these two, she best knew a woman named Celimon who was about forty, whose major task was to instruct the youngest priestesses and officiate at some of the less important rituals.

Her first task was to memorize every detail of those rites in which the maidens assisted, for if a mistake were made, a ceremony would have to be begun again. Two or three times Eilan had caused such an interruption. She felt foolish, but Miellyn assured her that they had all been through it.

Eilan was also instructed in the motions of moon and stars. She spent many night hours lying between Miellyn and Eilidh in a secluded part of the enclosure, watching the Great Wain swinging endlessly about the North Star, and the solemn march of the planets as they rose and fell and the Northern Lights flashed and circled in the summer sky. She learned that the earth went round the sun – of all the wonders, the hardest to believe. From all her early years in the Forest House these nights best captured her imagination; lying warmly cloaked on the damp grass with Caillean's voice floating above them in the darkness, intoning long stories of the stars.

She wished sometimes to learn to accompany the singing, but on one of the few occasions when she was allowed to spend some time with Caillean, she was told that women did not play the harp in the ceremonies.

"But why? Women can be bards now, can't they, like Dieda? And you play a harp, do you not?"

It was warm, and in the grove outside the walls one of the

younger priests from the Druidic college across the fields was practicing. He was not very good at it, but it was very hard to play a harp so badly that listening would be painful. Even though the melody halted, each note was pure and clear.

"My instrument is a lyre, Lhiannon's first gift to me, and I have played it for years, so no one dares object. And talent like Dieda's cannot be denied." Caillean's dark eyes flashed.

"It does not make sense. Why is it I cannot learn?" asked Eilan. However badly she might play, she could surely do better than that fellow outside, who did not seem to have noticed that as the day grew warmer his upper strings were going out of tune.

"Of course it does not make sense," Caillean replied. "A great deal that the priests do makes no sense; and they know it. That is one reason why I will not be allowed to succeed Lhiannon. Ardanos is aware that I know it too."

"Do you want to be High Priestess?" asked Eilan, her eyes rounding.

"Heaven forbid," said Caillean fervently. "I would be running head-on against the will of the priesthood – which is like a stone wall – every day of my life. Leadership is another thing the men wish to keep for themselves. I think it has got worse since they encountered the Romans. They wish to keep the weapons, and the harps, and everything else save for the suffering of childbirth and the toil of the cooking pot and the loom. I dare say they would like to say women cannot serve the gods, but no one would be foolish enough to believe that. But why do you want to learn to play a harp?"

Eilan said, "Because I love music, and I cannot sing."

"Your voice is soft but sweet, for I have heard it."

"Grandfather says that next to Dieda, I croak like a frog," Eilan said bitterly. "In our house it was always left to her to sing."

"I think he is mistaken; but this time I will not argue, for even I must admit that he is one of our greatest bards. Dieda has a very beautiful voice, perhaps from him. Next to such a voice as your kinswoman's we are all frogs croaking, child, so do not grieve. You can learn the stories of the gods, even if you cannot sing them as well as she; I think you will have no trouble becoming a spell singer anyway. We cannot all have the finest voices, even among the bards."

And, indeed, Eilan was taught to sing many of the spells she had to memorize, and a few of the simpler Words of Power were confided to her, even that first year.

One day when she was being instructed in spells by Caillean, the older woman asked, "Do you remember that night after Mairi's child was born, when I frightened away the raiders by throwing fire at them?"

"I will never forget it," Eilan said.

"Remember I told you that you could learn to do it, if you had the proper teaching?"

Eilan nodded, her heart beginning to pound, whether with excitement or fear, she did not know.

"Well, I will teach you now. The important thing to remember is that the fire cannot harm you; you have seen me handle it, and so you know within yourself that it can be done." She picked up the girl's slender white fingers in her own cool ones and breathed on the palm of Eilan's hand.

"Now," she said, "The important thing is to trust yourself. Reach quickly into the fire, and pick up a handful of live coals; the fire can only harm you because you believe it is in the nature of fire to burn; once you know its true spiritual nature, you can handle it as you would a handful of dry leaves. Fire burns within you as it burns on the hearth. How can one flame harm another? Let the spark of life within you welcome fire!"

Eilan quailed, but it was true that she had seen Caillean do this trick; and she trusted the older woman completely. She reached towards the brazier of live coals; heat touched her face, but Caillean said firmly, "Do not hesitate – do it quickly!" And Eilan thrust her hand into the flames.

On her cheeks she could still feel heat, but to her astonishment, the coals felt like a handful of winter snow. Caillean, watching her wondering face, said, "Drop it; quickly now." Eilan opened her fingers against a sudden blast of heat and the coals rolled on to the hearthstone. She stared at her hands in wonder.

"Did I really do that?"

"You did," Caillean said. The coal had reached a cloth lying in the hearth, which began to smolder. A strong stink of burning cloth rose suddenly from the singed edges as Caillean picked it up and blew it out.

Eilan stared at her in astonishment. "How did you know that in another moment it was going to burn?"

Caillean said, "I could feel you beginning to think and wonder – and doubt. Doubt is the enemy of magic. We are taught to do things like this to astonish the common people with wonders and marvels, or to guard ourselves in danger. But you must learn," she cautioned, "that it is not right to do miracles for the sake of merely astonishing the once-born. Even to preserve yourself against danger, you must be wary of doing what may seem miracles. It may not have been altogether wise to use it that night in Mairi's house; but done is done. Now that you know it is possible, you shall learn when it is right to use such things, and when it is not."

As the year's passage was marked by the festivals, the girls received not only the lore of the gods each festival honored but the meaning behind the tales, many of which, true in symbol, were not true in fact. They argued about the virginity of the goddess Arianrhod, and the fate of the bright son she so unwillingly bore; they analyzed the transformations of Gwion who tasted the brew in the cauldron of wisdom. They learned the secret lore of the Sacred King and the Lady of Sovereignty. And in the darkest days of winter, they contemplated the mysteries of the shadowy goddesses whose bloody faces and withered flesh were the embodiment of men's fears.

"But why do men fear old women?" Eilidh asked. "They do not feel that way about old men!"

"The old man becomes a sage, something for a man to aspire to," Caillean told them. "They fear the hag because she is beyond their power. With the coming of her moonblood a girl becomes a woman. She needs a man to become a mother, and a mother needs a man to protect her children. But the old woman knows all the secrets of birth and death; she has rebirthed herself and needs nothing. So of course the man, who knows only the first change that brings him to manhood, is afraid."

Lhiannon's name was sacred even when the younger girls giggled about their elders late at night in the Hall of Maidens, but Eilan could not help wondering if the High Priestess had gone through the rebirth Caillean had described. Old as she was, one could not imagine that any human grief or passion had ever touched her. She had lain with no man, borne no child; she drifted through the Forest House in a cloud of lavender scent and trailing draperies, her smile sweet and vague and distant as if she moved through her own private reality.

And yet Caillean loved her. Eilan could not allow herself to forget that the older priestess, with whom that night of Mairi's childbirth had given her so deep a bond, saw something in the High Priestess that she herself had not seen; but she would take it on faith that it was there.

When they began to teach the girls the disciplines that would give them access to the inner planes, Eilan applied herself with diligence. Such things – dreams and intuitions – had always come to her easily and without warning. Now she learned to bring the visions at will, and when it was necessary, to wall them away.

She learned the work of seeing visions in a bowl of water and the use of spells for far-seeing. One of the first things she saw through her scrying was the battle with the raiders who had destroyed her home.

"A blessing on the Lady of Vernemeton, if it is she who has sent this wind!" said Cynric, sniffing the mist that was blowing past him, heavy with the scent of the sea.

"She was as good as her word," answered Bendeigid beside him. "Since the third day after they burned my hall this wind has blown. When the scattered bands came back to load their curraghs with their spoils they found the breeze dead against them." He grinned mirthlessly. "We shall pin them between the strand and the sea!"

From near by came a hard-edged order, and the rhythmic tramp of hobnailed sandals came to a halt. Cynric grimaced, glad the wind had not carried the sound to the enemy. As well to go in with clarions shrilling than to let the raiders hear that ominous tread. The Britons were not nearly so orderly, but a great deal quieter.

He still found himself stiffening whenever the crest of a Roman helmet appeared through the mist. He had never expected to be fighting side by side with his enemy. But if, for the sake of a greater good, even Bendeigid could suspend his hatred, he supposed he could do the same.

Then Bendeigid laid a hand on his sleeve and Cynric halted, peering through the fringe of scrubby alders that stretched between them and the shore. He could smell woodsmoke and the rank odor of the privy trench – not very well tended. It was true, one could track vermin from the smell. He eased his shield down from his shoulder and got a better grip on his spear.

Cynric's heart was pounding oddly and his mouth was dry. *You longed for real battle, how can you be afraid?* he asked himself. *Would you have hidden behind Rheis's skirts if you had been there when they attacked the hall?* At the thought, his panic changed to fury.

Then the Roman trumpets blared. Bendeigid gave tongue with a guttural roar and Cynric found his own throat opening. Howling,

the Britons ran forward. Cynric pushed through the trees, spear
ready, and heard the Roman charge beating out an accompaniment
to the British cries.

As the Romans drove down upon the foe the Britons fell upon
their rear. A warrior turned, his form distorted by the mist to that
of a monster. He *was* a monster! Cynric's training took over and he
jabbed upward; felt the shock and heard the cry as the blade went
in. But he had no time to react, for another man was coming at
him. A swordstroke clattered on his shield. Side-vision showed him
the Roman troopers, cutting through the foe with mechanical
efficiency. Cynric jerked the spear free and swung, seeing in each
contorted face his enemy.

Cynric could not tell if half a day or half a lifetime had passed
when he realized there was no one attacking him any more. All
around him lay bodies, and Bendeigid was methodically giving the
mercy stroke to any that still lived. He was covered with blood, but
none of it seemed to be his own. Once he had fallen and thought
himself done for, but a legionary had stood above him, covering
him with that big oblong shield until he could rise.

He realized that you could hate someone and still admire them.
He would never love Romans, but he could see now there might be
something to be learned from them. At this moment, even his own
Roman blood did not seem so evil a thing. He heard a crackle of
flame and saw that Ardanos was directing the burning of the
enemy curraghs. The smoke stank of burnt meat, but the round,
leather-covered boats burned merrily. Cynric turned away, wondering if he were going to be ill.

But one boat had been kept back, and one of the raiders had
been saved alive, though blinded, to man it.

Ardanos lifted his hands to the skies, shouting something in the
old speech that only the Druids used. For a moment the breeze
died, then it backed and began to blow from landward. Ardanos set
his hand upon the rim of the curragh, holding it.

"I have called the winds to speed you," he told the man inside.
"If the gods love you, you will come to Eriu once more. Be you our
messenger, and take them this word," Ardanos said fiercely, "that
if you come again to these shores, the same will be done to every
one of you."

The vision faded, and Eilan sank back, shuddering. She had never
seen serious fighting, and it filled her with horror, yet she found

herself rejoicing fiercely as the raiders died. One of these men had certainly killed her mother and probably her younger sister, and set aflame the house in which she had been born.

She peered into the water, seeking the face of Gaius, but caught no sight of him. Had he fallen in some earlier skirmish with the enemy, believing her dead in the ruins of her home? Well, better that he should think her dead than faithless, she told herself, but she was surprised at how much, even now, the thought that he was the one who might have died brought her grief. The night they sat beside the Beltane fires they had seemed one being. Surely if he were killed, she could not help but know.

But presently the steady flow of her life in the Forest House washed the pain even from the memory of Gaius and what might have been.

With the others, she took her turn at gathering the sacred plants and herbs, learning which of them should be gathered by a particular light of sun or moon.

"This lore is older than the Druids," Miellyn confided to her once when they were paired. Miellyn, although she had come to the Forest House long ago, was not many years older than Eilan and the two, as the two youngest in the house, were often paired off in their work. Miellyn had chosen to become a priestess of the healing arts, and had already had extensive training. "Some of it comes down from the old days, even before our people came into this land."

It had been a wet spring, and along the banks of the brook that wandered through the fields behind the Forest House, the mugwort plants were waist high. The sharp pungent scent of their leaves was almost dizzying as she stripped them from their stalks. The priestesses used them to induce visions, and in an infusion to ease sore muscles.

"Caillean told me something of this," Eilan answered. "There was a time, she says, when there were no Druid priests in Britannia. When our people came they killed the priests of the tribes they conquered, but they did not dare to kill the priestesses of the Great Mother. Our own sacred women learned from them, and added the ancient knowledge to their own."

"It is true," Miellyn said, moving along the riverbank. "Caillean has studied these things more than I, and she is a priestess of the Oracle. They, at least, go back to a time well before the Forest House was built and long before the Order of Druids came to this island of Britain. They say that their first priestesses came here from an island far out in the western ocean that now is sunk beneath the waves. With them came the priest men called the Merlin, who taught the lore of the stars and of the standing stones."

For a moment they contemplated an almost unimaginable antiquity. Then a little breeze fluttered their skirts, and brought them back to the beauty of the green world around them.

"Is that feverfew or chervil?" Eilan pointed at a mass of low-growing bright green foliage with small jagged leaves.

"Chervil. See how tender the stems are? It has just sprung up here. Feverfew lives through the winter, and its stem is woody. But it is true, the leaves look much the same."

"There is so much to remember!" Eilan exclaimed. "If our people did not always live here, how did we learn all this lore?"

"Men are by nature wanderers," said Miellyn, "though you may not think it, rooted among us here. Every people has moved from somewhere, and had to learn the ways of the land from the people who were there before. The last of our own tribes came to this island only about a hundred years before the Romans, and from much the same part of the world."

"You would think the Romans would know more about us, then, if we were neighbors," said Eilan.

"They knew enough about our warriors to be afraid," Miellyn grinned fiercely. "Maybe that is why they spread such scandals about us. Tell me, Eilan, have you ever seen any man burnt on our altars? Or any woman either?"

"No; nor anyone put to death except for criminals," replied Eilan. "How can the Romans say such things about us?"

"Why should they not? They are ignorant men," said Miellyn scornfully. "They set down all their knowledge on bits of leather or waxed wood or tablets of stone and think that is wisdom. What good does it do a piece of stone to have knowledge? Even I, a young priestess, know it is the understanding graven in the heart that makes men wise. Can you learn the ways of the herbs from a book? It is not enough even to be told. You must seek out the plants yourself, handle them, love them, watch them grow. Then you can use them for healing, for their spirits will speak to you."

"Perhaps their women know more," said Eilan. "For I have heard the Romans do not teach the craft of letters to all their womenfolk. I wonder what wisdom the mothers pass on to their daughters that the men do not know?"

Miellyn made a face. "Perhaps they are afraid that if women learned bookcraft too there would not be enough work for scribes and the letter writers of the marketplace."

"Caillean said something like that, soon after I came here," Eilan said and shivered, though the day was warm, remembering the cold winds during the scrying. "But I have not seen much of her since then. I wonder sometimes if I have angered her."

"You must not pay too much attention to what Caillean says, or does not say." Miellyn cautioned. "She has suffered a great deal, and she is . . . immoderate in her opinions sometimes. But it is true the Romans do not think much of what women can do."

"Then they are foolish."

"I know that. You know that," Miellyn said. "But there are some Romans who do not yet know it. Let us hope that they learn it during our lifetime. Our own priests can be foolish too. Someone told me you wished to learn to play the harp. Have you heard Caillean play her lyre?"

Eilan shook her head. "Not often." Suddenly she remembered the occasion where Caillean had taught her to handle fire, and shivered.

Miellyn said, "You really must not mind Caillean's strange ways; she is very solitary. Sometimes for days she speaks to no one, except perhaps to Lhiannon. I know Caillean likes you; I have heard her say so."

Eilan looked at her and then quickly away. It had certainly seemed so that night at Mairi's, after Caillean had driven the raiders away. She realized now how unusual it had been for the older woman to reveal herself that way. Perhaps that was why she had avoided Eilan so much since then.

Miellyn had spotted a place where wild thyme grew beneath a tree and was using her little curved knife to cut the stems. The scent came sweet and sharp to Eilan's nostrils as she bent to gather it.

"Speak to her of her harp," Miellyn added then.

"I thought you said it was not a harp –"

"Indeed, Caillean went to considerable trouble to explain the difference –" Miellyn grinned. "The strings go into a box at the base instead of the side, but the sound is much the same. She knows many songs of Eriu. They are very strange indeed; somehow they all sound like the sea. She knows all of the old songs too, though because of our training we all remember more than most people. If they had been willing to train women as bards before so many of the priests had been killed, perhaps she would have been one." Irresistibly, Miellyn began to giggle. "Or she might have been the High Druid – if it is not blasphemy to say so – after your father."

"Ardanos is my mother's father, not mine. Dieda is his daughter," Eilan told her, gathering up the last of the thyme.

"And your foster brother is one of the Sacred Band?" Miellyn asked. "Truly you come from a priestly family. They will probably try to make you a priestess of the Oracle one day."

"No one has said anything about it to me," Eilan answered her.

"Would you dislike it?" Miellyn laughed at her. "The rest of us have our duties, and I, for one, am happy with my herbs. But the seeresses are the ones the people worship. Would you not like to be the voice of the Goddess?"

"*She* has not said anything to me," the girl answered, a little sharply.

It was no business of Miellyn's what Eilan might secretly long for, or the feelings that had stirred in her when she saw Lhiannon lift her arms in invocation to the moon. The longer she stayed here, the more vividly she remembered her childhood dreams, and every time she carried offerings to the shrine at the spring she stared into the water, hoping to see the Lady once more.

"I will be whatever my elders say. They know more about what the gods want than I."

Miellyn laughed. "Oh, perhaps some of them may; but I am not sure," she said. "Caillean would not say so. She told me once that the knowledge of the Druids is that which was given to all people, both men and women alike in the old days."

"And yet even the High Druid defers to Lhiannon," Eilan said, as she bent to cut a few leaves from a bunch of stitchwort she had found growing on the sunny side of a great rock.

"Or seems to," Miellyn said. "But Lhiannon is different, and of course we all adore her –"

Eilan frowned. "I have heard some of the women say that even my grandfather would not dare to cross her."

"Sometimes I wonder," Miellyn said as she sorted through the leaves Eilan had cut. "Cut them closer to the branch; we cannot use the stems. Do you know, I have heard that in the old days the laws required that any man who cut a tree must plant another in its place so the woods would never be less. That has not been done since the Romans came here; they cut trees and plant nothing, so one day there will be no trees in all Britain –"

"There seem to be as many as ever," said Eilan.

"Some seed and grow of themselves." Miellyn turned and gathered up the plants they had cut.

"What about the herbs?" asked Eilan.

"We have not cut enough to make any difference; enough shoots will grow up in a day or two to replace what we have taken. That is enough. I think it may rain; we should hurry back. The priestess who taught me herb lore used to say that the wilderness is the garden of the Goddess, and men cannot gather from it without replacing what they use!"

"I had not heard before, stated in just that way, but, but I think it is beautiful," Eilan said. "I suppose, if you think in centuries, that to cut down a tree is as foolish as slaughtering a breeding doe –"

"And yet some men believe – or seem to believe – that they have the right to do what they will to anything weaker than they are," Miellyn said. "I do not understand how the Romans can do what they do."

"The better ones among them would be as angry as you and I at some of the outrages," Eilan ventured. She was thinking of Gaius. He had seemed almost as angry as Cynric when he heard the story of the Romans on Mona. She could not imagine him slaughtering the helpless; and yet he must know perfectly well how short and dreadful a life could be expected by the Roman levies in the mines, ill-fed, poorly clothed, and breathing the poisoned dust of the ore they mined. If this punishment were limited to criminals and murderers it would be bad enough, but the byre-woman's husband?

Yet Gaius believed that the Romans were making civilized people of barbarians. Perhaps he had never really thought about the mines, because being taken to them had never happened to anyone he knew. Even she had not thought about it much until it happened to one of their own. But if she did not know what was going on, surely her father and grandfather did, and they had done nothing to stop it either.

The wind gusted round to the west and suddenly the clouds let loose their burden of rain. Miellyn squealed and pulled her shawl up over her head. "We'll be drowned if we stay here!" she exclaimed. "Pick up your basket and come! If we run, we'll be indoors before we're wet through."

But the girls were soaked by the time they came into the central hall of the priestesses. Eilan felt Miellyn had welcomed the opportunity to run.

"Get yourselves dry now, lasses, or you'll catch a rheum and I'll be using up all my medicines nursing you!" Latis, who was so old now she could no longer go into the forest to gather the herbs, cackled with laughter and shooed them towards the door. "But mind you come back then to lay out the herbs you've brought me, or they'll mildew and both the plants and your labor will be wasted!"

Skin still glowing from brisk rubbing, Miellyn and Eilan returned to the still-room. Built on behind the kitchen where heat from the ovens kept the air warm and dry, the rafters were festooned with bunches of hanging herbs. Woven trays upon which roots or leaves were spread to dry hung beneath them, turning lazily. Shelves with earthenware crocks stood along one wall, and bags and baskets of prepared herbs were stored along another, neatly labeled with the sigils of the herbalists' craft. The air was pungent.

"You're Eilan, are you not?" Latis peered at her. She looked rather like a dried root herself, thought Eilan, seamed and wrinkled with age. "Goddess help us, they get younger every year!"

"Who does, Mother?" asked Miellyn, hiding her grin.

"The girls they send to serve the Priestess of the Oracle."

"I told her she would be sent for training to the Lady soon," Miellyn said. "Well, Eilan, do you believe me now?"

"Oh, I believed you," Eilan said, "but I thought surely it would take someone older and with more skills than me."

"Caillean would say that they do not want anyone too learned near Lhiannon for fear she would ask too many questions. If the Priestess were forced to think about what she was doing, the Oracles she gives might not always serve the Druids' policies so conveniently."

"Miellyn, hush," Latis exclaimed. "You know you must not say such things – not even in a whisper!"

"I will speak the truth and if the priests object, I will ask them by what right they ask me to lie." But Miellyn lowered her voice. "Eilan, be careful; you are holding that basket aslant. We took enough trouble to gather these leaves, I do not want them dirtied by a fall to the floor."

Eilan readjusted the angle of the basket she was holding.

"There are some truths which should never be spoken aloud, not even in a whisper," Latis went on soberly.

"Yes," Miellyn said, "so I am told; and usually they are the truths that should be proclaimed from the rooftops."

"In the sight of the gods this may very well be true," replied the other. "But you know very well we are not in the presence of the gods, but of men."

"Well, if the truth cannot be spoken in a house built by the Druids," Miellyn replied stoutly, "where in the name of the gods can it be?"

"The gods alone know!" said Latis. "I have survived so long by sticking to my herbs, and you would do well to do the same. They, at least, speak true."

"Eilan doesn't have that choice," said Miellyn. "She'll be tied to the High Priestess for the next six moons."

"Remain true to yourself, child." Old Latis touched her chin so that Eilan could not look away. "If you know your own heart, you will always have one friend who does not lie."

The priestess had spoken the truth. With the coming of the next moon, Eilan was brought to Lhiannon and taught the ceremonious etiquette for attending upon the High Priestess in public, which, in effect, meant every time that Lhiannon went out of her own dwelling in the Forest House. She learned the rituals of robing Lhiannon for the ceremonies, which was more complicated than it looked; for from the beginning of the ritual, not even with a fingertip's weight could any human being touch the Priestess. She shared with Lhiannon the long ritual seclusion with which the Priestess prepared for the rites, and helped her through the physical collapse that followed.

That was when she learned the price Lhiannon paid for the great reverence in which she was held. For the delivery of the word of the gods there was a heavy reckoning. Vague and forgetful as Lhiannon, in her own person, might sometimes be, when she assumed the ornaments of the Oracle another power came upon her. She had been chosen, Eilan realized, not so much for force of will or wisdom, but because when it was needful, she was able to let her own personality go.

It was then, when the human identity had been put off with her ordinary clothes, that Lhiannon opened herself so that the Goddess might speak through her. And in those moments, she was a great priestess indeed – almost, Eilan thought, more than human. The price of becoming the vehicle for so great a power was both physical and mental, and Eilan's respect for the older priestess grew as she saw Lhiannon pay it without grudging the cost, or at least without complaint.

When Eilan left the Forest House and the woods around for the first time she was accompanying Lhiannon. It was then that she realized how the preceding weeks had changed her. Even the House of Maidens seemed remote and strange. When the newest novices scurried out of her way she scarcely noticed, and only afterwards realized that they had seen in her the same unearthly serenity she associated with Lhiannon.

It was, she supposed, a fairly ordinary Midsummer Festival. She had seen the Games and the market and the lighting of the big sun-fire many times before, but after her months of seclusion in the Forest House, the yammering of so many people was painful, and she shrank from the strong scents of humans and horses. Even the bright cloths the merchants had put up to shade their wares assaulted her senses.

Midsummer was a time when men put forth their strength in competitions, to entertain the gods and the people, and to strengthen the crops as they grew. But as Eilan watched the footraces and the wrestling it was the sweating bodies of the competitors that seemed the most gross and distorted of all. She could not imagine why she had ever wanted to lie with a man.

The winner of the Games was garlanded with summer flowers and escorted to preside over the ceremonies. Remembering what she had learned of the Mysteries, Eilan watched with a new appreciation. In time of need, or in some tribes every seven years, the new Year-King would have watched his predecessor burn, and even now some of the old sacredness attached to him. The Empire had killed or Romanized the heirs of the British princes, but so long as men were willing to offer their lives for the people, they could not eradicate the Sacred Kings, who each year stood surety for those who no longer understood their role.

If there were some great disaster, and a sacrifice were needed during the coming year, despite the Romans' prohibitions it was on this young man that the blow would fall. And, in recognition of his risk, he alone of all men was allowed to lie with whichever woman took his fancy – even a maiden from the Forest House if it was there that his eye should fall.

Eilan kept close to Lhiannon, watching as the warriors snatched brands from the great bonfire and vied to throw them high to make the crops grow. The people had grown rowdy with drink and the release of the festival. But no one would trouble her while she was with the High Priestess. Even the Year-King had never been known to push his rights that far.

She sat with Caillean and Dieda, glad of the protection of Lhiannon's presence and the hulking strength of her bodyguard Huw behind them, and hoped that the other priestesses who had come with them to the festival had fared as well.

It was not until several weeks had passed that she learned why her friend Miellyn had come away from the festivities so pale and thoughtful, and why she was so often ill. It was Eilidh who told her, one day when Miellyn was nowhere to be found, but by then everyone in the Forest House was buzzing with the news.

"She is pregnant, Eilan," Eilidh murmured and shook her head as if she still found it amazing. "By the winner of the games. Lhiannon was troubled and very cross when she learned of it, and has sent Miellyn to the seclusion of the hut by the white pool to meditate alone for a time."

"That is not fair!" exclaimed Eilan. "If he chose her, how could she deny him? It would be an impiety." Had the priests forgotten their own theology?

"The older priestesses are saying she should have kept herself out of his way. There is no shortage of women in this part of Britain, after all. I would have found a way to evade him if he had started looking at me!"

Eilan had to admit that she too would have sought some way to avoid being chosen. But when Miellyn reappeared among them, her loose robes no longer able to hide her rounding body, she had the sense not to say so.

And so the summer rolled on, and time came round to the second anniversary of her arrival at the Forest House.

By the time Eilan had assisted the High Priestess at half a dozen festivals, she had lost all enthusiasm for becoming the Oracle herself, but she knew that her desires would make no difference if she should be chosen by the Druids. She could not help knowing that the priests came to Lhiannon before each ritual, to help, they said, to prepare her. But once, when a half-closed door swung open, she saw the older woman slumped in trance as Ardanos droned into her ear.

She watched with extra interest that night when the Goddess was called down upon Her Priestess, wincing as Lhiannon twitched and muttered, garbling some answers while others came clear. It was like watching a horse fighting a tight rein, as if something within the Priestess struggled against the power that flowed through her.

They have bound her, she realized in horror as she sat by Lhiannon's beside that night when all was done. *They set spells upon her so that she could say only those words that accorded with their will!*

Perhaps that was why, despite the ritual, there were times when the Goddess did not come, and Lhiannon's answers arose from her own wisdom, or perhaps the words that the priests had taught her. It seemed to Eilan that those times were the most exhausting of all. And even when the trance was a true one, the Oracle could answer only those questions that were put to her; as time passed, Eilan began to suspect that the Druids controlled who was allowed to question her as well. A few genuine Oracles were indeed delivered; but only, Eilan discovered, in matters of small moment. And these, if they came from the Goddess, generally made little difference either to those who asked or those who heard.

Eilan's first reaction had been to protest, but to whom? Caillean was away, carrying a message from Lhiannon to the new queen of one of the tribes, and Miellyn too concerned about the coming child for Eilan to trouble her. By the time there was anyone she could have told, it had come to her that Caillean and Dieda, at least, must know already. It would explain some of their arguments, and the somewhat exasperated tenderness with which Caillean cared for Lhiannon.

And the High Priestess, above all, must understand what was being done to her. Lhiannon had chosen to come to the Forest House, and to remain in the power of the priesthood. If they were making her their mouthpiece, surely it was with her own consent and will.

It was in this state that matters stood when Eilan accompanied Lhiannon to the Beltane festival almost three years after she had been given to the temple.

eleven

G aius had not been in the Ordovici lands for almost two years
when the third Beltane since he lost Eilan arrived. His father
had not spoken again of the proposed marriage with the
daughter of Licinius, but had seconded him to the Governor's staff.
He had spent the past two seasons marching across Alba with
Agricola, engaged in what they fondly hoped was a pacification of
the lowland tribes. Raiders like those who had killed Bendeigid's
family were bad enough but it was the still free tribes of the North
who threatened the Empire's hold on Britannia. For a serving
officer of the Roman army, grief was an indulgence. Gaius did his
duty, and if the sight of some girl's bright hair and grave eyes set
his old wounds to aching he took care not to weep where anyone
could see.

He succeeded so well that when the campaign in Caledonia came
to a temporary halt he was rewarded by being sent to escort a party
of wounded men back to the Legion's permanent quarters in Deva
while the remainder of the Twentieth labored on a new fortress in
the Caledonian highlands. So it was that he found himself in the
South again, trotting down the road to the Hill of the Maidens
with a centurion at his side and a detachment of regulars tramping
along behind.

"We need a man we can trust to keep an eye on the festival, and
you're the only one available just now who can speak the language
well enough to pass. You'll have to face it sometime, lad," his
father had told him when he protested. "Best get it over with." But
not until Gaius saw the bare crown of the hillfort rising from the
sea of forest and heard the lowing of the assembled cattle did he
realize just how hard it would be. He reined in, staring, and the
centurion barked an order to halt the men.

"Looks peaceful enough," said the centurion. "Wherever you go, market fairs are pretty much the same. They can get ugly, though, when you mix religion in." The soldier laughed. Gaius had already found that the man was a garrulous soul who required a minimum of response from his audience. "I spent my first three years with the Legions in Egypt. A god for every day of the week, they had, and each one with his own festival. Had some pretty messy riots sometimes when two processions collided in the center of town."

"Oh?" Gaius asked politely, though he did not really care that much whether the man had served in Egypt or at the end of the world. This was the gate through which they had entered the festival grounds three years ago. He remembered how little Senara had jigged down the road ahead of them, laughing.

As before, he was wearing native clothing, for his assignment was to watch out for sedition at the festival, but that happy family with whom he had last come this way was no more. "What was Egypt like?" he said quickly, trying to wall the memory away.

"Oh, like everywhere else," the centurion said and yawned. "Great temples and dreadfully rich kings, and equally great poverty in the marketplace. It was warm though," he added and shivered. "I wouldn't mind a little of their sun right now; it's too cold and rainy here in Britannia."

Gaius looked up at the overcast sky. The man was right; he had not noticed the weather before. That was one thing that was different anyway. He did not think he could have borne to see this place again on a day of bright sun.

"You don't seem to mind it much, though," the centurion added enviously. "You were born here, weren't you? I'm from Etruria myself. Getting to be a rarity, these days, to find another native-born Latin in the Legions. I've served all over the Empire – Egypt, Hispania, Parthia. My cohort got cut to pieces in Parthia, and when they promoted me to centurion – probably because I was one of the few left alive – they sent me out here. If Apollo really discovered this country, I don't admire his taste."

"We'll dismount here," Gaius nerved himself up to it suddenly. "And leave a man with the horses. No room for them inside."

They heard lowing behind them as another contingent of cattle was driven in. The centurion bawled a command to the soldiers to move aside, and he and Gaius stepped back.

"No sense in getting under their hoofs," he added lazily. "I don't know about you, but I've better uses for my feet than having 'em stepped on by these cows. You ready to go in now?"

Gaius sighed. He would never be ready, but he was a Roman, and he could no longer run from his memories. He shivered and drew a fold of his mantle over his head.

"What's going on here anyway?" asked the centurion as they passed through the gateway in the wake of the cattle. "Is it some kind of festival for the farmers? They did that in Egypt – had a big white bull they called a god. Paraded him through the streets with garlands around his neck, and fanned incense over the cattle till you could hardly breathe. Trying to make them healthy, they said."

"Here, they throw herbs on the flames and drive the cows between the fires to bless them." Gaius answered him.

"Funny thing, how people keep fighting about religion, when really it's all the same. Seems to me it's the priests who make all the problems; most folks just want good harvests and healthy babies, just trying to get along. If it's not the cattle stampeding, it's the priests haranguing the crowds. Do the Druids run this festival?"

"Not exactly," said Gaius. "There's a priestess, something like a Vestal, who calls down blessings from their gods." For a moment he closed his eyes, once more seeing that veiled figure lifting her arms to the moon.

"Is she going to do the sacrifices?" They moved slowly towards the central square, for the herd of cattle was still ahead of them, lowing anxiously and pressing together at the strange sights and smells.

Gaius shook his head. "These days, anyway, the Druids or whoever runs their worship don't sacrifice anything except fruit and flowers."

"I heard they did lots of sacrifices – even human," said the centurion.

"Gates of Tartarus, no." Gaius remembered how indignant Eilan had been when he asked the same question. "Really, this festival's pretty tame. I was here once, and –"

"Oh, by Caligula's balls! Somebody's scared the cows," the centurion exclaimed, peering ahead of them. "That was what I was afraid of."

A big man in a checked robe had upset a lantern, and the cows were shifting about, lowing uneasily.

Beyond him an older man was haranguing the crowd. More than a hundred people had gathered to hear. Gaius edged forward to listen. This was why he was here, in case someone used the peaceful gathering to stir up rebellion. People in the crowd were yelling in agreement, ignoring the growing unease in the herd.

A lad came running with a bucket of water, splashing one of the shouters as he went by. The man turned, yelling, and the nearest cow threw up its head with a bellow, pricking its neighbor with a twisted horn.

"Oh, Hades, that's done it; those cows are going to stampede," Gaius shouted, even as one of the lead cows burst into a clumsy gallop, knocking into her drover and sending him head over heels into the crowd.

The speaker was still haranguing the crowd, but his audience were shouting at each other now. Two or three men were crowded off their feet, and a woman screamed, and then the whole front line of cattle burst into a lumbering run. A cow bellowed, swerving, and Gaius saw red on its horn. Somebody screamed. Men, women, and a few children surged backward, yelling.

Now everyone was pushing, trying to get out of the way. Within moments the central square was a confusion of motion and sound. Mothers reached for their crying children; one of the legionaries, not accustomed to cattle, was pushed off his feet and went down howling. Gaius struggled to keep his feet and was swept away from his men.

Someone grabbed at his arm. "Here, you look strong, you must help me; the Lady will fall." A tall, dark-haired woman in a blue robe gripped Gaius's arm and pulled him towards the edge of the square where an old woman swathed in a blue cloak had collapsed against two women in linen dresses with wreaths of green leaves over their unbleached linen veils.

Gaius reached out cautiously and the women let their burden sag into his arms. He blinked, recognizing the Priestess who had invoked the Goddess two years before. Carefully he lifted her, amazed at the fragility of the form within the heavy robes. Most of the people had fled, but cattle were still bucketing about angrily, or drifting in twos or threes with lowered horns and switching tails, lowing defiance at anyone who tried to herd them.

Near by lay the still form of the giant who accompanied the Priestess everywhere. "What's the matter with him?"

"Huw? Oh, he's all right," the older priestess said carelessly. "One of the cows gored somebody; he's afraid of the sight of blood."

Some bodyguard, Gaius could not help thinking. "We've got to get her out of the way of the cows," he said aloud. "Where shall I carry her?"

"This way." The taller of the two attending priestesses quickly led the way through the tumble of wrecked booths. Gaius settled his burden so that her head rested against his shoulder, relieved to hear the rasp of her breathing. He did not want to think what would happen to him if the High Priestess of Vernemeton died in his arms.

His nostrils flared at a sudden scent and he realized that the priestess had led them to the booth of a herb seller. The herbalist, plump and worried, was lifting the hanging rug aside so that Gaius could carry the High Priestess in. He knelt and laid her on the piled sleeping furs.

The place was dim and dusty, pungent with the fresh summery smell of the herbs suspended from the beams or shelved in linen bags. Gaius straightened, and his cloak fell back. From behind him came a sudden cry of surprise. Gaius felt his heart begin to thud heavily in his breast. Slowly, for suddenly he needed more courage than it had taken to face a charge of Caledonian tribesmen, he turned.

The smaller of the attending priestesses had thrown back her veil. From its shadowy folds he saw Eilan staring back at him. He felt the blood leaving his head; the world darkened, then flared into brightness as he got his breath again. *You're dead . . .* he thought. *You died in the fire!* But even when all other vision failed, shining down at him he saw Eilan's eyes. He felt a breath of air on his face and gradually his senses came back to him.

"Is it really you?" he croaked then. "I thought you had burned . . . I saw what was left of your house after the raiders came."

She stepped backward, motioning him towards the end of the booth, while the other priestesses bent over Lhiannon, and Gaius, his head still reeling, got up and followed her.

"I was away helping my older sister with her new child," she said quietly so they would not be overheard. "But my mother and little Senara were there." Her voice broke. Then she stopped and sent a quick guilty glance at the other priestesses.

In the dim light, wrapped in pale robes, she looked like a spirit. He reached out to her. He could hardly believe she was there, alive, unharmed. For a moment his fingers brushed cool linen, then she twitched away.

"We cannot talk here," she said breathlessly, "even though you are not in uniform."

"Eilan," he said quickly, "when can I see you?"

"That is not possible," she said. "I am a priestess of the Forest House, and not allowed —"

"You are not allowed to speak to a man?" *A Vestal*, he thought. *The girl I love is as forbidden to me as if she were a Vestal.*

"It is not so bad as that —" she said with a faint smile. "But you are a Roman, and you know what my father would say."

"Indeed I do," he said after a moment, and then thought of what *his* father would say. Had the Prefect let Gaius grieve, *knowing* there was no need? Along with his wonder at her presence came a surge of anger.

Looking into Eilan's hazel eyes, he realized suddenly that in all the time since he had left the house of Bendeigid, he had not felt so alive.

She shifted uneasily. "Dieda is looking at us; she may well recognize you. And Caillean, the older priestess —"

"I remember Dieda," he said harshly. "And I must get back to my centurion. Gods! I am glad to see you alive," he said, suddenly and intensely, but he did not move. The other priestesses were both looking at them now, and she raised her hand in a gesture of blessing.

"I thank you," she said in a voice that shook only a little. "Lhiannon is too heavy for any of us to lift. If you see Huw and he seems recovered, will you send him to us here?"

"To keep him safe from the cows," he said, and was rewarded by the sudden flicker of her smile.

"Go now."

"I must," he agreed. At that moment Lhiannon stirred; one of the women bent over and spoke soothingly to her, and hearing those low tones, it finally reached him that Eilan was a priestess of the Druids now.

He stumbled towards the entrance, and it was only when he was outside, blinking in the light, that he realized that he had not said goodbye or wished her well. Was she happy in the Forest House? Had she chosen that life, or had they forced her into it? But the door flap had fallen closed behind him. As he strode away, he heard Dieda's voice behind him.

"Eilan, what were you saying to that man? He walks like a Roman!"

"Oh, I don't think so," he heard Eilan say slowly. "Wouldn't he have been in uniform? The rest of them all were."

He slowed, amazed at her guile. It was at least partly her innocence that had at first attracted him.

Now where the devil had his centurion got to? He forced himself into motion again. Was the man likely to tell Macellius about this? And, more important, how would Gaius manage to see Eilan again? Now that he had found her once more, he could not simply let her go.

Behind him in the tent, Eilan clasped her hands over her pounding heart. It seemed almost impossible that the other priestesses could not hear it.

Lhiannon stirred, and murmured, "What happened? Was anyone hurt?"

"Some fool frightened the cattle and they stampeded," Caillean answered.

"How . . . how did I get here?"

"A passer-by carried you. Huw fainted – the great halfwit," Caillean said crisply. "No, your rescuer is gone; Eilan blessed him in your name."

Eilan, hearing, thought it lucky Gaius had not been wearing Roman uniform and wondered why. She wondered what he would look like in the uniform of the Legions. Handsome, she imagined, but then, he was nice-looking anyhow. She shook her head, knowing that she should not be thinking of him that way, certainly not here. That part of her life was over.

"First make certain that Huw is all right, then bring him in here." Lhiannon ordered. "If the cattle have stampeded, they probably cannot be rounded up at once, and we will be here for the rest of the day."

Eilan went out into the sunlight. She found Huw sitting on the ground, barely conscious, shaking his head dizzily.

"Is the Holy Lady safe?"

"No thanks to you, if she is," Eilan said crossly. "She fainted, and a passer-by carried her into the herb seller's booth."

"Where's all the cattle?"

Eilan looked around her and realized that Lhiannon had been wrong. The square was busy with folk setting up fallen booths and chattering, but there was not a cow to be seen.

"Only the gods know that, and maybe their drovers; they stampeded." The man who had been gored, she noticed, had been carried away by his friends. "That's why they gored that man; they were frightened," she said crisply.

"It was the Romans frightened them," Huw mumbled, getting

painfully to his feet again. "Marching in all clanking and glittering that way. A murrain on them; why did they come here anyway? Did they think the blessing of the cattle was some kind of unlawful gathering?"

"There'll be no blessing of the cattle this day," he went on, shaking his head, "I'd best carry the Lady home. With Romans around there's more likely than not to be some kind of trouble," he added in a grumbling undertone.

Not for the first time, Eilan wondered why Lhiannon tolerated this great oaf. He was little use to her as a bodyguard; Eilan could not see that he was any use at all. If she should be ever in the position of the Oracle priestess – little as she desired it – the first thing she would do would be to rid herself of the services of this great bobby.

About a month after Beltane, Eilan was summoned to Lhiannon, and found her with a man who reminded her oddly of Cynric, and a little girl of eight or ten years with light reddish hair sun-touched with gold.

Eilan smiled at the child, who returned her gaze bashfully. Lhiannon said, "Hadron is one of the Raven Brotherhood. Tell her your story yourself, Hadron."

"It is soon told," the man said. "I have a foster brother who has joined the Legions as an auxiliary, and he interceded for me or I would have been taken and sent to the lead mines. After his intercession, the penalty was removed and my life spared, and so I was given only ten years of exile from any Roman possession. I must now flee to the North, and I cannot take a girl child with me where I go."

"So what is the problem?" Eilan knew Lhiannon had the authority simply to take the girl into the Forest House without consulting anyone. The fact that she had not already done so meant that there was some difficulty.

"She seems to me to be too young for a place among us," Lhiannon said, frowning. "I do not know what to say to him."

"If that is all," Eilan replied, "I should be happy to care for her until she can be sent to fosterage elsewhere. Or is there a female relative to whom she might be consigned?"

"There is not," said the man. "For my wife was Roman born, and I know very little of her near kinfolk."

"So your child is partly Roman? Cannot you send her to her kin among them?" Lhiannon asked.

The man answered sullenly, "My wife quarreled with her kindred to marry me; she begged me with her dying breath to make certain her daughter never fell into their hands. I thought if I might leave her in the care of the priestesses . . ."

Lhiannon said sternly, "We are not a refuge for orphans. Although for one of the Brotherhood of the Ravens we might possibly make an exception."

Eilan looked at the child and thought of her own little sister, dead at the hands of raiders three years ago now. If Senara were alive, who was looking after her? She had looked forward to tending Miellyn's baby as a kind of substitute for her lost sister, but the older woman had miscarried the Year-King's child.

"I would willingly care for her, Lhiannon."

"That is why I called you. You are not yet committed to any very exacting duties here among us," Lhiannon replied. "Although this goes beyond the usual requirements. Still, if you will have it so, I will put this little refugee in your charge." She paused and asked Hadron, "What is her name?"

"My wife called her Valeria, My Lady."

Lhiannon scowled. "That is a Roman name; she cannot be called by it here."

"My wife had given up all her kin to marry me," said Hadron. "The least I could do was allow her to give her family name to her child."

"Even so, she must have a new name if she is to live here among us," Lhiannon said firmly. "Eilan, will you give her one?"

Eilan looked at the child, who was gazing at her with frightened eyes. She had lost all else; now she was to lose her father and even her name. Eilan said gently, "By your leave, I will call her Senara."

"That will do very well," said Lhiannon. "Now go; find her a place to sleep and suitable clothing. When she is of a proper age she may take vows among us as a priestess, if she wishes."

When Hadron had gone, Eilan looked once more at the little girl, who stood gazing raptly at the Lady.

"I am sorry to lay this upon you, Eilan. I have never had to deal with a child this age. What are we to do with her?" said Lhiannon.

"Perhaps she can run errands." Eilan put her arm around the little girl and smiled.

Lhiannon nodded. "Since she is not under vows, perhaps she could carry messages beyond our walls."

"She is a little young for that, but if you are truly uncertain about having her stay here, perhaps we should ask among the Romans," Eilan suggested. "Despite what Hadron said, her mother's people might want her. We should at least make inquiries."

"That is a good thought," Lhiannon agreed a little vaguely, her attention already flitting away. "Look after it, Eilan, if you will."

The little hand slipped trustingly into her own, and something in Eilan's heart that had been sore since she lost her sister at last began to ease. As they walked across the courtyard, she asked the child, "You are not unhappy to be called Senara? It was my sister's name."

"Not at all," the little girl answered. "Where is your sister? Is she dead?"

"Dead or carried off beyond the seas," Eilan replied. "Alas that I do not know." And then she wondered why she had not asked Caillean for some word of her sister's fate, and her mother's when the older woman was scrying. Was it perhaps that she preferred to think of Senara peacefully dead than living in slavery?

She looked at the child, seeking some sign of her Roman parentage, and thought of Gaius. As the Prefect's son, Gaius could find out if there was anything to be known. Before Valeria became Senara forever, she owed it to the child at least to try.

As Eilan showed her charge where she was to sleep and found a linen novice's gown that could be cut down for her to wear, she found herself thinking about Gaius as much as about the girl.

Where was he now? Was he thinking of her as eagerly as she was of him? Had he put some spell on her, that she could not only think of nothing else, but did not particularly want to? She sighed, remembering the strength of his voice, his handsome face and form; the slight accent with which he spoke her name, his lingering kiss at the Beltane fires.

I did not then realize fully what he wanted of me, she thought. *I was too young to know – or care. But now I am older, and I am beginning to understand. What have I thrown away?* The thought came to her then: *For the rest of my life am I to dwell unloved – until I am as old and loveless as Lhiannon?*

Who could she ask? Who could she tell? Dieda would understand, but separated from her own beloved, she would hardly sympathize. Caillean, mishandled and unloved so young, would be angry. And if Caillean would not understand, how could she expect it of anyone else here?

There was no one to whom she could describe the hungry need in her heart just to look on him once more, even if after that she should never set eyes on him again.

The next morning, as she was cutting bread and cheese for Senara, she asked, "Do you remember anything about your kin in the Roman town?"

"They are not in the town, Eilan. I think my mother's brother was some kind of Roman official; he wrote the letters for the Prefect of the camp, and other such things."

"Indeed?" Eilan stared at her. Surely the gods were smiling, for this man must be the secretary to Gaius's own father.

She thought for a moment of taking the child into her confidence, but after a moment's reflection decided against it. If a priestess of the Forest House should be discovered in the company of a Roman, no matter how innocent her motives, it would mean trouble for anyone involved. And would it be all that innocent?

twelve

━━━〜〜〜━━━

that very day, Valerius, who was secretary to Gaius's father, had arrived out of breath and looking shaken. "I have just heard that my sister is dead," he told Gaius.

"Tell me about it," suggested Gaius as they walked across the parade ground towards his father's offices.

"It's a long story," Valerius replied. "I lost contact with my sister when she married; I haven't seen her a dozen times in as many years."

"Did she move far away?"

Valerius gave a short laugh. "Only so far as Deva, but she married a man of the tribes, and my father disowned her."

Gaius nodded. It was bad enough for a Roman to marry a native woman of a princely house. He knew only too well how Roman society would view a daughter who ran off with a native lover.

"An old woman who used to be my sister's nurse and mine sent me the news of her death," Valerius went on, "and I found out by asking some questions about the trouble her husband's in. I've seen him only a time or two, but he had a foster brother who's with the auxiliaries who told me that Hadron is one of the Ravens and has been proscribed. The thing is, she left a small daughter, and I don't know what's become of the child. Didn't you know a couple of the Ravens?"

"I knew some of them, yes," said Gaius, thinking of Cynric. Considering the conditions of Cynric's birth, he did not wonder that he had joined a secret society dedicated to revenge. In similar circumstances, he thought, he might have felt much the same.

"Somehow or other I must find my sister's child. Hadron's foster brother is one of the auxiliaries, as I said, and he has no wife to whom he could consign a female child, which leaves me the girl's nearest relative. Can you think of me as the guardian of a little girl?

I have not seen the child since she was in swaddling clothes; I suppose she must be eight or thereabouts."

"First you have to find her . . ." said Gaius slowly. Cynric might know where Hadron had gone with his child. And in the process Cynric, who knew what it was to be separated from his beloved, might be able to help him see Eilan.

"Can you really help me?" Valerius slowed. They were almost at the Prefect's offices now, and the secretary was well aware of Macellius's disapproval of any contact between his son and his mother's people.

"Perhaps . . ." Gaius said cautiously. "I might know someone who could inquire for you."

He had heard that Cynric had been summoned south to ride with the legionaries who had been despatched to punish the raiders who had burned the house of Bendeigid. It had amazed him at the time, but revenge made strange bedfellows. The word was that Cynric was now working with the auxiliaries as a guide and interpreter. Gaius wondered if he had changed his mind or if he still belonged to the Ravens.

If he tried to contact Cynric through army channels, his father would hear, but he was bound to see the young Briton sooner or later, hanging around the taverns that served the fortress.

"May Bona Dea bless you!" Valerius reached out to clasp Gaius's hand. Then the door opened, and both men stiffened to military attention.

Only a few days later Gaius, making his way through Deva's crowded marketplace, saw Cynric standing head and shoulders above the crowd. His curls had darkened somewhat, and his face now bore the beginnings of a beard. Gaius shouted, saw Cynric frown, decide this young officer was no one he knew, and prepare to move on.

Gaius swore and thrust through the crowd to face him. "Wait, man – don't you know me?" He stopped, tensing as the blue gaze descended and darkened. Surely the lad wouldn't hold his own deception against him now, when he too was serving Rome! "I think I still owe you a drink for hauling me out of that boar pit," he said companionably. "There's a wine shop here; let's try its wares."

Gaius drew a breath of relief as Cynric's frown changed to a rueful grin. "I remember you now," he said, adding, "but I don't suppose your name is Gawen. What do I call you, Tribune?"

"As a matter of fact," Gaius said, "my mother named me Gawen and called me so until the day she died. I told you the truth as far as I dared. But in the Roman town I bear my father's name: Gaius Macellius Severus. My mother was a woman of the Silures; I bear the cognomen Siluricus after her."

"If I had known this at the time I would have killed you," admitted Cynric. "But a lot has happened since then. I'll drink with you, Roman, or whatever you may be."

In the dusty darkness of the wine shop, Gaius said, "I was sorry when I heard of the burning of your house; I could hardly have been more distressed if my own kin had been killed by those Hibernian bastards. I am glad that your father was not hurt, and more sorry than I can say that your mother died."

"She was my foster mother," Cynric remarked, "but for her sake I thank you. We have a saying in the North that blood binds for three generations, but fosterage for seven. And indeed my foster father's wife was as good to me as if I had been born to her."

"She was a gracious lady indeed," Gaius agreed. "And for your sake I grieve for her." If he had married Eilan he would have welcomed this man as a brother. And yet, by accident of birth, he and Cynric had been on opposite sides of this struggle until now. At least others than Romans commit outrages, he thought. "I saw the ashes of your home, but my father sent me north immediately thereafter. Perhaps I struck a blow or two on her behalf against those Caledonians. I was glad to hear that the Hibernian raiders were punished."

"At least I, too, got to strike a blow for them. That was the first time in my life I was not ashamed of the Roman blood in my veins." Cynric went on. "I think that Beltane when you guested with us was the last time we were all happy together. All who survived are scattered now."

"I was at the Hill of the Maidens this last Beltane," Gaius said carefully. "I saw Dieda, and Eilan your foster sister, there. I was glad to know she had survived."

"Aye," Cynric said shortly. "She is in the Forest House, a priestess of the Great Goddess. As for Dieda, she is Eilan's kin, but none to me. Nor likely to be, if she stays there!"

"I have a friend in the Legions –" Gaius said then.

Cynric laughed. "Well, I am not surprised at that –"

Gaius shook his head. "His sister married a Briton, and was cast off by her kin. They had a daughter, but the sister's dead now, and they say her husband is on the run. My friend wants to find the little girl."

"On the run . . ." Cynric said thoughtfully. "Why are you asking me?"

"Because they say he was one of those who fly at midnight –"

"Many birds fly at midnight." Cynric gazed into his wine. "What was the man's name?"

"Hadron," said Gaius. "His wife was called Valeria."

"I know little of birds," said Cynric, "but I can ask around."

"Could they have taken the child to the Forest House? Would your kinswomen know?"

"I could ask," answered Cynric.

I would rather ask her myself, thought Gaius, but he did not know how to say so. And how did he know that Eilan even wanted to see him again? If she was happy in the Forest House, would he be only breaking her peace to try and see her there? He had done his duty to Valerius. Should he make some excuse and disappear again?

He realized that he had been silent too long when Cynric refilled his cup from the jug of wine and shoved it back at him.

"There's more to this than a lost child," said the Briton. "What did you really want to say?"

"I must see Eilan again," Gaius burst out suddenly. "I swear I mean her no harm. I only want to know she is happy there."

For a moment Cynric stared at him, then threw back his head with a roar of laughter that turned heads all over the room. "You're in love!" he laughed again. "I should have recognized the symptoms. Isn't my own girl locked away behind those very walls?"

"But you're a kinsman," said Gaius seriously. "They'll let you talk to her. Can you arrange something for me?"

"Why not?" Cynric grinned. "I've never seen any reason to keep the priestesses all penned up. That's like something you Romans would do. Dieda won't see or speak to me since she went in there, but my foster sister is not a prisoner. I will see what I can arrange for you." He drained his wine cup. "Be at the edge of the path leading to the Forest House three days from now, an hour after noon."

As Eilan waited in the woods near the Sacred Grove in the unusual brightness of the early summer sunlight she was surprised to find that she was trembling. At first, when Cynric had spoken to her of a meeting with Gaius, it had seemed like the answer to an unusually fervent prayer. But she soon realized that the most dangerous thing in the world is an answered prayer. Her chances of keeping the meeting a secret were slim indeed. And no one would believe her if they were discovered.

In the end she had gone to Caillean for advice.

"There is nothing that you can do, since you have bidden him here, but to meet him as has been arranged," Caillean had replied. "But I am going to be within earshot every moment; so that if I am later asked I can swear that the two of you have exchanged no word that could not be spoken in the presence of the parents of either of you. Do you accept that?"

Eilan had bowed her head, then turned to go. In truth, she was even a little relieved. If she must speak to him in the presence of the priestess; there would then be no question of his asking of her anything . . . dangerous.

"Wait," Caillean had said. "Why did you bring this to me? Surely you could not imagine that I would approve!"

"I am doing nothing that betrays my vows." Eilan faced the other woman directly. "But I know how idle tongues can embroider a tale. I believe that you would advise me as you thought right, whatever you might feel!" And then she had turned once more, and gone. But she remembered with some satisfaction the flush of color that had stained the other woman's cheeks.

And so she waited, knowing that with the implacable watcher she had nothing to fear. If she had earlier been asked whether she was afraid of Gaius she would have unhesitatingly answered no; but as the shadows shortened, she became frightened, then terrified.

"Oh, Caillean." She turned to the other woman, who sat upon a stone at the edge of the clearing, working on a piece of embroidery. "What am I going to say to him?"

"Why should you ask me? I am hardly the person to advise a maiden on her dealings with a man," Caillean replied with a sardonic smile.

Eilan sighed. As time passed she realized that it would take a while for him to come all the way from Deva. But as she waited, she found her hand stealing into Caillean's.

Was she meddling in an affair which was, after all, none of her concern? No, she told herself firmly. It was clearly her duty to find out all she could about the child's surviving relatives. Thus fortified, she waited; and her heart began to pound when at last she saw his shadow upon the path.

It was the first time she had seen Gaius in the uniform and helmet of the Roman Legion; she was struck by how well it became him. He seemed taller under the crimson crested helmet, and the color set off his dark eyes. He came into the clearing and stopped short. If he was surprised to see two women instead of one, it showed only in the momentary flicker of his eyes. Saluting them, he lifted the helmet from his head and tucked it under one arm.

Eilan found herself staring. She had never before had more than a momentary look at a Roman officer in full uniform; and it emphasized the differences between them. *And yet*, she thought, *by their laws we are all Romans*. It was like a revelation to her.

He looked at her and smiled, and suddenly all the things she had meant to say to him vanished from her mind.

Gaius shifted his gaze from Eilan to the older priestess, wondering what on earth he should say. He had never once envisioned that their meeting would be attended by a third party. He had not chanced angering his father and risking the wrath of hers, to exchange a few guarded remarks in the presence of a veritable dragon.

But as he met Caillean's amused glance his anger cooled. If Eilan was a Vestal Virgin or the nearest thing to one to be found within the British Isles, he could hardly blame her for wanting a witness who could attest to her unbroken vows. He wondered how he could make it clear, she was as sacrosanct to him as a Virgin in the temple of Vesta. He remembered how overwhelmed he had been by her trust when she sat beside him at the Beltane fire, how touched by her innocence.

Caillean, of course, was another matter; he could tell at once that the older woman would not have trusted him – or both of them – out of her sight, and for Eilan's sake he was indignant. But he guessed that the priestess had been brought up on tales of Roman outrages. To the women of the Forest House the very fact that he was a Roman and a man was enough.

And the truth was that if Caillean had not been there, he might have kissed Eilan; she looked very enticing in the pale linen dress that set off the gold of her hair. He thought the garb must be some kind of standard dress among the priestesses, for Caillean was wearing the same kind of draperies, though hers were dark blue and unbecoming. Both had little curved daggers hanging from their girdles.

After a moment Eilan began to tell him about the girl in the house of the priestesses, not very coherently, but he knew at once that this must be the child of Valerius's sister. "But this is amazing," he exclaimed. "I think this must be the same girl I came here to speak about to you, the niece of my father's secretary. How old is she?"

"The Goddess must be guiding us indeed," said Eilan. "I do not think she has passed her tenth year."

"Oh, well, she is not old enough to be marriageable," he said, for Roman law did not permit the marriage of a girl under twelve. He added lightly, "That's good; otherwise Valerius would probably feel in honor bound to make some arrangement. Now he'll just have to marry someone else to have a home for her."

"That is not necessary," said Eilan. "The girl is well and happy where she is, and you may tell him so."

Gaius frowned; he knew that for Valerius, who came of a good old family, it would not be considered suitable that a kinswoman should live away from the family's protection. But Valerius had no other family to take care of the girl now, and perhaps Eilan's insistence that she would personally watch over the child's health and safety would be enough for him.

After all, in Rome, it was the greatest possible honor for a little girl to be taken into the temple of Vesta. For as long as she retained her ritual position she was treated like a queen, or an empress at least. Somehow he would make Valerius understand.

He realized that he was still making ineffectual remarks about the little girl, whom he had not even seen, when he saw Caillean glaring at him. They had already said everything they could legitimately say to one another, and were beginning to repeat themselves. It was time to say goodbye.

He paused, eyeing Eilan wistfully. He supposed he would never have another opportunity to speak with her in even this much privacy. He would have liked to bid her a proper goodbye, but he could certainly not do that under Caillean's eyes. And he should probably not expose himself to that kind of temptation anyhow. But Eilan was still looking at him, a question in her eyes.

"Eilan –" he stammered, for Caillean was watching as well. "You know what I would say to you . . ." He held out his hand, not daring to touch her, and then, as Caillean coughed, turned it to a formal salute of farewell. But he read Eilan's answer in her smile.

When he had withdrawn, Eilan ran to Caillean.

"So that is the Roman who has had you daydreaming to the

point where you can hardly be trusted to stuff a mattress with bracken. I cannot understand it; he does not seem in any way special to me."

"Well, I did not suppose that you would particularly like him," Eilan protested, "but he is well favored, is he not?"

"I cannot see that he is any more so than any other Roman," Caillean remarked. "Or for that matter any other man. To me your foster brother Cynric is much better looking. He has a gentler face and does not appear to think the world must revolve about his comings and goings."

Eilan supposed there was no accounting for taste; she herself did not think Cynric was particularly attractive, but Dieda certainly did. But Gaius was something different; to her he did not seem typically Roman, not in any way. Nor did Gaius himself appear to think of his Roman lineage as anything very special. *Certainly he could not if he was for a time thinking of abandoning it for marriage with me*, she told herself then.

She had never for an instant considered marrying anyone else; and as for men, the world was full of them. She hardly realized how much thinking of Gaius had come between her old life and what now seemed natural to her.

"Eilan, you are daydreaming again," Caillean remarked sharply. "Go and find Senara and tell her what you have discovered; and then go to Latis for your lesson. If you can manage to pay attention, some day you may be as skilled in the lore of herbs as Miellyn."

Thus admonished, Eilan went about her duties; but she could not resist going obsessively over and over every word she had said to Gaius and every word he had said to her. She could not believe she would never see or speak with him again; he seemed too much a part of her life even after their formal goodbye.

That night when she went in her turn to wait upon Lhiannon, the older woman looked at her with dismay.

"What is this I have heard? That you have been out of the temple to meet with a man? This is not the behavior expected of a priestess of the Forest House. I am disappointed in you," she chided.

Eilan colored angrily. But this was why she had asked Caillean to witness their meeting, after all. "I said not one word to him that could not have been spoken in the presence of all of you."

Lhiannon sighed. "I did not say you did, but the fact of the matter is that it was not spoken in the presence of all of us, and there will be talk. The Goddess be thanked, Caillean was there; but she should have known that we cannot afford to have even the suspicion of scandal, so it is she and not you who will be punished for it. But I beseech you before you do anything of this kind again, think that you have brought punishment down on the head of another. You are young, Eilan, and the young are always thoughtless."

"Punished? But that is not fair! What will you do to her?" Eilan asked apprehensively.

"I will not beat her, if that is what you are thinking," Lhiannon said smiling. "Even when she was a small child, I never beat her; perhaps I should have done. As for her punishment, that is for her to tell if she wishes."

"But, Mother," Eilan protested, "it was you who told me to find out if the child had any family."

"I did not say that you should inquire among the Romans," Lhiannon said irritably. Eilan wondered how in the world she could have been expected to find out about the relatives of a Roman child in any other way.

Later, among the priestesses, Eilan found an opportunity to speak to Caillean. "Lhiannon told me she had to punish you. Can you forgive me? Will it be too bad? She said she would not beat you."

"She will not," Caillean said. "There is a house in the forest where she will probably send me to spend time meditating on my sins while I clear away the brushwood and weeds with which it is surrounded and put the place in order. It's not much of a punishment; Lhiannon probably does not realize that it is actually a luxury to me to be alone with my music and my thoughts. So you must not think I am being ill treated."

"Alone in the forest? But won't you be frightened?"

"What should frighten me? Bears? Wolves? Wandering men? The last bears in this part of the world were trapped over thirty years ago. How long is it since you have seen so much as a wolfskin rug in the market? And as for men, you have good cause to know that I could frighten away any man alive. No, I am not afraid."

"I should be terrified," Eilan said somberly.

"I am sure of it; but I am not afraid of my own company. And I can think of my music as much as I wish, without a lesson or a duty interfering. So I shall be quite content," Caillean assured her. "There is nothing in this punishment – if she will call it so – to trouble me."

Eilan said no more, and she knew that at least when it came to waiting upon Lhiannon, she and Dieda would willingly share Caillean's duties between them. Well, that was no hardship; she loved Lhiannon in spite of her flaws, and she knew that her kinswoman loved her too. She would miss Caillean, though.

Now it occurred to her that if Lhiannon had been a different type of person she herself might have been beaten or severely punished. Whatever Caillean made of this penalty, it was Eilan who had brought it upon the older woman. For that she felt guilty, but not enough to regret her meeting with Gaius. She only wished she had been able to say half of what she wanted to, though what that was she could not have named.

When Caillean departed from the Forest House, Eilan realized that the older woman was really not much of a favorite with the other women there. Only Miellyn and Eilidh seemed to be truly her friends – and of course Lhiannon.

The weather changed as summer moved towards autumn. As the equinox approached there was rain, and late one evening, while the women in the House of Maidens were seated around the fire, Eilan found herself thinking of Caillean in her exile. Was the roof of the hut leaky? How did she react to the solitude and the silence of the forest?

The women had been inventing riddles, and at last, tired of this pastime, they asked Dieda to sing or to tell them a story.

Dieda acquiesced. "What would you like me to tell you?"

"Tell us a tale of the Otherworld," said Miellyn. "Tell us how Bran son of Febal voyaged to the western land. All the bards learn that one."

And so Dieda half told, half chanted, the tale of Bran and his encounter with the sea god Manannan, Lord of Illusion, who turned the sea into a flowering grove of trees, the fish into birds flying in the air, the waves into flowering bushes, and the sea creatures into sheep; so it seemed as if they sailed through a flowering grove. And when Manannan fell out of the boat, the waves rushed in, so that the sea god was cast upon the shore and all the other men drowned.

When she had finished they called for another tale, like little children sitting spellbound.

"Tell the story of the King and the Three Hags," suggested one of the women, and Dieda began as all tales were begun.

"A long time ago, times were better than now, and there were more gates between the Otherworld and this, and if I had been there, I should not now be here . . . well then, in a longer time ago than the oldest grandfather can tell, in a house on the borders of the Underworld, there lived a king and his queen . . .

"And it was on the eve of Samaine, when the gates between the world are open, and at the time between times, between the midnight of one year and the dawn of the next, there came to the door three hags. The first had a snout like a pig, and her lower lip hung down to her knees and concealed her garment; the second had lips both on one side of her head and a beard which hung down concealing her breasts; and the third was a hideous creature with one arm and one leg. Under her arm she carried a pig which was so much better looking than she was that it was as if the pig were a princess."

By this time all the women were laughing. Dieda herself smiled a little and went on. "The three hags came in and took three seats by the fire so that there were no seats by the fire for the King and his queen, who were forced to take seats by the door.

"Then the first of them, the one with the long lower lip, said, 'I am hungry; what have you to eat?' And they hastened to make her a pot of porridge; and she ate up the pot of porridge, and it was enough for a dozen men, and she cried out, 'You are stingy; I hunger still.'

"Now on this night no request of a guest can be denied; and so the Queen set herself and her serving maids to make more porridge for her guests and put some oatcakes on the hearth to bake. But no matter how much food they set before the guest, she growled, 'I am still hungry.'

"Then the second, the bearded one, complained, 'I am thirsty.' When they brought out a barrel of beer, she drank it all down at one draft and complained that she was still dry. And when they began to fear that the hags would eat all the provision for the winter to come, the Queen and the King went out and consulted together what they should do with their guests. And then one of the fairy folk appeared to them from out of a mound and gave the Queen good-day.

"'All the gods preserve you, good lady; why are you weeping?' And the Queen told them of the three hideous hags and their fear that the creatures meant to eat them out of house and home, and then to eat the King and the Queen. And the Fairy Woman told her what she should do.

"So the Queen went in and sat down to her knitting; and finally the first hag asked, 'What are you making, Granny?'

"And the Queen replied, 'Knitting a shroud, dear Aunty.'

"And the second hag asked through her beard. 'Who is the shroud for, Granny?'

"'Oh, for anyone I can find who is homeless this night, dear Aunty.'"

"And after a while the third asked, kissing her pig, 'And when will you be using the shroud, Granny?'

"And just then the King rushed in and cried out, 'The black mountain and the sky over it are all on fire!'

"And when they heard that, the three hags cried out, 'Alas, alas, our father is gone' and rushed out of the door, and they were never seen again in that country by any living man; or if they were, then I have not heard of it."

Dieda fell silent. After a long pause, while the wind wailed loudly around the building, Miellyn said, "I heard Caillean tell a story very like that, long ago; did you learn it from her?"

"I did not," said Dieda. "I heard my father tell it once when I was a very small girl."

"I suppose it is very old," said Miellyn, "and of course he is one of the greatest bards. But you told it as well as any Druid. You or Caillean could head the College as well as he."

"Oh, no doubt," Dieda scoffed. "And why not make us judges as well?"

Why not, indeed? Eilan wondered. Caillean would have had an answer to that, but Caillean was not here.

thirteen

O nce Gaius had reassured Valerius that his kinswoman was safe in Eilan's care in the Forest House, he made plans to leave again before his father could begin nagging him again about marriage. Since seeing Eilan, he was even more determined not to be married off to some Roman girl. Ever since the death of the Emperor Titus and the accession of Domitian everything had been unsettled, and Gaius knew that his father was looking about for alliances.

After a time he went out into the town. The morning had been warm and muggy, but now great clouds were building in the west, and he felt his hair ruffled by a cool wind. An old centurion had told him once that in this country there were two ways to tell the weather: if you could see the hills, it was about to rain; if not, it was already raining. The man had sighed then, homesick for the flat blue skies of Italia, but Gaius took a grateful breath of the damp wind. As the first drop of rain fell, the Romans began to scurry for shelter. But there was one man who stood still, as he did, turning his face to the sky.

Without much surprise, Gaius recognized Cynric.

"Join me for a cup of wine?" He gestured towards the wine shop where they had met before.

Cynric shook his head. "Thank you; I think I had better not. I'd rather that you could say that you haven't seen me. As a matter of fact it would be much better for you if you could say that you don't know too much about my comings and goings. That way I won't have to ask you to lie."

Gaius lifted one eyebrow. "Are you joking?"

"I wish I were. I shouldn't even stand about talking to you like this; though you can honestly say you encountered me by chance."

"Don't worry," said Gaius, looking around him. A gust of wind sent raindrops spattering across the road, sending up little puffs of dust as they fell. "All the good Romans are safe under cover, and won't care about two fools standing out in the rain! Listen, Cynric, I need to talk to you about Eilan . . ."

Cynric grimaced. "I beg of you, don't speak of that. That was quite the biggest mistake I've made this year; Lhiannon was furious with me. No real harm was done, but don't try to see my foster sister again." He looked nervously around him. "Even if you can afford it, I should not be seen talking to an officer of the Legions in full uniform. In fact, you'd better pretend you don't know me if we meet by accident again."

He added, "I won't be offended. Somebody finally figured out that I was still working for the Ravens, and it occurred to them that serving with the auxiliaries put me in a prime position to make trouble when the time comes. So they've proscribed me, and if I'm spotted within twenty miles of the Roman town, I could be sentenced to the mines – or to something worse – if there is anything worse. Farewell!" Cynric turned away.

Gaius blinked, realizing suddenly that Cynric no longer wore the insignia of Rome. That must be why he was willing to speak so plainly. He was still trying to think of something to say as his friend slid into a side street and disappeared, leaving him alone with the rain. Gaius checked the impulse to follow him. If Cynric were truly an enemy of Rome, even a quick death would be better than sending him to the Mendip lead mines.

"Don't try to see my foster sister again."

Cynric's words echoed in his head. Was this, then, the end to his hope of contact with Eilan? No doubt Cynric and his father were right. But as he pulled the garnet-colored folds of his military cloak over his head and started down the street, the moisture on his cheeks was not entirely from the rain.

Caillean paused in the doorway of the main hall, wincing as the cackle smote her ears. After more then two moons alone, she had forgotten how much noise women could make when they were all cooped up together. For a moment she wanted to turn and flee back to the solitude of her hut in the forest.

"So, you're back," commented Dieda, finally noticing her. "I wonder why, after the way Lhiannon has treated you. Having got free of us, I should think you would have kept going!"

"And why are *you* still here?" stung, Caillean replied. "The man you loved is away in the North with the Eagles after him. Is your place then not by his side?"

For a moment anger flared in the younger woman's face, to be replaced in a moment by something closer to despair.

"Don't you think I would have been away in a moment if he had asked me?" she said bitterly. "But his loyalty is given to the Lady of Ravens, and if I cannot be first with the man I love I will take the final vows of a priestess and not have one at all!" Her voice faltered as the other women turned, and Caillean gazed at her with reluctant pity, grateful that she had never been tempted to love.

"Caillean —" Eilidh hurried towards her. "I was hoping you would return today. Lhiannon is in her rooms. Go to her now. She never complains, but I know that she has missed you."

And well she might, thought Caillean wryly as she crossed the courtyard, pulling her shawl over her head to keep off the rain, *since it was she who sent me away!*

As always after an absence, Caillean was struck by Lhiannon's fragility. *She will not make old bones*, she thought now, looking at her. There was no obvious sign of illness, only an increasing translucence, but an instinct honed by years as a priestess told her that the older woman was being consumed from within.

"Mother, I am here," she said softly. "Were you wanting to see me?"

Lhiannon turned, and Caillean saw that her faded eyes were glistening with tears. "I have been waiting for you," she said softly. "Will you forgive me for sending you away?"

Caillean shook her head, feeling her own throat tighten, and crossed the room swiftly to kneel beside the High Priestess's chair.

"What is there to forgive?" she asked brokenly, laying her head on the older woman's knees. She felt her own tears begin to fall as Lhiannon touched her hair. "I should never have become a priestess, such a trouble to you I have been!" Suddenly, by that tender touch on her brow, a barrier that had begun to crack when she poured out her heart to Eilan so long ago was swept away.

"I never could tell you," she whispered, "at first I did not understand, and then I was ashamed. I am no pure maiden. In Eriu, before you found me, I was used by a man —" Her voice choked. There was a silence, and then the thin fingers began once more to stroke her hair.

"Ah, little one, is that what has troubled you? I thought there was something, but did not want to ask. You were not even a woman yet when I took you from Eriu. How could you sin? It is only that we do not speak of such things, because there are those who would not understand. We must preserve appearances. That is why I punished you for helping Eilan. But listen, Caillean, my dear one – whatever befell you before you came here is of no importance, not to the Goddess, and certainly not to me, so long as while you dwell in Her House you serve Her faithfully and well!"

Still weeping, Caillean reached up to clasp the older woman's arms. Despite occasional exasperation, she realized then that what she felt for Lhiannon was surely as deep as any love she might have had for a man, though it was different in kind. And she loved Eilan, whose sympathy had first enabled her to face these memories. But at least neither of these loves would ever conflict with her vows as priestess.

There had been moments, during the days of Caillean's exile, when the raindrops that fell from the eaves of the Forest House had seemed to strike Eilan's heart. Gaius was gone, and she would not see him again, that much had been made clear. It was a relief to have those thoughts interrupted when Caillean summoned her.

"You're back!" she exclaimed as she pushed through the woolen hangings at the door of Caillean's chamber. "No one told me! How long have you been here?"

"A day only," said the priestess. "I was with Lhiannon."

Eilan embraced her and stood back to look Caillean up and down. "It's done you no harm, anyway." She looked brown and healthy, and the little line that sometimes marred the blue crescent tattooed between her brows had smoothed away. "Have they quite forgiven you for my crime?"

Caillean smiled. "It is forgotten. And that, child, is why I sent for you. You have been here for three years now and done well in your studies. The time has come for you to decide if you wish to become truly one of us and take your vows."

"Has it been so long?" It was hard to believe that Mairi's daughter was already a thriving toddler three years old, and her older child nearly five. And yet at the same time it seemed to Eilan that she had always been here. Her old life was forgotten, and when she dreamed of Gaius it was always of his arms around her and his voice murmuring in her ear. She could not imagine living with him in the Roman world.

"Is Dieda to take her vows now too?" They were all aware of

Dieda's bitterness over what she saw as Cynric's defection, and now that he was proscribed, who could say when it would be safe for him to return? His commitment to the training of a warrior and his vengeance still commanded his first loyalty. *Like the loyalty that holds Gaius to his father's world*, Eilan thought.

"That is between her and the Goddess," Caillean said sternly. "Now we are speaking of you. Is it still your wish to persevere among us, little one?"

Dieda will make her vows, and so shall I, Eilan thought. *Why not, when neither of us can ever have the man we love?*

"Yes, it is. At least –" she hesitated – "if the Goddess still wants me, knowing that my love was first given to a man."

"That does not matter," Caillean smiled radiantly. "The Goddess no longer regards anything that happened to you before you made your vows. I have finally told Lhiannon what happened to me, and she has assured me that is so. I owe that blessing to you, my dear, and I am glad to be able to pass it on!"

"There are some who would not see it that way," Eilan said bitterly.

"You must not let them trouble you." Caillean set her hands on Eilan's shoulders and stared into her eyes, and it seemed to Eilan that the dark eyes of the priestess were like the sacred pool, in which past and future could be seen.

"Listen, little sister, and I will tell you the truth at the heart of the Mysteries. All the gods, and all the goddesses too, are one, whether we call her Arianrhod or Cathubodva or Don. The Light of Truth is One, but we see it as light reflects through crystals or prisms, in many colors. Each of the ways in which men and women see their gods – or their goddesses – has a part of that truth. We who live in the Forest House are privileged to see the Goddess in many ways, and to call Her by many names, but we know this first and greatest of all secrets, that the gods, whatever they are called, are all one."

"Then does this mean that the gods of the Romans are the same gods and goddesses we serve?"

"Indeed – that is why they carve their images with the attributes of both when they build their votive altars here. But it is true that while we in the Forest House know the identity of all gods by whatever name we may call them, we believe that we serve the Goddess in perhaps Her purest form, as the divinity in all women. And so we pledge ourselves to serve Her as Mother, Sister and

Daughter. This is why we sometimes speak of seeing the Face of the Goddess in the face of every woman."

For a moment the exaltation in Caillean's words held her, then Eilan felt a sudden spurt of anger. Why had they all been so angry at her interest in a Roman if their gods were all the same? Caillean had been present when she spoke with Gaius and knew how she felt about him. How could she say that those feelings would no longer matter once she had taken her vows? They were a part of her, as holy as the ecstasy she had felt sometimes when the presence of the Goddess filled her like moonlight glimmering on the sacred pool.

"What will be required of me?"

"You will take a vow to remain forever chaste unless you should be chosen by the god. And you will pledge that you will not speak foolishly of temple secrets to the unsworn, and that you will strive always to do the will of the Goddess and of anyone who shall command you lawfully in any of Her names."

Caillean paused, watching her and Eilan reflected on how much she loved her, and had come to love the other women and the life they had there. She met the priestess's dark gaze. "To all this I will willingly swear . . ."

"And you will demonstrate that you are mistress of the skills we have taught you, and that the Goddess is willing to accept you? You will understand that I cannot describe it – indeed they say that for each candidate the ordeal is different, so even if my oath did not forbid it I could tell you nothing more."

Eilan suppressed a shiver of anxiety. Living in the House of Maidens she had heard rumors of candidates who had failed and been sent away, or worse still, disappeared. "I understand, and I am willing," she said quietly.

"So be it, then," said Caillean, In Her name I now welcome you as a candidate priestess." She kissed Eilan on the cheek; and Eilan remembered that one of the younger priestesses had done this when first she came to the Forest House. For a moment the two kisses blurred; she blinked, dizzied by the sense that she was repeating a moment she had lived many times before.

"At the full moon before Samaine, then, you shall speak your vows in the presence of the priestesses. Lhiannon and your grandfather will be greatly pleased."

Eilan stared at her. She was certainly not doing this for their sake! Caillean had asked her to choose, but had her decision in fact been molded by her family's expectations and perhaps other forces dimly hovering in the shadows beyond perception.

"Caillean —" she whispered, reaching out to the priestess. "If I vow myself to the Goddess, it will not be because I am the daughter and granddaughter of Druids, or even because I will never see Gaius again. There has to be something more."

Caillean looked at her. "When we first met it seemed to me you had a destiny among us," she said slowly. "I feel it even more strongly now. But I cannot guarantee that you will be happy, child."

"I do not expect to be —" Eilan caught her breath on a sob. "So long as there is some *reason*, some purpose, in it all!"

Caillean sighed and held out her arms, and Eilan leaned against her, feeling the tightness in her throat ease as the other woman stroked her hair.

"There is always a reason, my dear, though it may be long before we understand it — that is all the comfort I can offer you. If the Goddess does not know what She is doing, what meaning is there in the world?"

"It is enough," whispered Eilan, hearing the other woman's heart beating, steady and slow, beneath her ear. "If I also have your love."

"You do . . ." Caillean's voice was almost too low to be heard. "I love you as Lhiannon has loved me . . ."

The full moon looked down from the heavens like a watchful eye, as if Arianrhod had personally decided to observe the ceremonies. As the chanting of the priestesses who had brought her here faded to silence, an inner chill pebbled Eilan's arms, though the night was warm. Had she been hoping for rain? It would have made no difference; if the Druids had allowed the weather to affect their rituals they would not have had much of a religion. She knew she should be glad that the skies had chosen to bless her initiation, but the moonlight made her uneasy.

At least the brightness should make it easier to follow the path, and all the priestesses had asked was that she walk through the forest back to the temple, which did not seem a great ordeal. Eager for it to be done, Eilan hurried into the shadows beneath the trees, away from the moon's implacable gaze.

She had been walking for scarcely the time it takes to spin a yard of thread when she realized that she was lost.

Controlling her breathing, Eilan turned. This, she supposed, must be the first test of her training, to see if she could use her inner senses to find her way. She drew on the steady power of the earth beneath her – that, at least, had not changed. The energies of moon and stars sang above, and as she opened herself to become the pillar that linked them, breathing out and in in regular rhythm until she knew herself to be at the center of the universe, the fear went away.

She opened her eyes once more. The panic was gone, but the moonlight that filtered through the leaves seemed to be coming from all quarters at once, and she had no idea in which direction the temple lay. Still, if she chose a direction and walked in it she should eventually get through the forest. Once, she had been told, all this island had been covered by trees, but now the land was dotted with roads and pastures and fields. Surely she could not walk for long without finding someone who could show her the way.

Humming softly, Eilan made her way forward, and only later realized that what she had been singing was the song the priestesses chanted at the rising of the moon.

As she walked, the dappled radiance of the moon transformed the world, and she understood why it had made her afraid. Each twig was outlined in silver; the leaves glittered, and light danced and flickered from every stone . . . but now Eilan realized that she was seeing something more than moonlight. Every living thing in the forest had its own glow – a radiance that increased until she could see almost as well as in the light of day. But it was not day, for this light was shadowless, a diffuse illumination in which the colors of the forest glowed like muted jewels. With a little shiver she understood that somehow she had passed the boundary that separates the fields of men from the Otherworld.

Truly it was as her teachers had told her; the Land of the Living and the world of men lay like the folds in a cloak, and where they touched, one could pass easily from one to the other. Or perhaps it was only sometimes that the worlds came thus closely together – at times like this, when the priestesses had sung the sacred songs.

The wood she had entered was filled with oak and hazel and thorn like any other. Now some of the trees she saw were familiar, but others were of no race she knew. Next to a thriving oak she glimpsed a tree with silver bark and little flowers of gold. A rowan tree bore white blossoms and red berries at the same time, though in the human world the flowering time had passed and the berries were not yet ripening on the bough.

Blossoms filled the air with a heady perfume. Now that she could see her way she walked with more confidence, her delight almost making her forget why she had come. Dimly she realized that this seduction of the senses might be the greatest danger, and tried to remember her goal. A lingering sense of duty, more than any other emotion, drew her to a halt in a small clearing where silver birches and rowans rustled in the fragrant breeze like maidens watching a festival. She closed her eyes.

"Lady, help me! Powers that dwell in this place, I honor you – " she said softly. "Of your favor, show me where I need to go . . ."

When she looked again, she glimpsed through the trees an avenue edged with rough stones. She moved along it, walking with the graceful pacing gait the maidens had been taught to use in the ceremonies. Presently the road passed between two great uprights carved with spirals and chevrons. Beyond them Eilan saw a pool whose waters glimmered as if reflecting the light of the hidden moon.

Hardly daring to breathe, Eilan moved between the great stones, and looked down into the pool. This at least had been part of her training, for one of her first skills was to see in the scrying bowl. A sudden wind ruffled the waters, and as they cleared she realized that the bowl had been like a candle to the sun beside the power of the pool.

In its depths Eilan saw the sea, glittering emerald and sapphire beneath a sky like translucent blue glass. As she stared, pool and forest and stones all disappeared and she floated like a bird on the wing above the waves. Embraced by those waters was an island girt with cliffs of red sandstone, crowned by white temples set among groves of dark trees. On the highest hill stood a temple greater than all the others, whose roof gleamed with gold.

Eilan swooped lower, and saw a white-robed woman pacing along the parapet, gazing out to sea. There was gold on the woman's neck and wrists, gold bound her brow, and her hair was like flame, but she had Caillean's eyes. A young man emerged from the temple and knelt before her, pressing his head against her belly. As the priestess blessed him, Eilan saw the tattooed dragons coiling up his arms. And it seemed to her that a voice like falling raindrops sang –

"Alas for the land beyond the wave –
Alas for the land that none could save –
The knowledge lost that gods once gave . . ."

Even as the singing faded, the scene changed. She had the sense that many years had passed. Suddenly the center of the island exploded in a great gout of ruddy flame, and the waters rose like a wall of green glass and swallowed trees and temples and all. Even as the island fell, a fleet of ships sped away from it, leaping through the water like frightened gulls. One with a dragon painted on its sail she followed as it arrowed through the water, faring northward until silver mists blotted out the sun's radiance, and the sea grew gray and green as the waters she knew.

Now she saw land once more, white cliffs and high grassy downs. Over hill and dale she soared, and came to a high, broad plain where long lines of men toiled with ropes, dragging great blocks of stone. Part of the henge was in place already and she could envision the rest of it. She had heard the Giants' Dance described often enough to recognize the great circle of stones. The man who was directing the work looked like her father, but he deferred to another who reminded her of Gaius, shorter and dark as a Silure tribesman, but vibrant with power. The second man gestured towards the henge, and she saw the dragons that had been tattooed upon his forearms ripple as the muscles moved.

A wind stroked the high grass of the plain, and when it passed, the scene had changed once more. Fascinated, Eilan watched as one image followed another. Coloring and cast of feature changed as each new people came into the land. But again and again she recognized an expression or gesture that was familiar – her grandfather's touch on a harp; Lhiannon's regal grace; and even herself, riding in a chariot like a queen. A tall man rode beside her, and she knew that it was he whose touch had given her access to her own power.

"All that has been will ever be;
The dragon rises from the sea;
Only the wise are truly free –"

came that clear voice from beyond the world.

The last image was of a hill of knobbed granite where the purple heather grew. Chill winds swept eastward from the sea, scouring the rolling fields. In this windswept place real trees grew only along the strait where the island fronted the grim bulk of the mainland. Even as she realized that she was seeing Mona, the scene changed, and Eilan saw men of her own race clad in white, and women in robes of midnight blue, their faces grim as they piled wood into great pyres.

For a moment she did not understand. Then a shiver of light rippled along the opposite shore. She blinked, recognizing Roman armor. The people of Mona saw it too, and suddenly the pyres were blazing. The priestesses danced forward, their shadows contorting as they screamed their spells. For a time the Romans hung back and their leaders harangued them, then the first rank went splashing into the water. The strait frothed as the Legion pushed across it. They came out dripping, but their swords gleamed red in the firelight. With grim precision they pursued the Druids, and their swords dripped with a brighter crimson as they slew all those they found.

For a time then all was silent. The fading firelight gave way to the cold grey of dawn. Ravens were already busy at the bodies. As Eilan watched, they rose suddenly upward, screaming, their wings darkening the sky.

> "While Eagles gorge, the Dragon sleeps,
> When Ravens fly, the Lady weeps,
> What hate has sown compassion reaps . . ."

As she heard the song Eilan felt her heart pierced by sorrow, and the vision blurred as tears filled her eyes.

When she could see again, she was standing beside the pool once more. But she was no longer alone. Mirrored in the water she saw a figure, and looking up she realized that it was a man wrapped in a spotted bull's hide with a headdress framed by hawk's wings and crowned by the antlers of a great stag. Her eyes widened, for this was a costume the Druids wore only for their most sacred ceremonies.

"Lord –" she gave him the salutation due his rank, "who are you?" For a moment he had reminded her of her grandfather, but she realized now that he was younger, despite the silver in his beard, and in his eyes shone a wisdom and power she had no more than glimpsed in any mortal man.

This is what Ardanos was meant to be! she thought then, like the great priestess she had glimpsed sometimes shining through Lhiannon in the rituals. This was the reality.

He smiled, and it seemed to her that the light brightened around them until the pool shone. "I have been in many shapes, and had many names. I have been the Hawk of the Sun, and the White Stallion, the Golden Stag, and the Black Boar. But here and now I am the Merlin of Britannia."

Eilan swallowed. She had heard something of this in her studies, for the Merlin was a title that had been borne by the Arch-Druid in previous years. But the soul to whom it belonged did not take flesh in every generation, and it was said that only the greatest of the Druids met him in the Otherworld.

She licked her lips. "What do you want of me?"

"Daughter of the Holy Isle, will you serve your people, and your gods?"

"I serve the Lady of Life," answered Eilan steadily. "And I would do Her will."

"This is an hour of omen, when many paths may meet, but only with your consent, for the way that opens before you will require that you give everything, and if you follow it you will find scant understanding or reward." He moved around the edge of the pool.

"And what do the omens say this hour is propitious for?" Close to, the reality of his presence was overpowering. Eilan was glad the old tales had taught her how to reply.

"It is propitious for the making of a priestess in the ancient way," he said gently. "They have told you that a priestess must be physically a virgin, but it is not so. A priestess of the Goddess gives herself at her own time and season, and when the power has passed through her, resumes her sovereignty. She gives, but is never taken. She is the initiator who sanctifies the Sacred King, that he may bestow the blessing on his queen, and life may be renewed in the land."

"And that is what you want of me?" Eilan realized that she was trembling. "How can I do it? I do not know how!"

"Not you, but the Goddess within you —" Eilan's breath stopped as he smiled. "And it is my office to awaken Her."

He released the hide, and as its stiff folds fell away she saw that he was naked, his body the image of the potent god. He smoothed the hair that curled away from her temples, and it seemed to her she would have fallen without the support of those strong hands. Then he bent to kiss her upon the brow.

Goddess! her spirit cried, and felt consciousness ignited by a white flame that surged downward as he kissed her lips, her breasts, and knelt to bless her womb. In that moment she was aware of her own essence as she had never been before, and yet at the same time, all selfhood was subsumed in Another, and whether that Presence was a part of her or she of it, or *Her*, Eilan could not say. What she knew beyond question was that in a sense that surpassed even the comfort of Gaius's arms around her, she was no longer alone.

Eilan burned and was not consumed, and it seemed to her that the voice she had heard sang in tones of flame –

> *"The enemy you would conquer, you must love . . .*
> *The law you would fulfill, you must defy . . .*
> *The thing that you would keep, you must now*
> *give . . .*
> *Thus will you have the victory . . .*
> *Daughter of Druids, through you the Dragon will*
> *be reborn."*

Her awareness flared with images of blood and splendor, battles and stone cities and a green tor above an inland sea, fire and sword and finally a fair-haired man with Gaius's eyes who rode to battle with the image of the Lady on his shield.

"I will!" came her reply. "But do not leave me alone –"

"*Daughter, I am always here*," came the reply. "*Thou art Mine, from age to age, while Time endures.*"

She knew that she had heard those words before, that this was only the renewing of an ancient bond, but the love that lapped her was becoming a sea in which she drowned, a light in which all awareness was consumed.

Eilan's next conscious thought was of floating in cool water. She sensed dark trees around her, and moonlight, and in the next moment many hands had hold of her and were lifting her to the shore. She blinked in amazement as she realized that she was lying beside the bathing pool in the stream below the House of Maidens.

Eilan tried to speak and found she could not. She realized then that what had happened to her was a mystery too deep for telling, even here. And yet she wondered that they could not see it, for the Divine Heat still blazed within her so that her skin dried as soon as they helped her rise from the pool. In silence the other women clad her in a robe of new linen dyed the deep blue that the consecrated priestesses wore.

"You have journeyed between the worlds; you have seen the

light that is without shadow; you have been purified . . ." said a voice Eilan recognized as Caillean's. She looked up, but it was the woman she had seen on the parapet in her vision who seemed to be standing there. "Daughter of the Goddess, arise, that your sisters may welcome you —"

The priestesses helped her to her feet and fell in behind her as she followed Caillean along the path that led to the Sacred Grove.

By the light of the torches that flickered among the trees Eilan saw that Lhiannon was waiting, attended by Eilidh. Beside her stood Dieda, her eyes as huge and dazzled as Eilan knew her own must be, and her hair clinging to her brow in damp tendrils. *What*, Eilan wondered, *happened to her?* Their eyes met, and all the barriers that the past years had built between them vanished; they remembered only that they were sisters now.

I am glad that we will be making our vows together . . . she thought. The testing was always the same, but each priestess received the vision the gods willed. Dieda, she supposed, would have found music. She looked at the other girl, and it seemed to her that the Goddess smiled back at her from Dieda's eyes.

Eilan looked around her and saw that they were all here — Miellyn and Eilidh and the others who had taught her for the past three years. But in each woman's face she saw a reflection of the light of the Otherworld, and in some of them, something more, a hint of faces she had seen in her visions, constantly changing and yet always the same.

Why do men fear death when we will live again? Eilan wondered then. The Druids taught that the soul could take many forms through the circling years, and she had always thought she believed it, but now she knew that it was true.

At last she understood Caillean's serenity, and the holiness that despite her fragility and fallibility, she sensed in Lhiannon. They too had been where she had gone, and no mortal accidents could change the truth of it.

She heard the words of the ceremony as if in a dream, and made her vows without hesitation, for the most important promise, the one that included and commanded all others, had already been made to the Goddess in the Otherworld. With the blood still singing in her veins, and the light of the Lady in her eyes, she scarcely felt the prick of the thorn as the blue crescent that proclaimed her priestess was drawn between her brows.

fourteen

~~~

It was the tradition in the Forest House that after the priestesses took their vows they should undergo a period of seclusion. Eilan was grateful. During the days that followed her initiation she lay as exhausted as Lhiannon after giving an Oracle, and even when she recovered physically, she found her attention focused inward as she tried to understand what had occurred.

Sometimes the Druid's words to her seemed impossible – a demented dream born of her frustrated love for Gaius. But when the priestesses gathered in the frosty darkness to salute the winter moon, Eilan would find her spirit lifted as the women's voices soared. At such times, when the moonlight filled her like a silver flame, she knew that what she had experienced was no dream.

Sometimes she found Caillean watching her rather curiously, but not even when the older priestess taught them the secrets of the Wise Ones who had come over the sea – the lore that only the sworn priestesses were allowed to learn – did Eilan feel free to speak of the Merlin and the destiny she believed he had offered her. For gradually she had realized that whatever ecstasies the other priestesses experienced in their initiations, this mystery had been for her alone. And so the dark days of winter passed and lengthened into spring, and the mark of the Goddess healed upon Eilan's brow.

Gaius lounged on the bench in his father's office at Deva, breathing deeply of the breeze that came through the open window and wondering how soon he could get away. For a year he had been attached to his father's staff, and he was tired of fortress walls. Spring was overwhelming the fields and woodlands. He could smell apple blossom on that breeze, and it made him think of Eilan.

"Most of the men will be taking leave for the Floralia, but I don't want too many of my officers away at one time." His father's voice seemed to come from far away. "When you're up for leave where will you go?"

"I hadn't thought about it," Gaius blurted out. Some of the officers used their free time to go hunting, but killing things for sport no longer particularly interested him. Really, there was nowhere he wanted to be.

"You might go and see the Procurator," his father suggested. "You haven't met his daughter yet."

"And if the gods are kind to me I never will," Gaius returned abruptly to the present and sat up. His father looked pained.

"Now, how could it possibly hurt you," Macellius inquired, obviously holding on to his temper, "just to see the girl? I think she's already fifteen years old."

"Father, I *know* she's marriageable. How stupid do you think I am, anyway?"

His father only smiled. "I haven't said a word about marrying her."

"You don't have to," Gaius said sullenly. If he could not have Eilan, he was damned if he would marry any woman in Britain – let alone one his father suggested.

"You don't have to be rude," his father said. "As a matter of fact, I was thinking of spending the holidays in Londinium, and –"

"Well, I wasn't," Gaius said, no longer caring what his father thought of his manners. He did not know where he would go but it would be as far away from Londinium as he could possibly get.

"I hope you're not thinking of that British girl again," Macellius commented, almost, Gaius thought, as if his father were reading his mind. If only he had left it at that. But Macellius went on to say, "I'm sure you've had the sense to put her out of your mind for good and all."

And that decided him. "As a matter of fact," he said deliberately, "I was thinking of going to see Clotinus." It had been after staying with the British lord, after all, that he had first met Eilan, and he could at least enjoy the memories.

Gaius enjoyed the trip southward, thinking of Eilan, and of Cynric who might have been his friend and was lost to him, through no fault of their own. Spring was advancing like a conquering army, and the weather was beautiful; mornings clear and cold, making him glad to be warmly clad, and days warm, bright and almost dry except for a sprinkle of soft rain late in the day.

Clotinus greeted him gladly and welcomed him, and although Gaius knew it was mostly that Clotinus wished to keep on the best of terms with the powerful Romans, he enjoyed it anyway. Gwenna had gone away to be married, so there was no one to trouble him.

The household of Clotinus, he realized, was not at all a bad place to spend a vacation. The food was good, and even Clotinus's remaining daughter, only twelve or so, was good company, and sympathetic enough when he told her that his father had tried to arrange a marriage for him with an unknown. She might well have been offering to console him on some subtle level but Gaius remembered – not before time, he thought – what his father had said about entangling himself with native women. If the girl was sending him any wordless signals, he pretended not to notice them.

But except for prayers dimly directed at Venus, he could think of no way to approach Eilan. In sleep he ground himself against his blankets, moaning, and waking, knew that it was of Eilan that he had dreamed.

I love her, he thought in self-pity, when the hopelessness of his situation overwhelmed him. *It isn't as if I meant to seduce and abandon the girl. I'd be happy to marry her if I could get the permission of all the people who seem to have made it their business to control our lives.* After all, he was twenty-three, and an officer – though a very minor one – in his Legion. If that did not make him old enough to marry at his own will, how old would he have to be?

One day when he was riding out under the excuse of hunting, he found himself traveling past the burned-out walls that once had been the house of Bendeigid, and he realized he must be somewhere in the vicinity of the Forest House. His leg ached a bit as he remembered the boar pit – it seemed to him very long ago – and the first time he had ever laid eyes on Eilan.

I cannot stay here . . . he thought suddenly. *Every tree and stone will bring back painful memories.* He had thought he could bear it. Certainly seeing old Ardanos from time to time in Deva had not troubled his peace. Perhaps he should ride south to visit his mother's people. It would not please Macellius, but he did not much care to please his father just now.

That night before the fire he spoke of it to Clotinus, who urged him to remain another day or two.

"There will be too many folk on the road till the festival," Clotinus pointed out. "You should stay until that is past at least and then you can travel in comfort."

"People won't bother me, but perhaps I should not travel in full uniform," said Gaius. "I will make better time and attract less attention if I wear the common dress of a Briton."

"That's true," Clotinus grinned sourly. "You are, in a sense, one of us. I daresay I can come up with something that will serve."

The next morning his steward produced clothing which fitted Gaius well enough: tan breeches and a tunic dyed green, in new cloth, clean and decent but not particularly luxurious, and with them a voluminous dark brown cloak of heavy wool. "The nights are still chilly, lad," Clotinus said. "You will need this when darkness falls."

When Gaius put it on his Roman identity seemed to fall away.

"You are no longer Gaius Macellius Severus in this garb." The old man eyed him oddly. Gaius grinned. "As I think I told you, my mother called me Gawen while she lived; now I look nothing else and I should use only that name."

Clotinus was quick to exclaim how well the clothing became him, yet somehow Gaius knew the man regretted the disappearance of his important-looking Roman guest.

"If I attend the festival, I will be just another Briton," Gaius went on. "Maybe I should have you send a message to Macellius that I am traveling in disguise!" He suspected his father would not be pleased, and the excuse of gathering information might justify this escapade.

When Eilan woke on Beltane morning she had the oddest feeling that Gaius was somewhere near. *Perhaps*, she thought, *he is thinking of me*. It was Beltane, after all, and all their most significant meetings had been at that festival. It was natural, in any case, that her thoughts should turn to him on this day when, throughout the land, the hearts of men and maidens were turning to love.

Here in the chaste sanctuary of the House of Maidens she should not be thinking of such things, or if she did, she should view them with the detached benevolence of one who existed far beyond such fleshly cravings. During the winter that had been easy. It seemed to her that the passion with which the Druid of her vision had touched her had been refined to a radiance as pure as an altar flame, and her vows of chastity no great sacrifice.

But now, when the sap was rising in the trees and every bud was bursting into flower, she was beginning to wonder. When she thought about her vision, her body flamed, and at night she

179

dreamed about lying with a lover who was sometimes the Druid and sometimes Gaius, and sometimes a stranger with the eyes of a king. *My body is still untouched*, she thought suddenly, *but my spirit is virgin no longer. Goddess, how will I bear this sweet pain?*

"Eilan, are you helping Lhiannon prepare for this evening's ritual?" Miellyn's voice brought her back to the world and she shook her head. "Then why not come out with the rest of us this morning and enjoy the festival? It will do you good to get some fresh air."

"The rest of us" turned out to include Senara, who was entirely delighted to be out of doors. It was a crisp bright day, and in the hedges the hawthorn glowed as if the light of the sun had settled on the boughs. The people were jammed together in a way that made Eilan, used to the peace and quiet after her months of seclusion, tremble. How quickly she had grown accustomed to silence and peace, or perhaps her initiation had altered her. She had always been a little uncomfortable in crowds, but she felt now as if she were walking about without her skin.

But Senara was in high spirits as she walked between them. She was fascinated by everything: a stall of round cheeses; a table where a seller of glass bangles had spread his glittering wares; and everywhere, the flowers.

Eilan had not seen so many people since last Beltane when she had met Gaius again. It seemed to her that everyone in Britain or the islands must be here, jostling, laughing, eating, drinking; and every craft from the making of cakes to rope-dancing.

"Will Lhiannon be here during the day?" Senara asked.

Miellyn nodded. "Ardanos will escort her. It is a part of her duty to show herself to the crowds at festivals." Miellyn paused, and added "And not the happier part. Between ourselves, I think she is very tired. Every year now, I wonder if it will be her last festival."

Seeing Eilan's face grow pale, she added, "Does it frighten you? Death is as much a part of life as birth; as a priestess you should know that."

But the crowds were so thick she could hardly hear what Miellyn was saying. A group of people were watching a man with a dancing bear; Senara cried out that she wanted to see, and they pressed forward for a better view. As people glimpsed the blue linen dresses of priestesses from the Forest House they parted before them till they stood at the ringside, watching the animal dance – or, at least, lumber heavily in a circle on its hind legs, which she supposed was as near as such a beast could come to dancing. The bear's muzzle was tightly wrapped with rope; she thought it looked miserable.

"Poor thing," she said, and Miellyn sighed.

"Sometimes it comes to me that Lhiannon is like that bear," the other priestess replied. "Always on display, never speaking her own words." Eilan gasped at the thought of comparing the High Priestess to a trained animal.

"And who leads her?" Senara giggled. "Miellyn, you should not say such things."

"Why not? Speaking the truth is usually considered to be a virtue," Miellyn said stoutly, and Eilan was reminded of Caillean. Her grandfather's treatment of the High Priestess seemed very different from the sovereignty that the Druid of her vision had proclaimed.

"I speak the truth as I see it; and when I see Lhiannon growing so feeble, I wonder –"

Miellyn did not finish her sentence, for at that moment the bear dropped to all fours and lumbered directly toward them. Senara shrieked and jumped away, but the crowd pressed in on every side. Eilan pulled back, stepping on a strange woman's dress, and hearing it rip.

"Watch where you are stepping!" the stranger said peevishly. Eilan apologized, trying to make herself smaller, and at that moment the bear surged forward again, his leading rope coming loose as someone cried out in alarm. The whole crowd pressed backward and when Eilan recovered her balance Miellyn and Senara had disappeared in the crushing crowd.

It was the first time in years that Eilan had been alone. She had grown accustomed to the constant chaperonage of the Forest House. Now it occurred to her that the supervision had another purpose than propriety; the presence of her sisters had helped to keep people away both physically and psychically. Alone, the tumult of alien thoughts and emotions buffeted her like a strong wind. She tried to draw strength from the earth for protection, but the strange faces surrounding her filled her with confusion. How did Lhiannon stand walking among the people when she was already half-tranced and opened to the power of the gods? So hemmed in by the crowd and the press of strangers was she that she could see nothing familiar; not even the avenue of trees that led towards the Forest House, nor the mound from which they gave the Oracles.

Once she glimpsed through the crowd what looked like a familiar blue gown; but when she neared it, it was the cloak of a complete stranger. Another time she thought she spotted a group of priestesses; but there were four of them, and by the time it occurred to her that her companions could have met with some others from the Forest House and that they could all be looking for her they had disappeared in the press of strangers again. The temporary landscape of the fair seemed as strange to her as the Otherworld. *This is ridiculous – shielding myself from other people's emotions was the first thing they taught us! I should simply ask someone*, she kept telling herself, but vulnerable as she was, she dared not speak to a stranger; for what would they think of a priestess who could not find the way back to her own dwelling place?

She moved through the crowds, trying to hold reasonless terror at bay. If she could just restore her defenses, she would ask someone in which direction the Forest House lay. Some day, no doubt, she would look back on this day with amusement, as an adventure. Only at the moment there could be no doubt that she was both lost and terrified.

A sudden movement of the crowd swept her almost off her feet; she lost her balance and collided with a man in a dark cloak. He murmured something, then started. "Eilan! Is it really you?" Strong hands seized her elbows and a familiar voice demanded, "Where did you come from?"

And Eilan looked up into the one face which of all the faces in the world she had least expected to see; the face of Gaius Macellius.

Wordless, she clung to him. He felt her trembling and pulled her closer. Abruptly the confusion around her was stilled by the circle of his arms.

"Eilan –" he repeated. "I did not dare dream I would find you here!"

But I did, thought Eilan dimly. *When I woke this morning my first thought was that you were near; why did I not trust it?*

His arms tightened around her; and in that moment she forgot all of Caillean's words of warning, all her own misgivings and fears. She knew only that she was happy.

She laughed a little shakily. "I'm afraid I lost myself; I was trying to return to the Forest House, or at least to the other priestesses who came to the festival, but I was not sure which way to go."

"The road is over there," he began, and then at her involuntary movement, broke out, "Must you really go back at once? I came to this – this part of the world, only in the hope of seeing you –"

She could hear, as clearly as if he had spoken, *I cannot bear to let her go now!*

"If you go we may never meet again," he burst out, his voice shaking as he spoke. "I think I could not bear it, to lose you again. Eilan . . ." His lips hesitated on the sound of her name like a caress; she felt it like a wash of cool fire across her skin. "You cannot leave me . . ." he murmured into her veil. "It is Fate that has brought you here, alone . . ."

Not precisely alone! she thought, smiling at the surging crowds around them. But it was true; only Fate, or the Goddess, could have brought her here, to his arms. Deliberately she set aside the training that had required a sworn priestess in the company of a man who was neither father, grandsire of brother to keep her eyes modestly cast down, and looked at him.

And what had she thought she would see? What could her eyes tell her, she wondered, seeing how strongly his hair still curled off his forehead, the stubborn jut of the jaw beneath the short beard he had grown on his last campaign, and the naked need in his dark eyes, that her heart did not already know? The inner and outer vision came abruptly together, and she saw at once the pinched face of the boy she had nursed four years ago, the strong features of the man he was becoming, and something else, a face battered by experience and discontent, its young promise being eroded by the years.

My poor love – she thought, *is that what you will be?*

"Must you really go?" he repeated, and she murmured "No."

Gaius swallowed, and lifted her veil back from her forehead. She felt him stiffen then, and realized that he had noticed for the first time the blue crescent drawn between her brows.

"I am a priestess," she said quietly and felt him flinch in understanding. But he did not let her go, and she did not pull away.

The very thought that she might not see him again was beginning to take the light from the sky. No doubt Caillean would have told her to leave him at once; but for once she would not do what the older priestess thought wiser, but what she wanted to do. And whatever came of it, this time, at least, Caillean could not be punished for it.

Two drovers blundered into them and backed away, eyeing them oddly as they caught sight of Eilan's blue robes. Gaius frowned and wrapped his brown cloak around her, pulling her veil back up to hide her bright hair.

"Let's get you out of this crowd, anyway," he muttered. His arm was still around her, strong and steadying, and as they walked on, neither knew quite where they were going, only that they were together, and it was away from the crowds.

"Tell me how came you here? I had no notion that you were in this part of the world."

"I think I came to see you," he began, and Eilan leaned against him, listening.

"It was Fate, or perhaps my father. At least I was heading the opposite way to where he wanted me to go! Is little Valeria well?"

"Senara – so we call her in the House of Maidens. Indeed, she is perfectly well and happy."

"I am glad to hear it," he answered, but she could tell that already Senara was forgotten. "Cynric is proscribed, did you know?" Gaius said then., "I met him before he left, and he told me to stay away from you . . ."

His voice faltered. What did he want to hear from her? wondered Eilan. Maybe only the sound of her voice, to know she was thinking of him. Couldn't he tell? She was aware of him with every sense in her body, every inch of her skin.

"Maybe he's right. My father has taken it into his head that I should marry some Roman girl, the Procurator's daughter in Londinium –"

"Will you obey him?" Eilan asked carefully, her blood pounding. Marriage! Why had he told her? She knew it changed nothing, but why should the thought give her such pain?

Somehow they had reached the edge of the fairgrounds. Another step would hide them in the shelter of the hazel trees. Last night, men and girls had wandered these woods to gather greenery and flowers and to lie with each other on the new grass. The forest still remembered; Eilan could feel the memory of their passion like an echo around her, conflicting with the tumult of the fair.

He turned to face her. "You know I will never marry anyone but you!"

"I cannot marry," she answered him. "My life is sworn to the gods . . ."

"Then I will never marry anyone," he said firmly.

But you will . . . Even as the irrational burst of happiness surged through her, foreknowledge tolled in Eilan's awareness. An image flickered in her mind of the woman who would be his wife. And why should Eilan resent her? Was she so selfish that she would wish Gaius to be alone for ever? Or had she wanted him to carry her away, to move heaven and earth to have her released from her vows? What words of men could erase the crescent set between her brows?

She stumbled over a tree root, and Gaius reached out to steady her. Blinking, she realized that they had entered the forest. The noise of the crowds was suddenly faint with distance, as if they had traveled miles away, as if they had stepped into the Otherworld. Great trees hid them in a leaf-dappled shadow. The sun had gone behind a cloud and a chill wind was beginning to blow. Was it going to rain? As if in answer, a few drops blew down on them, the beginnings of rain or perhaps moisture from the upper leaves.

"Eilan . . ." he whispered, and his grip tightened. "Please – Eilan!"

Turning, she felt the force of his need for her, and the world seemed to stop. From the moment the crowd had swept her away from Miellyn until now, thought Eilan, she had wandered in a dream. But she was awake now, and she could see both past and future with a terrible clarity. Perhaps Fate had brought them here, but what she decided at this moment would determine his future and her own – and perhaps other lives as well. Awareness pulsed outward, embracing other times in an ever-widening circle until she saw once more the bright-haired warrior who had been in her vision, with the Dragons on his wrists and the eagle-look she had learned to love in Gaius in his eyes.

Now it was he who was trembling. With clumsy fingers Gaius put back her veil and his hand, falling, brushed her cheek, for a moment clung there, and then, as if an irresistible force had drawn it downward, slipped along the softness of her neck and came to rest upon the swell of her breast beneath the opening of her gown. The turf stretched soft and green before them. She heard, like an echo, "*The Goddess is not worshiped in a temple made by human hands . . .*"

But it was forbidden – not six months ago she had sworn to give her virginity only to the Sacred King. And like an answer, the certainty came to her. *From this man of two bloods shall spring the King who is to be . . .* For this, the Merlin had initiated her. This was her destiny.

When they first met, she must have seemed to Gaius a child, but she knew herself immeasurably older now. Like an echo, the voice of the Merlin came to her:

"*A priestess of the Goddess gives herself at her own time and season, and when the power has passed through her resumes her sovereignty.*"

"By the rites of men we cannot be married," she said softly. "Are you willing to take me as your wife in the old way, as the priestesses mated with the men of the royal kindred, before the gods?"

He groaned as his hand curved around her breast, and she felt her nipple hardening against his palm. "Till death and after, by Mithras and the Mother," he muttered. "Eilan, oh, Eilan!"

When the Merlin touched her, the fire had flared from the crown of her head to her heels; but this flame seemed to rise upward from the earth, burning all other thoughts away.

She touched his face and he reached for her. A clumsy hand tangled in her hair and her veil fell unheeded to the ground. Then his lips claimed hers, no longer gentle but demanding, like a starving man. For a moment surprise held her still in his grasp; then she became aware of an answering hunger, and her lips opened, welcoming him.

As they kissed her arms went around his neck; her hair, released from its careful coils, tumbled down her back as hairpins scattered across the grass. Gaius groaned and pulled her against him. Now she could feel the hard strength of his body, and his need. His hands moved from her shoulders down her back, molding her body to his.

Eilan felt the strength going out of her knees. She clung to him, and her weight drew them both downward to the green grass. His lips moved to her cheek, her eyelids, and the soft skin of her neck as if he would devour her, and she arched against him, trembling. Her skirts had ridden upwards as they fell; his exploring hand moved down her body, paused a moment as he touched soft skin, and then brushed upward again beneath the cloth until it came to rest in the sacred place between her thighs.

Gaius grew suddenly still, breathing hard. Then he pulled away, his eyes wide and dazed, as if they had looked into too much light.

"Lady," he whispered. She could see the tremors shaking him, but somehow he was finding the control to act deliberately, dealing with their clothing, worshiping her body with an authority that grew until the light filled him also and she realized that he was not entirely Gaius any more.

"My King!" she whispered as the flame he had kindled seared along every nerve. "Come to me!"

He sighed then, sinking into her embrace as the sun into the sea, yielding to her even as she gave herself to him. In the distance she could hear shouting, as if it came from another world, and knew that the priests had lit the Beltane fires.

But a greater fire was blazing within her, and by that time, even if Caillean and all the women in the Forest House had been standing in a row watching them, Eilan would neither have known nor cared.

The day was far advanced and the sun was setting when Gaius finally stirred. Eilan drew reluctantly away from him; he reached for her once more and kissed her hard.

"I must return to the Forest House," she said very gently. "They will be looking for me." Indeed, Miellyn would be beside herself with worry. But if Eilan could manage somehow to get back into the enclosure unseen, they might believe that the crowds had kept them apart and she had somehow found her way back alone.

Even now, when passion had ebbed and she could think clearly once more, Eilan did not regret breaking her vows; the Goddess had known and had not intervened, proof enough that she had served a higher law. Part of the secret doctrine that Caillean had revealed in the months since Eilan's initiation was that before the coming of the Romans, the priestesses had taken lovers as they chose, or even married. It was only since the coming of the Romans that men had had the arrogance to control the private lives of their women. Caillean had never met the man who would tempt her to break her vows, but perhaps she would understand. On the other hand, Caillean would not agree with Eilan's choice of a lover, so perhaps she had better not tell the older priestess after all.

"Eilan, don't go back." Gaius raised himself on one elbow to look down at her. "I am afraid for you."

"I am the Arch-Druid's granddaughter; what do you suppose they would do to me?" she replied.

Her father had once said he would kill her with his own hands if she allowed what Gaius had just done, but this was not the moment to mention that. She was a woman now, and a priestess sworn, accountable only to her sisters and the gods.

"If I were there to protect you, it wouldn't matter what they tried," he said darkly.

"And would I be so safe if we ran away? Where could we go? The wild tribes of the North might accept me, but you would be in danger, and where else could we run beyond the reach of Rome? You are a soldier, Gaius, as bound by oaths as I. I broke one vow to fulfill a greater one, but that does not release me. I still belong to the Goddess, and must trust her to take care of me . . ."

"That's more than I can do –" he said then, rubbing his eyes.

"Nonsense. If you go back on active service you will certainly be in greater danger than I." Eilan clung to him once more at the thought of cold iron piercing the heart that now beat against her own, and as he kissed her again, all thoughts of the future were forgotten. For a little while.

fifteen

———〜〜〜———

Lying with a man had not, despite the whispered speculations Eilan remembered from the House of Maidens, destroyed her magic. At least the shielding spell she murmured as she eased through the kitchen gate and along the path to the Hall of the Priestesses appeared to prevent the few people who were about from noticing her as she passed.

In her own room she slid out of her gown and washed herself, hiding her stained shift until she should have time to soak the smear of maiden blood away. That done, she put on her night-garment and built up the fire, realizing that she was half frozen with cold, and famished. It was past the hour of the sunset meal. She ought to go to the kitchens and find herself something to eat; but she needed time to think about what had happened to her and Gaius. Or perhaps, she thought with unaccustomed self-mockery, she simply wished to close her eyes and relive their lovemaking again.

She might have expected that Gaius would be eager, but not that he would be so tender, holding back until he quivered like a drawn bow lest he go too fast and hurt her. But virgin though her body might be, the pleasure that pulsed through her had more than matched his. And in the final moments, when the ecstasy became almost too great for mortal endurance, it had seemed to her that once more it was the Goddess who encompassed her and received the gift of the God.

She sighed, noting the unaccustomed soreness and the sweet lassitude that weighted her limbs. *Will the Goddess strike me dead for breaking my oath*, she wondered, *or will my punishment be to weep in the night, remembering what I will never have again? Isn't that better than never having known it at all?* She pitied Caillean, scarred since childhood from her only experience of what men call love.

189

As day followed day, a certain equilibrium began to assert itself. Eilan attended Lhiannon at the rite of the full moon, and no lightning struck. The advanced training that followed initiation continued, both in skills and in lore, and as the days grew longer, they met with the older priestesses when weather permitted in one of the gardens or in the holy grove.

There were thirteen sacred oak trees, twelve in a circle, and the oldest, in the center, shading the stone altar. To Eilan, looking up at them, it seemed that even in the drowsy warmth of afternoon the trees still held something of the magic with which the moon had vested them a few nights before. Caillean's voice receded to a background murmur as Eilan gazed upward. Surely the light that glowed in their leaves was more than sunshine. All her senses seemed heightened since Beltane.

The voice of the priestess came into focus again. "In the old days there was a sisterhood of nine high priestesses, one for each region of this land. They stood behind the queen of each tribe, advising and supporting her."

Eilan sat back against the sturdy trunk of the oak tree, linking into its steady strength, and tried to keep her eyes open.

"They were not queens themselves?" Dieda asked.

"Their role was a less public one, though they were often of the royal line. But they were the initiators of kings, for when a king came to his hallowing, it was the priestess who became the channel by which the Goddess accepted his service, conferring a power that he in turn passed on to his queen."

"They were not virgins," Miellyn said sourly, and Eilan found herself suddenly wide awake, remembering the Merlin's words. Had she been the Goddess for Gaius? What then was his destiny?

"The priestesses lay with men when the service of the Lady required it," responded Caillean in a neutral tone. "But they did not marry, and they bore children only when it was the only way to preserve a royal line. They remained free."

"In the Forest House we do not marry, but I would not call us free," Dieda observed, frowning. "Even though the Priestess of the Oracle chooses her successor, the Council of Druids must approve her choice."

"Why did things change?" Eilan asked, need adding intensity to her tone. "Was it because of Mona?"

"The Druids say that our present seclusion is for our own protection," Caillean answered with the same careful neutrality.

"They say that only if we remain pure as Vestals will we be respected by Rome."

Eilan stared at her. *Then what I did with Gaius was not flouting the Law of the Lady, but only the Druids' rules!*

"But will we always have to live like this?" Miellyn asked wistfully. "Is there no place where we can speak the truth and serve the Goddess without interference from men?"

Caillean's eyes closed. For a moment it seemed to Eilan that the very trees stilled, waiting to hear what the priestess would say.

"Only in a place outside time . . ." Caillean whispered. "Protected by a mist of magic from the world." And for a moment then Eilan seemed to see what the older woman was seeing – mist drifting like a veil across the silver waters, and white swans singing as they took the air.

Then Caillean started and opened her eyes, staring in confusion around her, and through the trees they heard the gong summoning them to the evening meal.

For a time Eilan's anxieties were eased, but as the days lengthened towards Midsummer, she began to guess why the Goddess had not stricken her at once. At first, when the usual time came to seclude herself for purification according to the customs of the Forest House and there was no bloodsign, she was unconcerned; she had never been regular. But when the second month had come and gone, she became certain that the fertile magic of Beltane had worked on her only too well.

Her first, instinctive joy soon yielded to terror. What would Bendeigid say? Or do? She wept then, wishing that she could go back in time and seek the comfort of her mother's arms. Then, as the days went by, she wondered if instead of pregnancy some serious illness had seized upon her as punishment for her sacrilege.

All her life she had been healthy and strong, but now she grew sick whenever she tried to eat or drink; shudders racked her every day and she had no appetite for her food. She longed for harvest and thought wistfully of its fruits, as if they would not make her so sick. About all she could swallow without retching was the thinnest and sourest of buttermilk. Surely her sister Mairi's pregnancies had not tormented her this way, so this could hardly be an early symptom. Even the waters of the Sacred Well, when the priestesses gathered on the longest day to drink of them and see the future, racked her with icy shudders.

From time to time she sensed Caillean watching her, but the older woman was sick too; Eilan, who was perhaps closer to her than any other, did not know what ailed her. When asked, Caillean said that her moon cycle was troubled, but the older woman's ill-health only filled Eilan with greater fear. Surely Caillean could not be pregnant! Eilan wondered sometimes if her sin had cursed the whole Forest House, if her illness would spread first to Caillean, and presently kill them all. She dared not ask.

Caillean plucked a few thyme leaves from the bed Latis had growing in the inner court and rubbed them between her fingers, breathing deeply as the sweet scent hung in the moist morning air. Thyme was good for headaches, and perhaps it would clear hers. Today, at least, her womb had ceased the painful intermittent bleeding that had plagued her all summer, and perhaps this contact with the earth could ease the nagging sense of dread that had haunted her as well.

From the privies on the other side of the wall she could hear someone retching. She waited, wondering who had been awakened at such an early hour. Presently she glimpsed a figure in a white shift slipping through the archway as if she feared to be seen. For the first time in weeks Caillean's inner senses awakened and she knew who it must be, and with a sudden certainty, what was wrong with her.

"Eilan, come here!" It was the priestess-voice of command, and the girl was too well trained not to obey. With lagging footsteps, Eilan returned, and Caillean noted the pinched cheeks and the new fullness in the girl's breasts. Her own troubles must have been more distracting than she realized, she thought bitterly.

"How long have you been this way? Since Beltane?" she asked. Eilan stared at her, her face contorting. "My poor child!" Caillean held out her arms and suddenly Eilan was clinging to her and sobbing.

"Oh, Caillean, Caillean! I thought I was ill . . . I thought I was going to die!"

Caillean stroked her hair. "Have you had your courses during this time?" Eilan shook her head. "Then it is life, not death, you are carrying," she said, and felt the betraying release of tension in the thin body beneath her hands.

Her own eyes filled with tears. This was a dreadful thing, certainly, and yet she could not help feeling a desperate envy, remembering how her own body was betraying her now and not knowing if what had come to her was only the end of the fertility she had never used or the end of her life indeed.

"Who has done this to you, my darling?" she murmured into the girl's soft hair. "No wonder you have been so quiet. Why didn't you tell me? You cannot have thought I would not understand!"

Eilan looked up with red-rimmed eyes, and Caillean remembered that this girl did not lie. "It was not rape –"

Caillean sighed. "Then I suppose it was that Roman boy." It was not a question and Eilan nodded mutely. Caillean sighed again and looked off into space. "Poor child," she said at last. "If I had known at once, something might have been contrived, but you are three months along. We will have to tell Lhiannon, you know."

"What will she do to me?" Eilan quavered.

"I don't know," Caillean said. "Nothing very much, I imagine." There was an ancient law that demanded death for a priestess who broke her vows, but surely they would never apply that to Eilan. "Probably you will only be sent away – you were prepared for that, I suppose. But I am sure that is the worst," she added.

And if they try to punish her more harshly, thought Caillean with a spurt of her old energy, *they will have to reckon with me!*

"You wretch, you dirty little animal!" cried Lhiannon. A sudden purple suffused the High Priestess's cheeks and Eilan recoiled. "Who did this to you?"

Eilan shook her head, her eyes burning.

"You did this on purpose – you did not scream? Traitor! Did you mean to shame us all, or did you simply not think? Rutting like an animal in heat, after all our care for you –" Lhiannon sucked in breath, gasping horribly.

Caillean had suspected there would be a scene when the High Priestess was told, but it was worse than she expected. Lhiannon's health and temper had become increasingly precarious, and Caillean could see this was one of her bad days. But by then it was too late. Suddenly she slapped the girl, shouting, "Do you think this was a holy passion? You are no better than a whore!

"Lhiannon –" Caillean got an arm around the old woman's shoulders and felt some of the tension ease. "This is not good for you. Calm yourself, Mother; let me get you some tea." She passed her hand across the older woman's brow and Lhiannon sagged in her arms. One-handed, Caillean poured tea from the flask into a beaker and held it to Lhiannon's lips. A minty fragrance spread through the room. The High Priestess drank, then let out her breath in a long, shuddering sigh.

Eilan still stood numb and tearless before her. It had taken all her strength to come here. What happened next was in the lap of the gods, and at this moment, still appalled by Lhiannon's fury, she obviously found it hard to care. When Lhiannon roused, she seemed to have forgotten her fury.

"Sit down!" she said querulously. "It hurts my neck to look up at you."

Caillean pointed to a three-legged stool, and Eilan, still hot-eyed and resentful, complied.

"Very well," Lhiannon said in something closer to her normal tone. "Now what's to be done? I'm sorry I slapped you, but this upsets plans . . ." She stopped, frowning. "Well, we must manage something. I suppose we had better tell Ardanos."

"For the life of me I cannot see what he has to do with it," said Caillean. *Unless*, she thought, *it is his plans that have been upset by Eilan's disgrace!* "It's not as if she were the first to kindle from the Beltane fires, nor will she be the last, I am sure. It would be easier if Eilan were any other man's daughter. But Ardanos and Bendeigid will just have to live with it! Surely the fate of a priestess of Vernemeton is our own affair. Do you mean to say we cannot find the right thing to do?"

"I did not say that," Lhiannon answered fretfully, "but Ardanos should be told."

"Why? What law requires it except the Roman law which makes women no more than chattels of their menfolk?" Caillean grew angry. "Do you really have such respect for his wisdom?"

Lhiannon passed her hand over her eyes. "Why must your voice be so sharp, Caillean? You will give me a headache. You must know by now that it is not a question of wisdom but of power. By the treaty that protects this place, everything to do with the Forest House is in his charge."

"Yes, more's the pity," said Caillean bitterly. "Tell me, who appointed him to be the god?"

Lhiannon rubbed her left arm as if it pained her. "In any case he is one of Eilan's few surviving kinsmen, and it is only right to tell him," she said tiredly.

Caillean felt an unwilling pang of pity. Obviously Lhiannon was only too eager to unload the problem on to someone else's shoulders. In view of her poor health, perhaps this was not altogether surprising.

Eilan was still silent, as if this confession had taken all her strength. Her gaze was turned inward, as if what they said had nothing at all to do with her, or she no longer cared.

Say something, child! Caillean glared at her. *This is your fate we are deciding!* Caillean knew that Ardanos could not do anything to *her*; he had tried, but Lhiannon was fond of her fosterling, and they had come to a certain accommodation by carefully pretending that Caillean did not exist. She, for her part, tried to avoid attracting his attention, or opposing him; but for Eilan's sake she felt she would even try to face the old Druid down.

"Very well then, send for Ardanos," she said aloud. "But think twice before you put her into his power."

"Well?" Ardanos frowned at the three women who awaited him in the High Priestess's dwelling. "What has happened that is so important that you had to send for me?" Lhiannon looked fragile and tired, and Caillean loomed like a shadow behind her. Was it her health? he wondered with a sudden stab of alarm as he noticed Eilan sitting beside the window. Had they sent for him because the High Priestess was dying? She did not look that ill, and surely they would not have already told Eilan . . .

"Be clear about this," said Caillean clearly. "I did not send for you. And if it were my dying breath I would still deny that you have authority over the priestesses."

"Woman!" Ardanos thundered. "What –?"

"And don't you say 'Woman!' to me in that tone, as if they had nothing to do with you, as if your own mother had not been one," Caillean retorted furiously. "Men who do not fear the Goddess – who are they to speak for Her?"

Ardanos grimaced and turned back to Lhiannon. "Well, you had better tell me what all this is about," he said, none too gently. "It is for sure that I will not hear it from Caillean."

This was not a good time for him to leave Deva, he thought in irritation. With the Governor away fighting in Caledonia, some of the local officials had begun to presume on their powers. He needed to be back where his agents could keep him informed, and if necessary he could use his contacts among the Romans to prevent trouble.

Lhiannon made an odd strangled sound, coughed, and tried

again. "Eilan is pregnant by the Prefect's son, and we do not know what to do."

Ardanos looked at her in amazement, then his gaze traveled to Eilan. "Is this true?"

Eilan said in a low voice, "I always tell the truth."

"Aye," grunted Ardanos, his mind whirling with calculation. "I'll give you that; you're no liar, girl."

She looked as if she would much rather have told him nothing at all. Caillean moved to her side and took her hand protectively. He felt the anger rising. *Do these silly hens have any idea how devastating this could be?* The very survival of the Forest House depended on maintaining the myth of their purity! They must be made to understand!

"Why do you ask me?" His words rang with all the power of bardic training. "You know the penalty as well as I. It is death for a sworn priestess to lie with any man except the Sacred King."

Death. The word made a silence, even in the quiet of the room. Then Lhiannon moaned and Caillean moved quickly to catch her in her arms.

"You cruel, heartless old man!" she burst out. "And to think it is she who insisted on laying this before you!" She held the older woman against her, feeling for the pulse point at the neck. "Goddess! Her heart is leaping like a frightened horse! But you have not quite killed her, not this time." She straightened as Lhiannon moaned and stirred. "You know her heart is weak. Would you like to try again?"

Ardanos bent over her. He said quietly, "She has only fainted; she will recover." He felt more shaken than he had expected. "I did not know that it would upset her so."

He helped Caillean to lift the old woman, surprised at how light she was beneath the robes, and lay her on the bed, raised a little on pillows so that she could breathe. Caillean poured a few drops of some potion into a cup of water and set it to the High Priestess's lips. Ardanos saw the muscles of Lhiannon's throat constrict as she swallowed, and after a few moments her eyelids fluttered open once more.

Her eyes are still beautiful, Ardanos thought in surprise, *even now, when they are clouded by pain.* He would grieve when death took her, but that knowledge could not be allowed to interfere with what he had to do.

"Not death," she whispered. "Is there no other way?"

Ardanos glanced at Eilan, who sat huddled on her bench with her knuckles against her lips, staring at Lhiannon.

"I would say the same if it were my own daughter, Dieda. I thought at first that it was she –"

"Dieda doesn't matter –" Lhiannon said more strongly. "We cannot let them hurt Eilan!"

"Of course not," Caillean said soothingly. "Ardanos knows as well as you or I, that this penalty has never been exacted. After all, it is not as if this were an unknown thing."

"Well," Ardanos asked carefully, "what do you suggest we do?" It gave him a perverse satisfaction to see Caillean so subdued. Perhaps she would be less troublesome now.

"Miellyn's child was fathered by the Year-King, and in any case she miscarried, so the problem did not arise. But five or six years ago there was a case of this kind and the girl was quietly sent away."

"That is true," said Ardanos. "But the girl in question was not the daughter of an important Druid –"

"Nor the granddaughter of one," snapped Caillean. "So now we come to it; you are afraid that it will reflect upon you!"

"Be quiet, Caillean," said Lhiannon. "How can you sit here wrangling with Ardanos while this poor child" – she glanced over at Eilan – "is listening, not knowing whether she is to live or die."

Ardanos looked at his granddaughter; he could read nothing from her expression. Was she being stubborn or did she really not care? He shook his head in exasperation. The work they had done here must not be jeopardized by one silly girl. "Is this known among the others?" he asked, and Caillean shook her head. "Take care to keep it that way, and perhaps we can find a way –"

"Oh, that's kindness!" said Caillean sarcastically, "to do for your own granddaughter as much as you would for a stranger . . ."

"Be quiet, child," Lhiannon repeated tiredly. "You should not speak so to the Arch-Druid. He is trying, I am sure, to do the best he can for Eilan – and for us all."

Caillean looked skeptical, but she held her peace.

"In any case, you are not the only ones concerned here," Ardanos said grimly. The rape of a holy priestess, for that was what he would call it, whatever Eilan might say, was a torch that could set the whole of Britain aflame. He drew his cloak around him and looked down at them. There was one Roman, at least, who should be as anxious to see this handled discreetly as he. "I will go to Deva and speak with Macellius; maybe I will see the young Roman as well."

During the next month, Eilan's sickness subsided and during much of the time she felt as well as ever. Her loose robes concealed the changes in her breasts, and with a first child it would be some time yet before any rounding was visible in her belly.

She wondered what Gaius had said when he learned of her pregnancy. She was not sorry that she had lain with him, but she saw now the power of the forces arrayed against her, and it seemed to her that she had been a fool to think that things might change. Her visions of being a great priestess in the old way were dimming. Now she wanted only to be the mother of Gaius's child. But even then, despite Ardanos's parting words, she did not dare to believe that they would let her marry him.

At least Caillean and Lhiannon did not seem to believe that her condition disqualified her from participating in the rituals. Most of the time she spent memorizing the full-moon ceremony along with the other sworn priestesses.

It had become a point of pride with her to prove that her loss of virginity had not affected her ability to function as a priestess, so she set herself to memorize the minutiae of the rituals. Of them all, Dieda was her closest match in intelligence. When they were children they had worked to produce the best spun wool or the neatest embroidery and win Rheis's praise. In those days Eilan had pitied her kinswoman because Dieda's mother had died whereas she herself had always had a mother's loving care and had drawn back from competition. Dieda needed to be first; Eilan did not. But now she had a reason to excel.

Eilan had a good mind and, put on her mettle by Dieda, she used it to the utmost. Dieda's memory was more precise, and of course no one could match her singing; but, of the two, Eilan often proved to have the better understanding.

As Lhiannon spoke to them, Eilan found herself hanging on every word. The High Priestess had grown so frail that she found it hard to remember that Lhiannon was only in her sixties now.

Eilan wondered sometimes who would succeed her. It ought to be Caillean, but the Irishwoman had said the priests would never accept her. Miellyn was too outspoken, and bitter since the loss of her child, and Eilidh too retiring. It might be Dieda, she thought then, and wondered what it would be like to live here under her kinswoman's rule.

By the time the moon was at the full once more, Lhiannon seemed much better, but as the ritual progressed, they could hear her voice grow fainter. She completed the ceremony, but it was clear to all of them how much it had cost her. On the following day she collapsed, and this time, when she was put to bed, she could not find the strength to leave it again.

sixteen

~~~~~~~~

Ardanos might have found a certain satisfaction in telling Macellius Severus what his son had done, but, whatever he hoped for, in the Perfect he had met his equal. Macellius heard him out with great courtesy and then informed him quietly that Gaius had gone to Londinium to be married. And as soon as the Arch-Druid had gone away, he set about making it so.

Macellius had no doubt that Ardanos was telling him the truth. The only surprise was how he could have deluded himself about his son's passion. There was a stubborn streak in the boy that came from him, and a romantic streak that was his legacy from his mother. Macellius rubbed at his eyes. Moruadh had braved the displeasure of all her relations to marry him. He should not have underestimated the force of that wild, Celtic blood.

With so unruly a horse or slave he would have known to take sterner measures. Perhaps it was harder for him to discipline Gaius because so often he saw Moruadh looking out of her son's eyes. But marriage to a good Roman girl would settle the lad. As the Druid's footsteps receded along the tiled corridor, Macellius called for his secretary.

The sight of his employer's stormy face stopped young Valerius from making any of his customary jokes. He saluted smartly, and went in search of Gaius. He found him in the library, reading the account of Caesar's Gallic wars.

"I'll go at once." Gaius put down the scroll. "Do you have any idea what my father wants?"

"No. None. But I think he's angry," Valerius warned. "He had a visit this morning from the old Druid, Ardanos, and he came out looking like thunder, master Gaius."

"Oh? I wonder what the old fellow wanted?" Gaius asked,

feeling a tiny shiver begin to work its way up his spine. Ardanos had been in and out of the place since he was a child about some native problem or other. People were always turning up with requests, legitimate and otherwise, and when they proved too unreasonable, it was likely to put his father out of temper. There was no reason for this summons to have anything to do with Ardanos being Eilan's grandfather, but as he strode down the tiled corridor, he could not help worrying.

The elder Severus was holding a set of military orders. "You are to set out for Londinium at once," he barked out.

Gaius looked at him, startled. He opened his mouth to ask why, and realized that his father was in a towering rage.

"I told you to leave that girl alone!"

Comprehension began to dawn. Ardanos must have told the Prefect that he had been with Eilan. Had someone seen them? Surely Eilan had told no one. Gaius would have been happy to proclaim his love from the housetops; it was she who had insisted on secrecy.

"With respect, sir, I don't think —"

"No, you don't think. That's half the trouble," Macellius snarled. "I suppose you do know that you could hardly have done anything worse if you had hunted all over Britain, unless you had raped their High Priestess in broad daylight on their High Altar, or cut down their Sacred Oak. Do you want to get us all massacred?"

Macellius did not wait for an answer. "The folk around here need no excuse for rioting. No, not a word," he said with a peremptory gesture as Gaius would have spoken, "I trusted once to your word — and never again. I don't think for a moment that you raped the girl, but I can believe, all too easily, that you got her pregnant. I have no doubt whatever she's a very good girl in her own way, and that she deserves better of you than this. A sworn virgin, and the Arch-Druid's granddaughter!"

Gaius's mouth slowly closed again. Eilan pregnant! Eilan, carrying his child! He remembered the sweetness of her mouth and the softness of her body beneath him and swallowed, scarcely hearing his father's next words.

"I will not soon forgive you for putting me in a position where we cannot even make honorable amends, but, as things are now around here, I cannot even order you to marry her."

"But I want to —" Gaius began.

Macellius shook his head. "The South would explode as it did twenty years ago if the people heard of it, a fact of which the old man is very well aware. He's already wrung a concession on the levies out of me, and I daresay it won't end there. But at least he shall not use you against me. I have told Ardanos you were in Londinium, and that, my lad, is where you shall go. I'll give you a letter to Licinius, and with luck not see you again until you are properly married."

Gaius heard him in disbelief. "Married? But that's impossible!"

"We'll see about that," snapped his father. "Can you think of any other way to undo your folly? Ardanos has promised they won't hurt the girl, provided you stay away from her, and I can't think of any better way to make certain you never go near her again. You know that Licinius and I have talked of this, and dowry and settlements will be no problem. If she will still have you after this, you will marry that girl."

Gaius shook his head, trying to find words to protest, and his father glared at him.

"You will." he commanded softly but with so much concealed anger that Gaius did not dare protest. "I've gone to too much trouble to save you from your own folly to let you destroy yourself now. You set out in half an hour." His father scribbled his signature on a roll of papyrus and looked up at Gaius. "If you refuse I don't know what they'll do to the girl. You might try thinking of her for a change."

Gaius stared at him, trying to remember the Roman penalty for a Vestal who broke her vows; as he recalled, they buried them alive. He realized abruptly that nothing he could say would be taken as anything but self-defense. Indeed, he could endanger Eilan's life. Fear for her dried up the words in his throat.

Macellius rolled up the letter, sealed it, and handed it to his son. "Take this to Licinius," he instructed. "My orderly Capellus will go with you," he added. "I have already sent word to him to pack your things."

Within the hour, Gaius found himself on the road to Londinium with the massive figure of old Capellus at his side. All his attempts to begin a conversation were politely, but firmly rebuffed. When, almost desperate, he offered the man a bribe – he had to stop, to get word somehow to Eilan – the big man only snorted.

"No offense, sir, but your father told me you'd probably try that, and he paid me well to see you didn't go nowhere but directly to Londinium. And I works for your father and I don't want to be out of a job, see? So you relax sir, and do like the Prefect says. When you think it over, sir, it'll all be for the best, see?"

The journey to Londinium took the best part of six days. By the third day Gaius's natural optimism had begun to reassert itself, and he watched with increasing interest the neat villas that were springing up across the land. He could see now how untamed the West Country was still. But this ordered landscape was what the Empire was meant to be. He admired it, but he was not sure he liked it.

It was nearing dark when they passed the city gates and drew up in front of the Procurator's mansion, set between the Forum, where the treasury offices were located, and the new palace that Agricola was building, with its ornamental pools. He had been to Londinium several times as a child, and when he assumed the toga and officially became a man, but never since Agricola had become governor there.

The city had a gracious glow in the summer dusk, and a cool wind off the river dispelled the mugginess of the day. The scars of Boudicca's burning were mostly hidden now, and the Governor's building plans suggested the noble proportions of the city that would one day be. Of course it would never rival Rome, but in comparison to Deva it was a metropolis.

Gaius handed his letter to an imposing freedman at the portico and was bidden to enter and take a seat in the central courtyard. Here it was still warm, and fragrant with shrubs and flowers set round in pots. From the fountain came a tinkle of falling water and, somewhere in the rooms beyond the courtyard the music of a young girl's laughter. After a time an old gardener came out and began to cut flowers, probably for the table, but he knew, or feigned to know, none of the languages in which Gaius addressed him. For a time Gaius wandered about, glad to stretch his legs after the long day in the saddle. Presently he took a seat on a stone bench, all the fatigue of the journey overtook him, and he fell asleep.

Somehow the sound of a girl's laughter wove itself into his dream . . . Gaius started awake, staring about him, but there was no one to be seen except a heavy-set, middle-aged man on crutches, draped in a formal toga. Gaius sprang to his feet, flushing with embarrassment.

"Gaius Macellius Severus?"

"Yes, sir —"

"I should have known it." The old man smiled, "My name is Licinius, and your father and I have been friends most of our lives. It is a real pleasure to welcome his son. Is your father well?"

"He was when I last saw him a few days ago, sir."

"Good. Good. Well, young man, I had of course hoped he could get away to pay me a visit, but you are most heartily welcome in his stead. Given our arrangement, you can imagine that I've been eager to meet you."

Gaius had been telling himself all the way from Deva that he would not be hurried into any such ill-considered wedding, but he could not burst out into protest before the eyes of his father's old friend. He had agreed to this because of the danger to Eilan and knew he ought to be grateful Licinius was so kindly.

"Yes, sir," he said, temporizing. "Father did say something of this . . ."

"Well, I should hope so," Licinius said gruffly. "As I say, we've had it in our minds since you were born. By Mithras, boy, if Macellius had said nothing of this, I'd have wondered what he was using for a head these days." Despite its gruffness, this was the first wholly friendly voice Gaius had heard for a good many days, and, almost against his will, he was warmed by it. It was good to be welcomed. The Procurator took it for granted that he should be treated as a valued friend and a prospective son-in-law, and it had been a long time since Gaius had been made to feel a part of a family. He realized with a pang that the last time he had been made to feel so had been in the house of Bendeigid. Eilan, Cynric, what would become of them? Would he ever know? He had worried about this all the way to Londinium – he had to stop now.

"Well then, son," said Licinius, "You must be longing to meet your bride."

Speak up, Gaius said to himself. But he could not bring himself to put out the light that glowed in the old man's eyes, and mumbled something noncommittal instead. *They will punish Eilan if I try to see her again*, he reminded himself sternly. The best thing he could do for her would be to go through this ceremony as expected of him. *Or is that just an excuse to avoid a confrontation?* he wondered.

But Licinius had already beckoned to a well-dressed upper servant. "Send for the Lady Julia," he ordered.

Gaius knew that now was the time to say that he would have

nothing to do with this farce of an arranged marriage – but without waiting for him to reply, the Procurator had hauled himself to his feet.

"She'll be with you in a moment. I'll leave you young people alone to get acquainted." Before Gaius could find the words to stop him, he was limping away.

Julia Licinia had been keeping house for her father since her mother's death three years earlier. An only child, from girlhood she had assumed she would be married off to whatever man her father chose. He had told her that he had arranged a marriage with the son of Macellius; at least this meant she would not be given to some unknown patrician twice her age, as had happened to more than one of her friends. Trying to look unconcerned she plucked a ripening fig from one of the trees growing in the pots in the colonnaded atrium as her father came towards her.

He grinned broadly. "He is here now, my dear, Gaius Macellius the younger, your promised husband. Go and see what you think; it's you, after all, who is to marry him. But I think if you do not like the look of the young man, you'd be hard to please."

Julia stared at her father. She said, "I was not expecting this so soon."

And yet it occurred to her that there was no point in delay. She was eager to have something all her own; and certainly when she had borne this young tribune legionary a son, he would value her above all things. She was already used to running a household, but she wanted children who would love her. She was determined not to fail at giving her husband a son as her own mother had done.

"Nor was I," her father said good-naturedly. "I wanted to keep my little girl a bit longer. Now I'll probably have to marry some old widow to keep house for me. But the young man's evidently got himself entangled with some native woman, and Macellius feels that marriage will settle him. And so –"

A *native girl?* Julia's brows rose. She was aware that most fathers would not have spoken to a daughter so frankly, but she had always been as much a companion for Licinius as a child. "And so?"

"And so the young man's turned up on our doorstep, and it's time for you young folks to get acquainted with one another. I suppose you're eager to see him?"

"I must admit I'm curious." What sort of husband had she drawn? One escapade could be condoned, but if he was the type who habitually went after women, she was not sure she wanted him.

"Then run along, daughter," her father said. "I must say, if *he* doesn't like *you* he too will be hard to please."

In sudden panic Julia remembered she was wearing an old tunica, and that she had combed her hair very sketchily.

"Like this?" she asked. Flustered, she tried to adjust the folds of her dress to hide a berry stain.

"I'm sure it's you he wants to see, not your taste in gowns," admonished her father fondly. "You look perfectly lovely. He knows that you're my daughter, and that's really what matters. Run along and see what you think of him. Don't be silly, child."

Julia knew there was no appeal. Licinius was a kind father, even indulgent, but when he had once made up his mind, she could not tease or coax him out of it.

Once more Gaius heard the soft sound of girlish laughter, and for some reason he thought of Odysseus surprised on the beach by Nausicaa and her maidens; he could only stare as the girl herself slipped out from behind one of the flowering trees and came towards him.

A girl? A child, Gaius thought at first; for although he himself was not tall, the girl who entered barely reached his shoulder; she had a small well-shaped head with thick dark curls, loosely knotted at the nape of her neck. Her eyes were dark too, and met his fearlessly. She had evidently been eating berries, for her fine white wool tunic, and her lips, were stained pink with berry juice. His father had said she was fifteen, but she hardly looked more than twelve.

"You are Julia Licinia?"

"I am." She looked him up and down. "My father's promised me to some half-Roman barbarian, and I came here to have a look at him. Who are you?"

"I'm afraid I'm that half-Roman barbarian," he said a little stiffly.

The girl surveyed him coolly, and he felt as if he were waiting for some verdict of tremendous import; then she giggled.

"Well, you look Roman enough," she said. "I was prepared for some great blond barbarian whose sons would never look Roman born. It is true that our Governor's policy of teaching the sons of chieftains Roman arts and manners had been quite successful," she added consideringly, "but those of us with Roman blood must not forget to whom the Empire belongs. I would bear no babes whose portraits would look out of place among those of my ancestors."

Roman or Tuscani blood? Gaius wondered cynically, remembering that Licinius came from the same Etruscan country stock as his own father, and owed his rise in rank to merit, not ancestors. Those common origins were no doubt part of the bond. Gaius thought of Cynric, who was also half Roman, however unwillingly. At least he Gaius Macellius looked what he was supposed to be, and his father had spared no pains to have him accepted as such.

He said dryly, "I suppose I should be grateful that I pass your inspection."

"Oh, come," she said, "I am sure you want your sons to look like proper Romans no less than I do."

With a sudden pang he wondered, *And what of Eilan's child?* Would he be as fair as his mother, or show his father's breeding in his face? He made himself return Julia's droll smile. "Oh, I'm sure all our sons will be Roman and brave."

They were laughing together when Licinius returned. He peered, as if for confirmation, at Julia's rosy face, then said "That's settled, then."

Gaius blinked as his prospective father-in-law clasped his hand, feeling as if some great siege engine had run him down. But there was only Julia, small and smiling, at his side. She looked so harmless; like a child.

But she isn't, he thought. One meeting was enough to convince him. *Far from it. Harmless is the last word I'd use for her.*

"Of course," the Procurator said, "a wedding like this cannot be put together quickly. He was trying to be jocular. "People would certainly think that Julia had somehow misbehaved, being married off at a moment's notice to a stranger from nowhere. Local society and my family must have a chance to know and value you."

That was exactly the point of this wedding, Gaius thought wryly, except that he was the one who had misbehaved. But he could see that Julia would not want to be hurried into marriage with – as the Procurator had put it – a stranger from nowhere. She must be given a chance to be married as a respected member of her own community. And the delay would give him a chance to catch his breath and figure out what to do. Perhaps on closer acquaintance the girl would decide she did not like him after all, and even his father could not blame him for not marrying her then.

Licinius tapped the scroll from Macellius. "Officially, this transfers you to detached duty under my command. You may not think a young officer needs to know anything about finances, but when you come to command a Legion, you'll find your job easier if you know something about the system that keeps your men shod and fed! No doubt you'll find it easy duty after the frontier. It's not Rome, but Londinium is growing, and the women will make much of you with all the young officers on the Governor's staff gone off to the North."

He paused, and fixed Gaius with a hard stare. "It goes without saying," he added, "that there will be no improper behavior while you are here –" The Procurator went on, "You will live with Julia under this roof as if she were your sister, even though I will gradually let it be known that she has been your promised wife from infancy. But until after the ceremony –"

"Father," Julia protested, "do you really believe I would so disgrace both you and myself?"

Licinius's eyes softened as he looked at her. "I should hope not, girl," he growled. "I just wanted to make it clear to this young man."

"I should hope not indeed," Gaius muttered. But there was little danger; he found it hard to believe that Julia would ever be overcome by emotion. She was certainly different from Eilan, who had thought of his best interests before her own, and now was suffering the consequences.

Would they now hasten her into a marriage of convenience with someone more "suitable" as they were trying to do with him? He suddenly pictured her, beaten or bullied into compliance, tearful, wretched, perhaps weeping. She was, after all, of noble birth as the Britons counted such things, and an alliance with her family could be considered advantageous – as this marriage with Julia would be politically advantageous for his father – and, he supposed, for him.

But I am sure that if they try she will refuse it, he thought then. *She has more integrity than I.* Ecstatic as his union with Eilan had been, there had been moments when she had almost frightened him. Or perhaps it was his own response that had made him afraid.

Julia smiled with an appearance of timidity. It was, Gaius thought, assumed for her father's benefit; the last hour had taught him that anything less timid than Julia – except maybe one of Hannibal's war elephants – would be hard to imagine. But maybe her father still thought of her as a shy child; fathers were the last to know what their children were really like.

But that made him think of Eilan again; her father had trusted him, and look what had happened; he could not fault Julia's father for being more careful.

The duties of an officer attached to the Procurator's staff turned out to include a number of tasks which would probably have been easy for Valerius, but which for Gaius, whose tutor had been pensioned off several years ago, were as stressful to the mind as his first weeks in the army had been for his body. Fortunately these tasks were often interrupted by assignment to escort duty for visiting dignitaries.

He was not much used to cities, but he soon learned to find his way around well enough. Gnaeus Julius Agricola, the Governor, had instituted a program of building of which Londinium had been the first beneficiary. The Britons had been a pastoral people, whereas Roman life centered around the city, with its shops and baths, its games and theaters. A bridge linked Londinium with the south and other roads stretched away to the north and westward. Along these arteries came trade from every corner of the province, and the ships that anchored at the wharves carried goods from all over the Empire.

Shepherding the strangers gave him an excuse to explore, and expose him to visitors of high station. When Gaius got up the nerve to ask him, Licinius said that he had planned it that way.

"For of course, if this marriage is successful –" he said, and broke off without finishing the sentence. "You know, I have no sons; no child at all but Julia, and if things went as they should, she should be allowed to succeed me, and perhaps even attain to senator. But of course a woman, no matter how capable, can only bestow her rank on her husband. That is why it pleases me so much that she should marry the son of my oldest friend."

Only then did Gaius really understand Macellius's plan. Married to Julia, Gaius could legitimately aspire to the position for which his father's injudicious marriage had disqualified him. He would not have been human – nor Macellius's son – if he had been indifferent to the possibilities. Living in Londinium had already altered his perspective, and he was beginning to understand what he would have been giving up if he had run away with Eilan. Had she been ill used? He could only hope she knew that nothing on earth – short of his father's will or the threat to Eilan herself – could have made him abandon her.

He had not realized that Julia was aware of his troubles until she brought up the subject herself.

"Father told me," she said after the evening meal when they were sitting on the terrace together watching the late summer sunset gild the basilica's dome, "that you were sent here because you had formed some sort of alliance with a native woman, the daughter of a proscribed man. Tell me something about her. How old was she?"

Gaius felt his face flame and coughed to cover his confusion. It had never occurred to him that her father would have told her; but perhaps it was just as well to get things clear between them.

"A few years older than you are, I think." In truth, he supposed that Julia must now be just the age Eilan had been when he first met her. Though otherwise they were utterly different, Julia had the quality of innocence he had first loved in Eilan.

The Procurator had kept him busy, and so had local society. It was a heady experience for a young man of mixed blood. He had told his father once that he was not ambitious, but that was before he had realized what rewards wealth, and the right connections, could bring.

Julia smiled at him kindly. "Did you care very much about being married to her?"

"I thought I did. I was in love. Of course I had not met you then," he said quickly, wondering what love could possibly mean to Julia.

She looked at him, long and steadily. "I think you should see her again before we are married," she said, "just to be certain that you are not going to pine for her once you are married to me."

"I have every intention of being a good husband –" he began, but Julia either misunderstood or chose to pretend to. Her eyes were too dark; he could not read them. Eilan's eyes had been clear as a forest pool.

"Because," she said straightforwardly, "I do not want a man who would rather be married to someone else. I really think you should see her again, and find out what you want your life to be. Then, when you come back, I'll know that marriage with me is really what you want to do."

She sounded like her father, he thought grimly, when he was negotiating a contract; she sounded as if she thought marriage was a career. But then, brought up in the capital as she had been, that was probably exactly what she expected it to be! And what other career could there be for a Roman woman? What could she know of the fire that pulsed in the blood when the Beltane drums began, or the longing that ate at the heart like the music of the pipes the shepherds played on the hills?

In any case, his father had made it impossible for him to see Eilan; no doubt even Julia would be horrified if she heard that his beloved was the local equivalent of a Vestal Virgin. But Julia was already making plans, and once again Gaius felt as if he was in the path of a cavalry charge.

"Father is going to send you north with despatches for Agricola –"

Gaius raised one eyebrow, for he had heard nothing of this, but it did not really surprise him. Julia was the darling of every clerk in the *tabularium*, and when a change in orders was contemplated, they were always the first to know. *And the last one to know is always the man most concerned!* he thought.

"On your way you can make time to see this girl. When you come back you will be quite, quite sure that you would rather be married to me."

Gaius suppressed a smile, for she did not know as much as she thought if she imagined he would have much time for side trips on government service. But perhaps he could manage something; already his blood beat faster in his veins at the thought of seeing Eilan again.

Thanks be to Venus that Julia could not know what he was thinking, though there were times when he credited her with the powers of a Sibyl, or maybe all women had this kind of power. But Julia was chattering about her wedding veil, which was to be made of a fabulous material to be brought in by caravan from halfway around the world.

It would be rather a relief, he thought, even if he must travel to the wilds of Caledonia, to get back to the regular army again.

seventeen

s the summer ripened towards Lughnasad it did not seem to Eilan that Lhiannon grew any better. Sometimes the old woman's heart pained her, and always she was tired. Ardanos came daily, and at first he and the High Priestess would talk, but as the days passed, and her attention drew increasingly inward, he simply sat by her bedside in silence, and when he spoke it was with Caillean, or to himself. After these sessions, Caillean would be silent and pensive, but she had always been one for keeping her own counsel.

Eilan found it strange that as her own body was becoming a vessel of life, Lhiannon should be undergoing a parallel transformation, preparing to release her spirit – but in what world she would be reborn no one could say. Joy at the new life within her muted Eilan's own sorrow. But in those days the Forest House grew very silent, and all the women went about their tasks with mingled excitement and dread. For no one had yet dared to ask who Lhiannon's successor was to be.

It was fortunate that everyone was too distracted by Lhiannon's illness to take much notice of anyone else, but what would Eilan do when her belly could no longer be concealed by her loose robes? Not for a moment was Eilan allowed to forget that as far as Ardanos was concerned she was under sentence of death; she fancied that even Dieda regarded her with barely concealed contempt.

Miellyn was still mourning the loss of her own child and could offer no comfort. Only Caillean never changed toward her – but then Caillean had always been a law unto herself; the one thing that sustained Eilan when she grew most afraid was her awareness of the older woman's love.

She did not know when, if ever, she would see Gaius again; but remembering the kingly spirit she had glimpsed when they lay together, she felt certain they would meet again. She did not want to believe – as the Arch-Druid said – that he had hastily been married off to someone else. Even among the Romans the solemnizing of a marriage must demand more formality and time than that.

A month passed, and Caillean presided over the full moon rituals. Now it was obvious, nurse and care for her as they might, that Lhiannon was dying. Her feet swelled so that she could no longer even stagger to the privy. Caillean nursed her tenderly; no mother ever had a more devoted daughter. But still the fluid filled her body.

Caillean fed her herb brews and spoke of dropsy, and once they went far afield to find the purple flowers of the foxglove, which Caillean said were sovereign for an ailing heart. Eilan cautiously tasted the brew Caillean made of them, and found it bitter as sorrow.

But in spite of all their care, day by day Lhiannon grew weaker and more swollen and pale.

"Caillean –"

For a moment she doubted she had heard it; the call was like a breath drawn by the wind. Then the bed creaked. Wearily, Caillean turned. Lhiannon's eyes were open. Caillean rubbed the sleep from her own and made herself smile. Illness had consumed the flesh from the older woman's face so that the good bones showed with a terrible clarity. *It is almost over.* The unwelcome knowledge came to her. *Soon, only the essentials will remain.*

"Are you thirsty? Here's cool water, or I can stir up the fire and give you some tea . . ."

"Something hot . . . would ease me . . ." Lhiannon drew breath. "You are too good to me, Caillean."

Caillean shook her head. When she was ten years old and halfway to death with the fever, Lhiannon had nursed her back again, more than her mother or father would have done. Her feelings for the older woman went beyond love or hatred. How could you put that into words? If Lhiannon could not sense them in the taste of an infusion or the touch of a cool cloth on her brow, she would never know.

"I suppose there are those who think you are doing this so that I will make you my heir . . . Women cooped up together can be very petty, and it is true, you are a greater priestess than all of them put together . . . but you know better, do you not?"

"I know." Caillean managed a smile. "I am destined to live for ever in the shadows, but I will support whoever rules. Please the Goddess, it will not be for yet a while."

And who knows how long I will live after you? she thought then. Her strange bleeding had ceased at last, but fatigue dragged at her limbs as if they had been cast of lead from the Mendip mines.

"Perhaps . . . Do not be so sure you know everything, my child. Despite what people think, my Sight comes not always at the Druids' bidding. And I have *seen* you with the ornaments of a High Priestess and a mist that is not of this world blowing around you. A life path may have strange twists and turnings, and we do not always end up where we intend to go . . ."

Boiling water hissed in the little cauldron, and Caillean spooned in the mixture of yarrow and chamomile and white willow, and set it to steep beside the flame.

"Goddess knows I have not done so!" Lhiannon burst out suddenly. "We had such dreams when we were young, Ardanos and I – but he grew greedy for power . . . and I had none!"

You could have stood against him, thought Caillean. *You were the Voice of the Goddess, and for twenty years the people have lived by your words. And you don't even know what you have been saying! If you had ever allowed yourself to know, you would have had to act, for then it would have been real . . .*

But she bit back the words, for Lhiannon had given more hope to the people unknowing than Caillean with all her conscious wisdom, and that outweighed all her failings, whatever cynics like Dieda might say.

With a little honey to take away the bitterness, the tea was ready. Caillean slid her arm around Lhiannon's fragile shoulders and held the spoon to her lips. The sick woman's head turned fretfully, and her cheeks glistened with tears. "I am tired, Caillean . . ." she whispered, "so very tired, and afraid . . ."

"There, there, my dear; you are surrounded by those who love you," she whispered. "Drink this now, it will give you ease." Lhiannon swallowed a little of the bittersweet brew, and sighed.

"I promised Ardanos I would choose my successor . . . to serve his plan. He is waiting . . ." She grimaced. "Like a crow watching a sick ewe. It was to be Eilan, but she . . . must be sent away soon. Now he says I must choose Dieda, but I will not, and she would not, unless the Goddess –" a fit of coughing took her and Caillean hastily set the tea down, holding Lhiannon upright and patting her back until she was still.

"Until the Goddess shows you Her will," Caillean finished for her, and the High Priestess of Vernemeton smiled.

Lhiannon was dying. It was obvious to everyone – everyone except perhaps Caillean, who nursed her so devotedly and with a despairing tenderness, night and day, seldom stepping beyond the room where the sick woman lay. Even those of the priestesses who had always been suspicious of Caillean as an outlander had to admire her dedication now. Both Dieda and Eilan guessed what was coming – but it would have taken a braver woman than either one of them to name it to Caillean.

"But she is so skilled in healing," Dieda said as they carried Lhiannon's soiled bedding down to the river. "She must know."

"I suppose she does," said Eilan, "but admitting it would make it real." She looked at her kinswoman curiously. Apart from commenting sarcastically that the dirty laundry of a High Priestess smelled no different from anyone else's, and she could not see why a sworn priestess was required to wash it, Dieda had done her share of the work uncomplainingly.

It seemed odd that they should have become such strangers now, when they were sister priestesses. Working with Dieda these past weeks, when Caillean's attention was fixed on Lhiannon, reminded Eilan how close they had been as girls. Distracted by her thoughts, she tripped on a tree root.

Dieda put out a hand to steady her.

"Thank you," Eilan said in surprise. The other woman glared at her.

"Why are you staring?" said Dieda. "I don't hate you."

Eilan felt the hot color flare in her cheeks, then fade. "You know then," she whispered.

"You are the fool, not I," came the answer. "Cooped up with you and Caillean all this time I could hardly help overhearing something. But for the sake of our family's honor I have kept silent. If any of the other women know your secret, they did not learn it from me. At least pregnancy seems to agree with you. Are you feeling well?"

It was a relief to Eilan to speak of something other than Lhiannon's illness, and it seemed to her that Dieda felt that way as well. By the time they returned to the Forest House, they were more in harmony than they had been in years.

*

But a day came when even Caillean could not deny it any longer. Ardanos said that the priestesses must be summoned for the deathwatch. He looked grieved and gray, and Eilan remembered that her kinswoman had once said there was love between them. She thought it must have been a long time ago, or a very strange kind of love.

Certainly it was not at all what *she* would call love, thought Eilan, and surely she was an expert. But Ardanos sat close to the unconscious woman and held her hand; the priestesses slipped in and out to keep watch by twos and threes, and Caillean fidgeted lest they disturb Lhiannon.

"Why does she trouble herself? I do not think anything will disturb the High Priestess any more," Eilan whispered to Dieda, and the other girl nodded, but without words.

It was near sunset, and Ardanos had stepped into the air for a few breaths. Like all sickrooms, this one was hot and close, and Eilan could not blame him for a moment for wishing to escape it. Though it was nearly Lughnasad the light still lingered late. Sunset made a glare in the room, but the angle of the sinking sun told Eilan it would soon be gone. She had crossed the room to light the lamp when she became aware that Lhiannon was awake and looking at her with recognition for the first time in many days.

"Where is Caillean?" she whispered.

"She has gone to make you more tea, Mother," Eilan replied, "Will you have me call her?"

"No time," the High Priestess coughed. "Come here – is it Dieda?"

"I'm Eilan, but Dieda is in the garden; do you want me to call her?"

There was a strange, raspy, rustling sound, and Eilan realized the sick woman was trying to laugh.

"Even now I cannot tell one from the other," Lhiannon whispered. "Do you not see the hand of the gods in this?"

Eilan wondered if Lhiannon had sunk into the delirium she had been warned might come before the end. The High Priestess said harshly, "Call Dieda; my time is short. I do not rave; I know very well what I am doing and I must finish before I die."

Eilan hurried to the door to summon Dieda. When they returned, the dying woman smiled as they stood side by side.

"It is true what they say," she whispered. "The dying see clearly.

Dieda, now you must bear witness. Eilan, daughter of Rheis, take the torque that lies beside me – take it!" she gasped for breath, and with trembling hands Eilan picked up the ring of twisted gold that lay on the pillow. "And the arm rings . . . Now put them on . . ."

"But only the High Priestess – Eilan began, but the old woman's eyes held hers with such terrible fixity that she found herself twisting the necklace to open it, and sliding it on. For a moment it seemed cold, then it settled about her own slim throat, warming as if grateful to be close to human flesh once more.

From Dieda came a small, strangled sound, but the rattle in Lhiannon's throat was louder.

Then the High Priestess rasped, "Be it so. Maiden and Mother, I see the Goddess in you now . . . Tell Caillean –" She was silent a moment as if struggling for breath, and Eilan wondered if the old woman was delirious, or if it were she. She reached up once more to touch the heavy gold.

"Caillean is yonder, Mother; shall I summon her?" Dieda asked.

"Go," whispered Lhiannon with more strength than she had before. "Tell her I love her . . ."

As Dieda hurried out, the gaze of the dying woman fixed on Eilan.

"I know now what Ardanos wanted when he bade me choose you, child, and instead the gods brought Dieda into my hand. He was wrong about you, and yet he did the Lady's will all the same!" Her lips twisted with what Eilan realized was laughter. "Remember – it is important! Perhaps even the Goddess Herself could not tell you two one from the other. Nor the Romans – I see now –" and she was silent again. Eilan looked down at her, unable to move.

She was silent so long that Caillean, returning, asked, "Does she sleep? If she can sleep, then perhaps she may live another moon –" and then, tiptoeing to Lhiannon's side, caught her breath on a gasp and whispered, "Ah, she will never sleep more –"

Caillean knelt beside the bed and kissed Lhiannon on the brow, and then, very tenderly, closed her eyes. With every moment that passed more expression was fading from the dead woman's face, so that she no longer looked asleep; she did not even look like Lhiannon any more. Eilan hugged her arms, and winced as she felt the hard metal of the arm-ring. She felt dizzy, and cold.

Then Caillean stood, and as her gaze focused on the ornaments Eilan was wearing her eyes widened. Then she smiled.

"Lady of Vernemeton, I salute you in the name of the Mother of all!"

Ardanos, coming into the room behind Dieda, bent over the dead and then stood back again. "She is gone," he said in a strange, flat, voice. He turned, and something flickered in his eyes as he, too, saw the golden ornaments that Eilan wore.

The other priestesses were crowding around them, but it was old Latis the herb mistress who pushed forward and bowed, saying with a strange deference that terrified her, "I pray you, Voice of the Goddess, tell us everything the Holy Lady said with her last breath to you."

"Lhiannon, may the Goddess rest her, chose an uncommonly awkward season for her dying," Ardanos said sharply. "For we must have a priestess of the Oracle at the rites at Lughnasad, and obviously we cannot use Eilan!" He surveyed the two women before him grimly.

The three days of ritual mourning were past, and Lhiannon laid in her grave; Ardanos was surprised at how much it still hurt when he looked around this chamber where he had always met with her and remembered she was gone. He supposed he would continue to miss her for a long time, but he could not afford to show his grief now. Caillean sat frowning, but Eilan stared at him with wide, unreadable eyes. He glared back at her.

"You know as well as I do that it is superstition to believe that only a virgin can serve the shrine, but for Eilan to bear the power of the Goddess right now would be dangerous both for her and her child," agreed Caillean.

Sexual abstinence was necessary during performance of the great magics – a magic such as the complete surrender of body and spirit necessary for the Goddess to speak through a mortal.

For the power to flow freely, the spirit must be detached from the senses. Thus it was forbidden to do those things that would increase their attraction and clog the pathways, such as eating the flesh of some animals, drinking mead or other liquors, or lying with a man.

"Lhiannon should have thought of that when she chose her," the Arch-Druid replied. "It will not do, you know. It's bad enough that she is still here. But a *pregnant* High Priestess? Impossible!"

"I could take her place in the ritual –" Caillean began.

"And how would we explain *that* to the people? We could have justified a temporary substitution on the grounds that Lhiannon was ill, but they know that she is dead. Transitions are always delicate. People are wondering if the new High Priestess will survive her ordeal, whether the Goddess will still come to them now that Lhiannon is gone."

He rubbed his forehead. None of them had had enough sleep for far too long. Caillean's eyes looked dark and haunted, and despite the bloom of pregnancy, Eilan seemed anxious and strained. And well she might be, it occurred to him then. Lhiannon had put them all in a quandary when she chose the girl.

"I tell you this – whatever madness came on Lhiannon at her ending, I will not allow it to destroy all that we have labored so hard to build!" He sighed. "There is no help for it. We shall have to choose again. There is a precedent; old Helve tried to pass her power to – what was her name? – that poor mad girl who died. And then the council chose Lhiannon."

"You would like that, wouldn't you!" Caillean began, but Eilan, who had been silent for so long the Arch-Druid had almost forgotten she was there, got to her feet suddenly.

"Not until after the ordeal!" she said loudly. Spots of color flamed in her cheeks as the other two stared at her. "They named a new High Priestess after the chosen one failed to carry the power of the Goddess in the ritual, didn't they? What kind of talk do you think there will be if I do not even attempt it? Everyone in Vernemeton knows that Lhiannon chose me."

"But the danger!" exclaimed Caillean.

"Do you think the Goddess will strike me dead? If what I did was such a sin, then She is welcome to do so!" Eilan exclaimed. "But if I survive, you will know that She has chosen me indeed!"

"And what do you propose that we should do with you if you live?" he said acidly. "Your condition will be showing soon, and the Romans will have a good laugh when they see our High Priestess wallowing around with a belly like a pregnant cow!"

"Lhiannon thought of a way," said Eilan. "It was the last thing she said to me. Once the ritual is over, Dieda must take my place and you must pretend that it is she who had to be sent away. You yourself cannot tell us apart, Grandfather, and you have known us both since we were babies!"

Ardanos eyed her narrowly, calculation spinning in his brain. The wretched child might indeed have solved their problem. If the ritual killed her, as was most likely, they would have every right to choose her successor, and if Eilan died in childbirth, Dieda would already be in place, ready to take over with no one the wiser. They would do well enough, he told himself, with either girl, for neither would ever think herself quite secure in her office. If the High Priestess needed the support of the priesthood, she would do what she was told.

"But will Dieda agree?" he asked.

"Leave her to me," Caillean replied.

Still wondering at the summons, Dieda faced Caillean in the chamber that had for so long been Lhiannon's.

"Ardanos has agreed to let you substitute for Eilan after the ordeal of the Oracle. Dieda – you must help us now," said Caillean.

Dieda shook her head. "Why should I care what Ardanos wants when he has never cared about me? Eilan has brought her troubles on her own head. I will not consent to this deception, and you may tell my father so!"

"Fine words, indeed, but if you are always determined to do exactly the reverse of what Ardanos decrees, then his will still rules you. I suppose if I had told you he opposes this you would have agreed?" Caillean replied.

Dieda stared at the older priestess, her mind whirling.

"He doesn't at all like it, you know," Caillean added, watching her intently. "He would rather reject Eilan now and make you High Priestess in her place. I think he agreed to suggest the substitution only because he thought you would react in just this way . . ."

"High Priestess?" Dieda exclaimed. "I would never escape from this place then!"

"It would only be temporary, after all," Caillean reflected. "As soon as Eilan's babe is born she would return to take up her duties, and then, in any case, you would have to go away –"

"Would you let me go north to be with Cynric?" Dieda asked suspiciously.

"If that is what you desire. But we had thought of sending you to Eriu for advanced training in the skills of a bard . . ."

"You know perfectly well it is what I have always wanted most!" Dieda exclaimed. Caillean looked at her steadily. "Then it seems there is something I still can promise or deny you. If you do this for Eilan – and for me – I will see that you are allowed to learn from the greatest poets and harpers in Eriu. If you do not, Ardanos will surely make you Priestess, and I will make sure that you rot within these walls."

"You would not," Dieda said. But she felt a chill of fear.

"You shall see," Caillean responded calmly. "There is no alternative. It was Lhiannon's wish, and I will do her will as we all have always done."

Dieda sighed. She did not want to see anything evil happen to Eilan. She had loved her once, but after the past few years she found it hard to love anyone. It seemed to her that the other girl had been a great fool. She had had the kind of love Dieda had been denied and thrown it away. Nor could she see why Caillean should care. Still, she would not cross her. Caillean could be a good friend or a dangerous enemy – both to her and possibly to Cynric as well. Dieda had dwelt in the Forest House long enough to know just how much influence the Irishwoman wielded in her quiet way.

"So be it," she said. "I pledge to stand substitute for Eilan until she is delivered if afterward you will be responsible for giving me my desire."

"I will," Caillean lifted one hand. "And may the Goddess bear witness. And no one alive can say I have ever broken an oath."

Half a moon had passed since Lhiannon's passing, and they were come to the Feast of Lughnasad. Eilan waited with Caillean in the separate dwelling where the High Priestess had so often prepared for the rituals. Hearing sharpened by anxiety alerted her to the scuff of sandaled feet outside the door. Then it swung open, and she saw the hooded figure, seeming impossibly tall in the half-light, standing there. She could just make out the shapes of the other Druids behind him.

"Eilan, daughter of Rheis, the Voice of the Goddess has chosen you. Are you prepared to give yourself to Her completely?" Ardanos's voice tolled like a great bell, and Eilan felt her belly tighten with fear.

Now all the tales she had heard in the House of Maidens rose up to sweep her careful reasoning away. It hardly mattered whether the Goddess really cared about what she had done with Gaius, Eilan thought despairingly. To survive the ritual without damage would require a miracle. *I meant only to challenge the Druids, but I have challenged Her, daring Her wrath this way. Surely the Goddess will strike me down! And what will this do to my child?* Eilan wondered. But if the Goddess would punish an unborn baby for what the mother had done, She was not the loving Presence Eilan had sworn to serve.

Ardanos was waiting for her answer — they were all waiting, watching with hope or judgment in their eyes — and slowly she calmed. *If the Lady does not want me as I am, I do not wish to live.* She took a deep breath, fighting her way back to the decision to which in the sleepless nights since Lhiannon's death she had come.

"I am ready." Her voice trembled only a little. At least her own father was in the North somewhere with Cynric. She was glad. She did not think she could have met his eyes.

"And do you declare yourself a fit vessel for Her power?"

Eilan swallowed. Was she? The night before she had doubted it, and wept on Caillean's shoulder like a terrified child.

"*Fit? Who is, if you put it like that?*" Caillean had asked. "*We are all only mortal; but it is you who have been chosen. Why else have you been preparing for so many years?*"

The Arch-Druid was watching her like a hawk waiting for some betraying rustle in the grass, waiting for her to perjure herself so that she would be in his power. She realized dimly that he was enjoying this.

Lhiannon thought I was fit, she told herself then. Only by going through with this could she justify Lhiannon's dying choice, and the choice she herself had made when she gave herself to Gaius beneath the trees. It had seemed to her then that she was affirming a more ancient law of the Goddess than the one pledging her to chastity. To refuse this test was to admit that act of love had been a sin. She lifted her chin proudly. "I am a fit and holy vessel. Let the earth rise up and cover me, let the sky fall down and crush me, and let the gods by whom I swear forsake me if I lie!"

"The candidate has been questioned, and she has sworn —" Ardanos said to the Druids who attended him. He turned to the priestesses. "Let her now be purified and prepared for the ritual —"

For a moment he looked at her, and pity, exasperation, and satisfaction seemed to war in his gaze. Then he turned on his heel and led the men from the room.

"Eilan, you must not tremble so," Caillean said softly. "Don't let that old buzzard scare you, there is nothing to fear. The Goddess is merciful. She is our mother, Eilan, and the Mother of all women, the maker of all things mortal. Do not forget it."

Eilan nodded, knowing that even if this moment had come to her in the ordinary course of events she would still have been afraid. If she must die, it should be at the hands of the Goddess, there was no need to perish of fear beforehand.

The curtain stirred again and four of the youngest priestesses, among them Senara and Eilidh, came into the room carrying pails of water from the sacred spring. They stopped just inside the door, looking at her in awe. *The hand of the Goddess has descended on me*, she thought, and it seemed that she saw in their faces something of that same wonder with which she herself had always looked on Lhiannon. They were all young; not one of them, except Eilidh, even as old as she was herself . . .

She wanted to cry out, "Nothing has changed; I am still Eilan –" but in fact everything had changed. Yet when they stripped off her gown and she looked down, she was startled that her body still looked so little altered.

But these were virgins. So it was not surprising that they should not see the slight changes her pregnancy had made. As Eilan had done so often for Lhiannon, the girls helped her to bathe. She stood shivering in the chilly room, feeling the icy touch of the clear water on her body as, curiously, a purification; as if somehow it were dissolving away not only the last traces of her contact with Gaius, but the whole of her previous life.

It was an entirely new Eilan who allowed them to robe her in the ritual garments. About her forehead they bound the traditional garland. As she felt the vines tighten around her forehead, she had a moment of dizziness, and wondered if this was the first, faraway touch of the Goddess.

She felt strange and light-headed, altogether unlike herself; vaguely she recognized hunger. The sacred herbs in the potion given her at the commencement of the ritual must be taken on an empty stomach, lest they make her very ill. Caillean had once said that she believed that Lhiannon's ill health was partly caused by her protracted use of these herbs. Briefly Eilan wondered if before long her own health would be endangered as well. Then she smiled, thinking it would be time enough to worry about her future if she survived this evening.

They brought her the chased golden bowl with the magical potion of Vision. She knew that it contained berries of mistletoe and other sacred herbs; she had more than once seen Miellyn gathering those herbs. The sacred potion also contained various mushrooms; the common people avoided them, as much for their sacred character as for belief that they were poisonous, and certainly they were useless as food. The priestesses knew, however, that taken in small quantities they could amplify the ordinary clairvoyance in which she had been trained.

Trembling, Eilan did as she had often enough seen Lhiannon do, and took it from Eilidh's hands. Caillean had been right, she thought as she raised the bowl to her lips. She had assisted in this ritual so often that she did know what to do.

And from her ceremonial sips she had thought she knew what to expect from the potion as well. But as she tipped it upward, she realized that the priestess was required to drain it at a single draft because otherwise no one would ever have been able to get it down. It was intensely bitter, and when she had swallowed it, she began to wonder if it was poison after all. That would have been a good way for Ardanos to get rid of her. But Caillean had assured her that she would prepare the herbs herself and let no one else have access to them, and she had to trust her.

Her head swam and for a moment her stomach revolted. Perhaps her punishment was beginning now. But after a short, sharp struggle she controlled herself, swallowed a few sips of water to clear her mouth of the taste and closed her eyes, waiting.

Presently, the acute feeling of sickness passed. Eilan closed her eyes against the wave of dizziness, and sat down, waiting to recover her balance. Vaguely she remembered that this, too, had been part of the procedure with Lhiannon. At the time, Eilan had thought it the weakness of age. But Lhiannon had really not been so old. Would she, too, age before her time? Well, she could only hope she would have a chance to grow old!

There was a little stir in the room, and the young girls drew away. Eilan realized that Ardanos was standing before her. She lifted heavy eyelids to look at him, and he met her gaze with an unsmiling stare.

"Eilan, I see they have prepared you. You look very beautiful, my dear. The people will be sure the Goddess has come to them . . ." The kindly words sounded strange from his lips.

Will they? she wondered muzzily. *And what do you think, old man, if you believe in the Goddess at all? By your rules, these garlands should be withering on my brow!* But it no longer mattered; she felt as if she were floating above all this, with every moment she drifted further away.

"The drink is taking her swiftly," he muttered, and gestured to the maidens to stand away. "Listen, my child – I know you can still hear me . . ." His voice slipped into the melodic intonation of ritual as he went on.

Eilan knew that he was saying something of great importance, something that she must remember ... what, she was not certain. Time passed, and he was no longer there. Did any of it matter, she wondered then? She felt as if she were floating above a green darkness. The very tops of the trees were far below. She was being carried in something – a litter – then they set her down and helped her to stand. She could feel Caillean beside her and someone else, she thought it was Latis, on her other side. They took her hands and drew her into the procession towards the torches that ringed the sacred mound.

Eilan was aware enough to hang back for a moment when she saw the three-legged stool. There had been some reason why she should not sit there; some sin upon her soul. But her attendants drew her forward, and she thought that if she could not remember it, perhaps it made no difference.

They had sacrificed the sacred bull already and shared its meat among the people. The priests had played out the ritual in which the young god wrested the harvest from the old. Now it was time to seek omens for the autumntide. In the east the harvest moon was rising, golden as the ornaments that her priestess wore.

Look down on me, Lady, Eilan fought to form the prayer. *Ward me well!*

One of the attendant priestesses had placed in her hand the little curved golden dagger of ritual. She raised the dagger, and with one swift movement plunged it into her fingertip. She felt a sharp pain, and one heavy drop of blood gleamed on the surface; she held it over the golden bowl, letting three drops of blood fall. The bowl was filled to the brim with water from the Sacred Well, and floating on the surface were leaves of the sacred plant, the mistletoe. Planted by no human hand, and growing between air and earth, it partook of the very nature of the lightning which had engendered it.

Now they were turning her; she felt the hard wood against the backs of her knees and sat down. There was a moment of dizziness as the priests lifted her and carried her to the mound. The attendant priestesses had drawn back.

As the priests began to sing Eilan felt as if she were falling, or perhaps rising, borne away by the song in some direction that had no relation to ordinary reality. She wondered why she had been afraid. In this place she floated; needing and wanting nothing, content simply to be ...

A blaze of torches assaulted her eyes; below her all the assembled crowd seemed to blur into a single face. Their eyes upon her were like a weight, a positive physical pressure drawing her back to a place that was in, and yet not of, the world.

"Children of Don, why have you come here?" Ardanos's voice seemed very far away.

"We seek the blessing of the Goddess," a male voice replied.

"Then call Her!"

Eilan's nostrils flared as smoke swirled around her, heavy with the scent of sacred herbs. Involuntarily she breathed in and her breath caught; the world whirled and she fought for balance; she heard a voice whimpering and did not know it was her own. From below rose the sound of many other voices, calling, calling:

Dark Huntress ... Bright Mother ... Lady of Flowers, hear us ... Come to us, Lady of the Silver Wheel ...

I am Eilan ... Eilan ... She clung to her own identity, crying out as the need in those voices assaulted her until she felt their pressure as a physical pain. At the same time, another pressure was building up behind her, or perhaps within her, demanding that she let it in. Spasms shook her body as she fought; she felt terror as the Self that she knew was constricted between them; she could not breathe. *Help me!* her spirit cried.

She slumped forward, seeing the glimmer of water before her, and a voice that seemed to come from *within* her said then:

"Daughter, I am always here. To see Me, you have only to gaze into the Sacred Pool."

"Look into the water, Lady —" a voice that was very near commanded. "Look into the bowl, and *see!*"

An image was forming in the troubled surface of the water, but as it cleared Eilan saw that the face reflected there was not her own. She jerked back in panic, and heard the voice once more.

"My daughter, rest now. Your spirit will be safe with Me ... "

With the words came a tide of love that Eilan remembered, and with the same trust with which she had given herself to Gaius she sighed and slid away into the warm comfort of the Lady's arms.

As if from a great distance, she was aware that her body was straightening, she was putting back her veil, lifting her hands to the moon.

"Behold, the Lady of Life has come to us!" in a great voice Caillean cried. "Let us welcome her!"

And the sound of many voices rose like a tide and carried her to a place where she could watch the body she had left behind move and speak with wonder, but with no fear.

As the cheering subsided, the High Priestess sank back on to the seat once more; the identity that filled her waiting in a timeless patience for the response of humankind.

"There are the questions the people bring to you," the Arch-Druid said, and because he spoke to her in the old speech of the Wise Ones, it was in that language that the Goddess answered him.

After each question the priest turned to the people and said something in the common language. From that far-off realm from which Eilan was listening it seemed to her odd that his statements, if they were translations, had so little to do with what the Goddess replied. That did not seem right, but perhaps she had not heard him clearly, and in this place in which she had found refuge it was hard to care.

The questioning went on, but as time passed, she found her perceptions becoming more and more disjointed. It seemed to her that Ardanos frowned then and leaned close to her.

"Lady, we thank you for your words. It is time to leave this body through which you have spoken. Hail now, and farewell!" He plucked the sprig of mistletoe from the golden bowl and shook droplets of water over her.

For a moment Eilan was blinded, then her body convulsed. Pain stabbed through her and she fell into darkness on a shimmer of silver bells.

When awareness began to return Eilan realized that the priestesses were singing. She knew the song; it seemed to her that once she had sung it but, aching and dizzied as she was, she could not sing now. They had removed the constricting garlands from her head, and someone was bathing her brow and hands. Someone gave her water to drink and a voice murmured in her ear. *Caillean* . . . She felt herself lifted and settled into the carrying chair.

"*Hail unto Thee,*" the women sang.

"*Jewel of the night!*" the Druids replied.

"*Beauty of the heavens . . . Mother of the stars . . . Fosterling of the Sun . . .*" The priestesses held up their white arms to the silver moon.

"*Majesty of the stars . . .*" they sang, and with each chorus, "*Jewel of the night!*" the deep voices of the men replied.

A long time later, it seemed, Eilan found herself back in her own bed in the House of the High Priestess. The light of the torches was no longer assaulting her eyes, and the effects of the sacred drink must be wearing off at last, for she found that she could think clearly once more. For some reason a fragment of an ancient ballad was floating in her mind.

"After they stripped her ornaments away, and burned her sacred flowers . . ." She could not remember where it had come from, but she knew that her garlands had been thrown on the fire; the sweet scent of their burning had filled the air. Now other things came back to her – the singing of the priestesses, the silver moon.

But though she knew there had been questions, Eilan found she could not remember a word of her replies. Whatever they had been, the populace had seemed to find them satisfactory.

And the Goddess, she thought then. *She did not strike me dead after all!* At least not yet, though she might yet come to wish She had done so. Eilan's stomach was still unsettled; she felt as if she had been beaten with sticks and would no doubt feel even worse tomorrow. But it was her belly, not her womb, that was aching. She had faced her ordeal and survived.

"Good night, Lady," said Eilidh from the doorway. "May you rest well."

Lady . . . thought Eilan. It was true, then. She was Lady of Vernemeton now.

A few days later Caillean summoned Dieda to the High Priestess's rooms. Eilan sat by the fire, looking pale and strained.

"The time has come for you to keep your word. Eilan is well enough to travel now, and we are sending her into hiding to bear her child."

"This is ridiculous. Do you really think no one will notice the change?" Dieda said bitterly.

"Since she became High Priestess, she has been veiled so much of the time that few of the women in the house will know the difference, and no doubt they will put it down to the effects of the ritual."

Cynric would know, Dieda thought with longing, wishing he would appear and carry her away. But it had been over a year since she had heard from him. Even if he knew, would he have come?

"Your father is grateful to you," said Caillean.

Dieda grimaced, *And well he should be. If I had insisted on leaving here to marry Cynric, what would have become of this fine charade?*

"Dieda." For the first time Eilan spoke on her own behalf. "We have been like sisters. For the sake of the blood we share, and because you, too, know what it is to love, please help me!"

"At least I had better sense than to give myself to a man who would abandon me!" Dieda said tartly. "Caillean has vowed to send me to Eriu. *Sister*, what will *you* promise me?"

"If I remain High Priestess I will try to help you and Cynric. If I fail in this, you have the knowledge to destroy me. Will that be enough for you?"

"That is true." Dieda found herself smiling strangely. And when she had finished learning from the Druids of Eriu, she would be able to raise blisters on a man's skin with a word, or charm any bird or beast with her song; she would have skills of which these pious fools did not dream. She realized suddenly that it was only the constraints of the priestesses that irked her. She could learn to enjoy wielding power.

"Very well, I will help you," she said, and held out her hand for the veil.

eighteen

～～～

despite the tales the Romans of Londinium told about the North, traveling through northern Britain at the end of summer was no hardship for a young and healthy man. It did not rain every day, and the air was sweet with the smell of curing hay. As Gaius traveled up the eastern side of Britain through country that grew ever wilder, he observed the woods and hills with a professional interest, for on his previous campaign they had marched up the western coast through Lenacum, and the eastern was new to him. With Capellus, his father's orderly, once more at his side, the details of making camp and tending the horses were handled efficiently. And his own British tongue was enough to win them a welcome when they had to seek shelter at a native holding.

As Gaius moved further north, more of the talk was of the Governor Agricola's campaigns. From a newly retired veteran who managed one of the posting stations he learned that in the previous year the appearance of a Roman fleet off the Caledonian coast had struck the natives with such panic that they had attacked in desperation, and succeeded in savaging the already weakened Ninth Legion before Agricola sent his cavalry around to attack their rear.

"It was bad, my boy, very bad," admitted the station-keeper, "with them demons howling like wolves in the middle of our camp and men falling over tent lines as they tried to get to their arms. But somehow we held them, and I won't forget the moment when suddenly we could see the glitter of our standards and knew that day was coming at last." He took another long drink of the thin wine and wiped his mouth with the back of his hand.

"Then, I'll tell you, we found our courage, and when the Twentieth finally came up to help us we were ready to tell them they were too late for the party and should go home! But the General kept the men to their work. If those painted devils hadn't scuttled back to their pestilent woods and marshes, we'd have mopped them up entirely. But I suppose we had to leave something for you young glory-hounds to do!" He laughed and offered Gaius more wine.

Gaius suppressed a smile. He had learned something of the battle from men who had been sent home to Deva, but it was interesting to hear the story from someone who had actually been inside the camp when the Caledonians attacked it.

"Ah, the General is a great man! After last summer, even those who hung back and whined about the danger are singing his praises. He'll find work for you, no doubt about it, and you'll start your career with some honors behind you! I wish I was coming with you, lad, so I do!"

Licinius had said nothing about the possibility of actually serving with the Governor, but Gaius wondered suddenly if the messages he carried were at least partially intended to bring him to Agricola's attention. As a provincial governor, Agricola was unusual in that he had got on quite well with his procurators. A word from Licinius might indeed be useful.

In the previous campaign Gaius had been no more than one of a gaggle of young officers, all eager for glory and depending heavily on their centurions. He had been impressed by what he had seen of their commander, but there was no reason for the General to remember him. Ambition stirred within at the thought of winning his commander's esteem.

Presently Gaius left the hunting runs of the Brigantes behind him and moved into even wilder country where the folk spoke a dialect he did not know. Rome might conquer these lands, he thought, as he rode over barren heaths and through shadowed forests, but he wondered if she could ever rule them. Only the need to prevent the wild Caledonians and their Hibernian allies from tearing at the richer fields of the South — as they had destroyed the house of Bendeigid — could begin to justify a Roman presence here.

The long northern twilight was deepening the sky to violet when Gaius rode into Pinnata Castra, the fortress the Twentieth Legion was building above the firth of the Tava where the fleet had made so impressive a showing the summer before. Stone walls were already rising behind the stout palisade, and the leather tents of a marching camp had been replaced by barracks and stabling of timber that looked as if they could stand up even to a winter in these wilds. The place seemed all the larger because it appeared to be almost empty.

"Where is everyone?" he asked as he rode under the legionary wild boar emblazoned on the gate and presented his orders to the officer on duty.

"Up there." The man waved vaguely towards the North. "The word is that the tribes have united at last under a Votadini chieftain called Calgacus. The Old Man's been chasing 'em all summer, laying down marching camps behind him like stepping stones. You'll have another week's riding to catch him, but tonight at least you can sleep under a roof and put a hot meal inside you. No doubt the Prefect will give you an escort in the morning; it would be a shame to get picked off by an ambush after you've come so far!"

By this time Gaius was less interested in a meal than in soaking himself in the legionary bathhouse, but he was glad enough for the dinner once he was clean again, and his host, who was clearly lonely and a little nervous, left here with his small command, seemed glad to welcome him to his quarters and have someone new to talk to.

"Did you hear about the Usipii mutiny?" asked the Prefect as the remains of the sauced grouse on which they had been dining were cleared away.

Gaius set down his wine cup – it had been a rather nice Falernian – and looked expectant.

"A bunch of raw Germans, you know, fresh from their dismal marshes, sent up to Lenacum as levies. They mutinied and stole three ships – ended up sailing all the way from west to east around the coast of Britannia."

Gaius stared. "Then Britannia *is* an island . . ." That question had been a topic of dinner-table debate for as long as he could remember.

"It would seem so," the man nodded. "Eventually the Suevi caught the survivors and sold them as slaves back to the Roman side of the Rhenus, and so we learned the story!"

"Remarkable!" said Gaius. The wine had done its work, and he was beginning to feel nicely toasted. It would make a good story to tell Julia when he got back to Londinium. He was a little surprised to realize that he was thinking of it as something to share with her – but it was a tale whose ironies could only be appreciated by someone from his own world. Eilan would not have understood at all. He realized that he was really two people – the Roman who was betrothed to Julia, and the Briton who loved Eilan.

The next day it began to drizzle. Gaius snuffled and coughed as they moved forward through the sodden landscape, thinking that it was no wonder they said the tribesmen could dissolve into the heather at will. It seemed to him that the hills were dissolving into the sky, and the woods into the soil, and he and his horse into the mud through which they toiled.

At least, he thought dismally, he was riding. He pitied the legionaries who had to slog along this road weighted by all their weapons and gear. Sometimes they saw sheep on a hillside, or the little black cattle the natives herded, but except for an arrow that flashed by Gaius's head from the trees as they were fording one of the streams, there was no sign of hostile forces anywhere.

"Good news for us, but maybe bad for the army," the decurion who led his escort said somberly. "If the warriors aren't guarding their own hunting runs, it can only mean they really have united at last. No one can deny they're good enough fighters when their blood is up. If the tribes had been able to join forces when Caesar came, the Empire would still end on the coasts of Gaul."

Gaius nodded and pulled his brick-colored cloak more tightly around him, wondering what fate had inspired Licinius to send his messages at just the moment when perhaps the most formidable confederation of British tribes ever to assemble was about to attack the army that Agricola had led north . . .

"You have news from Martius Julius Licinius? Tell me, is he well?"

The man who emerged from the large leather tent was only of middle height, and without his armor almost slender, but despite the raindrops glittering in his graying hair and the shadows around his eyes, he projected an aura of authority that would have identified him even without the cloak, of scarlet so deep it was almost purple, that he wore.

"Gaius Macellius Severus Siluricus reporting, sir!" He drew himself up and saluted, ignoring the water that dripped from the brim of his helmet. "The Procurator is well, and sends you his dearest greetings. As you may read in his letters, sir –"

"Indeed." Agricola held out his hand for the packet and smiled. "And best read under cover before they dissolve from damp. You must be wet as well, after your ride. Tacitus here will take you over to the officers' campfire and see to your billeting." He indicated a tall, saturnine young man whom Gaius later learned was his son-in-law. "Now that you are here, you had best wait for the conclusion of the fighting so that I can send a report home with you again."

Gaius blinked as the Governor withdrew into his tent. He had forgotten the man's charm, or perhaps it had never been directed at him personally when he was just one junior officer among many. Then Tacitus took his arm, and, wincing a little as his stiffening thigh muscles protested, Gaius followed him.

It was very good to sit around a campfire with his brother officers once more, eating hot lentil stew and hard bread and drinking sour wine. Only now did Gaius realize how much he had missed that camaraderie. Once the other tribunes had been reminded of his previous campaign experience and realized he was not just a parade-ground soldier they accepted him, and as the wine jug went round, even the rain that was still beading on his cloak did not seem so cold. The tension he sensed around him was only to be expected, and morale seemed high. The loricas of the men on duty were scoured and shining despite the weather, and new paint gleamed on battered shields. The young staff officers with whom he was sitting seemed serious, but not afraid.

"Do you think the General will be able to bring Calgacus to battle?" he asked.

One of the other men laughed. "More likely to be the other way round. Can't you hear 'em?" He gestured into the windy darkness. "They're up there all right, howling and painting themselves blue! The scouts say there's thirty thousand men up on Graupius – warriors of the Votadini and Selgovae, Novantae and Dobunni and all the other little clans we've been chasing these past four years, and Caledonians from northern tribes whose names even they don't know. Calgacus will give us a battle, no doubt of it; he has to, before they all start remembering old feuds and begin to fight each other instead!"

"And how many," Gaius asked carefully, "have we?"

"From the Legions, fifteen thousand: the Twentieth Valeria Victrix, Second Adiutrix, and what's left of the Ninth," said one of the tribunes, who by his insignia, was attached to the Second.

Gaius looked at him with interest. The tribune had joined the Legion since Gaius had been in Londinium, but there must be others here from his father's Legion whom he would know.

"And eight thousand auxiliary infantry, mostly Batavians and

Tungri, some Brigantian irregulars and four wings of cavalry." This was from a troop commander, who shortly thereafter took his leave to return to his men.

"Well, that's not so unequal, is it?" Gaius said brightly, and someone laughed.

"It would be no problem at all, except that they hold the higher ground."

On the upper slopes of the peak the Romans called Mons Graupius, the wind was colder. The Britons gave the mountain other names – the Old Woman, ancient and enduring, Deathbringer and Winter Hag. As the night wore on, it was in her latter aspect that Cynric was meeting her. Here, the gusts of rain that fell in the valleys were coming down in bursts of sleet that stung his cheeks and fell hissing into the fires.

The Caledonians did not appear to mind. They sat around their campfires, draining skins of heather ale and boasting of tomorrow's victory. Cynric pulled his checked cloak over his head, hoping that it would hide his shivering.

"The hunter who boasts too loudly at dawning may find himself with an empty cookpot when night falls," said a quiet voice at his elbow.

Cynric turned and recognized Bendeigid, his pale robes a ghostly blur in the darkness.

"Our warriors have always chanted thus before battle – it raises their spirits!"

He turned and gazed at the men around the fire. This lot were Novantae of the White Horse Clan, from the south-east coast of Caledonia, where the Salmaes firth ran in towards Luguvalium. But at the fire beyond them Selgovae men were drinking, their hereditary enemies. The volume rose and he saw the figure of their commander lit suddenly as someone threw a new log on the fire. The chieftain threw back his head, laughing, and the light flamed anew in his pale eyes and his red hair.

"We're on our own ground, lads, and the land itself will fight for us! The Red-cloaks are driven by greed, which is a cold counselor, but we burn with the fire of freedom! How can we fail?"

The Novantae, hearing his words, left their own fire to gather around him, and in moments the two groups had become a single mass of cheering men.

"He's right," said Cynric. "If Calgacus has been able to persuade this lot to stand together, how can we fail?"

Bendeigid remained silent and, despite his bold words, Cynric felt the serpent of anxiety that had been gnawing at him since night fell begin to stir once more.

"What is it?" he asked. "Have you had an omen?"

Bendeigid shook his head. "No omens – I think the odds for this fight are so evenly balanced that even the gods will not wager on its outcome. We have the advantage, true, but Agricola is a formidable opponent. If Calgacus, great leader though he is, underestimates him, it could be fatal."

Cynric let out his breath in a long sigh. He had fought so hard to prove himself to these tribesmen, who had begun by mocking him as the son of a defeated people even when they did not know his blood was tainted by that of Rome, defiance had become second nature. But with his foster father he need not pretend.

"I hear the singing, but I cannot join in it; I drink, but my belly remains cold. Father, will my courage fail me tomorrow when we face the Roman steel?" At times like this, he could not help wondering if he should have run off with Dieda when he had the chance.

Bendeigid turned him so the Druid could look into Cynric's eyes. "You will not fail," he said fiercely. "These men are still fighting for glory. They do not understand their enemy as you do. But in battle your despair will only make you more terrible. Remember that you are a Raven, Cynric, and what you will seek down there tomorrow is not honor, but revenge!"

That night Gaius lay listening to other men's breathing and wondering why sleep came so hard. This was a drier bed than any he had slept in for some time, and he had been in battles before. But his other fights, he reflected, had been unexpected skirmishes that were over almost as soon as they had begun.

He sought for some distraction, and suddenly found himself remembering Eilan. During the journey north it had been Julia he thought of, imagining her amusement at some bit of odd gossip or army tale. But he could never admit to Julia the things that in this moment of darkness were haunting him –

Surrounded by all these men I feel alone . . . I want to lay my head on your breast and feel your arms around me . . . I am alone, Eilan, and I am afraid!

Finally he passed at last into an uneasy slumber, and in his dreaming it seemed to him that he and Eilan were together in a hut in the midst of the forest. He kissed her, and realized that her body was rounding with his child. She smiled at him and pulled her gown tight over her belly so that he could see; he laid his hand upon the hard curve and felt the child move within and thought that she had never been so beautiful. She opened her arms to him and drew him down beside her, murmuring words of love.

Gaius fell into a deeper sleep then. When he woke, men were stirring around him, pulling on their tunics and fumbling to lace their armor in the dim gray hour before the dawn.

"Why isn't he putting the Legions in the battle line?" Gaius asked Tacitus in an undertone.

They sat their horses with the rest of the General's personal staff on a little hill, watching the light infantry spread out in a long line below the mountain with the cavalry to either side. The pale light gleamed on the smooth tops of their bronze helmets and their spear points, and glinted on their mail. Rough pasture rose towards the lower slopes beyond them, where the dry grass gave way to broad swathes of garnet-brown bracken and the paler purple of heather. But much of the topography of Graupius could only be guessed at, for the lower part of the mountain was hidden by armed men.

"Because they're under strength," the answer came. "The Emperor siphoned off men from all four Legions, remember, for his German campaign. As a result, three thousand of our crack troops are kicking their heels in Germania while the Chatti and the Sugambri laugh at them, and Agricola will have to use every trick he knows to compensate. He's got the Legions formed up in front of the entrenchments where they can support us if we fall back, but he hopes it won't come to that."

"But it was the Emperor who ordered the Governor to secure northern Caledonia, wasn't it?" Gaius asked. "Domitian is a soldier. Wouldn't he know –?"

Tacitus smiled and Gaius felt suddenly like a child.

"Some would say," he answered softly, "that he knows all too well. Titus gave our Governor a hero's honors for his successes in Britannia, and when this campaign is over Agricola's term as Governor will be done. Perhaps the Emperor feels there is not room for two victorious generals in Rome."

Gaius looked towards their Commander, who was watching the deployment of his troops with grave attention. His armor, of dagged scale over mail, glittered in the growing light, and the horse-hair crest of his helmet stirred slightly in the breeze. Beneath the mail, tunic and breeches were snowy white, but in the early morning light his crimson cloak glowed balefully.

Years later, on a visit to Rome, Gaius read the passage from the biography of Agricola in which Tacitus described that day. He had to smile at the speeches, which had been elaborated for literary effect in the best rhetorical tradition, for while they had both heard the General's words, the wind brought them only fragments of the harangue of Calgacus, which Gaius no doubt understood much better than Tacitus.

Calgacus had begun first; at least they could see a tall man with hair the color of a fox-pelt striding back and forth before the most richly dressed of the enemy, and assumed it must be he. Echoing from the slopes behind him, phrases drifted across the open ground.

". . . they have eaten the land, and behind us remains only the sea!" Calgacus gestured northward. ". . . let us destroy these monsters who would sell our children into slavery!" The Caledonians began to roar approval, and the next words were lost. When Gaius could hear again, the enemy leader seemed to be talking about the Iceni rebellion.

". . . ran in terror when Boudicca, a woman, raised the Trinobantes against them . . . do not even risk their own people against us! Let the Gauls and our brothers the Brigantes remember how the Romans have betrayed them, and let the Batavians desert them as the Usipii have done!" There was a little stir in the ranks of the auxiliaries from those who understood this as Calgacus continued his appeal to the Caledonians to fight for their liberty, but a word from their commanders calmed them.

The tribesmen were crowding forward, singing and shaking their spears, and Gaius trembled, hearing in that wild music a call that awakened memories almost too old for him to have words for them, of songs that he had heard among the Silures when he was a babe in arms. And the hidden side of his soul, the mother's side, wept in answer, for Gaius had seen the Mendip mines, and the lines of British slaves being marched on to ships for sale in Rome, and he knew that what Calgacus said was true.

The Romans, understanding the tone if not the words, were stirring angrily. It was in that moment, when it seemed that their discipline, if not their loyalty might break, that Agricola raised his hand and reined his white horse around to face them, and his officers drew close to hear what he would say.

The General seemed to speak quietly, like a kindly father reassuring an excited child, but his words carried. He spoke of the distance they had covered, their courage in going beyond the boundaries of the Roman world, and gently pointed out the dangers of trying to retreat through such a hostile country.

". . . a retiring general or army is never safe . . . death with honor is preferable to life with ignominy . . . Even to fall in this extremest verge of earth and of nature cannot be thought an inglorious fate."

As for the Caledonians, whom Calgacus had called the last free men in Britain, in Agricola's version they became fugitives, ". . . the remaining number consists solely of the cowardly and spiritless; whom you see at length within your reach, not because they have stood their ground, but because they are overtaken." For a moment, listening to that calm and kindly voice destroy the Caledonian vision of glory, Gaius almost hated him. But he could not deny the General's conclusion, which was that a Roman victory today could bring an end to a struggle that had gone on for fifty years.

It seemed to Gaius that in this man he saw the essence of what Macellius meant by a Roman. Despite the fact that Agricola's family was of Gaulish extraction and had risen through successful public service first to the middle rank of equestrian and then to senator, he made Gaius think of the old heroes of republican Rome.

Licinius's clerks held their master in affection, but in the way Agricola's officers watched him Gaius sensed something else, an intensity of devotion that kept them steady even when the savages on the mountain began to raise their courage to battle heat by war cries and beating on their shields. Apparently this attitude extended to the men under Agricola's command, and Gaius, observing that stern profile and hearing the General speak as calmly as if he had been conversing in his tent with a few friends, thought suddenly, *This is the kind of devotion that makes Emperors*. Perhaps Domitian was right to be afraid.

The Caledonians were ranged upon the rising ground, their ranks rising in tier upon tier above the plain. Now their chariots came rushing down the slope with the horsemen ranging about them, agile ponies careering at full tilt with their drivers swaying on the wickerwork platforms while the spearmen they carried shook their weapons and laughed.

To Gaius they were an image of beauty and terror. He understood that he was seeing the warrior soul of Britannia as Caesar and

Frontinus had seen it, sensing that after this it would never be seen in all its glory again. The chariots hurtled forward, turning at the last moment as their javelins thudded into the Roman shields, and the warriors ran out along the poles between the horses, throwing their swords glittering into the air and catching them again. They had come to this battle as if to a festival, and the sun glinted from torques and armrings. Some had mail and helmets, but most fought in brightly checked tunics or half naked, their fair skin painted with spiraling designs in blue. Gaius could hear their boasting above the rattle of the chariot wheels, and felt not terror but a terrible sorrow.

One of the tribunes protested loudly as Agricola dismounted and a man came up to lead his horse away, but the faces of the others set grimly at this evidence that whatever happened to his army, Agricola would not flee. *They would give their lives to protect him,* thought Gaius, *and so,* he realized suddenly, *would I.* Some of the General's personal staff were dismounting as quiet orders set others cantering down the lines. Gaius reined back, uncertain what to do.

"You." The General gestured him closer. "Get down to the Tungri and tell them to spread out further. Tell them that I know it weakens the center, but I don't want the enemy outflanking us."

As he kicked his pony into a gallop, Gaius heard the thunk of javelins slamming into shields behind him and realized that the British chariots had pulled away and their first line of infantry were moving in. He bent over the animal's neck and urged it to better speed. The space between two armies that were closing for the first, devastating exchange of missiles was no place to be. He saw the gleam of the Tungrian standard before him and the line parted to let him through; then he was gabbling his message, moving behind the men as they began to press sideways, and watching from the corner of his eye as the enemy attack expanded outward.

The British warriors were good, he thought as he saw them deflecting Roman spears with their round shields. Their greatswords were longer even than the Roman spatha, slashing weapons blunt at the tips but wickedly sharpened along the side. The Roman trumpets blared and Agricola's center bulged forward, closing with the enemy.

Gaius knew he could do no more good here with the infantry, but the General had given him no further orders; with sudden decision he kneed his mount further down the line to join the cavalry there. Over the heads of the auxiliaries he saw the battle lines breaking up into a close, confused struggle in which the Caledonians had no room to swing their longer swords. This was the Batavians' favorite kind of fighting; they pressed forward, stabbing with their gladii and smashing enemy faces with the bosses of their shields. There was a shout from the Romans as the first line of foes gave way, and Agricola's center began to advance up the lower slopes of the mountain after them.

More slowly, the infantry to either side tried to follow them, but now the British chariots, seeing their lines thin and sensing a weakness, plunged towards them, bouncing on the rough ground. In another moment they were in among the infantry like wolves in a sheepfold, savaging the footsoldiers with sword and spear. Someone screamed at the men to close ranks; men and horses and chariots swirled in confusion; Gaius saw a blue-painted warrior loom up before him and thrust with his spear.

In the moments that followed, things happened too fast for thinking. Gaius stabbed and parried as weapons flared around him. A chariot plunged towards him and his pony whirled, throwing him hard against the back horns of his saddle. He felt the spear wrenched out of his hand and ducked as a javelin sped towards him. The missile clanged on his helmet, caught for a moment in the crest and fell away. Gaius blinked dizzily, understanding now why only officers wore crests on their helms in battle, but the pony, wiser than its master, was already carrying him out of danger.

For a moment he was clear; Gaius tugged his spatha from its sheath and straightened. He could see now that the chariots, having failed to break through the Roman lines, were becoming entangled within them. A chariot lurched towards him on the uneven ground; wood crunched as a wheel hit a boulder and it slewed round. He saw the driver hacking at the traces. Whinnying wildly, the horses sprang free, joining the others that careered in panic through the battle, knocking down friend and foe.

Battle was fairly joined now; the slopes of Graupius seethed with knots of struggling men, clumping and unraveling and knotting again in a constantly shifting tapestry. But it appeared to Gaius that little by little, the Romans were gaining ground.

Then a spear seemed to thrust up from the ground before him with a snarling face behind it; his pony reared as he whacked the shaft aside with his sword and slashed downward. Red covered the blue designs as the blade bit, then the horse leaped forward and the face was gone, and Gaius was slashing and guarding with no time for thinking at all.

When he next had a moment to focus, they were well up the mountain. From the left he heard shouting; the Caledonians who had been watching the battle from the summit were now descending, leaping down the slope with appalling swiftness to take the Romans from the rear. Could Agricola see it? Gaius heard once more the bray of the Roman trumpets, and grinned as the four wings of cavalry the General had been reserving swung into action at last. They outflanked the Britons and hammered them against the anvil of the infantry; then the true slaughter began.

Calgacus's force had lost all cohesion. Some men were still fighting, others tried to flee, but the Romans were everywhere, killing or making prisoners only to slay them in turn as yet more enemy warriors came their way. Gaius saw a gleam of white near by and spotted Agricola in the middle of the battle with only two tribunes and a couple of legionaries to guard him. He turned his mount that way.

As he neared them, one of the tribunes shouted. Three Britons, their finery soaked in blood and armed only with knives and stones, were charging. Gaius kicked the pony hard. He swung and his blade tore a crimson gash through the chest of the first man. Then his horse stumbled on something soft; Gaius felt himself falling, released his shield and wrenched himself free as the animal went down. He saw a knife flash and felt pain sear his thigh; the horse tried to struggle to its feet and the knife flared again, sinking into its neck; the animal jerked and went back down.

Gaius got up on one elbow, sank his own dagger into the Briton's chest and then used it to cut the throat of the dying horse. Then, grimacing as his thigh began to throb, he started to get up, searching around for his shield and sword.

"You all right, lad?" Agricola was looking down at him.

"Yes, sir!" he started to salute, realized that the dagger was still in his hand, and sheathed it again.

"Fall in, then," said the General, "we still have work to do."

"Yes –" Gaius began, but Agricola was already turning away to give someone else an order. One of the tribunes helped him to his feet, and he tried to catch his breath.

Blood had dyed the bracken at his feet a deeper crimson. The field seemed a mass of broken men and weapons, and those enemies left alive were scattering, pursued by the cavalry. The Romans on foot followed more slowly as the Caledonians fled towards the forest on the other side of the mountain. Agricola ordered some of the men to dismount and beat through the wood while the others circled round behind it.

It was at the edge of the wood as dusk was falling that Gaius whirled to face a man who sprang out at them. He swung instinctively, but he was tired and the blade turned in his hand, taking the warrior on the side of the head and bearing him to the ground. He drew his dagger and bent over the man to finish him, and swore as a bloody hand seized his arm. He lost his balance and came down on top of his enemy; the two of them rolled over and over, fighting for possession of the blade.

Gaius's arm began to shake as muscles that had never quite recovered from the old wound where the boar stake had gone into his shoulder began to give way. Panic tapped his last reserves of energy, and his fingers closed on the other man's throat. For a moment they heaved, the dagger digging uselessly into his armor. Then all the fight went out of the other man and he lay still.

Shaking, Gaius pulled himself upright and plucked the weapon from his enemy's nerveless fingers. He bent over to finish the job he had begun and found himself staring into Cynric's dazed eyes.

"Don't move!" he said in British, and the other stilled. Gaius looked quickly around him. "I can save you – they're beginning to take hostages. Will you surrender to me now?"

"Roman." Cynric spat, but weakly. "I should have left you in the boar pit!" It was then that Gaius realized the other man had recognized him as well. "Better for me . . . and for Eilan!"

"You have as much Roman blood as I do!" Guilt added venom to Gaius's reply.

"Your mother sold her honor! Mine died!"

Gaius found himself pushing down on the blade, and at the last moment realized that was what Cynric wanted him to do.

"You saved my life once. Now I give you yours, and Hades take your damned British pride! Surrender, and another day you can fight me." He knew this was foolish; even lying in his blood Cynric looked dangerous. But saving him was the only thing he could do for Eilan.

"You win . . ." Cynric's head fell back in exhaustion, and Gaius saw new blood seeping from the gashes on his arms and thighs, ". . . today . . ." Their eyes met, and Gaius saw the hatred still burning in his eyes. "But one day you will pay . . ." He fell silent as the wagon that was picking up the wounded creaked towards them.

Gaius watched two battered legionaries load him in with the

others, his satisfaction in the Roman victory dissipating as he realized that he had lost his friend as surely as if he had seen Cynric die before his own eyes.

With darkness Agricola called off the pursuit, not wishing to risk his men on unfamiliar ground. But for the Caledonians who survived it was not yet over. Far into the night the Romans could hear women calling as they searched the battlefield. Over the next few days returning scouts reported an ever-widening circle of devastation. The land that had once supported a thriving people was now a silent world in which the bodies of women and children killed by their own men to save them from slavery gazed blankly at the heavens, and the smoke of burned housesteads darkened the weeping sky.

When the numbers were finally tallied it was estimated that wounds or battle had accounted for ten thousand of the enemy; while only three hundred and sixty Romans died.

As Gaius rode along the column of men marching south to winter quarters, he remembered the words of Calgacus: "*To ravage, to slaughter, to usurp under false titles they call Empire; and where they make a desert, they call it peace.*"

Certainly the North was peaceful now, the last hopes for British freedom as dead as the men who had defended it. It was *this*, more than the fact that the despatches he carried included a very flattering description of his own conduct on the battlefield, that made Gaius realize that he must become entirely a Roman now.

nineteen

━━━━〰〰〰━━━━

despite Agricola's hopes, the pacification of the North was not to be neatly accomplished with a single battle. And though the people of Rome danced in the streets when the triumphant account of Mons Graupius was proclaimed, a great deal remained to be done to secure the victory. The despatches that Gaius bore southward included an order for him to return as soon as his wounds were healed, for the Governor was not inclined to let so useful a young man go to waste in Londinium.

One of Gaius's assignments was to visit the compound where they were keeping the more important prisoners. Cynric was still there, scarred and embittered, but alive, and grimly triumphant that Calgacus had not been captured to grace Agricola's triumph in Rome. Indeed, no one seemed to know what had happened to the British leader. There were rumors that the Druid Bendeigid was hiding out in the hills.

"I was taken in arms, and expect no mercy," said Cynric in a momentary softening, "but if your general has any regard for you, ask him to pardon the old man. I pulled you out of the boar pit, but he saved your life. For that, I think you owe him something, don't you?"

And Gaius had agreed. In truth, his debt was greater than Cynric knew, and since it could not be proven that Bendeigid had fought against Rome, Agricola was willing to let word be circulated through the North that the Druid could safely return home.

In the event, it was not until the Governor himself headed south to prepare for his return to Rome that Gaius was given leave to do the same. And so it was the end of winter by the time he found himself on the road to visit his father in Deva, free at last to follow the instructions Julia had given him months before to make his peace with Eilan.

Winter in the North had been black and chill, with bitter winds and nights that seemed to have no end. Even this far south the air was brisk, though the first buds were beginning to tip the branches with green, and Gaius was glad of his wolfskin cloak. In Britain even the deified Julius had sometimes worn three tunics, one above the other, against the cold.

It felt strange to ride through a country that was at peace. It seemed to Gaius that everything must have changed since last he saw it, as if he had been gone for years. But as he neared Deva, the raw wind that blew in off the estuary was the same, and the dark mountains that hung on the western horizon were the brooding shadows that had haunted him since he was a child. He rode past the mighty embankments of the fortress to the main gate, and found the timber stockade that crowned them only a little more weathered than he remembered. It was he himself that had changed.

His footsteps rang on the stone pavement of the praetorium as he strode towards his father's office. Valerius looked up as he entered, frowning for a moment until Gaius began to strip off his wrappings. Then he grinned. But it was when Macellius emerged from the inner office that Gaius realized he was not the only one to have grown older.

"Well, my boy! Is it you indeed? We had begun to fear that the Governor would take you back to Rome with him. He wrote very favorably about your work up there, lad, very favorably indeed." Macellius held out his arms, and clasped Gaius in a hearty embrace, cut short, as if the older man were afraid to betray himself if he held on to his son for too long.

But Gaius had felt how his father's fingers gripped him, as if he needed to reassure himself that his boy was there in the flesh, alive. He had no need to ask if Macellius had been worried; he did not think that settling the petty squabbles of men in winter quarters and tallying up stores had put the new gray in the Camp Prefect's hair.

"So how long are we to have the pleasure of your company before they need you back in Londinium?"

"I have a few weeks of leave, sir." Gaius forced a smile. "I thought it was time I came home for a while." With a pang he realized that Macellius had not said a word about his wedding. *The old man must realize that I have grown up at last!*

But Macellius no longer needed to ask about it. Since the battle of Mons Graupius Gaius had somehow begun to take his marriage to Julia for granted. But now that the familiar hills of Deva were bringing back old memories he wondered. Could he really go through with it, and if he did not, what would he do?

But Gaius had found out one thing about himself in these last months: he was ambitious after all. Agricola was a great man, and he had been an excellent Governor, but who could say whom Domitian would send after him? And there were things about this land that even Agricola could never understand. The old Britannia of the tribes was dead. Its people would have to change and become Romans, but how could some Gaul or Spaniard understand them? To make this country the gem of the Empire could require the leadership of someone both British and Roman. Someone like himself, if he made the right moves now.

". . . invite a few of the senior officers to join us for dinner," his father was saying. "If you're not too tired?"

"I'm fine," Gaius smiled. "After the roads in Caledonia, it was a pleasure to ride here."

Macellius nodded, and Gaius could see the pride radiating off of him like heat from a fire. He swallowed, suddenly realizing that Macellius had never before given him such unqualified approval – and how much he needed to see that glow in his father's eyes.

It was usual for the High Priestess to spend some time in seclusion after the great festivals, recovering from the ritual. The women of the Forest House had become accustomed to this when Lhiannon ruled them, and no one thought it odd that after Eilan's first appearance as High Priestess her recovery should be protracted.

And once she was up and about again, they might have been disappointed that she did not participate much in the life of their community, and so often went heavily veiled, but they were not surprised. Lhiannon was the only High Priestess that most of them had ever known, and during her last years she had kept mostly to her rooms, served by Caillean, or by her chosen attendants. In any case a period of retreat was required so that the new Oracle could commune with the gods.

And the reclusiveness of their new High Priestess was less intriguing a topic of gossip than the disappearance of Dieda. Some were sure that she had gone voluntarily, angry because she had not been chosen High Priestess. Others suggested that she had run away to join Cynric, whom several had seen when he visited the Forest House in the company of Bendeigid.

But when someone heard from a woodcutter that a pregnant woman was living in the hut in the forest, the solution to the mystery became appallingly obvious. Dieda must be with child; she had been sent to live in the isolation of the forest until she should be delivered of her shame.

The truth, of course, was so impossible that no one guessed it. In the event, Dieda's part in the deception was not even very taxing, for after the battle of Mons Graupius the Governor had forbidden all public assemblies lest they spark unrest. This far south they had heard only rumors of the destruction; for most folk, getting in food for the winter was a more pressing concern. At the feast of Samaine folk had to make do with the little divinations of apples and nuts and the hearthfire, for there was no fair or festival, and no Oracle.

As for Eilan, she spent the winter snug in the round hut in the forest, visited from time to time by Caillean, and attended by an old woman who did not know her name. She made a little altar to the Goddess as Mother by the fireside, and as she watched her belly ripen, she wavered between joy in the new life that was growing within her and anguish because she did not know if she would ever see her child's father again.

But it was the natural course of things that even the longest winter should one day give way to spring. Though there were times when Eilan had felt that she would be pregnant for ever, the feast of Brigantia was approaching, when her child should be born. A few days before the festival Caillean appeared in the doorway, and though these days she came easily to tears or laughter, Eilan felt so glad to see her that she thought she would weep.

"There is fresh oat bread that I baked this morning," she said. "Sit here and join me in my noon meal –" She hesitated. "– unless you feel that I contaminate you by my forsworn presence?"

Caillean laughed, "Never," she replied. "If it had not been for the snows, I would have come before."

"And how are things in the Forest House?" Eilan asked. "How does Dieda in my place? Tell me everything; I am very dull here; growing like a vegetable!"

"Surely not." Caillean smiled. "Perhaps a fruit tree come to harvest not in autumn but spring. As for Vernemeton, Dieda performs your duties faithfully, though perhaps not as well as you would do. I promise you I will come when your child is born. Send me word by the old woman when the time comes."

"How will I know?"

Caillean laughed, not unkindly. "You were present when your sister's second child was born. How much do you remember?"

"What I remember of that time is the raiders, and how you carried fire," Eilan said meekly.

Caillean smiled. "Well, I think it will not be long now. Perhaps you will deliver on the Feast of the Maiden – your hands were busy this morning, and such restlessness is often seen when a child stirs in readiness to be born. And I have brought you a gift, a garland of white birch twigs, sacred to the Mother. See – I will hang it above your bed that it may bring you good fortune at Her hands." She rose and drew the wreath from her bag.

"The gods men follow may seem to shun you, but the Goddess cares for all Her daughters who stand where you stand now. After the festival I will come again, though it will be no pleasure seeing Dieda in your place there."

"How delighted I am to hear your opinion," someone said from the doorway, the sweetness of her voice intensifying the sting of her words. "But if you do not like me in the role of High Priestess, surely it is a little late to be saying so!"

A figure heavily veiled in dark blue was standing there. Eilan's eyes widened and Caillean flushed angrily.

"Why have you come here?"

"Why not?" Dieda asked. "Do you not think it gracious of the High Priestess to visit her fallen kinswoman? All of our dear sisters are aware that someone is living here, you know, and have concluded it is me. I will not have a shred of reputation left when I eventually 'return'."

Eilan's voice shook. "Did you come only to gloat over my shame, Dieda?"

"Strangely enough, I did not," Dieda put back her veil. "Eilan, in spite of all that has been between us, I wish you well. You are not the only one who is alone. I have had no word of Cynric since he went north, and he has sent no word to me. He cares for nothing but the fate of the Ravens. Perhaps when this deception is over I should go north instead of to Eriu and become one of the warrior women who serve the goddess of battles."

"Nonsense," said Caillean tartly. "You would make a very poor warrior, but you are a gifted bard."

Dieda shrugged helplessly. "Perhaps, but I must find some way to atone for serving Ardanos's treachery."

"Do you truly call it so?" asked Eilan; "I do not. I have had time to think, living here, and it seems to me that the Lady has allowed this to happen to Her priestess so that I may understand the need to protect all the children of this land. It is peace, not war, that I will work for when I return."

Dieda looked down at Eilan. She said slowly, "I never had any wish for a child by Cynric or any other man. And yet I think that if I were bearing a child to Cynric, I might feel as you do." Her eyes were glistening with tears and she dashed them angrily away. "I must return before busy tongues have time to spin too many tales. I came only to wish you good fortune; but it seems that even here, Caillean has forestalled me."

She turned, pulling her veil over her face once more, and before either of them could find words to reply, was gone.

Every day, it seemed, the light lasted a little longer. The branches blushed with returning sap and the swans began courting in the marshes. Though winter storms might still come to lash the land, there was a sense that spring was coming. The men who worked the land took down their plowshares from the rafters, and the fishermen began to caulk their vessels, and the shepherds stayed out all night on the cold hillsides with the lambing ewes.

Gaius rode out, listening to the sounds of new life all around him, and counted the days. It had been Beltane when he and Eilan lay together, and since then nine moons had passed. She would be giving birth soon now. Women died in childbirth sometimes. He watched returning waterfowl unraveling across the sky and knew that whether he married Julia or not, he had to see Eilan once more.

The higher he rose among the Romans, the more he could do for Eilan and their child. If it were a son, perhaps Eilan would let him raise him. She certainly could not keep him in the Forest House. It did not seem so unlikely; his mother's people had been willing enough to give him up completely into his father's hands.

As he rode back to the fortress his thoughts went round and round. It would be hard to tell her that they could not be married, at least not yet. If Julia did not give him a son, well, he sometimes thought divorced couples were more common than married ones in the Roman world. When his position was assured perhaps they could marry; at least he could give his child a good start in the world. Would she believe that? Would she forgive him? He bit his lip, wondering what he would say to her.

But mostly his heart beat hard simply at the thought of seeing Eilan again, even at a distance; just to know that all was well with her.

Of course, there was still the problem of *how* he was going to get in to see her. At length he realized that he would have to trust to the gods to help him.

The Legate who commanded the Second Adiutrix Legion had retired the preceding winter and it was just at this moment that his replacement arrived. Gaius knew that his father would have more than enough to do helping the new Commander settle in. When he announced he was going off for a few days' hunting, Macellius hardly had time to say farewell.

It was at the festival of the goddess the Britons called Brigantia that celebrated the end of the winter that Gaius rode once more past the Hill of the Maidens, just at that time when the young men dressed in costumes of straw and carried an image of the Lady from house to house to give Her blessing in exchange for cakes and ale. But here, he had heard, the priestess who was the Voice of the Goddess came out to proclaim the coming of spring to the people. In the wood outside the village Gaius changed into the British clothing he had brought along. Then he joined the others who were gathering to await the priestesses. From conversations overheard around him, he learned that this year the crowd was bigger than usual.

"The old Priestess died last autumn," one of the women told him. "And they say that the new one is young, and very beautiful."

"Who is she?" he asked, his heart beginning to beat heavily in his breast.

"The Arch-Druid's granddaughter, I am told, and some whisper there was more than chance in her choosing. But I say that the old blood is best for the old ways, and who should be better fitted for such a task than one whose fathers and mothers before her have served the gods?"

Eilan! he thought. How could it be? Had she lost the child? If she was really High Priestess, how was he ever to see her again? He waited with ill-concealed impatience for nightfall, and grew silent with the others as they saw the procession of white-robed maidens emerge from the timber gate of the Forest House and come towards them down the avenue. At their head walked a slender woman with a scarlet cloak over her white gown. Beneath the thin veil he could see the glint of golden hair. She came crowned with light and attended by harpsong. *Eilan* . . . his heart cried. *Can you feel me near you, Eilan?*

"Out of the winter's darkness I have come –" she said, and her voice was like music. Too much like music, thought Gaius; Eilan's voice had been sweet to him, but it had not this resonance. He pressed closer, trying to see. This woman's voice sounded as if she were a trained singer.

"Light-bearer am I, and bearer of blessings. Now comes the springtide; new leaves shall spring soon from the branches, and the rainbow flowers. May your beasts bear in abundance; good fortune to your plowing. Take now the light, my children, and with it my favor."

The Priestess bent, and they lifted from her head the crown of candles. As they lowered it to the ground before her, Gaius saw her face for the first time in full light. It was the face he had dreamed of, and yet, even in a single moment of illumination, he knew it was not Eilan. He remembered, now, how beautifully Dieda had sung.

He pulled away, shaking. Had the woman got it wrong or was Eilan the victim of some dreadful deception?

"Hail to the Lady!" the people cried. "Hail to the Holy Bride!" Cheering, the young men touched their torches to the candle crown and began to form the procession that would carry the light to every hut and farm. It was certainly Dieda, and she must know where Eilan was. But he could not approach her now.

He turned away and recognized another face in the crowd. At this moment, danger meant nothing.

"Caillean," he whispered harshly. "I must speak to you! In the name of mercy – where is Eilan?"

In the half-light he felt sharp eyes on him; he heard a voice speaking in a whisper, "What are you saying?" A hard grip closed on his hand. "Come away from this crowd; we cannot speak here."

He went unresisting. It seemed to him that if death should descend on him, it would be no more than his due. But when they were beyond the crowd, he stopped in his tracks and turned to the priestess.

His voice was low and hoarse. "Mistress Caillean, I know how Eilan loved you. In the name of any god you cherish, tell me – where is she now?"

Caillean pointed to the dais where the white-veiled woman presided over the festivities.

"Cry out and betray me if you will, but do not lie to me." Gaius stared into her eyes. "Though every man here should swear that is Eilan, I know better. Tell me if she is alive and well!"

Caillean stared back at him with widening eyes in which he read amazement, anger, and fear. Then she let out her breath in an explosive sigh and pulled him after her, further away from the circle of torchlight where Dieda was lifting her hands to bless the crowd. As he followed Caillean into the shadows, Gaius told himself that the catch in his throat was only from the smoke of the fires.

"I should tell them who you are and let them kill you," she said finally. "But I, too, love Eilan, and she has had enough pain."

"Is she alive?" Gaius's voice cracked.

"No thanks to you," Caillean retorted. "Ardanos would have put her to death when he heard what you had done! But he was persuaded to spare her, and she told me everything. Why did you never come for her? Is it true that you have married someone else as we were told?"

"My father sent me away —"

"To Londinium," she confirmed. "Then it was one of the Arch-Druids's lies that you had been married off to some Roman girl?"

"Not yet," he said. "But I have been on service and was not free to come. If Eilan was not punished, why do I not see her here?"

Caillean looked at him with contempt; and Gaius felt it withering him. At last she said, "Would you expect her to be out here dancing when she has just given birth to your son?"

Gaius's breath caught. "Is she alive? Is the child?" It was dark here, away from the fires, but it seemed to him that Caillean's stern expression softened.

"She is alive, but weak, for the birth was hard; I have been very frightened for her. You do not seem to me worth dying for, but seeing you might be the medicine she needs. The gods know I am no judge. I care nothing what Ardanos might say. Come with me."

Caillean was only a dark shadow in the night as she led him around the crowd and back along the road, away from the Forest House and the Hill of Maidens. When they could no longer see the light of the fires, Gaius asked, "Where are you taking me?"

"Eilan is not in the Forest House now; she has dwelt in a little house in the deepest part of the woods since the child began to show." After a moment Caillean added hesitantly, "I have been very troubled for her. Women are sometimes very sorrowful after they have had a child, and the gods know that Eilan has enough reason to be unhappy; perhaps when she sees that you have not abandoned her, she will recover more quickly."

"They told me that if I did not attempt to see her, she would not be mistreated –" he protested.

Caillean laughed, a brief bitter sound. "Ardanos was furious, of course, the wretched old tyrant. He is convinced that only if you Romans think of our priestesses as Vestals will you protect them. But the choice of the Goddess had fallen on Eilan, and he could not deny it, when Lhiannon with almost her dying breath had proposed this deception."

Caillean did not speak again. After a time Gaius saw through the trees a small glimmer of light against a greater darkness.

"There is the house."

Caillean's voice came soft in his ear. "Wait in the shadows while I get rid of the old woman." She opened the door.

"The blessing of the Lady to you, Eilan; I've come to keep you company. Annis, I'll care for her now. Why don't you go out and enjoy the festival?"

Presently he saw the old woman emerging, well-swaddled in shawls, and as she passed down the pathway he drew back beneath the trees. Caillean stood in the open doorway behind her, framed by the light. She gestured, and as he came forward, heart thumping like a charge of cavalry, said quietly into the golden glow behind her, "I have brought you a visitor, Eilan." He heard her going out to keep watch behind him.

For a moment Gaius's eyes were dazzled by the light. When he could focus again, he saw Eilan lying on a narrow bed, at her side the bundle that he knew must be the child.

Eilan forced her eyes to open. She supposed it was kind of Caillean to come to her, but why should she bring a visitor? She did not want to see anyone except Caillean, but she had been sure the older priestess would be busy with the festival. A dull curiosity stirring within her, she opened her eyes.

A man's shape was standing between her and the light. Her grip on the child tightened in instinctive alarm and the baby made a little squeaking sound of protest. At that, the man took a quick step forward, and as the light fell full upon his face, she knew him at last.

"Gaius!" she exclaimed, and at once burst into tears. She saw him redden, shifting uncomfortably from foot to foot, unable to meet her eyes.

"I was sent to Londinium; I had no choice," he said. "I wanted to come to you."

"I'm sorry –" she said, though she was not really sure why she was apologizing, "I seem to weep very easily these days."

His gaze flicked swiftly to her, and then to the bundle.

"Is this my son?"

"No other," she said, "or do you really think perhaps that because –" suddenly she was crying so hard she could hardly speak – "that because I gave myself to you, I would lie down for any other man who came along?"

"Eilan!" From his face, she could see that the thought had never occurred to him, and did not know whether to be flattered or indignant. His hands clenched and unclenched. "Please! Let me hold my son."

Eilan felt her tears ceasing as abruptly as they had come. She looked up at Gaius, for the first time really seeing him as he knelt beside her, and lifted the baby into his arms. He looked older and grimmer, fine drawn by hardship and with a shadow in his eyes as if he too had known pain; on his cheek was a new scar. But as he held the child she saw his face begin to change.

"My son –" he whispered, gazing at the crumpled features, "my first-born son . . ." Even if he went through with his marriage to the Roman girl, thought Eilan, this moment was hers.

As the baby's pale blue, wandering eyes met those of his father and seemed to fix on him, Gaius's arms tightened protectively around him. All the hardness had gone from his features now; his focus was entirely on the baby, as if he would do anything to safeguard this child who lay so trusting and helpless in his arms. It came to Eilan that even when Gaius had been making love to her she had never seen him look so radiant. She recognized the Father-face of the God.

"What sort of world will this be for you, little one?" Gaius whispered, his voice cracking. "How can I protect you, give you a home that will be secure?" For a long moment he and the child seemed lost in mutual contemplation; then the baby burped suddenly and began to chew on his thumb.

Gaius's gaze returned to Eilan, and as he set the child once more within the curve of her arm she realized that, wan and exhausted though she might be, to him she was the Goddess as well.

"So, how do you like him, my dear?" she said gently. "I have called him Gawen, the name that your mother gave you."

"I think he is beautiful, Eilan." His voice was shaking. "How can I ever thank you for this great gift?"

Run away with me! her heart cried. *Carry us both away to some land where we can all live together and be free!* But the lamplight glinted balefully on the signet ring he wore, and she knew that there was no such country, beyond the reach of Rome.

"Make a world that will be safe for him." She echoed his own words. She remembered her vision; in this child the blood of the Dragon and the Eagle had mingled with the old line of the Wise; the saviors of Britannia would come from his line. But for that to happen he must live to be a man.

"Sometimes I wonder if that is possible." His gaze went inward, and she saw the grim shadow once more in his eyes.

"You have been in battle since I saw you," she said gently, "you did not get that scar in Londinium . . . Tell me."

"Have you heard about the battle of Mons Graupius?" Gaius's voice grew harsher. "Well, I was there." As the story poured out of him in a succession of images, she flinched, feeling the horror, and the pity, and the fear.

"I knew that something had happened," she said in a low voice when he was done. "There was a night, a moon after Lughnasad, when I felt that you were in great danger. I spent the following day in terror, but the feeling passed off after nightfall. I thought then that perhaps you had been fighting, but though I could sense nothing more I was certain that you had survived! You are part of me, my beloved. Surely if you had died, I would know!"

Gaius reached out blindly and took her hand. "It is true. I dreamed I was in your arms. No other woman will ever live in my heart as you do, Eilan. No other woman can give me my first-born son! But –" His voice cracked. "I cannot acknowledge him. I cannot marry you!"

His face working, he looked down at the child. "When I could not find out what had happened to you, I kept telling myself that we should have fled together when we had the chance. I could have endured a life on the run if we were together – but what kind of a life would that have been for you, and what kind of life for *him?*" He reached out and touched the baby's cheek.

"He is so little, so soft," he said wonderingly. "If anything tried to harm him, right now I think I could kill it with my bare hands!" Gaius's gaze flicked from the child to Eilan and he grew red, as if embarrassed by his own emotion.

"You said to make the world safe for him," he went on in a low voice. "As things are now, I can think of only one way to do that. But you will need as much courage as some ancient Roman matron of the Republic." At the moment neither thought it odd that despite their great Emperors, Romans always invoked the days of the Republic whenever they wished to call great virtue to mind.

"You are trying to tell me that you are going to marry your Roman girl," Eilan said harshly. She was crying once more.

"I have to!" he exclaimed. "Don't you see? Mons Graupius was the last stand of the tribes. The only hope of mercy for your people now is in rulers who are both Roman and British, like me, but my only hope of gaining power in the Roman world is through alliance to an important family. "Don't cry," he begged raggedly. "I have never been able to endure your tears, my little one. Think of him." He gestured toward the sleeping baby. "For his sake, surely we can bear whatever we must."

You will not have to bear what I do, she struggled against her tears, *what I have already borne!*

"You won't be alone for ever, I promise you that," he said. "I'll claim you as soon as I can. And," he added disingenuously, "surely you know that among our people a marriage is not indissoluble."

"Yes, I have heard that," Eilan said acidly, sure that if he was marrying into a noble family, that the union would be as tight as the girl's kinfolk could make it. "But what is she like, this Roman girl? Is she beautiful?"

He looked at her ruefully. "She has not half your beauty, my precious. She is a little thing," he added, "but very determined. There are times when it seems that I have been thrown unarmed into the arena to face a war-elephant, or a savage wild animal unarmed, as I have heard is done with criminals in Rome."

Then she will never let go of him, thought Eilan, but she managed a smile. "Then you do not . . . really care about her?"

"Darling," he said, kneeling at her side, and the relief in his voice made her want to laugh, "if it were not that her father is the Procurator, I give you my word, I would never have looked twice at her. With his help I can become a senator, even a Governor of Britain one day. Think of all I could do for you and the baby then!"

Gaius bent over the child and once more that fierce protectiveness flickered in his eyes. Then, sensing that Eilan was watching him, he looked up again.

Eilan continued to stare until she saw him becoming uneasy again. *Caillean was right*, she thought with bitter resignation, *he has fallen in love with a delusion and persuaded himself it is reality – like every other man!* Well, that should make it easier to tell him what she had to say.

"Gaius, you know that I love you," she began, "but you must believe that even if you were free to offer me marriage I could not accept you." She sighed, seeing confusion flicker in his eyes.

"I am High Priestess of Vernemeton, the Voice of the Goddess, did not they tell you? What you hope to be among the Romans, Gaius, among my people I already am! I risked my life to prove myself worthy, and the ordeal was every bit as dangerous as your battle. I can no more give up that victory than you can throw away the honor you have won!"

He frowned, trying to accept it, and Eilan realized that they were really far more alike than he knew. But it seemed to her that he was prompted by ambition, while she – if that were not also a delusion – was obeying the will of the gods.

"Then, though no one else knows it, we will work together – said Gaius finally, his gaze returning to the child. "And with a Governor and a High Priestess for parents, what might this little one not do? Who knows; perhaps he will be Emperor himself someday."

At that, the baby opened his eyes, considering them both impartially with his vague gaze. Gaius picked him up again, cradling him awkwardly. "Be still now, Lord of the World," he whispered as the baby squirmed, "and let me hold you."

At that thought – that anything so small and pink could ever grow up to be Emperor – his parents laughed.

twenty

━━━∿∿∿━━━

Gaius returned to Londinium in a kind of bittersweet daze. He had found Eilan, and lost her. He had been forced to leave the child she had borne him, and yet, he had a son! At times, as the capital and Julia drew nearer, he wanted to turn his horse and gallop back to Eilan, but he could find no way they could stay together as a family. And he remembered how stern her face had grown when Eilan told him what being High Priestess meant to her. For a few moments she had not looked like his Eilan at all. It chilled him to think of the risk she had run to prove herself worthy, and how she had risked his son!

And yet she had wept when they parted. So, to be truthful, had he. If Eilan thought he got any pleasure from the thought of being married to Julia Licinia, she was very much mistaken. As he breasted the last hill and saw the tile roofs of the city basking in the afternoon sun, he reminded himself that he was only doing this for her sake and for the sake of their child.

It was twilight by the time he reached the house of Licinius. The Procurator had not yet returned from the tabularium, but Gaius found Julia in the women's atrium. Her eyes lit up at the sight of him; making her prettier than he had ever seen her. Not, of course, as pretty as Eilan; but then no one could be as beautiful as Eilan had become. Still, Julia might become very handsome in time.

She greeted him demurely. "So you are back from the West Country, Gaius."

"As I stand before you, what would you say if I told you I was still in the North?"

She giggled. "Well, I have heard that the spirits of the slain sometimes appear to those they leave behind." Suddenly she was frightened, and the mirth went out of her voice. "Gaius, tell me you

are only teasing me and that I truly see you here, alive and well!"
Abruptly he realized how young she was.

"I am flesh and blood," he said wearily. But since he had been
here last he had seen death and dealt it; he had seen his future in
the eyes of a new-born child. Before, he had been a boy. He was a
man now, and had learned to think like one. No wonder if Julia
was confused by the change.

Julia came forward and touched his arm. "Yes – you are alive,"
she said, more steadily. "And you have seen your British girl?" She
gazed up at him.

"I have seen her –" he began, searching for a way to tell her what
had happened. Julia had a right to know what kind of a husband
she would be getting if she married him.

But before he could get the words out, he heard Licinius's halting
step on the mosaic floor and the moment was lost.

"So you're back, my dear fellow." Licinius seemed genuinely
glad to see him. "I suppose this means we shall soon be having a
wedding here."

"I hope so, sir," Gaius said, and hoped they thought his hesitation
had been modesty. Perhaps it was just as well, for if Julia had
refused to marry him, what hope had he of fulfilling his promises
to protect Eilan and their child?

Julia smiled radiantly. Perhaps being married to her would have
its compensations. She caught his glance and blushed.

"Come and see my wedding veil," she said invitingly. "I have
been working on the embroidery for months. It's all right to show it
to Gaius now, isn't it, Father?" she asked.

"Yes, my dear, of course, but I still think you should have been
content with a linen veil. That was good enough for a Roman
woman in the days of the Republic, and it should have been good
enough for you," Licinius grumbled.

"And look at what became of your Republic," Julia said
impertinently. "I wanted the most fashionable veil that could be
had – and I think you did too!"

The veil was indeed beautiful, of sheer, flame-colored silk, which
Julia was embroidering in gold thread with fruit and flowers.

When she had left them, Licinius took Gaius quietly aside.

"I have set the date for the formal betrothal at the end of this
month, before the unlucky days at the beginning of March. Your
father cannot be present, but the Legate should be able to do
without him for a time by April, when my augurs have found a

favorable day for the wedding. It is short notice, but I think we can be ready. Otherwise it would be the second half of June before the season was auspicious, and while you have been off winning honors among the Caledonians my daughter has had to wait an extra year to be married." He smiled benignly. "If that's quite all right with you, my dear boy?"

"Oh yes, quite –" Gaius said faintly. And what would they all do, he wondered, if he said it was not? He wondered why Licinius bothered to consult him at all.

Then Julia came back into the room, and as she reached out to him, he realized that he could not betray the trust in those dark eyes. He and Eilan had never really had a chance; at least he might be able to give some happiness to this Roman girl.

A watery sunlight streamed through the door of the hut in the forest, for it had been raining earlier. Eilan moved slowly about inside. Putting on her clothes, part of her awareness turned to the small sounds the baby made in his sleep. Her strength had returned more quickly after Gaius's visit, but it still hurt to move. She had been much torn by the birth, and she was easily tired.

The baby slumbered in his basket, wrapped in an old shawl. Eilan stopped for a moment to admire him. To her, Gawen was all the more beautiful because she fancied she could see a blurred reflection of his father in the nub of his nose and the dark feathering of his brows.

She sat for a moment contemplating her child's face. *Gawen* . . . she thought, *my little king!* What would Macellius – supposing he should ever hear of his grandson – think of that? She wanted to pick him up but she had so much else to do, and he was sleeping peacefully. So peacefully, in fact, that she bent close to catch the small sound of his breathing. Reassured, she straightened again.

One garment at a time, with long rests between them, she managed to dress and to comb and braid her long hair. Ordinarily Annis would have helped her, but she had been sent to the village to replenish their supplies. Having preserved her secret so long, it would not do to have the old woman present when Ardanos arrived.

Eilan wrapped the braid around her head in a matronly style that was new to her. Perhaps she could face him with more confidence if he saw her as a grown woman instead of a frightened child.

What did the old man want? Reason told her that he had come

to order her back to the Forest House, but again and again she had to repress a chill of fear. Did he mean to send her away after all?

She thought wildly of following Gaius, if he was not yet married. Or Mairi might shelter her, unless their father forbade it. Caillean had told her that Bendeigid was back from the North, gaunt as a winter wolf and much embittered by the ruin of their cause. But so long as he lived quietly at his elder daughter's steading, the Romans were unlikely to bother him.

Once Eilan got her strength back she could care for herself and her child by hiring out to some farm. A healthy boy could always earn his keep. It might be wiser, though, not to say who his father was. She herself was skilled in all manner of household work, spinning and weaving, milking and churning; if she had to support herself and her son, she certainly could. She sighed and sat back on the bed, knowing that these were only fantasies.

She had heard that the Roman Vestals could leave the temple when they reached the age of thirty, but here the only release for a High Priestess was the funeral fire. She remembered that Ardanos's first reaction to her pregnancy had been to sentence her and her unborn child to death, and there was Bendeigid's threat to strangle her with his own hands. But surely, if they meant to kill her, they could already have easily done it.

By the time the Arch-Druid's shadow fell across the doorway she had worked herself into a state of numb apprehension.

"I am glad to see you are better," he said neutrally, looking down at her.

"Oh yes, I am feeling quite well, Grandsire."

He scowled. "Indeed I am your grandsire, and you will do well to remember it!"

He strode to the basket, looked down at the child for a moment, then lifted it in his arms. "But you have made your bed, and now we must all lie in it. This masquerade has gone on long enough. Three days should be enough for your milk to dry off, and then you will return to the Forest House to prepare for the spring rituals. As for your son, he will be fostered elsewhere." He turned and started towards the door.

"Stop!" Eilan cried out. "Where are you taking him?" She felt anguish swelling in her throat and remembered how their hound bitch had howled when Bendeigid took her puppies out to be drowned because she had mismated with a neighbor's terrier.

He regarded her unblinkingly. "Believe me, it is better that you do not know. I pledge you that he will be perfectly well and safe. Perhaps, if you do everything you are told, we may let you see him from time to time."

Eilan wondered why she had never noticed before how cruel Ardanos looked when he smiled, and how very long and sharp his teeth were. "You cannot," she cried. "I will care for him. You must not take him from me. Oh, please, I beg you –"

Ardanos's bushy brows met. "Why such surprise?" he asked with edged control. "Did you suppose you could nurse your child before all the priestesses in the House of Maidens. Be reasonable."

"Give him to me," she cried. "You cannot have him." She snatched at the wrapped bundle in her grandfather's arms, and the baby, waking, began to scream.

"You little fool, let him go."

Eilan's legs would no longer uphold her, but she clung to his knees. "I beg you, I beg you, Grandfather! You cannot," she was babbling, "you cannot take my son from me . . ."

"I must, and I will," Ardanos said fiercely, thrust outward with his knee and wrenched his robe free. As she collapsed he carried the wailing infant out through the open door.

And then there was only the dappling of sunlight, as innocently mocking as a baby's smile.

"Is this your revenge, you monster?" Caillean banged the door shut behind her and stormed into the room, too angry to appreciate the fact that in his quarters in the Roman town, the Arch-Druid had a door to slam. By Roman standards the house would have seemed plain and small; its straight, plastered walls and sharp corners seemed unfriendly to British eyes.

Ardanos looked up from his meal, agape, and she marshaled the words stored up during her ride from Vernemeton.

"You wicked, cruel old man! I promised Lhiannon before she died to help you. But that does not make me your slave or your torturer!"

He opened his mouth to speak but she raged on. "How could you treat Eilan – your own daughter's child – that way? I tell you I will be no part of this; let her keep her child or –" she drew breath, "or I will appeal directly to the people and let the Goddess judge between us."

"You would not –" Ardanos began.

"Try me!" Caillean retorted implacably. "I assume that you have some use for her or you would not have let her survive," she continued more moderately. "Well, I tell you, unless Eilan is allowed to have her child with her she will die."

"I suppose it is not surprising that the girl should be such a fool, but I did not expect it of you," he said when she let him get a word in at last. "Stop exaggerating. Women do not die so easily."

"Do they not? Eilan was bleeding again when I found her. You almost lost her, old man, and then where would all your plans be? Do you truly believe Dieda would be as pliant to your will?"

"In the Goddess's name, what do you want of me, woman?"

"Don't dare to speak of the Goddess; you have shown me over and over that you know less than nothing of Her," Caillean said angrily. For the sake of Lhiannon who – the gods know why – loved you and believed in your plans, I have helped you so far.

"But you cannot intimidate me as you did Lhiannon, nor frighten me; I have too little to lose. I would be willing to go to the priests and let them judge between us. Treating with the Romans and interfering with Oracles is a nasty business, or at least they would think it so, not understanding –" she stopped to sneer – "your high purpose."

"Why are you doing this? Eilan is no kin of yours." Ardanos was gazing at her as if he really did not understand.

Caillean sighed. She had loved Lhiannon as a mother, but she was coming to realize that Eilan was like a sister, or like the daughter she had never had – and never would, now that her moonblood had ceased to flow. Barren as she was, and in a way that would have been impossible when she was younger, she understood Eilan's passionate need to keep her child.

"It should be enough to know that you really cannot stop me. I suggest that you believe that, Ardanos, for you have more to lose than I. Do you think the other priests of your Order would not inquire why this child should live at all? You have a hold over Eilan while she knows you can take her child; you have – thanks be to all the gods at once – none over me."

The Arch-Druid looked thoughtful, but even as she began to hope that she was convincing him, Caillean realized that what she had said was not strictly true. Ardanos threatened her by threatening Eilan.

"Bring the baby back, Ardanos," Caillean, who in her years with Lhiannon had learned all about compromise, softened her voice. "Even if Eilan has the child with her, they are still in your power.

Do you think it is a small thing to have the Priestess of the Oracles in the hollow of your hand?"

"Perhaps I did act a little hastily –" he said finally. "But what I told the girl was true. If she flaunts her son at the Forest House we might as well proclaim her shame to the world. How do you suggest we maintain the deception if I let her keep him there?"

Caillean's shoulders slumped as she realized that she had won. "I have thought of a way –"

The day appointed for Gaius's wedding dawned clear and bright. Gaius woke when the spring sun shone in through his window, and blinked as it glowed blindingly on the whiteness of the toga draped across the chair. In the past year he had been required to wear the garment at the social and diplomatic occasions at which he had accompanied his prospective father-in-law and had become a little more used to handling its draperies, but he still found it awkward. Agricola boasted that he had taught the sons of British chieftains to wear the toga, but Gaius wondered. He had been brought up as a Roman, but he was still more comfortable in uniform or in the tunic and trews of the tribes.

He sat up, surveying the garment in dismay. His father, who had come in from Deva the day before and was sleeping in the same room, turned over and lifted one eyebrow.

"I do think they could invent a better ceremonial garment," Gaius grumbled, "or at least something more convenient."

"A toga is more than a garment," said Macellius. "It is a symbol." He sat up and to the amazement of his son, who was never at his best the first thing in the morning, began to discourse on the toga's honorable history.

But presently Gaius started to understand. Even, or perhaps especially, here at the far end of the Empire, the right to wear the white toga of a citizen was a way of distinguishing between the masters of the world and those they had conquered, and the narrow purple stripe of the *eques* that marked his tunic an honor dearly won. And that was very important to men like his father. Compared to that, the comfort of the garment was irrelevant.

Much as he would have liked to toss the offending piece of cloth out of the window, it was just one of the things he had to accept when he threw in his lot with Rome. At least the toga was woolen, and so was the tunic he would wear beneath it. Though the April wind blew chill and rainy he would not freeze.

Sighing, he allowed himself to be bathed and shaved by his freedman, slipped into his tunic and sandals, and then set to work trying to figure out how to drape the thing. After a few moments his father, his face gone so wooden that Gaius felt sure he was suppressing a grin, took the toga away from him. Deftly he arranged the pleats of white wool to hang down in front of the left shoulder, adjusted the drape across the back and under his son's right arm, and then drew the remainder carefully across his chest and over the left shoulder in the other direction so that the folds were draped gracefully over his arm.

"There now." He stepped back and surveyed his son indulgently. "Stand up a little straighter and you could pose for a statue."

"I feel like one," Gaius mumbled, afraid to move lest the whole arrangement come undone. This time his father did laugh.

"Never mind; it's natural for a bridegroom to be nervous. You'll feel better when it's all done."

"Did you?" Gaius asked abruptly. "When you married my mother, were you afraid?"

Macellius stilled, and for a moment his eyes clouded with remembered pain. "I felt joy when she came to me and every day of our lives together until she was gone . . ." he whispered.

As I did when Eilan lay in my arms . . . Gaius thought bitterly. *But I have consented to this mummery, and have no choice but to go through with it now.*

The sight of the haruspex who had been called in to take the auspices for the marriage did nothing to improve his mood. In the noon sunlight the man's bald red head and long skinny legs made him look like one of his own chickens and Gaius was cynically certain that whatever spots he found on the entrails of the unfortunate fowl would indicate it was an auspicious day. With most of the dignitaries of Londinium standing about it would be exceedingly inconvenient to cancel the festivities. In any case, the augurs had already been consulted weeks ago to select the proper day.

The atrium, its pillars twined with greenery, was crowded with what seemed to be an appalling number of people; he recognized a couple of wrinkled prune-faced elderly dowagers whom he had met in Licinius's house several times over the last few months. He noticed that they really smiled, if not actually at him, at least somewhere in his direction. Maybe they were happy for Julia; if they only knew how mixed a bargain she was getting they would frown!

In due course the sacrificer declared it a very good day for a wedding and offered congratulations. No day on which Julia had decided to be married would dare to be unfavorable.

There was a little murmur as the sacrifice was cleared away and the bride entered on her father's arm. Gaius could see little but the hem of her white tunica beneath the crimson flamma, the famous veil. One of Licinius's secretaries unrolled the marriage contract and began to read in a nasal drone. Most of it had been completed at the ceremony of betrothal: the amount of the *coemptio* which Gaius was offering, and the sum which Julia would bring to the marriage, the fact that she was to remain "in the hand" of her father as a legal part of his family, and would retain her own property. It had been explained to him that these days that arrangement was more usual, and no one would think the less of him. There was a provision that he could not divorce Julia except for "grievous misconduct", which must be attested by at least two noble matrons. Gaius would have laughed if anything now could have made him laugh; anyone less likely to misbehave than the dignified Julia, he simply could not imagine, and she had made it too clear that she wanted this marriage to jeopardize it. Even her sober demeanor today could not hide the triumph in her eyes.

"Gaius Macellius Severus Siluricus, do you agree to the terms of this contract, and are you willing to take this woman as your wife according to the law?" his father asked then. Gaius realized that they were all looking at him, but still it seemed an endless time before he could say the words.

"I am willing —"

"Julia Licinia?" Her father turned to the girl and repeated the question. Her agreement came a good deal more swiftly. The secretary presented the document to each of them for signing and then carried it away to be registered in the archives.

Gaius felt as if his freedom were going with it, but the Roman gravity that went with the toga did not require him to smile. A sweet-faced lady, identified as the daughter of Agricola, came forward, took Julia's hand and led her to Gaius. He felt a pang of guilt as her small fingers tightened on his.

There were prayers then, a great many it seemed, invoking Juno and Jupiter, Vesta and every other deity who might be assumed to be concerned with the preservation of hearth and home. He and

Julia were given a bowl of grain and a flagon of oil to offer to the fire on the altar. As it crackled in the flames the scent of cooked food came suddenly from the dining hall off the atrium, mingling in a rather sickening fashion with the incense that had been burned. The feast was almost ready. Julia put back her veil. He took the cake of rough spelt wheat – he hoped they would have something better to eat at the feast to follow – broke it and thrust a morsel between Julia's lips. She repeated the gesture, saying the appointed words that made them legally one. The ritual had acquired its own momentum, and from now on he had only to go through the motions.

He sat through the wedding feast in the dining chamber, as lavish as Licinius's purse and Julia's pride could make it, in a kind of daze. He was aware that the tables were laden with an amazing variety of things. People spoke to him; he accepted congratulations from an elderly friend of Licinius and agreed that yes, he was indeed lucky to be getting a splendid girl. The old senator lingered, insisting on telling him anecdotes of Julia as a toddler; he had known her all her life. Somewhere near by two of the magistrates were discussing in low tones the Emperor's upcoming German campaign.

Slaves, murmuring congratulations, served them, not the meat of the sacrifices, but tender roast chickens, roast pork and delicate cakes of fine wheat bread. And there was a liberal amount of wine; which Gaius, drinking everything he was given, soon decided was better than he had thought. An almost endless stream of guests kept coming and offering him congratulations; he had seldom seen Macellius look so happy.

As the feasting continued, Gaius drew on all his reserves of courtesy and self-control, while at the back of his mind wondering what Eilan would think of all this nonsense, whether she would ever know or appreciate what he was doing for her and for their son.

Julia giggled at the rude jokes of the mountebanks who entertained them, but he was not sure whether she really understood them. This part of the ceremony was traditionally to encourage the begetting of children; the clowns seemed very eager to make sure nobody could possibly miss the point. The sight of food was beginning to revolt him, but he continued to make a pretense of eating, and agreed for the ninetieth time that Julia was a lovely girl and he a very lucky man.

Julia was beginning to look sleepy; she had accepted a second and then a third glass of the wine, and since it was considerably stronger than what Licinius served at his everyday table, her normal vivacity was muted. Gaius envied her condition; he was still, unfortunately, quite conscious.

It was growing dark. From outside he heard shouting, and grinned foolishly when the Master of Ceremonies announced that the moment for the bridal procession had arrived. It was all quite ridiculous really, for since Macellius had no house in the town, the new couple was only moving to the far wing of Licinius's mansion, but Julia was apparently determined not to miss a single tradition on her big day.

It was just as well that he was not really expected to carry off his bride, thought Gaius as he gripped Julia by the wrist with simulated roughness and pulled her after him. In his current state of unsteadiness he could have been held off by an old woman and a lame dog.

The Master of Ceremonies handed him a bag full of gilded walnuts and small copper coins; he indicated that Gaius should scatter them to the beggars outside who frequented weddings just for this. Julia had a similar bag which matched her crimson veil. The litter bearers ceremoniously carried them out of Licinius's house, down the avenue to the forum, past the new Governor's palace and the tabularium, preceded by flute players and singers and surrounded by torches, and finally circled back to the entrance of the new apartment that had been made ready for them. Gaius suppressed a desire to giggle. He scattered coins and heard the blessings of the crowd. Only a little further now . . .

The whitethorn torch sent a flickering light through the doorway, banishing shadows and evil magic. Gaius, whose head had been somewhat cleared by the chill air, wished it could banish memory. Someone handed Julia a bowl of oil with which to anoint the doorposts and the strands of white wool with which to adorn them.

The elderly dowagers kissed Julia, murmuring wishes for her happiness, and after a moment's thought kissed Gaius too; this touched off a regular storm of embraces, kisses and congratulations. Macellius, a bit drunk – the first time Gaius had ever seen his father affected even a little by wine – embraced them both; Licinius kissed Julia and Gaius, and said it had been a splendid wedding.

Then Gaius lifted her, marveling once more at how light she was in his arms, carried her over the threshold, and kicked the door shut behind him.

He could smell fresh paint on the walls, competing with the incense and the scent of Julia's flowers. She stood still before him, and with more tenderness than he had thought he could muster he lifted the flamma away.

Her wreath was wilting; the six locks of hair that her maid had so carefully curled unraveling around the neck of her gown. She looked far too young to be married. Before he could speak she led the way to the altar in the center of their own atrium, and stood waiting expectantly.

He pulled the end of his toga up to cover his head and saluted the little terracotta statues that represented the family gods.

"By fire and water I welcome you as my wife and priestess of my home —" he said hoarsely. He poured water across her hands and held the towel for her to dry them; then handed her the taper from which to light the fire.

"May the gods bless us at bed and at board; and grant that I bear you many sons," she answered him.

The bridal bed had been made up against the wall. He led her towards it and fumbled to undo the peculiar knot with which her woolen girdle was tied, wondering how many eager grooms had lost patience and simply cut the thing loose. At least now he could unwind himself from the swaddling folds of his toga.

Julia lay in the big bed with the covers drawn up to her chin, watching him. In the morning the bloody sheets would be ceremoniously presented to the dowagers as evidence of consummation; but Gaius would not even have to be present. And in any case he did not doubt that Julia – always practical – had provided herself with a little bag of chicken blood in case he should be too drunk to perform. Almost every bride had sense enough for that, he had been told.

But he was not that drunk, and if he did his duty with more efficiency than passion, at least he was gentle, and Julia was too innocent to expect more.

twenty-one

E ilan did not return to Vernemeton until March, for despite
Caillean's promise to bring her son back to her, it took some
time to recover from the shock of losing him. Once she had
wept herself out she came to understand that even when he was
restored to her it would not be the same.

After a few days her breasts ceased to ache and she knew that
another woman would feed her little one now. Another woman
would hold him close during the long night hours and pat the
bubbles away and comfort him, would have the sweet labor of
bathing the firm little body. Someone else would lean over his
cradle and sing the lullabies her mother had taught her. But not
Eilan. She could not – she must not – or all she had suffered to
achieve was lost.

It was announced that the High Priestess was ill to cover the
transition, and late one night Eilan was brought back to the Forest
House and Dieda was spirited away, bound for further bardic
training in Eriu as promised. By the time she returned, it was their
hope that everyone would have forgotten there had ever been two
maidens in Vernemeton who looked almost the same. With Cynric
still a prisoner, it was clearly impossible for Dieda to go to him
even if she had desired it. In the end, Dieda seemed reconciled to
the prospect of learning from the bards of a land that had never
been touched by Rome.

Only now, as she resumed her duties as Priestess of the Oracles,
did Eilan realize how isolated she would henceforward be. Part of
this was the result of the seclusion forced on Dieda as part of the
deception, but it was also a result of her change in status. As was
her right, Eilan honored Caillean, Eilidh, Miellyn and young Senara
by choosing them as her primary attendants, but she saw little of
the other priestesses except at the ceremonies.

271

From time to time in the past the Forest House had sheltered women or children like Senara who had need of care. It was therefore unusual, but not unheard of, to take in the young woman called Lia and the infant the Arch-Druid had brought to her to wet-nurse and install them in the roundhouse next to the herb sheds where visitors usually stayed. Nor was it even so surprising that Caillean should take the baby to the High Priestess, saying that she might be cheered by holding a young child.

After that first joyful reunion, Eilan wept copiously; for it seemed to her that Gawen, being nursed by Lia, had somehow become almost more Lia's child than hers. Nevertheless it seemed a miracle to her that Ardanos, even under duress, had kept his word. She wondered sometimes how Caillean had persuaded him, but did not dare to ask.

Naturally her partiality for the child caused gossip. But Caillean took the precaution of confiding to old Latis – in strictest confidence – that the child belonged to Eilan's sister Mairi, born of a father unknown, and had been sent here because Mairi was thinking of marrying again. Within a week the story was all over Vernemeton, as they had expected. But although there were some who believed the baby was Dieda's, no one appeared to suspect he was Eilan's. And with most of the women the boy soon became a pet.

Eilan felt guilt for the damage to the reputations of her sister and the girl who had been like a sister to her. But after all they had assented, however reluctantly. Worse was the torment of not being able to acknowledge her child. But she must not – she would not – and, as week followed week, confession became less and less possible.

It seemed to Eilan that time went by very slowly under this uneasy reprieve; Ardanos had returned from Deva, and, almost gloating, reported that Macellius's son was married to the daughter of the Procurator in Londinium. She had known this must happen, but she could hardly keep from weeping, though she resolved not to in the sight of Ardanos.

She had to believe that both she and Gaius had made the right decision, but she could not help wondering about the woman whom she could not keep from thinking of as her rival. Was she beautiful? Did he speak words of love to her, from time to time? Eilan was the mother of his first son; did that not count for something? Or was she forgotten? And if she were, how would she ever know?

But time went on – as it always does, no matter what shifts are taken to ignore its passing – and the festival of Beltane came upon her, when she must serve again as the voice of the Oracle.

Eilan had thought that she had resolved her doubts when she became High Priestess. Perhaps they were returning now because of the child. In the dark hours of the night she wondered if this time she would be punished for her blasphemy, though by daylight she reasoned that if she had lived through the first time, the Goddess was unlikely to be insulted now. If the Power she had felt during her initiation was a delusion, then she had given up Gaius for nothing. But if Ardanos did not truly believe in the Goddess he served, then it was *he* not she, who was committing the blasphemy. If she meant to continue in this role, it was essential to learn whether it was the Arch-Druid's interpretation or the Goddess Herself that was the lie.

As Eilan was preparing and purifying herself, it occurred to her that drinking from the golden bowl would be more dramatic done in the sight of the people, and resolved to speak of this to Ardanos when she saw him again. He readily agreed to the change, as if surprised that she should have thought upon the matter at all.

This time, Eilan herself mixed the herbs she would be drinking, and made certain substitutions, retaining those that would increase vision and leaving out the ones that detached the senses from the will. As a result she was vividly aware of the vast hush that descended over the assembled gathering. She could feel their reverence and expectation. From a purely public point of view she could understand it. She knew that the people responded to her beauty as they had never responded to Lhiannon's faded charm. But there must have been a time when Lhiannon too had been young and very beautiful. Had it never been any more than this – a drama staged by the priests of whom her grandfather was foremost? Surely the first time she sat in the Oracle's chair the Power that spoke through her had been real.

Eilan drank, and felt the familiar dip and lift of the trance state take her. Remembering how the potion had affected her before, she slumped in her chair with lids half-closed so that Ardanos would not see the intelligence in her eyes. And this time, when the Arch-Druid began his incantation she was aware that instructions were being interspersed into the spell. It was clear what was wanted – and why.

Now she understood why Ardanos wanted a Priestess of the

Oracles who did not rely on inspiration. She had heard him speak before of all the benefits to Britain that would come from the civilizing influence of the Romans. In fact she remembered his saying something like this on that evening in her father's house before she knew who Gaius really was. Well, at least the Arch-Druid could not be accused of inconsistency.

In her last meeting with Gaius she had learned enough to agree that – for now – Ardanos might even have the right idea. Used wisely, the Oracle could be a powerful tool to bring peace to Britain. So long as Ardanos was Arch-Druid, and so long as his policies were indeed the path of wisdom, perhaps what they were doing was not even so great a sin. But if Eilan were to be something more than Ardanos's instrument; she would have to understand what was going on in the world outside her walls. Potentially, the High Priestess of Vernemeton could exercise an influence that went far beyond her role as Oracle. By learning what her grandfather was doing, she had also taken on the responsibility for deciding whether or not to co-operate, and how far.

Eilan believed that something other than her own hidden will had spoken through her before. But no single human could carry the full power of a goddess. When a divine spirit possessed a body, it not only became accessible, but took on some of that body's limitations; it had to work with the material at hand.

Goddess, help me! her spirit cried. *If You are there, Lady, and not just my delusion, show me how to do Your will!*

Ardanos's invocation ended, but the expectation of the crowd around her was building. As the smoke of the sacred herbs billowed from the fires, Eilan felt a Presence building up behind her.

Lady, I am in Your hands. With a sigh, Eilan allowed control to slip away. She had the sensation that soft arms were holding her, but at the same time she knew that her body was sitting up, and the One whose power now flowed through it was fixing Ardanos with a radiant smile.

Grandfather, she thought, *be careful! Can you not see Who has come to you now?* But he had turned to the people, and was leading them in the invocation, and she knew he could not see. Her awareness turned inward then. *Goddess have mercy!* her spirit cried. *He works for the good of his people – give him the wisdom to do the right thing – for the sake of us all!*

And in the silence of the place to which she had come, it seemed to her that there was a reply.

"*Daughter, I care for all my children, even when they quarrel; and for all times, not only the one you are living through. My Light may be your darkness; and your winter the prelude to My spring. Will you accept this, that a greater good may come?*"

"I will, but do not leave, me, for You are all I have," she answered, and once more that Voice spoke within her.

"*How could I leave you – do you not know I love you as you love your child?*"

The Lady's love surrounded her. Eilan allowed herself to sink into it as into her own mother's arms. As if from a great distance she was aware of Ardanos's questions. She remembered the answers he had told her to give, but they no longer seemed important. Knowledge came to her; she knew what she said in reply, and yet the Self who spoke those words, this time in the language of the people, was not the Eilan she knew.

Eilan could not tell how long it went on. In that state where she rested now there was no time at all. And yet a time did come when she heard her own name called. She moaned and tried to turn away. Why should she return? But the cool air with which they were fanning her and the drops of water that splashed her face and hands could not be ignored. They drew her back into her body once more.

She shuddered and gasped, and suddenly she was herself, Eilan, once more, looking at the awed faces of the people around her with wide eyes.

Ardanos was instructing the people to depart in peace. There was almost a hint of smugness in the satisfaction that filled his smile.

He does not understand, Eilan thought then. *He thinks he did it all* . . . But if the Arch-Druid did not understand the power of the Goddess he said he served, it was not for her to enlighten him. She could only trust that the Lady knew Her own business, and would continue to watch over them.

Gaius spent the first months of his marriage fighting the awareness that it was based upon a lie. He suspected that Julia was more enamored of being married than she was of him, but she was cheerful and affectionate, and as long as he was reasonably attentive, she seemed satisfied with his companionship. He could only thank the gods for the innocence, or perhaps the lack of emotional depth, which prevented her from realizing a relationship between a man and a woman ought to be a great deal more.

Licinius, who believed that a young couple should not be separated in the first year of their marriage, had arranged for Gaius to serve as an *aedile* in charge of government buildings in Londinium, which would give him some of the experience in public service necessary to advance his career. At first he had protested lack of background, and wondered if his father-in-law had got him the job simply so that Julia could continue to keep house for him, but he found that although his staff of slaves and freedmen could do the work, they needed the authority of a man of status to deal with the rest of the government. Presently, he realized that a childhood spent listening to his father deal with the problems of maintaining a major fortress had prepared him for his new responsibilities quite well.

"Treasure the time you have with Julia now, my lad," Licinius would say, patting him on the shoulder, "for you'll be parted often enough in the future, especially if you're assigned duty in Dacia or some other post on the frontier." They both knew that the path of promotion led all over the Empire; a long-term provincial post such as Camp Prefect or Procurator was awarded only at the end of a career.

These were the crucial years, when the name a young man made for himself – and the contacts – determined how far he would rise. Soon Gaius would need to spend some time in Rome itself; he found himself looking forward to it. Meanwhile he applied himself to understanding the workings of government in the smaller reflection of the capital that Londinium had become.

More quickly than he could have imagined, a year went by. From time to time disturbing news came from Rome. The Emperor had got himself elected to the office of Consul for the next ten years, and Censor for life in addition to the powers he already had. The patricians muttered darkly that it was a plot to gain control over the Senate, but did little more, for at the moment the army was quite happy with their Emperor, who had raised pay by one-third. As an officer Gaius could not object to that, but it was clear which way the wind was blowing. Even more than his predecessors, Domitian seemed to regard the remaining democratic institutions of Rome as outdated, and certainly inconvenient.

A few months after their marriage, Licinius had engaged a tutor – primarily for Julia, he said – so that she might learn to speak better Greek and more polished Latin, and Gaius, to his chagrin, was urged to share these lessons. "For if you go to Rome, it will be necessary for you to speak good Greek; and a more aristocratic Latin," he pointed out.

Stung, Gaius had protested. From his earliest boyhood, Macellius had insisted that tutors should be engaged, and that he became as fluent in Latin as in the tribal Celtic language of his mother's kin.

"Plain Latin is good enough for me," he protested.

"No doubt it's good enough for an army camp," Julia argued, "but believe me, it would be better to speak to the Senate in Celtic than in that vulgar dialect of Deva."

Gaius felt like protesting that his Latin was no worse than that of Macellius; but it was true that Macellius had never had to speak to the senators of Rome. And it would do him no harm to learn the language of educated men everywhere, which would always be Greek. But the lessons did not go on for long. By the end of the summer Julia was pregnant and so queasy much of the time that the tutor was dismissed.

But by this time Gaius was conversing with the Greek house slaves whenever he had the opportunity, including Charis, Julia's chambermaid, who had herself been born on Apollo's own island of Mytilene. One of the freedmen who worked for him had originally come to Britain as a secretary to a former Governor, and was glad enough to earn a few extra sesterces by correcting Gaius's accent and making him copy out the speeches of Cicero to improve his Latin style.

He was resolved that when Julia's child was born and she felt well enough to resume her lessons – if she ever did – he would have far surpassed her.

And so the winter passed. By their first anniversary, Julia's sickness had subsided. She did not protest when her father proposed that Gaius join a hunting party for boar in the woods north of Londinium, escorting a wealthy senator with interests in the wine trade who claimed to have undertaken the hazardous journey all the way there for the sake of the hunting. Licinius did not think a great deal of the man's skill, but admitted his political power, and flattered the man by assigning his own son-in-law to escort duty.

Julia, far from resenting his absence, was a little relieved to have him out of the house. Like most men, Gaius appeared to feel that any admission of difficulty was a plea for help. Since he could not help her, and indeed, was the cause of her condition, he was inclined to react with annoyance if she mentioned ill health or anxiety. Her father was not much better, and she had too much pride to unburden her heart to the slaves.

And so, on the morning Gaius left to go hunting, Julia sought the temple of Juno. Her maid Charis complained about walking all the way, but ungainly as she had become, Julia was sure the jolt of a wagon or the sway of a litter would have made her queasy again.

Nor did she mind when the eunuch who watched the door told her she must wait until the priestess should have time for her, for the interior of the temple was dim and cool after the brightness and dust of the street outside, and she was quite content to sit there for a time, gazing up at the painted statue.

Domina Dea . . . she prayed, *I thought it would be so easy. But the slaves gossip about women who have died in childbirth when they think I cannot hear. I'm not afraid of that, Goddess, but what if my baby should die? What if I am like my mother, who bore only one child who lived beyond a year? My father has political power and Gaius can fight battles. But the only thing that I can do is give them a legitimate heir.* She pulled her veil across her face so that no one could see that she was weeping. *Help me to deliver a healthy son . . . please, Goddess, please!*

She started as the eunuch touched her shoulder, then wiped her eyes and followed him to the inner chamber, ignoring the nagging pain in her lower back.

Juno's high priestess was a woman of middle years, her face painted to look younger, whose hard eyes silently priced Julia's jewels and gown. But she greeted Julia with an effusive warmth that sparked lively caution in the girl.

"You are worried about the birthing." The woman patted her arm. "And it is your first, so it is only natural that you should be afraid . . ."

Julia pulled back a little, eyeing her warily. Didn't the woman understand that it was not for herself that she feared?

"I want a son," she began, and coughed at the wave of scent as the priestess bent closer.

"Of course you do. And if you make an offering, the Goddess will help you."

"What kind of animal should I buy for the sacrifice?"

"Well, dear —" The woman looked down at her rings. "We really have enough of that sort of thing. But they are building a lavish temple for Isis down near the wharfs, and it would be a pity if Juno should be left looking like a poor relation. Surely she will give you what you want if you offer a generous gift to her shrine."

Julia stared at her, understanding all too well, and rose heavily to her feet. "Indeed," she said dryly. "I must go now, but I thank you for your good counsel."

She turned on her heel, wishing she had the height to make an impressive exit, and stalked from the room, leaving the priestess gaping behind her. As she crossed the threshold, the ache in her back became a stabbing pain that for a moment took her breath away.

"My lady —" Charis reached out to help her.

"Go summon a chair for me," Julia told her, supporting herself against a pillar. "I believe I will ride home after all."

Gaius did not return to Londinium until late in the evening, having seen to it that the distinguished guest got the trophy he wanted, and taking leave of him with some relief. When he came in, he discovered all in chaos; for during his absence, Julia had gone into premature labor and borne him a daughter. He received the news from Licinius, who said all had been over for an hour or two, and Julia was asleep.

It was time to toast the birth of his first child, said Licinius, holding out a dusty clay flagon with a Greek seal. It was all too clear, Gaius thought, that his father-in-law had already been celebrating.

"I do not know how to thank you for this great gift," he said somewhat drunkenly. "I have always wanted to be a grandfather; and if the child is only a daughter, well, I do not mind that; Julia has been as good a child to me as forty sons, and she brought you into our family. No doubt that your next child will be a boy."

"I certainly hope you are right," Gaius said. It would not be his fault if she did not, since he had begotten one son already.

"I put this wine away when Julia was born, to be drunk when my first grandchild was born," Licinius said, removing the seal. "Drink with me, my son; and don't spoil it by putting too much water with it."

Gaius had had no supper and would much rather have had a cup of ale with a bowl of beans or a roast fowl, but with the household in such disarray he'd be lucky to get some cold bread and meat if he could corner one of the household slaves. He resigned himself to going to bed half drunk, and joined Licinius.

"To your daughter," Licinius said. "May she be as good to you as Julia has been to me."

Gaius drank and then the old man proposed a toast to his son.

Gaius blinked and sputtered, and his father-in-law elaborated, "Surely you will have a son next year."

"Oh, yes, of course."

But as Gaius lifted his goblet it was of Eilan and the son he already had that he was thinking. By now the boy would be a year old. Was he walking? Had the fuzz of dark hair turned to gold?

And then of course they had to drink to Julia; if the serving woman had not come in at around that point to say he might see her, Gaius would have been very drunk indeed. Grateful for the interruption, he followed the woman to the bedchamber.

Julia struck her husband as very small, small and pale. Tucked in her arms was the tiny swaddled form of the child.

Julia looked up at him and began to cry. "I'm so sorry. I did so want to give you a son – I was so sure . . ."

Made generous by the thought of Eilan's son, far to the west, he stooped and kissed her. "Don't cry," he said. "We will have a boy next time, if the gods wish it."

"Then you accept her?"

The slave woman picked up the child and held it out and they all looked at him expectantly. After a moment Gaius realized what he was supposed to do and took the baby, rather awkwardly. He looked down into the crumpled features, waiting for the tide of tenderness that had overwhelmed him when he held his son. But his only emotion was amazement, for it seemed to him impossible that something so tiny could be real. He sighed.

"In the name of my ancestors I claim this child as my daughter," Gaius said loudly. "Macellia Severina shall be her name."

Just after Beltane, Bendeigid sought audience with the Lady of Vernemeton. By this time Eilan had settled into her role as High Priestess, but it still seemed strange that her own father, a powerful Druid, should seek permission to visit her. Yet she sent an equally formal reply that she would gladly receive him, and when he appeared in her outer chamber that afternoon, she made ready to give him a cordial welcome.

Truth to tell, Eilan did not feel all that cordial. She could not help but remember that it was her father's refusal even to consider her marriage to Gaius that had placed her in a position in which, while she had comfort and honor, had also made her a stranger to her own son. She made certain that Gawen was out of sight and hearing for the afternoon. Bendeigid at least would know that

Mairi had not borne another child, and Gawen was getting to look more like his father.

She set out a pitcher of fresh water, newly drawn by Senara from the Sacred Well, and indicated to Huw that he could let her visitor come in. It gave her a certain pleasure to have her bodyguard looming over them. His bulk made even her father, who was a big man, seem small. She had thought that to be the recipient of such dog-like devotion would make her uncomfortable, for Huw had gratefully transferred his loyalty to her as soon as she emerged from her ritual seclusion and began to go about again, but he never intruded. He was simply there, and she gradually came to appreciate his usefulness in getting rid of visitors, or, as now, to overawe them.

"How may I serve you, my father?" she said coolly, remaining seated. Her tone was the same as she would have used to any highly placed Druid. Indeed, his time in the North had changed him. He was still a powerful man, but the comfortable solidity she remembered had been worn away until he was all sinew and bone.

Bendeigid stopped short, eyeing her oddly. What was he seeing, she wondered? Not the daughter he remembered, for certain. The face she saw when she looked into the Sacred Pool had lost its girlish roundness, and suffering and responsibility had given a certain air of watchfulness to her shadowed eyes. But perhaps those subtle signs of maturity would be less striking than her golden ornaments and the crescent between her brows.

Although she had pushed the sheer veil of fine, dark blue linen back from her face, its folds were draped about her head and shoulders. She had continued to go veiled in the fashion Dieda had adopted to aid in the deception; and by the time it might have been safe to go without it, she had grown used to its protection. It seemed to lend an air of authority; certainly it added to her mystery.

"I only wanted to pay you my respects, daughter – or should I say Lady," replied the Druid. "It has been long since we met. I wanted to be sure that you were well . . ."

It has taken you long enough, she thought grimly. But she could see that the past few years had not been easy for him either. It was not entirely Huw's bulk that made him seem smaller; his hair had gone completely gray and there were new lines around his mouth and in his brow. He had always been stern, but now purpose burned in his eyes like a dark flame.

Bendeigid accepted the silver-bound wooden cup she handed him and sat down on a bench. Eilan took her seat in the great carven chair.

"Surely that is not the only reason you have come here, my father," she said calmly.

"Lhiannon was old." He looked into his cup and then back up at her. "I can well understand that she did not wish her country torn by war – and that may be why the Goddess has counseled peace for the past few years. But now there is a new time and a new priestess. Did you not know about the battle the Romans call Mons Graupius? Have you heard how the Votadini lands are become a desert in which a few survivors scratch for a living where once was a thriving tribe?"

Eilan lowered her gaze away from his. Indeed she had heard of the battle, from one who had fought in it, and Gaius had told her how that winter the starving survivors had come to the gates of the fortress to be fed. It was true that the Romans were the invaders, but she knew it was the defeated tribesmen who in despair had fired their own villages and slaughtered their animals to keep them out of Roman hands.

"Voice of the Goddess, tell me – the tears of captive women fall down like rain and the blood of our slain warriors shrieks from the ground, why does She not hear them? Why has the Goddess not answered our prayers, and why does the Oracle still counsel us to keep this miserable peace?"

He surged to his feet, reaching out to her, and Huw took a heavy step into the room. Eilan drew a long breath to conceal her astonishment and gestured the man away. She had always assumed that her father was deep in the Arch-Druid's counsels. Was it possible that he did not know how Ardanos had been manipulating the Oracle all these years?

"Surely my father knows I speak only such Oracles as are given to me," she said soothingly. *If he knows, then I have told him the truth – and if he does not, then I have told him nothing he does not know.*

Indeed, what she had said was a greater truth than even Ardanos knew, for although Ardanos translated her answers to questions as he saw fit, when the Goddess filled her and she spoke directly to the people, it was the Goddess who agreed or disagreed with the policies of the Arch-Druid as She chose. So far, at least, Her counsels had been sufficiently peaceable that he had not questioned them.

Bendeigid rose and began nervously to wander about the room. He said, "Then I must entreat you to pray to the Goddess to avenge us. The spirits of the women of Mona still cry out for vengeance."

She frowned. "Has Cynric sent you to say this to me?" She knew that Gaius had taken him prisoner, and saved his life and freedom by making him one of the hostages, but did not know what had happened to him after that.

"He was captured," growled her father, "They were going to send him to Rome to amuse the Emperor, but he killed his guards and won free."

"Where is he?" she asked in some alarm. If the Romans caught him now a quick death was the best fate he could expect from them.

"I do not know," the Druid said evasively. "But there is a great anger growing in the North, my daughter. The Romans are pulling back. The Ravens were not all killed in that battle, and their wounds are healing. If the Goddess does not rouse the land against the Romans, be sure that Cynric will."

"But I speak only to those who attend the festivals at the Hill of the Maidens," Eilan said uncomfortably. "The Cornovii and Ordovices primarily, some Demetae and Silures, and a few of the wilder folk from the hills. What have we to do with Caledonia?"

"Can it be that you do not understand your influence?" He faced her directly. "The Romans have taken our lands and subverted our chieftains and forbidden most of our religious rites. The Oracle here at Vernemeton is one of the few things that remains to us, and if you do not think that the words of the Goddess are repeated from one end of Britannia to the other you are a fool!"

He does not know that Ardanos influences the Oracle, Eilan thought then, *but he suspects it*. While she pretended ignorance he could not openly ask her support for an insurrection. But eventually matters were going to come to a head.

"I have been very isolated . . ." she said softly. "But pilgrims do come to make their prayers at the sacred well. Let those who have news come to drink the waters on the new moon of each month, and if the veiled priestess who attends them talks of ravens, let them speak to her there."

"Ah, Daughter ! I knew you would not betray your breeding!" he exclaimed, his gaze kindling. "I will tell Cynric –"

"Tell him I make no promises," she interrupted, "but if you wish me to pray to the Goddess for Her help, I must know what to ask! I can give you no assurances how She will reply . . ."

With that, Bendeigid would have to be contented. Eilan sat for a long time in thought when he had gone. Clearly Cynric was doing his best to start a rebellion, and without her support, he would certainly fail.

But the Druid had apparently also realized that she was a grown woman now and would make her own decisions. It was almost worth all she had suffered to face him from such a position of power. But with that power came a responsibility she could not avoid, not when there might come a day when her father and foster brother faced the father of her son across a battlefield.

And if that happens, what will I do? Eilan closed her eyes in anguish. *Dear Goddess, what will I do?*

As Julia's child grew they took to calling her "Cella", for it seemed ridiculous to refer to something so tiny by such a long name. But Gaius waited in vain for the bond he had felt with little Gawen when first he saw him in Eilan's arms. Was it then something that happened only between a man and his first-born son? Or was it because he did not have such a bond with the child's mother?

At least Julia did not seem to find it odd that he would have little interest in a girl-child. And Cella was a placid baby who soon promised to be pretty, and was the delight of her grandfather's heart. Julia spent much of her time with the infant, dressing her in beautifully embroidered clothes, which seemed to Gaius a waste of time, and by the time the girl was a year old, Julia was pregnant again. This time she was absolutely positive it would be the longed-for son. A soothsayer, consulted at Julia's behest, promised that a son awaited birth but Gaius was not so certain.

In the end, however, he did not have to suffer with his wife through this pregnancy. The wars in Dacia had been going badly. Gaius felt a pang at hearing the Second Legion was to be withdrawn and the fortress they had built in the North destroyed. He supposed that it had become apparent that the North could not be held without a far greater investment of men and materiel than the Empire could afford. A lot of lives would have been saved, Gaius thought grimly, if they had had the sense to see that three years earlier!

He took to spending his spare time at the army post, listening to the news. On orders from the Emperor, the new Governor,

Sallustius Lucullus, had commanded that all the northernmost fortresses be abandoned, their walls pulled down and their timber buildings burned so that nothing would remain that could be of use to the enemy. The Twentieth marched down from the North and settled back into their old quarters in Glevum, but no one knew for how long.

It was the Second Legion, however, which was ordered from Deva to Dacia. Macellius, announcing that he was too old to go dragging across the Empire, decided that the time had come to retire and started planning a new house in Deva. But Gaius was surprised by an invitation from the new legionary Commander to join his staff and sail with them. What amazed him almost as much was the fact that even Licinius did not object when he indicated that he would like to accept the offer.

"We'll miss you, lad," the old man said, "but it's time that you were attending to your career now that you've started your family. Haven't I been singing your praises all over Londinium for just this reason? It's a pity you won't be here for the birth of your second child, but it was only to be expected. Don't worry about Julia – I'll take care of her. You do your duty and come back covered with glory!"

twenty-two

———～———

dieda returned to the Forest House in the middle of May, a little over four years after she had gone into exile in Eriu. For once the day was sunny, and Eilan received her in the garden, hoping their meeting might be eased by a more informal setting, but she had asked Caillean to stay with her just the same. She sat up straighter, her veil sliding down over her shoulders, as Dieda came through the gateway, and Caillean hurried forward to greet her.

"Dieda, my child, it is good indeed to see you. It has been too long —" They embraced ceremoniously, pressing cheek to cheek.

Dieda was wearing a loose gown of white linen in the Irish style, lavishly embroidered, with a bard's mantle of sky blue edged with golden fringe and held with a golden pin. Her hair, confined by an embroidered band, fell down in ringlets but, despite the festive raiment, her manner seemed strained.

"Ah, I had forgotten the peace here —" said Dieda, looking around her at the glossy green of the mint beds, and the silvery foliage of lavender where the bees buzzed among the purple flowers.

"I am afraid you will find us quiet indeed after all the kings and the princes of Eriu." Eilan found her voice.

"It is a fine land, certainly, and very appreciative of singers and poets and all kinds of makers of music, but after a time one begins to miss one's own country."

"Well you certainly have the very lilt of Eriu in your voice, my child," observed Caillean. "It is good to hear that music again!"

Certainly nobody who heard her speak could confuse us now, thought Eilan. It was not only a matter of accent but of depth and timbre. Dieda's voice had always been pleasant, but now she used it like a well-tuned instrument. Even ill words said in such a beautiful voice could be forgiven more easily.

"I've had time and enough to acquire it," said Dieda. Her gaze slid to Eilan. "It seemed half a lifetime I was away."

Eilan nodded. She felt herself to be a century older than the girl Lhiannon had chosen as her successor five years ago. But there was a petulant twist to Dieda's mouth. Did she still resent being sent away?

"It has been long enough for half a dozen new girls to come to us," she said evenly. "A promising group – I think that most of them will eventually take their vows."

Dieda looked at her. "And what had you in mind for me?"

"Teach these girls as much as you can of the skills you have learned!" Eilan leaned forward. "I don't mean only hymns to make our rituals more beautiful, but the ancient learning, the lore of the gods and heroes as well."

"The priests will not like it."

"They will have nothing to say about it," said Eilan. Dieda's eyes widened. "These days the chieftains buy Latin tutors for their sons and teach them to recite Virgil and appreciate Italian wines. They are doing their best to turn our men into Romans, but they do not care what women do. The last sanctuary for the old wisdom of our people may be here at Vernemeton, and I would not have it lost!"

"Things have changed indeed since I went away." For the first time, Dieda smiled. Then her eyes fixed on something beyond Eilan, and her expression changed.

Gawen was running towards them with his nurse trailing behind him. Eilan's hands twisted in the folds of her veil as she fought the compulsion to reach out and take him into her arms.

"Moon Lady! Moon Lady!" he cried, then stopped and peered up into Dieda's face. "*You're* not the Moon Lady!" he said disapprovingly.

"Not any more," Dieda said with a strange smile.

"This lady is our kinswoman Dieda," Eilan said through stiff lips. "She sings as beautifully as any bird."

For a few moments the boy looked from one to the other, frowning. His eyes were the same changeable hazel as Eilan's, but his hair was dark and curling like his father's, and he would have the same broad brow when he was a man.

"My Lady, I'm sorry," Lia said breathlessly, catching up with him and reaching for his hand. "He got away from me!"

Gawen's lower lip began to quiver and Eilan, recognizing the signs, gestured to the nurse to let him be. *I suppose we have spoiled him*, she thought, *but he is so little, and I will lose him so soon!*

"Did you want to see me, my heartling?" she asked softly. "I cannot play now, but if you come to me at sunset we will go down and feed the salmon in the Sacred Pool. Will that make you happy?"

Solemnly Gawen nodded. She reached out to touch his cheek, and her breath caught as he grinned and the dimple suddenly appeared. And then, as swiftly as he had come, he darted back to his nurse and let her lead him away. The day seemed to darken when he had gone.

"That is the child?" Dieda said in the silence after they had disappeared. As Eilan nodded, fury flared in her blue eyes. "You are mad to have him here! If he is discovered we are all lost! Have I spent four years in exile so that you could enjoy the pleasures of motherhood as well as the honor of being High Priestess?"

"He does not know I am his mother," Eilan whispered brokenly.

"But you can see him! They did not kill him, or you! You owe that to me, O holy Moon Lady of Vernemeton!" Dieda began to walk up and down, vibrating like one of her own harp strings.

"Have some pity, Dieda," Caillean said sternly. "The boy will be fostered out in a year or two, and no one knows."

"Whose child do they think he is then?" Dieda spat over her shoulder. "Poor Mairi's, or perhaps mine?" In their faces she could read the answer. "So. Now that I have finished your exile, I will also have to bear your shame. Well, when they see me with the boy perhaps that rumor will die. For I warn you, I do not like children at all!"

"But you will stay, and keep silent?" Caillean asked bluntly.

"I will," Dieda said after a time, "for I believe in the work you are doing here. But Eilan, hear me, for I have said this to you before, when I agreed to the substitution – if ever you betray our people, then beware, for I will be your doom!"

The new moon was already high in the sunset sky, adding a silver gleam to the opalescent waters of the Sacred Pool. The salmon had come when summoned, and taken the cake Gawen offered almost from the boy's hand. Eilan waited until she could hear his prattling die away into the silence of the evening, then drew her veil over her face and took the path up to the shrine they had built around the spring that fed the pool.

Her maidens thought it a great grace in their High Priestess to take her turn to minister to those who came to the Forest House for counsel. And often enough, that was all that Eilan did, serving as a sympathetic ear for the troubled, or referring those with more tangible problems to one of the spell-women or herbalists. But since learning of Cynric's plans for insurrection, she climbed this path with a little tremor, dreading those nights when the one who waited would whisper of ravens and rebellion.

It was cool in the shrine; Eilan pulled her mantle more closely around her, letting the murmur of running water soothe her. The water trickled from a fissure in the rock with a leaden figure of the Lady set into a niche above it, and splashed into the channel that led to the drinking well and the Sacred Pool.

Source of life . . . she prayed, bending to cup some of the icy water in her hand and touch it to lips and brow. *Sacred water, forever upwelling, fill me with your serenity*. Then she lit the lamp below the image, and settled herself to wait.

The moon was high in the sky when she heard the dragging footsteps of someone who was either ill or exhausted forcing himself up the path. Her throat tightened as the dark figure appeared in the doorway. It was a man, wrapped in a coarse sagum that might belong to any farmer, but below the cloak old blood stained his trews. When he saw her, some of the tension went out of him in a long sigh.

"Rest, drink, receive the Lady's peace . . ." she murmured. He dropped to his knees and scooped water from the channel, visibly struggling for control.

"I have been fighting . . . the ravens flew over the battlefield," he whispered, looking up at her.

"Ravens fly at midnight as well," she answered. "What have you to say to me?"

"The rising . . . was set for midsummer. Red-cloaks found out about it somehow, attacked us —" He passed his hand over his eyes. "Night before last."

"Where is Cynric?" she asked, her voice low and quick. Was her foster brother still among the living? "What does he want from us here?"

The man shrugged hopelessly. "Cynric? On the run, probably. There may be more like me coming, needing a place to lick their wounds."

Eilan nodded. "Behind our kitchens a path goes off into the

forest. It leads to a hut our women use sometimes for meditation. Go now. You can sleep there, and someone will come with food." His shoulders sagged, and she wondered if he would have the strength to get that far.

"Blessed be the Lady," he murmured, "and a blessing on you, for helping me." He heaved himself to his feet, saluted the image, and then, more silently than she would have thought possible, was gone.

But Eilan sat for a long time after he had left her, listening to the plash of the water and watching the hypnotic flicker of lamplight on the wall.

Goddess, she prayed, *have pity on all fugitives; have pity on us all! In a month it will be Midsummer; Ardanos will want me to tell the people to accept this latest blow, and my father will want them to rise and avenge the Ravens in blood and fire. What should I say to them? How can we bring peace to this land?*

She waited for what seemed a long time, but the only vision that came to her was that of water continually welling forth from the rock and running away down the hill.

Gaius sat writing in his quarters in the fort at Colonia Agrippensis, listening to the rain. He supposed that Germania Inferior was not really wetter than Britannia, but it had been a rainy spring. Sometimes the two years he had been gone, first in the lands north and west of Italia and now here, where the gorge of the Rhenus ended and it began its meanderings through flat marshes towards the northern sea, seemed only weeks. But today it felt to him as if he had been away from home for centuries.

He dipped his quill into the inkpot and began to form the letters of the next sentence in the letter he was writing to Licinius. Two years of regular correspondence, he reflected wryly, had made him almost as facile a writer as his slave secretary; at first it had been hard, but he had come to appreciate the value of a private correspondence.

"*. . . the last of the legionaries who a year ago followed Saturninus into rebellion have been judged and, for the most part, split up and integrated into other legions,*" he wrote carefully. "*The Emperor's new order of only one legion per camp is causing some inconvenience, and a great deal of work for the engineers. I do not know if it will discourage conspiracy, but it may be a good thing to have our forces spread more evenly along the border. Has the order been implemented in Britannia?*"

For a moment he paused, listening to the regular tramp of hobnailed sandals on stone as the watch went by, then bent to his work again.

"The word here is that the Marcomanni and Quadi are restive again, and Domitian has had to pause in his campaign against Dacia to deal with them. My advice would be to make an ally of King Decebalus if possible, and use the Dacians to deal with the Marcomanni. The Emperor, however, has not yet included me among the select circle of his advisers, so who knows what he will do?"

He smiled, knowing that Licinius would understand his humor. He had been in the Emperor's presence several times before he was transferred from the Second Legion in Dacia to a cavalry command in Germania, but he rather doubted that Domitian was aware of his existence.

"Training with my wing of cavalry goes well. The Brigantes stationed here are fearless horsemen, and very grateful to have a commander who can speak to them in their own language. The poor beggars must be as homesick as I am. Give my love to Julia and the children. I suppose Cella must be quite a big girl now, and it is hard to believe that little Secunda is more than a year old.

"I think of Britannia as a haven of peace compared to the frontier of Germania," he went on, *"but I suppose that is an illusion. I overheard one of the new men in my command talking about ravens, and suddenly I am wondering about that secret society that we used to hear of years ago . . ."*

Once more he paused, telling himself that the anxiety that had suddenly overwhelmed him was only his reaction to the rain, but before he could return to his writing, someone knocked on his door with word that the Legate wanted to see him, and he pulled on his cloak and left his quarters, wondering what it could be.

"It's new orders, tribune," said his Commander. "And I must say I'll be sorry to lose you, for you were shaping well here —"

"Is the wing being transferred?" Gaius looked at him in some confusion, for a wave of camp gossip usually preceded any move of this kind.

"Just you, lad, more's the pity. You're being transferred to the staff of the Governor in Britannia. Seems there's been some kind of local dust-up, and they need a man with your particular background there."

The Ravens . . . thought Gaius, and Cynric's face as he had last seen it, sullen with hatred, came to mind. *I shall pay more attention to my premonitions from now on.* He could see Licinius's hand in this summons. As one officer among many on the frontier, only the greatest good luck would bring him to the attention of anyone who could offer useful patronage. But if he could prevent a rebellion . . .

Licinius was no doubt congratulating himself at finding a way for his son-in-law to do his duty and at the same time advance his career. Only Gaius would know, or care, that to do so he must destroy a man who had been his friend. He made some kind of polite response to his Commander, scarcely hearing the reply, and went back to his quarters to pack his gear.

As the days ripened towards Midsummer, whispers of the fate of the Ravens' rebellion circulated through the land. Eilan had hoped that the Governor would forbid public assemblies in response to the rising, but it seemed that the official line was to discourage popular support by refusing to recognize that anything was wrong. But from the refugees, Eilan learned that Cynric had gone back to his friends in the North and raised a force from the survivors of Mons Graupius with men of the Ravens to lead them. That was easy enough, for the Romans had simply withdrawn from the desert they had made, leaving the people with nothing to sustain them but their hatred.

But then he had attempted to raise Brigantia, where the severity with which Venutius's rebellion had been put down had been followed by some attempt to rebuild the province. It was probably some man of the Brigantes, thought Eilan, or perhaps, remembering Cartimandua, a woman who had betrayed them, having decided that a limited prosperity in chains was preferable to the Roman sword.

By ones and twos more of the Ravens made their way southward, anguished by grief or sullen with despair. They were tended by Eilan's most trustworthy women, given new names and clothing and sent on their way. They told her that Cynric was still in the North with a remnant of unwounded men, being hunted by a special detachment from the Legions. The Caledonians had melted back into their hills, but the Ravens were clanless men, and had no homes to flee to when they could fight no more.

The ones who came to the Forest House were only Cynric's age, but hardship had made old men of them. Eilan looked at them with anguish, for some, like her own Gawen, showed their Roman blood in their faces. In her vision, she had seen that it was necessary for the blood of Rome and the tribes to mingle. But the Merlin had not said whether this would occur in friendship or through generation after generation in which men planted their seed and died, leaving grieving women to carry on.

Ardanos and Lhiannon, remembering the rape of Mona, had chosen a policy of accommodation as the lesser evil; her father and Cynric seemed to feel that death was preferable to slavery. As Eilan watched Gawen grow, she knew only that she would protect her child.

And so the lengthening days brought them at last to Midsummer, and the priestesses of the Forest House went out to the Hill of the Maidens to perform the ritual.

Even from the avenue Eilan could see the glow of the great bonfires atop the mound, and the fiery arcs the torches traced against the dark sky. The drums pulsed with a heavy insistence, their beat deepening to thunder as the young men of the countryside competed to toss their torches highest. Kings and armies might come and go, but the real struggle – sometimes it seemed to Eilan the only struggle that mattered – was the one that men waged each year to protect their fields and nurture the young crops.

In the distance she could hear the lowing of the cattle that had already been protected by driving them between the sacred fires; she smelled woodsmoke and cooked meat and the sharp fragrance of mugwort and hypericum from her garland.

"Oh look," said Senara, beside her. "See how high they are throwing the torches, like shooting stars!"

"May the crops grow as high as the torches rise!" Caillean answered her.

They had brought a bench for Eilan to sit on until it was time for the rite of the Oracle; she huddled there gratefully, letting the murmured conversation of the other women eddy around her. It was not only the crops that were growing, she thought, listening to Senara's commentary. The frightened eight-year-old who had been given into her care five years ago was becoming a leggy maiden with a promise of beauty in her long bones and amber hair.

There was a last crescendo from the hill, and then the fires appeared to explode outwards as lads snatched brands from the bonfires and raced down the hill in every direction to bear their protecting sun-power to the fields. The drumming settled to a hypnotic heartbeat, and Eilan felt the familiar flutter of approaching trance.

It will be soon now, she thought, *and then, whatever comes of this night's work, it will be done.* For the first time in years she had mixed the most powerful trance herbs into the potion, afraid that without their help her own fears might keep the Goddess from coming through. She knew that Ardanos was anxious as well, though his face did not show it. He was like a carven image, she thought, a shell in which the spirit flickered ever more fitfully, and she had seen how much he needed the support of his oaken staff. One day, perhaps soon, he would be gone. There had been times when she hated him, but in the past years they had come to an unspoken understanding. And there was no telling who his successor would be.

But that was a fear she could face once this night was past. The procession was beginning to move now. Eilan allowed Caillean to assist her to her feet and started up the hill.

The Druids were chanting; their song pulsed through the warm air.

> *"Behold, the holy priestess comes,*
> *Sacred herbs are in her crown;*
> *The golden crescent in her hand . . ."*

Even after five years, there was always that moment of surprise when Eilan felt the first wave of expectation from the assembled crowd. And she had certainly forgotten the nausea, and the sickening lurch in consciousness as the drugs began to take hold. She fought back the flicker of panic as the world whirled around her. She had sought this; whether out of faith or cowardice she was not sure, but this time she *wanted* the world to go away.

Lady of Life, to You I entrust my spirit. Mother, be merciful to all your children!

Years of practice had given her full control over the techniques of focus and breathing that loosed the spirit from the body. The herbs in the potion aided the process, as if her head had been shattered like a broken bowl so that Other could flood into her, tossing her consciousness aside like a leaf on a stream.

Eilan felt the priestesses assisting her into the chair, and the unsettling sensation of falling even though she knew they were lifting her. Her spirit swung between earth and heaven; there was a slight jerk as they set the chair atop the mound, and she was free.

She was floating in a golden mist, and for a time it was enough simply to enjoy the sense of being safe, protected, and at home. Suspended in this certainty, the fears she had left behind her seemed transitory, even absurd. But the silver cord that still tied her to her body would not entirely release her, and presently, ever reluctantly, the mist thinned enough so that she could see, and hear.

She looked down upon the huddle of blue robes in the tall chair and knew it for her body, dimly illuminated by the embers of the great bonfires to either side. The priests and priestesses made a circle with the people behind them, pale robes on one side and dark on the other in two great curves of light and shadow. The great mass of folk who had come for the festival darkened the hillside; points of fire winked from the booths and tents of the encampment that had sprung up around it. Beyond stretched the patchwork of field and forest, with the pale glimmer of roads cutting through the trees. Without curiosity she noted a swirl of motion in one part of the crowd, and further off a more regular movement along the road from Deva, and the gleam as metal caught the light of the setting moon.

The Druids were invoking the Goddess, twining all the incoherent imaginings of the people into a single, mighty image which was at the same time as various as there were people to echo their call. Eilan saw the power they were raising as a swirl of multicolored light and pitied the fragile human form into which it was descending. Now her body was almost hidden; the energy was taking shape; she saw a female figure, heroic in stature and splendid in form, though the features could not yet be seen.

Eilan drew closer, wondering what face the Lady would wear for this gathering.

And in that moment, the disturbance in the crowd reached the center; she saw the red gleam of swords and heard male voices harsh with anguish crying, "Great Queen, hear us! Cathubodva, we call you – Lady of Ravens, avenge your sons!"

Ardanos turned, his face contorting, to silence them, but the intensity of emotion in that call had done its work. A whirl of dark-winged shadows fluttered across the circle as a sudden chill wind stirred the fires; and the figure in the chair seemed to expand suddenly and sat bolt upright, flinging the veil aside.

"I hear your summoning, and I come," she said in the language of the tribes. "Who is it that dares to call on Me?"

The murmur of fright that had swept the circle faded to absolute silence as a man limped into the circle of firelight. Eilan recognized Cynric, a bloody bandage around his head and a naked sword in his hand. "Mother, it is I who call you – ever have I served you! Lady of Ravens, arise now in wrath!"

The chair creaked as the figure who sat there leaned forward. In the firelight Her face and Her hair were as red as Cynric's sword. Ardanos looked from one to the other, straining to stop this; but the force that linked them was too strong and he did not dare.

"Well indeed have you served me ..." Her voice scraped the silence. "Severed heads and dismembered bodies are your offerings, blood the libation you pour upon the ground. The wails of women and the groans of the dying are your sacred music; your ritual fires are fueled by the bodies of men ... You have called me, red raven. What would you, now that I have come?"

She smiled terribly, and Midsummer though it was, the wind was suddenly icy, as if Cathubodva's darkness had killed the sun. The people began to edge backward. Only Cynric, Ardanos, and the two attendant priestesses held their ground.

"Destroy the invaders; strike down the despoilers of our land! Victory, Lady, is what I demand!"

"Victory?" Hideously, the battle-goddess began to laugh. "I do not give victory – I am the battle-bride; I am the devouring mother; death is the only victory that you will find in my arms!" She raised her hands and the folds of her cloak flared out like dark wings. This time even Cynric recoiled.

"But our cause is just ..." he faltered.

"Justice! Is there ever justice in the wars of men? Everything the Romans do to you, men of your blood have done to each other, and to the peoples who were before them in this land! Your blood feeds the earth whether you die in the straw or on the battlefield – it makes no difference to Me!"

Cynric was shaking his head bewilderedly. "But I fought for my people. At least tell me that our enemies will also suffer one day ..."

The Goddess leaned forward, staring at him, and he could not look away. "I see ..." She whispered. "From the bright god's shoulders the ravens are flying – no more shall they counsel him. Instead it is an eagle he welcomes. He shall become an eagle, betrayed and betraying, suffering in the branches of the oak tree until he becomes a god once more ...

"I see the eagle put to flight by a white horse that gallops from across the sea. Now the eagle joins with the red dragon, and together they fight the stallion, and the stallion battles dragons from the North and lions from the South . . . I see one beast killing another and arising in its turn to defend the land. The blood of all of them shall feed the earth, and the blood of all of them shall mingle, till no man can say who is the enemy . . ."

There was silence in the circle when She had finished, as if folk did not know whether to hope or fear. From further away came the moaning of cattle, and a sound like drumming, though the musicians were still.

"Tell us, Lady –" Cynric croaked as if he found it hard to get the words out. "Tell us what we should do . . ."

The Lady sat back, and this time her laugh was low and amused.

"Flee," She said softly. "Flee now, for your enemies are upon you." She lifted her head and looked around the circle. "All of you, go swiftly and quietly, and you will live . . . for a while."

Some of the people began to shift away from the fires, but the remainder stayed staring as if enchanted.

"Go!" She flung up her hand, and a wing of darkness swept the circle. Startled into movement, people began to push against their neighbors like the first rolling pebbles in an avalanche of stones. "Cynric son of Junius, run," she screamed suddenly. "Run, for the Eagles come!"

And as the people fled the distant drumming became a present thunder and the Roman cavalry charged.

Gaius let the impetus of the charge sweep him forward, willing his awareness to confine itself to the movement of the horse beneath him, and the riders to either side, the rising ground, the running shapes of men and women and the glow of the flames. He tried to banish the memories which colored his perceptions, but he kept seeing a full moon and dancers, Cynric walking hand in hand with Dieda, and Eilan's rosy face lit by the Beltane fires.

The anterior horns of the saddle jabbed his buttocks as the slope steepened; he gripped with his knees and settled lance and shield, scanning the fleeing figures for armed men. Their orders had been clear enough – to avoid slaughtering a peaceful population, but to keep the fugitive rebels among them from getting away. The Legate had not explained how, in the confusion and darkness, that was to be done.

Still cursing the fate that had sent him after Cynric and the Ravens at this of all places, Gaius saw a glint of metal, a white face contorting in fear or fury. Responses trained into him by ten years as a soldier moved his arm without the need for decision. He felt the jerk and tug as the lance pierced flesh and pulled free again, and the face disappeared.

The charge was slowing; they reached the flattened hilltop and saw it almost deserted, though people were streaming away on every side. A terse order to his optio sent riders swinging outward in pursuit. His mount half-reared as a white figure waved its arms wildly, mouthing something about sacred ground. Gaius kneed the animal in a rocking canter around the perimeter, looking for Cynric, heard the clash of metal on the other side of the mound in the center, and headed toward it.

And suddenly his mount was plunging, whinnying in terror as a wing of shadow swirled around it and someone screamed. It was not fear he heard but anger, anguish; a cry that contained all the horror and fear and fury of all the battlefields in the world; a shriek that turned the bowels to water and shivered the bones. Every animal that heard it for a moment was maddened, and every human felt the spirit within him gibber with fear. Gaius lost his reins and his lance and clung to his pony's mane as the world whirled around him. The face of a Fury hung before him, haloed by seething tendrils of shining hair.

His mount plunged onward and he came into the leaping firelight; all around him men stood frozen as if by some spell. Then his horse came to a shivering halt and people began to move again, but he could still see the terror in their eyes. He took a deep breath, realizing that surprise was lost, and looked around.

Some of the Druids were supporting a man in white whom he realized in shock must be Ardanos; he looked very old now. The blue-robed priestesses were easing what looked like a bundle of cloth out of the chair on the top of the mound. As his battle fury drained away, Gaius felt suddenly very tired.

Another rider, his optio, appeared at his side. "They've scattered, sir."

Gaius nodded. "But they can't have gone far. Set the men to scouring the area. They can report back to me here."

Stiffly he swung his leg over the pony's neck, slid to the ground, and walked forward, the horse plodding behind him. As he neared, Ardanos stirred, looking at him pleadingly.

"It was not my doing," he mumbled. "Called the Goddess – suddenly Cynric was *there*!"

Gaius nodded. He knew the Arch-Druid's policies well enough to believe him. It was the woman whose shriek had paralyzed them who had given the rebels the extra moment they needed to melt into the crowd. He continued walking towards the group of women. Somehow he was not surprised when Caillean turned, staring at him defiantly, but it was the woman who lay on the ground he wanted to see.

He took another step and found himself staring down at a woman's face; white, unconscious, identifiable only in its broadest outlines with the Fury who had appeared to him. And yet with a sick certainty he knew that it was She, and at the same time that it was Eilan.

twenty-three

———~~~———

as the Romans hunted Ravens in the days that followed the fight at the Hill of Maidens, Gaius felt as if he had become two people, the one dispassionately reporting the results of the operation to the Commander in Deva and then returning to Londinium to repeat the story to the Governor, while the other tried to reconcile the mask of fury he had seen there with the image of the woman he loved. Julia hovered about him with wifely solicitude, but after the first nightmare, they both agreed that for a time it might be better if he slept alone.

Julia did not seem to mind. She was as affectionate as ever, but during the two years he had been away her focus had shifted to her children. The girls were growing fast, miniatures of their mother, although there were times when Gaius thought he saw a gleam of Macellius's determination in his elder daughter's eyes. But though they were dutiful, he had become a stranger. It hurt a little to hear their laughter cease when he entered the room, and it occurred to him that perhaps if he could find the time to get to know them better the distance between them would disappear.

But he could not bring himself to try to bridge it, not now, when his heart was telling him that whatever love had remained between him and Eilan had been swept away by the Power that possessed her. At times the strain of concealing his anguish made him want to howl. Gaius was relieved when the Commander at Deva requested him to return for consultation, a postscript indicating that his father was hoping that instead of staying in the fortress, Gaius could pay him a visit in the new house he had built in the town. Perhaps it would be easier there to reconcile the conflict that was tearing at him.

"Have they captured any more fugitives from the Raven

conspiracy?" Macellius poured wine for Gaius and handed him the cup, good but not gaudy, like the dining chamber itself and the mansion that surrounded it. His father's place was one of the better houses that had been built around the fortress, evidence of a growing civilian presence as the country settled down. Gaius shook his head.

"That fellow Cynric – he was their leader, wasn't he?" Macellius said then. "Didn't you capture him at Mons Graupius?"

Gaius nodded and took a long drink of sour wine, wincing as the movement stretched the healing slash on his side. He had not noticed it until the fight at the Hill was over, but it was more annoying than serious; he had had far worse on the German frontier. The shock of realizing that the Fury who had cursed them all was Eilan was his worst wound. After a moment he realized that his father was waiting for an answer. "I did – but later he got away."

"Seems to be good at that," observed his father, "like that bastard Caractacus. But we got *him* in the end, and eventually somebody will betray your Cynric too, someone from his own side . . ."

Gaius stirred uncomfortably at the pronoun, hoping his father would not remember that Cynric was Bendeigid's foster son. It would have saved everyone a lot of trouble, he thought grimly, if he had killed Cynric when he had the chance.

"Ah well," the older man continued, "nobody blames you for not catching him, and wherever the survivors run to, it's not likely we'll see them here . . ." He looked around him with what Gaius could only characterize as a smug sigh.

"Not likely," his son agreed. "Are you really comfortable here?" After retiring from the army, Macellius had built his mansion, almost immediately been elected a decurion and was rapidly becoming a pillar of the community.

"Oh yes, it's a nice place. Settled down a lot in the past few years, and the town is growing. The amphitheater is a draw, of course. More shops every day, it seems to me, and I've just coughed up a goodly sum to pay for the new temple."

"A miniature Rome, in fact," Gaius said, smiling. "All you lack is a coliseum for the Games."

"Gods preserve me." Macellius held up one hand, laughing. "No doubt I'd have to pay for those as well. This business of being a city father is highly overrated. I hardly dare open my door for fear I'll be given the honor of contributing to something new!"

But he was laughing, Gaius observed, and thought that he had never seen his father so contented.

"There's one thing I'd not grudge the money for, though," said Macellius, "and that's to send you to Rome. It's time, you know. You'll get a good recommendation from the Governor after this last bit of service, and you can't rise much further on the kind of patronage your father-in-law and I can give you. Has Licinius said anything?"

"He's mentioned it," Gaius said cautiously. "But I can't go until everyone's satisfied that things will stay quiet here."

"I can't help wishing Vespasian had lived longer." Macellius frowned. "There was a stingy old fox for you, but he knew how to pick good men. This cub of his, Domitian, seems determined to rule like an Eastern despot. He's banished the philosophers, I hear. Now I ask you, what harm could a lot of prosy old bores do?"

Gaius, remembering his own desperation when his old tutor had droned on about Plato, felt a sneaking sympathy for the Emperor.

"In any case, he's the man you'll have to impress if you want a good posting, and though I'll miss you, a procuratorship somewhere in one of the older provinces is the logical next step in your career."

"I'll miss you, too," said Gaius quietly. And that was true, but he realized that he would not particularly miss Licinius, or even Julia and the girls. In fact, he thought he would be glad to get away from Britain for a while, to some place where nothing would remind him of Cynric or Eilan.

Gaius finally set out for Rome on the ides of August, attended by a Greek slave called Philo, a gift from Licinius, who swore he could be depended upon to drape a toga decently and send his master out each morning looking like a gentleman. In his saddlebag was the Procurator's annual report on the economy of the Province, which gave Gaius the status of official courier and carried with it the right to use the military post houses.

The weather held fair, but even so it seemed a weary journey. The further south they traveled the drier the country became – to Gaius's northern eyes a desert, though the officers at the posting houses laughed to hear him say so and traded stories of Egypt and Palestine, where the desert sands scoured monuments older than Rome. He found himself wishing that like Caesar he could while away the time by writing his memoirs, but even if he waited forty years to do so, he doubted anyone would be interested in reading them.

Even Julia's chatter would have been welcome, though these days all she seemed able to talk about was the children. But children were what he had married her for, he reminded himself; children, and social standing. And so far everything had gone more or less to plan. Only, as he passed through the endless miles of slave-farmed estates in Gaul, Gaius found himself wondering if this pursuit of rank and position was really worth it. And then they would come to the next inn, or the next villa belonging to one of Licinius's friends. In the arms of whatever pretty slave girl they sent to warm his bed he could forget both Julia and Eilan, and in the morning he would tell himself that it was only his fatigue that had been speaking, or perhaps a natural anxiety about how he would do in Rome.

Once he reached Rome, it began to rain, heavily and continuously, as if making up for lost time. The kinsman of Licinius with whom he was staying was hospitable enough, but Gaius very quickly became tired of jokes about bringing his British weather with him. And it was not even true, really, for in Britannia there was an honest chill to the rain, but Rome was not so much cold as plagued by a pervasive and pestilent damp. Forever after, Gaius's memories of that time were linked to the alkaline smell of damp plaster and the reek of wet wool.

Rome was mud and smoky skies; the rank smell of the Tiber and the exotically spiced cooking fires of a hundred different nationalities. Rome was white marble and gilding and heady perfumes; the blare of trumpets and the shrieking of market-women and the eternal, sub-aural hum of more people, speaking more languages than Gaius had ever imagined existed, crammed together on seven hills whose contours had long ago disappeared beneath this encrustation of humanity. Rome was the pulsing heart of the world.

"And this is your first visit to Rome?" The lady to whom Gaius was talking favored him with a laugh that tinkled like the silver bangles she wore. Exquisitely curled women and elegantly draped men crowded the atrium of Licinius's cousin, who was giving the party, and conversation hummed like bees in an orchard. "So what do you think of the Mistress of Nations, diadem of the Empire?" her painted eyelids drooped coquettishly. This was another question Gaius had heard so often he had been forced to memorize an answer.

"I think the splendor of the city far eclipsed by the beauty that adorns it," he said gallantly. He would have said "might," and "power," if he had been talking to a man.

This earned him another burst of tinkling; then his host rescued him and bore him away to the peristyle, where toga-clad men were grouped like figures on a piece of statuary. He joined them with some relief. Even among the men, there were dangers, but at least he understood them. Roman women produced in him something of the same paralysis he had felt when he first met Julia.

But she was straightforward by comparison to the ladies he was meeting now. One or two of them had invited him to bed, but a lively sense of self-preservation had kept him free of such entrapments. Rome attracted the best of everything, and if he needed a woman, there were courtesans who demanded nothing of him but his money, and whose arts could banish anxiety, for a little while.

Moving in Roman society was like leading a cavalry charge across icy ground – exhilarating while it lasted, but you never knew when some treacherous bit would bring you down. Gaius wondered if Julia could have held her own in that company. And as for Eilan – it was like trying to imagine a wild antelope, or perhaps a wildcat, among a herd of high-bred racing mares to picture her here: both were beautiful, but different orders of being entirely.

"I understand that you served under Agricola in Caledonia . . ."

Gaius blinked, realizing that one of the older men was talking to him. He caught the flicker of a broad purple stripe on the tunic and straightened as if he were facing a superior officer, racking his brains to remember the man's name. Most of his host's friends were from the equestrian class; he had done well to get a senator here.

"Yes, sir, I had that honor. I had hoped to call upon him here in Rome."

"I believe that at present he is residing on the family estates in Gaul," the Senator said neutrally. Marcellus Clodius Malleus, that was his name.

"It is hard to imagine him resting." Gaius grinned. "I had supposed he would be putting the fear of the gods into the enemies of Rome somewhere on the frontiers or bringing the Pax Romana to one of the provinces."

"Indeed, one might think so." The Senator's manner warmed perceptibly. "But you might be wiser not to say so until you are sure of your company . . ."

Gaius stilled, thinking once more of icy ground, but Malleus continued to smile.

"There are many here in Rome who appreciate Agricola's qualities, qualities that appear ever more admirable each time we learn of some mishandled campaign by one of our other generals."

"Then why doesn't the Emperor employ him?" Gaius asked.

"Because victory for Roman arms is secondary to keeping the Emperor in power. The more people clamor for Agricola to be sent out as General, the more our "lord and god" suspects him. In another year he will be due for a major consular appointment, but as things are now, his friends must advise him not to accept it."

"I can see the problem," said Gaius thoughtfully. "Agricola is far too conscientious to fail deliberately, but if he does well, the Emperor will feel threatened by his success. Well, he will be remembered with honor in Britannia, whatever happens in Rome."

"Tacitus would be happy to hear you say that," said Malleus.

"Oh, do you know him? I served with him in Caledonia." The conversation moved into a general discussion of the northern campaign, which the Senator proved to have followed closely. It was only as the guests were being herded to the gardens for a display by some Bithynian dancing girls that the conversation became personal once more.

"I'm giving a small dinner party three weeks from now –" Malleus laid a friendly hand on Gaius's arm. "Nothing elaborate, just a few men whom I think you will find interesting. Would you honor me by attending? Cornelius Tacitus has promised to be there."

From that day forward it seemed to Gaius that the superficial round of parties and entertainments that had begun to exasperate him took on a new dimension. It felt as if he were at last penetrating the veil with which Roman society protected itself against outsiders, and if it was only one segment of that society, and perhaps a dangerous one, even that was preferable to dying of boredom.

A few days later Licinius's cousin, whose agnomen was Corax, took Gaius with him to the Games in the new Coliseum that Domitian was building on the site where Nero's overwrought palace had once stood.

"There's a certain appropriateness in the location," Corax observed as they took their seats in the section reserved for the equestrians, "since Nero himself put on Games such as Rome had never seen before, especially when he was trying to convince everyone that that odd Jewish sect – you know, the Christians – had caused the great fire."

"Did they?" Gaius was looking around him. They had arrived between fights, and slaves were replacing the bloodstained sand.

"You hardly need deliberate sabotage to start a fire in this city, my lad," his host said wryly. "Why do you think every district has a fire watch to which we all contribute so willingly? But this was a particularly bad one, and the Emperor needed a scapegoat to counter the rumors that he had started the blaze himself!"

Gaius turned to stare at him.

"New buildings, lad, new buildings!" Corax explained. "Nero fancied himself an architect, and the people who owned the property where the fire started wouldn't sell. The fire got out of hand, and the Emperor needed someone to blame. The Games were really quite horrid – no skill involved at all – just a lot of poor souls who died more like sheep than like men."

Gaius was suddenly glad he had not captured Cynric after all. Such a fighter would certainly have been sent here, and he did not deserve it, though surely he would have not been a sheep but rather a wolf or a bear.

Trumpets blared and a shiver of expectation ran through the vast throng. Gaius felt his own heartbeat quicken and was reminded oddly of the moment before battle; it was the only time he had been in the presence of so many thousands, all nerving themselves up to make blood flow. But at least in war both sides were at equal risk. It was other men's blood these Romans were offering, not their own.

He had seen bear baitings at home, of course, as entertainment for the Legions. There was certainly a fascination in some of the pairings of wild beasts imported for the Games. A lion and a giraffe, for instance, or a wild boar and a panther. Corax told him that on one occasion a pregnant sow had been fighting and actually farrowed a piglet during her death throes. But the real focus of the afternoon was on the most dangerous of all animals – man.

"Now we shall see some skill," said Corax as the mock combats finished and the first of the gladiators, hide and armor alike oiled and gleaming, stalked across the sand. "This kind of thing is what makes the Games worth seeing. Those fights in which they throw in untrained prisoners of war or criminals, even women and children, are simply a stupid slaughter. Here, for instance, we have a Samnite and a Retarius —" He indicated the first gladiator, wearing greaves and a visored helmet crowned with a tuft of feathers and armed with a shortsword and big rectangular shield, and his more agile opponent, flourishing his net and trident.

Gaius, trained to judge fighting men, found his professional interest engaged. All around him bets were being placed with an intensity that almost matched that of the fighters. Corax kept up a running commentary, and it was not until the Samnite fighter was down with the net-man's trident at his throat that he realized that the man giving the thumb's down signal from the purple-hung box was the Emperor.

The trident thrust and the Samnite convulsed and then was still, his bright blood staining the sand. Gaius sat back, licking dry lips, his throat raw from cheering. He must have been intent indeed not to hear the trumpets announcing the entrance of the Emperor. From this distance he could see only a figure in a purple tunic, wrapped in a mantle that glittered with gold.

Later that night, as Corax's masseur pummeled him after his soak in the bath, Gaius realized that his whole body was a mass of aching muscles, which had been tensed against one another as he watched the Games. At the time he had not noticed.

But he felt also a great sense of release. Going to the Coliseum was indeed like being in a battle, like that moment when all existence is simplified into a single struggle, and you are carried beyond yourself and become one with a greater whole. For a moment, it seemed to him he understood why the Romans loved their Games with such a passion. However perverse and pointless it seemed, they were moved by the same force that had enabled the Legions to conquer half the world.

The night of Malleus's party was cold and windy, but the streets were choked as usual with food sellers and barbers, men hawking pots and every other kind of street merchant, hoping for one more sale before darkness forced them all indoors. As Gaius's litter bearers forced their way towards the Aventine, it occurred to him that he had almost become used to the noise, as he had grown accustomed to the clatter of iron-shod cartwheels on cobblestones that made the night almost as noisy as the day.

But as they turned on to the main avenue he heard a new sound. The litter stopped, and he stuck his head through the curtains to see. A religious procession was making its way along the road; he glimpsed shaven-headed priests in white robes and women in veils. The women were wailing, their lamentations punctuated by the sibilance of shaking sistrums and the deep boom of a drum.

Despite the warmth of his toga Gaius found himself shivering, for the mourning touched something that deeply disturbed his urbane persona, and even the easy competence of the man he was at home.

Even without understanding its cause, he felt that anguish as his own. It was like the mourning in the Mithraeum when the bull is killed. Another group of priests went by, and then more women, their gliding gait reminding him of the priestesses at home, and then a litter on which he could see the black-veiled statue of a golden cow. For a few moments longer the drumming pounded in his ears; then the procession passed.

When Gaius finally got to it, the dinner party proved to be a gathering of the kind that he had come to feel represented the best in Roman society. The food was simple but well prepared, the company urbane and well informed. Gaius felt outclassed, but these were men from whom he could learn.

The topic that had been proposed was "pietas," the wine mixed half and half with water so that everyone remained focused enough to discuss it seriously.

"I suppose one question is whether there is more than one true religion," Gaius said when his turn to speak arrived. "Of course each people has its faith and should be allowed to keep it, but here in Rome you seem to worship more gods than I ever knew existed. Just tonight, for instance, I saw some kind of procession that sounded oriental, but most of those following it looked Roman."

"That must have been the Isia," observed Herennius Senecio, one of the more important of the guests. "The followers of Isis celebrate her search for the dismembered body of Osiris at this time of year. When she has gathered the pieces she reanimates his body and conceives the sun-child Horus anew."

"Do not the British tribes have a festival at this time also?" asked Tacitus. "I seem to remember processions around the countryside with masks and bones."

"True," replied Gaius. "At Samaine the white mare goes around with her followers and the people invite the souls of their ancestors to reincarnate in the wombs of the women of the tribe."

"Perhaps that is the answer then," said Malleus. "Though we all have different names for the gods, they are all in essence the same, and therefore to worship any of them is piety."

"For instance, the god whom we call Jupiter is known by his oak tree and his thunderbolt," said Tacitus. "The Germans worship him as Donar, and the British as Tanarus or Taranis."

Gaius was not so sure. It was hard to imagine any Celtic deity being worshipped in a great temple like the one dedicated to Jupiter in the Forum. At one party he had met a woman they said was a Vestal and he had observed her with curiosity, but although the woman was marked by a certain dignity and certainly more decorum than most of the Roman women he had seen, there was none of the nobility he associated with the women of the Forest House. Curiously, it was easier to identify the Egyptian Isis, whose procession he had just seen, with the Great Goddess Eilan served.

"I think, that our British friend has put his finger on a real problem," said Malleus. "Surely that is why our fathers fought so hard to keep foreign cults like that of Cybele and Dionysos from taking root in Rome. Even the temple of Isis was burned."

"If we include all the peoples of the world in our Empire," Tacitus countered, "then we must also include their gods. I would never deny that, for I think that there is more honor, more purity of morals, and more of what we would call piety in the hall of any German chieftain than in most of the mansions of Rome. There is no harm in that, so long as the rituals that preserve the State are given first priority."

"That seems to be what the deified Augustus had in mind when he allowed his cult to spread through the Empire," Malleus replied. There was a short silence.

"*Dominus et Deus* . . ." someone said softly, and Gaius remembered hearing that was how the Emperor liked to be addressed these days. "He goes too far! Will we return to the days when Caligula trotted out his favorite horse for everyone to worship?"

Gaius looked around and realized in some surprise that the man who had spoken was Flavius Clemens, some kind of cousin of the Emperor.

"*Pietas* is the essence of reverence and obligation between men and the gods, not adulation for a mortal!" Senecio exclaimed. "Even Augustus insisted that "Roma" be coupled with his name. We do not worship the man, but his genius, the god within him. To believe that a mere human has the wisdom and power to govern an Empire like this one would be impiety indeed."

"Well, in the Provinces the cult works as a force for unity,"

Gaius observed brightly in the even more uncomfortable silence that followed. "When nobody knows what the Emperor is like personally, all they can do is to worship the idea of a Divine Ruler. Whatever their personal religion, everyone can come together to burn incense to the Emperor."

"Everyone except the Christians," someone observed, and, except for Flavius Clemens, they all laughed.

"Well, there's no need to persecute them and make more martyrs," Tacitus pointed out. "Their appeal is mostly to slaves and women. And they have so many factions, they can be depended upon to destroy each other if we only leave them alone!"

Sweets and cheese were served then, and the conversation passed to other things. These were all civilized men, after all, not likely to be swayed by religious enthusiasm. But Gaius could not help wondering if piety, duty, and mutual obligation were enough to nourish the human soul. Perhaps people were driven to cults such as that of Isis or the Christos by the aridity of the State religion, or perhaps the bloody rituals of the Coliseum had become the real religion of Rome.

The other thing he was beginning to realize was that among the thinking men of the city – the men whose company he was increasingly coming to value – there was a growing opposition to the Emperor. These connections would not bring him the patronage he needed to advance in his career. If it came to a choice between ambition and honor, which would he choose?

Shortly after Gaius's arrival, the Imperial Procurator's staff of busy freedmen went to work to digest the content of the report from Licinius that he had carried and analyze its implications for the Emperor. Yet the city fathers retained enough authority so that this information must be delivered to them eventually, and Gaius discovered that the influence of his new friends was sufficient to win him an invitation to address the Senate and meet the Emperor afterward.

On the morning he was to appear, Gaius had himself shaved with special care – though he sometimes thought that the bearded Ardanos and Bendeigid were less barbarian than he was himself, he did not think he could explain that to the assembled conscript fathers.

It was very early when he arrived at the Senate and was given a seat beneath a statue of the deified Augustus, who stood on his pedestal looking as cold and cross as Gaius felt. The senators entered by ones and twos, talking softly, followed by the secretaries with their piles of wax tablets, ready to record the debates and decisions of the day. This, reflected Gaius, was where the lords of the world decided the fates of nations. On this marble floor they had debated the defense against Hannibal and the invasion of Britannia. The river of time flowed strongly in this chamber; in comparison, even the pride of the Caesars was only a ripple on the stream.

Just as the opening invocations were beginning the Emperor arrived, resplendent in a purple toga sewn all over with golden stars that made Gaius blink. He had heard of the *toga picta*, but had thought it was only worn by a general presiding over his triumph. It was rather disturbing to see it worn here, and he wondered if Domitian wanted to be seen as a conqueror, or was simply fond of finery. This was the first time Gaius had seen his Emperor at such close hand. The youngest son of the great Vespasian had the bull neck and well-muscled shoulders of a soldier, but Gaius read petulance in the twist of his mouth and suspicion in his eyes.

It was almost time for the noon recess before Gaius was beckoned forward to read Licinius's report on the finances of Britannia. There were a few questions, mostly on the subject of resources, and one from Clodius Malleus that allowed Gaius to mention the part he had played in controlling the latest rebellion. Despite some recent tutoring in oratory, he felt he must have bored them, but at the end of his speech, they voted him a perfunctory round of applause and – as Licinius had foreseen – confirmed that for the next year a reasonable percentage of the tax money they had collected might be retained in Britain. Since this was why Licinius had sent him in the first place, Gaius was hardly surprised.

The meeting with Domitian afterwards was brief. On his way to another engagement, the Emperor was already removing the gorgeous toga, but he stopped long enough to give Gaius a careless word of thanks.

"You've been in the army?" he asked.

"As a tribune with the Second Legion. I had the privilege of serving under you in Dacia," Gaius said carefully.

"Hmm ... Well, I suppose we'll have to find you something to do in the Provinces then," said the Emperor without much interest, turning away.

"*Dominus et Deus*," said Gaius, saluting, and hated himself for saying the words.

On the way home Gaius shared a litter with Clodius Malleus. It was the first time they had been able to talk privately all day.

"And what did you think of the Senate?" the older man asked.

"It made me proud to be a Roman," Gaius answered truthfully.

"And the Emperor?"

Gaius was silent. After a moment he heard the Senator sigh. "You have seen how things are," Malleus said softly. "Such patronage as I have to offer must be given carefully, at least for now. But if you are willing to face the risks that this bond might bring you, along with its potential rewards, I would be happy to accept you among my clients. I can arrange for you to serve as Procurator for army supplies in Britannia. Ordinarily it would be somewhere else in the Empire, but I think you would be most useful to us in the land that you know best."

That collegial "us" made something in Gaius that the Emperor's lack of interest had chilled awaken to warmth again. The Rome that his father and Licinius had taught him to honor might be dead, but it seemed to Gaius that under the leadership of such men as Malleus and Agricola the spirit of Rome might revive.

"I would be honored," he said into the silence, and knew that like the decision he had made after Mons Graupius, this choice would determine the course of his life from now on.

twenty-four

——— ~~~~ ———

the priestesses worshipped at the new moon in the Sacred Grove behind the Forest House, following a ritual that men had not invented and were not allowed to see. Caillean watched as the novices filed in to complete the circle, feeling rather like a mother hen counting her chicks, or perhaps, observing the pale glimmer of their gowns in the half-light, cygnets about to become swans.

For a moment there was silence as the circle was completed. She moved into position before the stone cairn that was their altar, Dieda to her left and Miellyn to her right, in the place that was usually her own. But tonight Eilan was sick with cramps and the place of the High Priestess had fallen to Caillean. It felt strange to stand here, and strange not to feel the younger woman's familiar energy balancing her own.

Dieda lifted her hand, and the silence was broken by a shimmer of silver bells.

"*Hail to thee, thou new moon, guiding jewel of gentleness,*" sang the maidens, nearly a round dozen, all of them come to the Forest House since Eilan had become High Priestess. The most recent arrivals had been drawn by Dieda's music. When old Ardanos had schemed to get his two kinswomen into Vernemeton he had wrought better than he knew. Caillean listened to those pure voices offering their praise to heaven and sighed in pure content.

> "*I am bending to thee my knee,*
> *I am offering thee my love;*
> *I am bending to thee my knee,*
> *I am giving thee my hand*
> *I am lifting to thee mine eye*
> *Oh, new moon of the seasons!*"

With each phrase they were bending, then reaching upward in supplication, eyes fixed on the silver sickle above, so that their chanting became a dance. Now they began slowly to move sunwise around the circle, arms uplifted to the sky.

> *"Hail to thee, thou new moon,*
> *Joyful maiden of my love!*
> *Hail to thee, thou new moon*
> *Joyful maiden of the graces!*
> *Thou art traveling in thy course,*
> *Thou art showing us thy shining face,*
> *O new moon of the seasons!"*

Caillean let her gaze unfocus and allowed the rhythm of the chanting to carry her ever deeper into trance. Each time it grew easier. There had been a barren period in her life when nothing seemed to have meaning any more. But thanks to the Goddess, that seemed to be over. With the ending of her blood cycles, the floodgates of her spirit had opened, and with each season she felt ever more strongly the tides of power.

And it is because of you, Eilan, she thought, sending her awareness winging towards the dark bulk of the Forest House beyond the trees. *Can you hear how sweetly your daughters are singing now?*

Unbidden, her own arms were opening; the girls that circled the altar seemed to move in a haze of light.

> *"Thou queen-maiden of guidance,*
> *Thou queen-maiden of good fortune,*
> *Thou queen-maiden, my beloved new moon of the*
> *seasons!"*

Once more the bells shivered sweetly and the singing faded to silence; but it was a charged silence now, pregnant with power. Caillean reached out and felt the shock of completion as the other two grasped her hands; a second shift told her that the maidens had joined hands in a circle around them.

"Know, O my sisters, that the moon power is the Power of women, the light that shines in the darkness, the tides that rule the inner planes. The maiden moon governs all growth and all beginnings, and so it is that we draw on her power for those purposes for which our help has been requested. Sisters, are you willing to lend your energy to the work that we do now?"

There was a murmur of assent from the circle, and Caillean planted her feet more firmly in the cool grass.

"We call upon the Goddess, the Lady of Life, whose garment is the starry heavens; She is the virgin bride, the mother of all living, the wisdom beyond the circles of the world. She is all goddesses, and all the goddesses are one Goddess; in all Her phases, in all our faces, as She shines in the heavens, She shines within us all!" It was as if she sought to breathe against the wind. "Goddess, hear us –" she called.

"Goddess, be near us –" the others echoed her.

"Goddess hear us now!" The tension was almost unbearable; she could feel it thrilling through the hands braced against her own.

"For the healing of Bethoc, mother of Ambigatos, we raise this power!"

She heard Dieda intone the first note of the healing chord and a quarter of the circle joining her, the sound low and thrilling as a harp string, but deeper, sweeter, louder, continuing on and on. Then came the second note; now half the circle was singing; and the third, as the chord built and was completed on a high note above which Dieda's voice rose in a clear descant like a lark winging into the sky. It was a principle used by the harpers of Eriu in their magic, but it had been Eilan's idea to apply it to singing, and Dieda who worked out the technique of it and taught the girls. It was like being inside a harp to stand in the midst of that singing. And gradually, as their voices blended, Caillean began to touch the spirits of the others as well.

I am soaring with wings of light. Caillean could not tell whose thought that had been, nor did it matter, for at this moment when they were linked together she felt the same.

I see rainbows around the moon . . . in the sunlight . . . in the waterfall . . . all the world is shimmering . . .

Cool water . . . a fire's warmth . . . softness of a duckling's down . . . my mother's arms . . .

In this melding of sound all the senses were confounded. Only Dieda's mind remained distinct from the others – critical, and still unsatisfied.

Breathe now, and hold . . . Tanais is wavering. Wait, wait – Rhian should come in now with the fifth note – that's better. Now let's lift it, moving up the scale – stay with me, all of you – maintain the harmony!

The last irregularities disappeared. The women's joined voices moved upward together to become the Voice of the Goddess. For a time even Dieda's inner monologue ceased. Caillean felt some tension in the other woman relax as the chord vibrated with inhuman intensity. And though Caillean herself was self-taught, and had no words to describe the *rightness* of what she heard, she was singer enough to apprehend the ecstasy of a trained musician experiencing perfect harmony.

It took an effort for Caillean to collect herself, to reach out to the energy that was pulsing around her and gather it in, holding in her mind the image of the sick woman they were working for. She could see it now, a mist of power that grew brighter with every breath.

Caillean drew the Power inward, projecting upon it the image until they could all see it, shimmering above the pile of stones. The sound built until it seemed she could bear it no longer. Her arms were rising – all their arms were lifting unbidden as the Power fountained upward in a pillar of light, a surge of pure sound to send strength to the sick woman. And then it was gone. They settled back, breathing as if they had been running, knowing they had succeeded.

They raised the Power twice more that night for healing, and a last time, gently, to replenish some of the energy they had lost. When it was over, a measure of peace had returned even to Dieda's eyes. And then, with a final murmur of thanks, they filed back to the Forest House for food and bed. But Caillean, tired as she was, went to the separate building where the High Priestess had her chambers to tell Eilan how it had gone.

"You do not have to tell me –" said Eilan as Caillean came into her room. "Even from here I could hear you, I could feel the Power." The older woman looked lit up from within.

"It's true, Eilan. This is the work we were meant for! When I was a child serving Lhiannon, this is the kind of thing I dreamed of, but then the Druids penned us up here, and the vision was lost. With all my knowledge, I did not know how to find it again until you showed me the way."

"You would have found it . . ." Eilan sat up in bed and forced a smile. She still felt out of sorts and achy, as she often did at this time of the moon. More and more, she had become convinced that in ages past Caillean had been one of the greatest of priestesses. So much of what they were doing now in the Forest House came in spurts of certainty, as if they were not inventing it, but *remembering*. She supposed that she herself had been a priestess too, but while she had vision, there were times when Caillean was able to summon up an amazing power. "I have often thought that you should have been chosen High Priestess instead of me."

Caillean gave her a quick glance. "Once, I would have thought so too," she said. "I do not want it now."

"Sensible woman! But none the less, if you had to, you could do it." There was more silver now in Caillean's dark hair, thought Eilan, but otherwise she looked little different from the woman who had delivered Mairi's child ten years ago.

"Well I don't have to do it now," Caillean said briskly. "Only to get a few decisions out of you! We have had a rather odd request. A strange fellow from that Roman sect they call Christians wants to live in the old hut in the forest. He calls himself a hermit. Shall I say he may stay there or send him away?"

"He may as well," said Eilan, considering. "I don't intend to send any more of our women there for punishment, nor, I suppose, do you, and the Ravens have all found new hiding places." It gave her a pang to think of a stranger living in the place where she had borne and suckled her child, but there was no point in sentimentality.

"Very well," said Caillean. "And if Ardanos objects I can point to the precedent set when they let Christians build the chapel of the white thorn on the Isle of Apples below the Sacred Well."

"Have you been there?" Eilan asked.

"Long ago, when I was much younger," Caillean replied. "The Summer Country is a strange land, all marsh and lake and meadow. If there's any rain at all, the Tor turns to an island. Mist lies on the land sometimes so that you think the next turning will bring you to the Otherworld; and then a flare of sunlight cuts through the clouds and you see the holy Tor with its ring of stones."

Listening to Caillean, Eilan felt as if she could almost see it. Then she *was* seeing it, in a flash of vision as unexpected as it had been transitory – but Caillean had been in the vision too, gliding through the mists towards the hill in a flat-bottomed boat poled by the little dark men of the hills, with several of the novice priestesses huddled in the stern. But Caillean stood upright, with gold upon her neck and brow.

"Caillean," she began, and from the widening of the other woman's eyes, something of what she had seen must have shown in her face, "you will be High Priestess on the Isle of Apples. I have seen it. You will take the women there."

"When –" Caillean began, and Eilan shook her head.

"I don't know!" She sighed, for the vision, as so often happened, had been only a glimmering. "But it sounds a safe place, hidden from Roman eyes. Perhaps we should think about installing some priestesses there."

Gaius's new position kept him much on the move about the country. Since for the time, the main supply depot had been established at Deva, now occupied by the Twentieth Legion, it made sense for him to move his family to a pleasant estate that they called Villa Severina, south of the town. Julia was not happy about leaving Londinium, but she settled in to country life with a stoic resignation, and a year after their arrival in the West gave birth to twin girls whom she named matter-of-factly, Tertia and Quarta. The latter was so tiny they soon took to calling her Quartilla instead.

"But why?" asked Licinius. The old man had come to pay a visit to see his new granddaughters.

"Can't you guess?" Julia asked, but without humor. "If she were a jug, we would have to name her half-pint, not quart at all." Her father looked at her oddly, and she realized that it was not much of a joke – but then Quartilla was not much of a baby.

She found it hard to warm to the twins. When her belly grew so large, she had been certain she was about to bear Gaius a strapping son at last. Surely to go through such a hard labor with no more result than a pair of daughters, one of whom was sickly, was a reason for depression?

She recovered slowly, for she had been much torn during the delivery, and when it became clear that she could not nurse these children herself, gave them up to wet nurses with hardly a pang. The sooner she was fertile once more, the sooner she could try again for a son. The Greek physician had hinted that it might be dangerous, but he was only a slave, and Julia's threats kept him from saying anything to Gaius or her father.

Next time, she swore, *I will build a temple to Juno in Deva if I have to – but next time it will be a boy!*

Yet, as the children grew, Julia became accustomed to living most of the time among the gentle hills south of Deva and staying in her father's house in Londinium only during the wintertime. Licinius loved the children, and was already looking around for families with whom to ally them in marriage.

Gaius was a somewhat indifferent father, but she had expected no more. She knew that when she was unwell he sometimes slept with one of the slave girls, but so long as he did his duty in her bed as well she could hardly object to it. She had married to gain the status of a matron and to give her father an heir. Her relationship with Gaius was one of mutual respect and affection; for a Roman girl of good family anything else would have been unseemly.

Observing the scandals and divorces that occurred even in the pale imitation of Roman society that was Londinium, it seemed to her that she and Gaius were one of the few couples who had managed to preserve the old Roman values. Her marriage was a good one, and there were even times, seeing her daughters playing together in the garden of the villa, their bright tunics like flowers against the greenery, when Julia felt that perhaps she had not done so badly as a mother.

And soon after the twins celebrated their second birthday, she was pregnant once more.

After a long rainy spell, when the children chafed and whined at being kept inside, the weather had turned warm at last. Julia sat on the veranda they had built along the front of the house when they added the wings to either side. Ostensibly she was going over the household accounts, but actually she was dozing in the sunshine. Her hands rested lightly on the round of her belly, where she could sense the movements of the child within, surely a son. He had not moved much lately and she supposed that the warm weather had made the baby as torpid as she was.

Julia lay still, eyes half-closed against the sunshine, listening to the singing of the birds and the voices of the household slaves as they busied themselves about the tasks of the farm. Gaius used to say that Julia's household always ran with the efficiency of a Legion making camp. She knew without checking where each of her servants would be and what he or she would be doing at each hour of the day.

". . . playing in the garden." That was the voice of the strapping Gaulish girl whose job it was to keep track of the children.

"That they are not!" Old Lydia, who ran the nursery, replied. "The twins are eating their noon meal, and Cella is helping the cook make pies. But Secunda is just at that age when if they are unwatched they will go exploring –"

"She was in the garden . . ." the girl said weakly.

"And where were you? Flirting with the master's groom again?" Lydia replied. "Well, she can't have gone far. You get out there and find her, and I will call some of the men to help you. But I promise to personally see you whipped if any harm has come to the child! What were you thinking of? You know the mistress must not be worried with her time so near!"

Julia frowned, debating whether to get up and speak to them. But this pregnancy had sapped her energy and her will, and surely Secunda would turn up soon.

In the distance she heard more voices, and Gaius's deep tones questioning. *Good,* she thought then, *they have got him out looking. It is high time he bestirred himself more on the children's behalf.*

She lay back again, knowing that she ought to relax for the sake of her unborn child, but as the moments wore on, she found tension bringing her upright again. She could hardly hear the calling now. How far had Secunda gone?

The shadow on the sundial had moved almost to the next hour when she heard muted voices and footsteps crunching on the gravel of the path. They had found her then – but why were they so silent? Secunda ought to have been wailing if her father had paddled her as she deserved. A chill swept through Julia's body. She hauled herself upright, clinging to the pillar, as the little procession emerged from among the trees.

She saw Gaius's dark head and tried to call out to him, but words would not come. Then the gardener moved aside and she saw that he was holding Secunda in his arms. But even asleep she had never seen her little girl lie so still.

"Why isn't she moving?" Her lips twitched soundlessly.

Gaius came forward, his face working, already blotched with tears. More water dripped from Secunda's pink gown, and her black curls were plastered tight to her skull. Julia stared, shock sending ice through her veins.

"She was in the stream," he said hoarsely, "at the edge of the field. I tried to breathe life back into her. I tried . . ." He swallowed, looking down at the small closed face, pale as marble now.

No, thought Julia numbly, Secunda would never breathe again. She blinked, wondering why the world had gone so dim around her. Then she felt a wrenching pain in her belly.

The next few hours were a confusion of grief and pain. She remembered hearing Gaius swear he would have the Gaullish girl flayed, and Licinius trying to calm him. Something was wrong with

Secunda . . . She tried to get up and go to her, but her women kept pushing her back down. And then the ache in her belly would begin again. In her more lucid moments Julia knew this was wrong. She was familiar with the pangs of labor, but she was barely six months along. *Gods, if you have any mercy, make it stop. You took my daughter – don't let me lose my son!*

It was nearly dawn when she convulsed and felt a last hot gush of blood between her thighs. Lydia bent over her, swearing softly. Julia felt the pressure as the woman jammed more cloths between her legs to stop the bleeding. But for a moment she had glimpsed something else, something small and purplish that did not move.

"My son." Her whisper was a thread of sound. "Let me hold him, please!"

Weeping, Lydia brought something wrapped in a bloody cloth and laid it in the curve of her arm. The face had been wiped clean, and she could see the tiny, perfect features, like the petals of a blighted rose.

She was still holding him when they finally let Gaius in to see her.

"The gods hate me," she whispered, tears sliding from her eyes.

He knelt beside the bed, lifted the damp hair from her brow and kissed her with more tenderness than she expected. For a moment he looked down at the stillborn child, and then, gently, he drew a fold of cloth across its face and lifted it. She made a convulsive movement to stop him, but she could barely move. For a moment he stood with the child in his arms, like any father about to acknowledge his new-born son, then handed the still form to Lydia to take away.

Julia turned her face into the pillow, sobbing. "Let me die! I have failed, let me die!"

"That's not true, my poor darling. You still have three little girls who need you. You must not weep so."

"My baby, my little boy is dead!"

"Hush, my love." Gaius tried to soothe her, looking at his father-in-law, who had come into the room behind him, in appeal. "We are not yet old, my dear. If the gods will it, we may yet have many children –"

Licinius bent down to kiss her as well. "And if you have no son, my dear child, what of that? You have been a better child to me than many sons, that I vow to you."

"You must think of our living children now," said Gaius.

Julia felt despair well up in her. "You never paid any attention to Secunda. Why should you care about the others now? You only care that I have lost your son."

"No," Gaius said very quietly, "I do not need you to give me a son. You must sleep now." He got to his feet, looking down at her. "Sleep heals many griefs, and in the morning you will feel differently."

But Julia, remembering the delicately carved features of her little boy, did not really hear.

As the slow weeks of Julia's recovery wore on, Gaius found that he was saddened more by her grief than any feelings of his own. He had been away from home when Secunda was born, and had no great attachment to her. Nor could he bring himself to grieve overmuch for one of four girls.

Yet when he thought of the son they had lost, he could not help thinking about his son by Eilan. In Roman society, adoption of a healthy boy from another family was a traditional solution. If Julia had no male children, and after a consultation with the physician that began to seem improbable, she was less likely to object if he claimed Eilan's son. And he was fond of his daughters, although he felt no such bond as he had to his first-born boy.

But there was time and enough for that once Julia had her health again. Hoping it would at least distract her from her grief, he agreed to take Julia on a pilgrimage to the shrine of the Mother Goddess near Venta, but the journey did little to help her recover her health and spirits, and when he offered to move the family back to Londinium, she did not want to go.

"It is here that our children are buried," she told him. "I will not leave them here."

Gaius privately considered this unreasonable. Despite native beliefs that the land of the Silures held the entrance to the Otherworld, it seemed to him that no earthly place could be nearer or further off than any other to the Land of the Dead, but he gave way to Julia's whim and they remained.

Towards the end of that year news came that Agricola was dead as well.

"*As Tacitus is fond of saying*," wrote Licinius Corax, "'*It is a principle of human nature to hate those whom we have injured.*' *But even our Divine Emperor could find little in Agricola to justify his anger, and so our friend escaped official disfavor. Indeed, the*

*Emperor was remarkably solicitous throughout Agricola's ill-
ness, and though there are those who whisper that the General was
taken off by poison; for myself, I think the cause was a heart
broken by witnessing Rome's dishonor. It may be that he is well
out of it, and it is we who will soon wish that we had gone
on before. Be glad that you are safely out of sight in
Britannia . . ."*

In the following year Licinius retired and came to make his home
with them, and so they added another wing to the Villa Severina,
and the final year of Gaius's service as Procurator for supplies
began. He had hoped that when he completed his term of office
Senator Malleus would be able to arrange to have him appointed to
a higher position, but that year brought disturbing news. The
Emperor was growing ever more autocratic and suspicious. As a
military leader he had been reasonably successful, but he seemed to
take his successes as proof of divine favor, and was doing his best,
wrote Licinius's cousin Corax, to destroy what power remained to
the patrician class.

Gaius wondered if this would be the spark that set the embers of
rebellion aflame, but the next thing they heard was that Herennius
Senecio and several others had been executed for treason.

Gaius understood that his career was likely to be on hold for
some time. His patron Senator Malleus, while not accused, had
found it prudent to retire to his estates in Campania. And so, when
Gaius completed his term as Procurator, he put off the visit to
Rome with which he had planned to follow it and, like his patron,
decided to devote himself for a time to developing the productivity
of his lands.

Now he began at last to establish a stronger friendship with his
remaining daughters, but Julia remained depressed and sickly.
Though they still shared a bed, it was becoming ever clearer that
she was unlikely to give him a son.

By now Eilan's child would be ten years old. Even a father who
was not precisely in the Emperor's favor could guarantee the child
a better future than a British priestess who must hide the very fact
of his existence, and surely Julia would rather raise a son of his
than a stranger's child – although he could never be quite sure what
Julia would feel. But after all, Gaius could assure her – and it
would be the truth – that the boy had been fathered before he ever
set eyes on her.

The Forest House was scarcely an afternoon's ride away. His son could be living just over the next hill, reflected Gaius, gazing southward through the trees. But he found himself oddly afraid to face Eilan again. Did she hate Rome? Did she hate him? The girl he had loved when he was a boy was gone, transformed into the terrible priestess of Vernemeton. Sometimes it seemed to him that the woman he had married was gone too, all the playfulness that had attracted him dead with her son.

Gaius had been reasonably successful in his career, though he had hardly fufilled his father's dreams. But it occurred to him that he had little to love. In his life he had often been lonely, but his father's discipline, or that of the army, had kept him too busy to worry about it. But as the year wore on Gaius found that though managing the estate exercised his body it left his mind free to roam, and he was haunted by dreams of his childhood.

Perhaps it was all the time he was putting in on the land that was stimulating his memories from that age when all the world was wonderful and new. He had not allowed himself to think about his mother when he was a child, but he dreamed of her now. He felt her holding him, heard her sweet lullabies and woke in tears, calling to her not to leave him alone.

But she had gone away to the Land of the Dead, and Eilan had left him for the Goddess she served, and now Julia was withdrawing from him as well. Would there ever be anyone, he wondered, who could simply love without trying to change him, whose love would endure?

Then Gaius would remember how he had felt when he held his son in his arms. But whenever he began planning how to find the boy, he would flinch from the possibility that when they did meet, his son would not care after all. And so he did nothing.

One day when Gaius was riding out after the wild pigs that had been rooting in his gardens he realized that he had reached the woodland above the Forest House where Eilan had given birth to their son and found himself reining his horse down the path. He knew that Eilan would not be there, but perhaps there was someone who could give him news of her. Even if she hated him, she could hardly refuse to give him news of their son.

At first he thought the place deserted. The promise of spring was blushing in the branches with their hard buds of green, but the thatched roof of the hut was ragged and weather-bleached, and the ground littered with sticks blown down in the last storm and last year's dead leaves. Then he saw a thin haze of smoke filtering up through the thatching. His pony snorted as he reined in and a man peered out at him. "Welcome, my son," he said, "Who are you and why have you come?"

Gaius gave his name, eyeing the fellow curiously. "And who might you be?" he asked. The man was tall, with a sun-browned face and night-dark hair, dressed in a coarse goat-hair robe above an untidy straggle of beard.

Gaius wondered if he were some homeless wanderer who had taken refuge in the unused building; then he saw the crossed sticks that hung from the man's neck on a thong and realized he must be some kind of Christian, perhaps one of those hermits who were, in the last two or three years, springing up from one end of the Empire to the other. Gaius had heard of them in Egypt and Northern Africa, but it was strange to see one here. "What are you doing here?" he asked again.

"I have come to minister to God's lost ones," the hermit answered. "In the world I was known as Lycias; now I am called Father Petros. Surely God has sent you to me because you are in need. What can I do for you?"

"How do you know it was God who sent me to you?" Gaius asked, amused in spite of himself by the man's simplicity.

"You're here, aren't you?" asked Father Petros.

He shrugged and Petros went on. "Believe me, my son, nothing happens without the knowledge of the God who set the stars in their places."

"Nothing?" Gaius said with a bitterness that surprised him. He realized that at some point during the past three years, perhaps when he heard of the death of Agricola, or perhaps while he was watching Julia's suffering, he had ceased to believe in the gods. "Then perhaps you can tell me what kind of deity would take a son, and a daughter, from a mother who loved them?"

"Is that your trouble?" Father Petros pulled the door wider. "Come in, my son. Such matters are not explained in a breath, and your poor beast looks tired."

A little guiltily, Gaius remembered how far the pony had carried him. When he had tethered the animal with a long enough lead to let it reach the dry grass, he went in.

Father Petros was setting out cups on a rough table. "What can I offer you? I have beans and turnips and even some wine; the weather is such, here, that I cannot fast as often as I did in a warmer climate. I drink nothing but water, myself, but I am permitted to offer these worldly things to such guests as come to me."

Gaius shook his head, realizing he had happened upon a philosopher. "I will try your wine," he said, "but I tell you plainly; you will never convince me your god is either all-powerful or good. For if he were all-powerful, why can he not prevent suffering? And if he can and does not, why should men worship him?"

"Ah," said Father Petros, "I can tell by that question that you have been trained in the Stoic philosophy; for the words are theirs. But the philosophers are wrong about the nature of God."

"And you, of course, are right?" Gaius's tone was belligerent.

Father Petros shook his head. "I am only a poor minister to such children as seek my counsel. The only Son of God was crucified and returned from the dead to save us; that is all I need to know. Those who believe in Him will live eternally in glory."

It was the usual childish oriental legend, Gaius thought, remembering what he had heard about the cult in Rome. He supposed he could see why the story appealed to slaves and even a few women of good family. Suddenly it occurred to him that this fellow's ramblings might interest Julia, or at least give her something to think about. He set down his cup.

"I thank you for your wine, Father, and for your story," he said. "May my wife call upon you? She is devastated with grief for our daughter."

"She will be welcome whenever she comes," Father Petros replied graciously. "I am only sorry I have not convinced you. I haven't, have I?"

"I'm afraid not." Gaius was a little disarmed by the man's regret.

"I am not much of a preacher," said Father Petros, looking somewhat crestfallen. "I wish Father Joseph were here; I am sure he could convince you."

Gaius thought it highly unlikely, but he smiled politely. As he turned to go, there was a knock at the door.

"Ah, Senara? Do come in," the hermit said.

"I see you have someone with you," a girl's voice replied. "I'll come another time, if I may."

"It's all right, I'm just leaving." Gaius pushed aside the flap of leather that covered the door. Before him was one of the prettiest young girls he had seen at least since his first sight of Eilan, so long ago. But of course he too had been very young then. She was about fifteen, he thought, with hair the color of copper filings in a blacksmith's fire and eyes very blue, dressed in an undyed linen gown.

Then he looked at her again and realized where he had seen her before. Despite the Celtic coloring, there was a distinct look of his father's old secretary Valerius in the line of her nose and jaw. That would explain her knowledge of Latin.

It was not until he was untying his horse that he realized he could have asked – what was it the hermit had called her, Senara? – how he might arrange a meeting with Eilan. But by that time the doorflap had closed behind her, and one of the few things he knew about women – not that he knew that much, and since his marriage he felt he knew even less – was that it was never wise to ask one woman about another.

It was well past sunset by the time Gaius reached the villa, but Julia's greeting, if subdued, was friendly. Licinius was already awaiting them in the dining room.

Macellia and Tertia were playing with a toy chariot on the veranda; they had dressed Julia's pet monkey in baby clothes, and were trying to stuff it into the chariot. He rescued the little animal and handed it to Julia. Sometimes he wondered how three small girls and one woman, with only seven servants, could make so much chaos in one house.

The little girls screamed, "Papa! Papa!" and Quartilla came running to join them. Gaius hugged them all round, called for Lydia to take charge of them, then went into the dining room with Julia.

She still had the monkey on her shoulder; it was about the size of a baby, and for some reason, seeing it dressed in baby clothes annoyed him. He couldn't imagine what Julia wanted with the creature; it was a hot-weather animal and had to be cosseted as if it really were a child. Of all places to keep such a pet, Britain was certainly the worst; even in summer, he supposed, it was too cold for the little animal. "I wish you'd get rid of that wretched beast," he snapped irritably as they sat down to the meal.

Her eyes watered. "Secunda was so fond of it," she whispered.

The comment made him wonder, not for the first time, if Julia had lost her mind. Secunda had been six years old when she died, and he didn't think she had ever paid the slightest attention to the monkey. Still, if it pleased Julia to think so ... Seeing Licinius's warning glance from across the table, he sighed and abandoned the subject.

"What were you doing today?" she asked, making an obvious effort to speak cheerfully as the servants brought in the boiled eggs, a platter of smoked oysters and salt fish, and a selection of salad greens dressed with olive oil.

Gaius swallowed a piece of onion too quickly and coughed, mentally editing his day. He reached across the table for a fragrant roll of fresh bread. "I was trying to track those wild pigs and ended up on the other side of the hills," he began. "The old hut in the woods down there has a new tenant, some kind of a hermit."

"A Christian?" asked Licinius dubiously. He had never had any good to say of the oriental cults that were invading Rome.

"Apparently so," said Gaius neutrally, letting the girl take his plate away while others brought in the dish of ducklings sauced with plums soaked in sweet wine. He dabbled his fingers in the bowl of scented water and wiped them. "At any rate he believes that his god rose from the dead."

Licinius snorted, but Julia's eyes filled with tears. "Does he really?" The helpless look in her eyes wrung Gaius's heart even while it exasperated him. *Whatever gives her comfort.* He put down the duck wing, turning on his dining couch to face her.

"Do you think he would let me come and speak to him? Will you allow me to go?" she asked pleadingly.

"My dear Julia, I want you to do whatever will give you comfort." He meant it in all sincerity. "Whatever makes you happy will please me."

"You are so good to me." Her eyes filled with tears again. She gulped apologetically, and fled from the room.

"I don't understand her," admitted Licinius. "I raised her to live a virtuous life and honor her ancestors. I loved the child too, but all of us will die one day, be it late or soon. I chose well for my girl," he added. "You have been kinder to her than I could be, even though she did not give you a son."

Gaius sighed and reached for the wine. He felt like a monstrous deceiver, but held his peace. He had become responsible for this woman's happiness, and to hurt her feelings was the first of many things he did not want to do. But he could not help thinking that Eilan would never have been foolish enough to be seduced by some Christian monk's ramblings.

When the sweets had been cleared away, Gaius went to the room where Julia was supervising as the little girls were put to bed. Gaius was glad to see the monkey had escaped; feeling very mean-spirited, he hoped it would run off and, if they were lucky, get caught by a marauding dog.

The slave trimmed the wick and he and Julia stood for a moment, watching the soft light flickering on smooth cheeks and dark lashes. Julia spoke a phrase of blessing, and touched the amulet against fire that hung on the wall. Of late she had become very superstitious. Of course a fire would be disastrous, but the house was newly built and not at all drafty. On the whole he had rather more faith in the fire-fighting abilities of their household slaves than in most goddesses or charms.

As they came out into the hallway, she said, "I think I will go to bed now."

Gaius patted her shoulder and kissed the cheek she presented. He might have expected that. The idea was that by the time he came to bed she would be – or pretend to be – so deeply asleep that he would not disturb her. He might as well not have a wife at all. And how could she expect him to give her another child if she would not sleep with him?

But it was pointless to censure her. He wished her a good night and turned towards his office in the other wing of the villa, where a scroll containing the latest installment of Tacitus's *Life of Agricola* was waiting for him.

And there he discovered where Julia's monkey had taken refuge; it was on his desk and had defecated, evil-smelling monkey excrement, all over his papers. He shouted with rage, grabbed the little beast and flung it with all his force into the yard. He heard an odd crunch and then a whimper, then nothing more.

Good. If the creature was dead, he would not mourn; and tomorrow he would have no compunction in telling Julia that a dog must have caught it. The Christian priest could comfort her; though he had heard that they preferred to have nothing to do with women. At the moment, he wished that he need not either.

twenty-five

———〰〰〰———

G aius woke in the early morning. Today, whatever else happened, he must do something about finding his son. Ardanos must know how to contact his granddaughter. He was not anxious to talk to the old man, whom he suspected of being as much a fanatic in his own way as Father Petros, but he could see no alternative. The only problem that remained was how to find Ardanos, who no longer lived near Deva.

But while he lay contemplating the problem, he heard a peremptory knock on the front gate, and his steward complaining as he went to answer it. Gaius threw on a robe and slid out of bed, carefully, so as not to wake Julia. A legionary was waiting in the front courtyard with a request from Macellius for a visit. Gaius raised one eyebrow. Officially, his father was retired, but he was aware that the old man had made himself a trusted adviser to the Twentieth Legion's young Commander.

If he were gone when Julia discovered the death of her monkey, he would not have to face her tears. Gaius rode through the town and directly to the gates of the fortress, exchanging salutes with the guard on duty, who knew him well from his stint as Procurator.

"Your father said you would probably arrive before noon," said the soldier. "You'll find him with the Legate in the Praetorium."

On the bench outside the Commander's office he saw a weary-looking woman. She was a Briton of the dark-haired, pale-skinned type like his mother's people; somewhere between thirty and thirty-five, he guessed, dressed in a gown of saffron wool rather lavishly embroidered with gold. Gaius wondered what she had done, and when the legionary on duty ushered him into the presence of the Commander and his father, he put the question.

"Her name is Brigitta," his father answered with distaste. "She calls herself Queen of the Demetae. When her husband died, he left

330

his fortune in equal shares to her and to the Emperor, and she seems to feel this gives her the right to rule his kingdom. Sound familiar?"

Gaius licked dry lips. It was common practice for a rich man to split his estate between his own family and the Emperor in hopes that the Imperial co-heir would make sure the other heirs got their share. Agricola had done the same thing.

The Legate looked from Gaius to his father. Clearly it did not sound familiar to him.

"Boudicca." Gaius said succinctly. "Her husband tried the same thing, but the Iceni had debts to some fairly prominent senators. When he died, they moved in, and she tried to resist. She and her daughters were rather . . . badly treated and she raised the tribe in a rebellion that nearly swept us out of this land!" That was the specter that Macellius was seeing when he looked at the unhappy woman sitting outside, especially since the Demetae were one of the tribes that counted descent through the mother's line.

"Oh, *that* Boudicca," said the Legate. He was called Lucius Domitius Brutus, and he seemed to Gaius rather young for such a major posting, but he was reputed to be a good friend of the Emperor.

"*That* Boudicca," Macellius echoed disgustedly. "So you see, sir, why the tribune over at Moridunum scooped her up as soon as the will was read, and why we cannot simply carry out the terms of the will as they stand, no matter how much they benefit the Emperor."

"On the other hand," said Gaius, "it should also be clear that this woman must be handled like blown glass. I assure you that every native in this country will be waiting to see what we do." A thought occurred to him. "I don't suppose she has children?"

"A couple of daughters somewhere, I've heard," said Macellius wearily, "but I don't know what has become of them; they are only about three or four, worse luck, or I'd have them properly married off to a citizen. I have no particular stomach for this business of war against women and children; but if women will mingle in politics, what can we do? Rumor has it that she – or those who would like to use her – have sent messages seeking alliance with the Hibernians."

Gaius shuddered, remembering the raid on Eilan's home. "Take her to Londinium," he suggested. "If she's sent to Rome her people will think she's a prisoner, but if she's set up in a fine house in the city they may think she's betrayed them. Tell her that unless she lives in Londinium she won't see a sestercius of her husband's gold."

"It might work," Macellius said, considering. He turned to the Legate. "I agree with my son's suggestion. You've already got a detachment ready to strengthen the garrison at Moridunum; they can carry the news."

"She'll be a hostage then," Domitius Brutus said. This he could understand.

As he left the office, it occurred to Gaius that the daughters, however young, could still be a danger. The woman stirred a faint pity; she looked so forlorn.

"Where are your little girls?" he asked in the British tongue.

"Where you will never find them, Roman, and I thank the gods," she said. "Don't you think I know how your legionaries treat young girls?"

"Not little children!" Gaius exclaimed. "Come now; I am a father myself with three little daughters about the age of yours. At most we would find them suitable guardians."

"I will spare you that trouble." she said fiercely, "They are well taken care of!"

A legionary came up and touched her on the arm. When she flinched, he ordered, "Do come along quietly, lady. We don't wish to bind you."

She looked wildly around her, and her gaze settled on Gaius. "Where are you taking me?"

"Only to Londinium," he said soothingly. He saw her face crumple, with relief or disappointment he did not know, but she went quietly enough.

The legionary on guard watched her go and said to Gaius, "You'd never think she would associate with known agitators, not to look at her now; but when we picked her up, it was reported she'd been seen about with a notorious rebel: Conmor, Cynric, or some such name as that. He's said to be still in the area."

"I know him," Gaius said. The legionary stared, "You, sir?"

Gaius nodded, recalling the high-hearted boy who had pulled him out of the boar pit. Was Cynric still in contact with Eilan? If they caught him, Gaius could ask how he could arrange a private meeting.

"Gods," said Macellius, closing the door of the Legate's office behind him and following Gaius down the corridor, "all this makes me feel old!"

"Don't be ridiculous," Gaius answered him.

"The Legate wants me to do something to calm things down among the people. Use my old contacts, he says."

Perhaps Brutus was not as stupid as he looked, Gaius thought. Macellius's ability to get co-operation from the tribes had been legendary in his day.

"But I'm tired of picking other people's chestnuts out of the fire. Maybe I'll move to Rome. It's been a long time since I've seen the city. Maybe I should go to Egypt where I would be warm for once."

"Don't be foolish," Gaius chided. "What would my little girls do without their grandsire?"

"Oh, come, they hardly know I'm alive," said Macellius. But he seemed pleased. "Of course if you had a son it would be different."

"I – well, I may have a son one of these days," Gaius broke out in a sweat. Macellius himself had told Gaius about Eilan's pregnancy, but when he had seen her and the baby in the hut in the forest, it was clear that the birth had been kept secret. If Macellius did not know that Eilan had borne him a son, Gaius did not think he should tell his father now.

Eilan dreamed that she walked beside a lake in a half-light that could have been either dusk or dawn. A light mist hung above the waters, obscuring the further shore; the mists were silver, and a silver sheen was on the waters; wavelets lapped softly against the shore. It seemed that across the water drifted singing, and out of the mists came swimming nine white swans, as fair as the maidens of the Forest House when they saluted the moon.

Eilan had never heard anything so beautiful. She moved down to the edge of the lake, stretching out her hands, and the swans circled slowly.

"Let me come to you, let me swim with you!" she cried, but from the swans came the answer, "You cannot come with us; your robes and ornaments weigh you down ..." They began to swim away, and Eilan's heart was torn with loss.

Eilan stripped off her heavy gown, her veils and mantle, and cast the golden torque and armlets of the High Priestess aside. As her shadow glimmered in the water, it was the shape of a swan. She cast herself into the lake ...

As the silver waters closed over her head she woke to the familiar timbers of the Forest House in the dim light of dawn. For a few moments Eilan sat still, rubbing her eyes. This was not the first time she had dreamed of the lake and the swans. Each time, it seemed harder to return. She had told no one of her trouble. She was High Priestess of Vernemeton, not some silly girl to be frightened by an odd dream. But each time it happened the dream was more vivid, and the role she played while waking more and more unreal.

Someone was pounding on a door. Oddly, it was the gateway to her garden. Faintly she could hear the voice of the young priestess who guarded it raised in protest.

"Who the mischief do you think you are? You cannot simply walk in from nowhere and ask to see the High Priestess, certainly not at this hour."

"Forgive me," answered a deep voice. "I think of her still as my foster sister, not the High Priestess. Ask her, please, if she will speak to me!"

Eilan threw on a shawl and hurried out on to the porch. "Cynric!" she exclaimed. "I thought you in the North somewhere!" She stopped short. Clinging around his neck was a small, dark-haired child of two or three; another girl, perhaps five years old, hid behind his cloak. "Are they yours?"

He shook his head. "They belong to an unfortunate woman, and I have come to beg you to give them shelter in the name of the Goddess."

"To give them shelter?" Eilan repeated stupidly. "But why?"

"Because they stand in need of it," Cynric returned, as if it were the most natural thing in the world.

"What I meant was, why here? Have they no kindred to care for them? If they are not yours, why have they become your responsibility?"

"Their mother is Brigitta, Queen of the Demetae," said Cynric uneasily. "She tried to claim the kingdom when her husband died and is now a prisoner of Rome. We feared her daughters would be held as hostages, or worse, if they fell into Roman hands."

Eilan looked at the children and thought of her own son. She pitied their mother with all her heart, but what would Ardanos say? This was one of those times when she could have used Caillean's counsel, but the older woman had gone down to the Summer Country to visit the Sacred Well.

"You know they are too young to claim for the Goddess."

"All I am asking is that you keep them safe and secure!" Cynric began, but before he could say anything else there was more noise outside.

"My lady, you cannot see the Priestess now; she is with a guest."

"All the more reason I should be with her," a voice said, and Dieda came into the garden. At the sight of Cynric she cried out, and he turned hastily to see her. She had been told about his activities when she returned from Eriu, but this was the first time she had seen him.

"The children are not mine!" he exclaimed as the color left her face and then flamed back again. "Queen Brigitta sent them here for sanctuary."

"They should be taken to the House of Maidens, then," said Dieda, mastering herself, and held out her hand. But her eyes were still on Cynric.

"Wait," said Eilan. "I must think. The Forest House cannot afford to entangle itself in anything political."

"Without the consent of the Romans?" Cynric said scornfully.

"It is easy for you to jeer," Eilan began, "but you must remember that we exist by sufferance of those Romans you are so ready to dismiss. We should at least consult with the Arch-Druid before we commit ourselves to something that might look like support for a rebellion."

"With Ardanos?" Cynric spat. "Why not with the Legate in Deva himself? Maybe we should go to the Governor of Britain and ask his leave."

"Cynric, I have risked a great deal for you and your cause," Eilan reminded him soberly. "But I cannot risk the Forest House by taking in political fugitives without Ardanos's leave." A quick word sent her attendant running down the path towards the nearby house that had been built for the Arch-Druid.

Cynric said, "Eilan, do you know the fate to which you will be abandoning these girls?"

"Do you?" she snapped. "Why are you so sure Ardanos will refuse?"

"Regarding what?" said a new voice, and they all turned, Eilan frowning, Cynric flushed with anger, and Dieda pale with some emotion Eilan could not name. "Your woman encountered me just outside," Ardanos explained.

Eilan pointed to the children.

"There is nothing I can do for Brigitta," Ardanos said when she was done. "She was warned about what would happen if she claimed the right to rule. But she will not be harshly treated; even the Romans would not make that mistake twice in one century. As for the girls, I do not know. They could be trouble, later on."

"But not yet," said Eilan decisively. "And I will not hold children responsible for their parents' crimes. Senara and Lia can tend them. If we give them new names and treat them like any other children they should be safe enough for a time. No one will think anything of it." She smiled bitterly. "After all, I have a reputation for sheltering motherless children!"

"I suppose so," said Ardanos dubiously. "But Cynric had better get well away. For where he is, I have noticed, trouble follows." He glared at the young man, and Dieda went pale. "The Romans may not care about the girls, but they will certainly be looking for you!"

"If they try to interfere with me they may find more trouble than they bargained for." Cynric said fiercely.

Eilan sighed, thinking that rather than a raven, he should have been called a stormy petrel. But she knew better than to argue with Cynric, or with Dieda. All she could do was to try and keep the peace a little longer. Sometimes it seemed as if the whole weight of Britain lay on her shoulders – and that all her kin were conspiring to keep it there.

Senara was summoned to take the children to their new quarters, and Eilan went on to her duties, leaving Dieda and Cynric to make their farewells. Later that afternoon, she heard weeping in the shed where they dried the herbs. It was Dieda.

The other woman started up, her eyes blazing, then seemed to deflate when she saw who it was. Although their relationship was no longer close, at least Dieda felt no need to dissemble. But Eilan knew better than to try to touch her or offer comfort.

"What is it?" she said.

Dieda scrubbed at her eyes with the corner of her veil, making them even redder. "He asked me to go with him –"

"And you refused." Eilan kept her voice deliberately neutral.

"To live the life of an outlaw, always skulking in the forest, afraid of every sound, always wondering if tomorrow I would see him marched off in chains or slain by Roman swords? I could not do it, Eilan! Here at least I have my music, and work to do that I believe in. How could I go?"

"Did you tell him so?"

Dieda nodded. "He said that if I felt that way I could not truly love him; that I was betraying our cause . . . He said that he needed me . . ."

I'm sure he did, the idiot, thought Eilan, *and never wondered whether she needs* him *at all!*

"It is your fault!" Dieda exclaimed. "If it were not for you, I would have married him long ago. Then perhaps he would never have become an outlaw!"

With an effort, Eilan stopped herself from pointing out that Dieda had sworn the vows of a priestess of her own free will. Even when Eilan returned to the Forest House after Gawen's birth, she could have gone to Cynric instead of to Eriu. The poor girl did not want logic, she needed someone to blame.

"And now all I can think of is the way he looked at me! It may be months or even years before I know how he is, or what is happening to him! At least if I were with him I would know!" Dieda wailed.

"I don't suppose you care one way or another for my approval," Eilan said softly. "Whatever you think of my choices, you know that I have learned to live with them. But I too have wept in the darkness, wondering whether I did the right thing. Dieda, you may never be sure – all you can do is the work that is given to you, and hope that the Goddess will explain the reason for it all some day."

Dieda's face was turned away, but it seemed to Eilan that her sobs were diminishing.

"I will tell the maidens that you are ill and cannot take them tonight for the singing," she went on. "No doubt they will be glad of a holiday."

It seemed to Eilan that the problem of Brigitta's children had been solved, but only a few days later, just before the evening meal, her attendant told her that a Roman sought audience.

Gaius leapt to mind but a second thought told her he would never dare come here. "Find out his name and business," she said evenly.

In a few moments the girl returned. "Lady, it is Macellius Severus who begs the favor of a word with you." She added, "He used to be the Camp Prefect of Deva –"

"I know who he is." Lhiannon had received him once or twice, but Macellius was now retired. What, in the name of all the gods, could he want with her? The only way to find out was to ask. "Tell him to come in," she directed. She straightened her gown and after a moment's thought drew her veil down over her face.

Presently Huw shouldered through the entrance with another

man behind him. *Gaius's father . . . the grandfather of her son . . .* From behind the veil Eilan eyed him curiously. She had never seen him before, and yet she would have known him anywhere. Overlapping visions showed her the weathered features of the old man and the strong lines of nose and brow that had been repeated in his son, and were just beginning to emerge from the childish curves in the face of her own.

Huw took up position beside the door and Macellius came to a halt before her. He drew himself up and bowed, and Eilan knew suddenly where Gaius had got his pride.

"My lady." He used the Roman term, *Domina*, but his British was quite good otherwise. "It is very kind of you to receive me –"

"Not at all," she replied. "What can I do for you?" She supposed it had to do with one of the approaching festivals as it had when he had waited upon Lhiannon.

Macellius cleared his throat. "I understand that you have given sanctuary to the daughters of the Demetan Queen –"

Suddenly Eilan was very glad that she had put on the veil. "If that were true," she said slowly, desperately wishing that Ardanos or Caillean, were here to help her, "why would it matter to you?"

"If it were so," he echoed, "we would want to know why."

The words of Cynric came into her mind. "Because it was told to me that they stood in need of it. Can you think of any better reason?"

"I cannot," he answered her, "and yet their mother is a rebel who threatened to raise the whole West against Rome. But Rome has been merciful. Brigitta has been sent in protective custody to Londinium, and will not be harmed. Nor have we demanded death for her kin."

The little ones will be glad to know their mother is safe, thought Eilan, remembering how unnaturally silent they had been. But why? Was it possible that Macellius desired peace between Rome and the Britons as much as she?

"If this is true I am glad to hear it," she said, "but what do you want of me?"

"I should think it would be obvious lady. These girls must not become a rallying point for some future uprising. Brigitta herself is not important, but in times of tension, any pretext will serve."

She said, "I think you may rest easy on that point; if they were among the maidens of the Forest House no political use would be made of them."

"Not even when they are grown?" he asked. "How do we know that they will not be given to men who will try to rule the Demetae by right of marriage to the Queen?"

He was right to wonder she thought. It was exactly the sort of thing that Cynric would try. "How would you avoid it?"

"The best way is to have them fostered in loyal Roman homes; and when they are grown, find them good solid husbands with Roman sympathies."

"And that is all that would happen to them in Roman hands?"

"That is all," Macellius replied. "My lady, you cannot believe that we make war on babes and little children?"

She was silent. *That is exactly what I have been brought up to believe.*

"Is it your will that we shall always be paying for atrocities committed by others? On the sacred island, for instance?" said Macellius, as if he could hear what she was thinking.

That is what Cynric believes, but the decision is mine. And it is I whom the Goddess must tell what to do. For a few moments longer Eilan was silent, seeking the inner stillness in which she could hear.

"It is not," she said, "but I would lose the trust of my own people if I appeared too eager to believe you. I have heard Brigitta's daughters are both still too young for anyone to think of marriage. They have been through a great deal. Surely it would be more merciful to let them stay wherever they are a few months, or even a year, until the furor has died down. By then everyone will know how you have treated their mother. Passions will have cooled, and there will be less outcry if people learn they are in your hands."

"And will they then be given to us?" Macellius said, frowning.

"If all is as you say, I swear by the gods of my tribe that they will." Eilan set her hand upon the torque around her neck. "Prepare to receive them in your house in Deva at the Feast of the Maiden next year."

His face lightened, and Eilan's breath caught as she saw on his lined face Gawen's flickering smile. If only she could tell him who she was, and show him his grandson, safe and strong!

"I believe you," Macellius said. "I can only hope that the Legate will believe *me.*"

"Vernemeton is hostage for my honesty," she gestured around her. "If I betray it, we are within easy grasp of his hand."

He said, "Lady, I would kiss yours; but your guard is eyeing me most suspiciously."

"You cannot do that," she said, "but I accept your good will, my lord."

"And I yours," Macellius said, and bowed once more.

When he had gone, Eilan sat for a time in silence, wondering if she had betrayed her people or saved them. Was it for this that the gods had worked to bring her here? Was it for this she had been born?

Caillean returned from the Summer Country late the next day, looking tired, but elated. When the older woman had bathed, Eilan sent Senara to ask if she would take her evening meal by Eilan's fire.

"How that child has grown!" Caillean commented as Senara went out to fetch the meal. "It seems just yesterday she came here, and now she is the same age as you were when I first met you, and almost as beautiful!"

With some surprise Eilan realized that Senara was indeed a young woman, old enough for vows; one day soon she should be pledged as a priestess. There had been no word from the girl's Roman relatives for years, and she had no reason to think there would be any objection. But for this at least there was no hurry.

"And what have you been doing this bright sunny day, my dear child?" Caillean asked as Senara set the food down.

A strange look passed over the girl's face. "I walked by that little house in the forest. Did you know, a hermit has come to live there?"

"Indeed, we gave our permission. He is a strange old man from somewhere in the South, Christian, is he not?"

"He is," Senara answered with that same strange look. "He has been kind to me."

Caillean frowned. Eilan knew that she would say it was not suitable for a priestess of the Forest House to be alone with a man, no matter how staid or elderly. But after all, the girl was not sworn to them; besides, she had heard somewhere that Christian priests swore themselves to chastity. In any case, Eilan thought wryly, she herself was no one to question a young girl's modesty.

"My mother was a Christian," Senara said. "May I have your permission to visit this priest and take him some food from our kitchen? I would like to learn more about what my mother believed."

"I do not see why not," Eilan answered. "That all the gods are one God is a part of our most ancient teachings. Go, and learn which face of Him the Christians see . . ."

They ate for a time in silence.

"Something has happened," said Eilan finally, watching Caillean's face as she stared into the flames.

"Perhaps –" Caillean answered her. "But I am not entirely sure what it means. The Tor is very powerful, and the lake . . ." she shook her head. "I promise that when I understand what I felt there, you will know. In the meantime –" her eyes lost their softness as she looked up at Eilan. "I am told that something has happened here as well. Dieda says you had a visitor."

"Visitors, rather; but I assume you were speaking of Cynric."

"I meant Macellius Severus," Caillean said. "What did you think of him?"

Eilan thought, *I could have wished for him as my father-in-law.* But she could not, after all, say that to Caillean. She compromised by saying, "He seems both kindly and fatherly."

"That is how the Romans take more and more of our world," said Caillean. "I would rather they were all evil without compromise. When even *you* can think well of Macellius, who will rebel?"

"Why should we rebel against them? You speak like Cynric."

"I could do worse," said Caillean.

"I do not see how," Eilan said resentfully. "Even if we must have a Roman peace, what is wrong with that? Peace is certainly better than war however it comes."

"Even a peace without honor? A peace in which everything that makes life worth living has been taken away?"

"The Romans can be honorable –" Eilan began, but Caillean interrupted.

"I would have thought you the last person to say so!" Her voice trailed off into an appalled silence, as if she had realized that whatever she said could only make it worse.

But I do say so, thought Eilan, feeling her flush of shame die away. *Gaius's mother married Macellius to bring peace, and I let Gaius marry a Roman girl for the same reason.* She wondered what sort of person his Roman wife was, and whether she had made him happy. Not all women sought peace, she knew, remembering Boudicca, who had started a rebellion, and Cartimandua, who betrayed Caractacus, and Brigitta, whose daughters she was sheltering, but she had made her decision, and she would stand by it.

"Cynric is wrong," she said finally. "What makes life worth living is not the glory that warriors sing of, but tended cattle and tilled fields and happy children around the fire. I know that the Goddess can be as terrible as a sow-bear when her cubs are threatened, but I think She would rather see us building and growing than killing each other. Isn't that why we have tried to recover the ancient ways of healing here?"

She looked up at last and met Caillean's dark eyes, and was startled to see that they held appeal.

"I have told you the reasons I have to hate men and fear what they can do," the older priestess said softly. "It is very hard sometimes for me to believe in life; it would be so much easier to go down fighting. There are times when you make me ashamed. But when I looked into the Sacred Well, it seemed to me that it overflowed in a hundred little rivulets that sank into the ground and carried its healing power throughout the land. And then, for a little while, I did believe."

"We must do something about that well," said Eilan softly, taking Caillean's hand and, like an echo, she seemed to hear the singing of the swans.

The next time Gaius was in Deva he called upon his father. Over a cup of wine, the talk came round to Brigitta of the Demetae. "Did you ever find her daughters?" asked Gaius.

"In a manner of speaking," his father replied. "I know where they are, and you will never guess where it is."

"I thought you were going to find them Roman foster parents."

"I will, when the time comes, but for now I think that the Priestess of the Oracles is the best guardian they could have." As Gaius gaped, his father went on. "She is a young woman, and I feared she would sympathize with young hot-heads like Cynric, whom, I tell you plainly, I would hang if we could lay hands on him, but she was surprisingly reasonable. As you might guess I have had an informant there for years, a servant of the priestesses, but this is the first time I have seen the Priestess myself."

"What did she look like?" Gaius's voice cracked, but Macellius did not appear to notice.

"She was veiled," he said. "But between us we worked it out that she'll keep the girls until tensions have eased, and then turn them over to us to be fostered in Roman homes, and contracted to Roman husbands; I think even Brigitta will be inclined to agree to this, if it is put to her. And I mean to put it to her. I feared that some of the agitators around her would make the girls the cause of another holy war, which, I need hardly tell you, would go hard with us, after Domitian's losses on the frontier."

He paused, and looked hard at his son. "I wonder sometimes if I made the right choices for you, lad. I thought Vespasian would live longer; he was a good Emperor, and would have seen to your career. After all our planning, you are living on your lands like a British chieftain after all. Even your marriage to Julia —" he broke off. "Can you forgive me?"

Gaius stared at him. "I did not know there was anything to forgive. I have made a life for myself here, and this is my home. Regarding my career, well, there is plenty of time."

No Emperor lives for ever, he thought, remembering what Malleus had said in his last letter, but even to his father he would not say that aloud. When he thought of Rome he remembered crowds and filth and the detested toga. He might have liked a little more sun here in Britain; but he felt little desire for southern climes.

And as for his lack of a male heir, he wondered if this was the time to tell Macellius about Eilan's son. Was it really she whom his father had seen? It was a great relief to know that she could be so moderate. Even if he could not see her; he knew that she was safe and well. It was not that he did not love his daughters, and Gaius knew that Licinius loved all the children. But Roman law counted only male children. It might not be fair, for in effect he would be disenfranchising little Cella, but the law was the law, like it or not.

In the end it seemed safer to say nothing. What remained unspoken – and he had found this out the hard way – he need never regret.

twenty-six

————〜〜〜————

aillean woke, shaking, to the gray light of early dawn. *It was only a dream.* But the images were still vivid, more real, even now, than the curtains of her bed and the breathing of the other women near by. She sat up and stuck her feet into slippers, and then, shivering, took her shawl down from its hook and wrapped it around her.

But the warm wool did not comfort her. When she closed her eyes she could still see the expanse of silver water where white mists wreathed and swirled. Eilan stood on the other side, but with each moment the waters grew wider, as if a strong current were carrying her away. It was the emotion that went with the images that terrified her, the overwhelming surge of anguish and loss.

It is only my own fears speaking, she told herself, *a dream that will disappear with the dawn*. Not all dreams were prescient. She got up and drank some water from the flask.

In the end, a grey veil of cloud had swirled between her and Eilan, cutting her off from the world. *Death is like that* ... The thought would not go away. The ordinary fantasies of sleep dissipated like the mist of morning when one awakened. A great dream – a dream of power – became ever more distinct as one puzzled over it. It could not be ignored.

As the other women began to stir, Caillean realized she could not stay here to face their curious eyes. Perhaps in the garden she could find the serenity she needed to deal with this. But one thing was clear, she must tell Eilan.

That year the Beltane celebrations had ushered in a bounteous summer, and the woods around the Forest House were vivid with flowers. Eilan had allowed herself to be persuaded to go out to gather herbs with Miellyn, and Lia and the children had come

344

along. Beneath the trees the creamy primroses and bluebells still flourished, but golden buttercups were already beginning to star the meadows, and white hawthorn hung heavy on the bough.

Gawen gleefully showed off his knowledge of the forest to Brigitta's two girls, who hung on every word, wide-eyed and admiring. Eilan smiled, remembering how she and Dieda had followed Cynric about when they were small. Listening to their laughter, she realized how much Gawen had missed having other children to play with, and knew that it was not only the girls who would soon be leaving her. Gawen would have to be fostered out soon.

It was noon before they returned, flushed and chattering and crowned with flowers. "Caillean is waiting for you in the garden," said Eilidh as Eilan came in. "She has been sitting there all morning. She would not even come in to eat breakfast, but she assures us that nothing is wrong."

Frowning, Eilan passed on into the garden without removing her wide-brimmed straw hat, for the day was warm. Caillean was sitting on a bench by the rosemary bed, motionless as if she were meditating, but at Eilan's step she opened her eyes.

"Caillean, what is it?"

The other woman looked up, and Eilan flinched at the utter calm in those dark eyes. "How many years now have we known one another?" Caillean asked.

Eilan tried to reckon it up in memory; they had met when Mairi's younger child was born. But in truth it seemed longer, and there were times when she remembered those odd glimpses of knowledge that had come to her and thought that they had been sisters in more lives than one.

"Sixteen years, I think," she said at last, doubtfully. It had been near to winter then; but no, it could not be, for the wild Hibernians were raiding, and it was certain they would not sail if they were afraid of being caught by winter storms. It had not been snow, but rain, she remembered. That had been a bad spring. And she had come to the Forest House as a novice priestess the summer that followed.

"Has it been so long? You are right. Mairi's child is nearly old enough to be wed, and Gawen is eleven winters old."

Eilan nodded, remembering with sudden vividness how Caillean had visited her in her exile in the hut in the forest, and how the older woman had held her hands and sponged her brow while the child was being born. She had thought those memories would never fade or dim; now they were like a dream long gone by. The work that she and Caillean were doing in the Forest House seemed far more vivid now.

"And now we have two of Brigitta's daughters within the House," Caillean said thoughtfully. "But within a year they will go to the Romans to be fostered."

Eilan said, sighing, "I hate to think Brigitta should lose her children."

"I would waste no sympathy on *her*," Caillean answered her. "I doubt she lost any sleep over what it would do to her children when she let Cynric persuade her into plotting rebellion."

Eilan knew this was most likely true; but as a mother she remembered her anguish when Ardanos had taken Gawen away. "Why do you speak of these things now?" she asked. "I cannot believe you have waited here all morning just to count over old memories as a Roman moneylender counts his gold!"

Caillean sighed. "There is something I must say to you, and I know not how to say it. So I speak of all manner of meaningless things. Eilan, I have had such warning as they say comes to each priestess before her death. No, I cannot explain —"

Eilan felt cold congealing around her heart, despite the warmth of the sun. "What do you mean, a warning? Are you in pain? Perhaps Miellyn knows some herbs —"

Caillean returned quietly. "I have had a dream, and I think it means that this life will soon end."

Caillean, dying? Stunned, all Eilan could find to say aloud was, "But how?"

Caillean replied quietly, "Truly, I know not how to tell you; perhaps it is something one can understand only when it comes."

Oh aye, Eilan thought. *It is true: I too am a priestess, even if not a very good one.* In Caillean's presence she remembered that, though she often doubted it at other times. Since her last meeting with Cynric she had been most aware of herself as a pawn in his combat with the Romans, as with Ardanos she was aware above all else of the way he wished to use her to keep the peace with Rome. For the past few seasons the tribes had been quiet, but she heard tales of troubles among the Romans. Cynric would be quick to take advantage of any weakness if the Romans should rebel against their Emperor. Would Gaius join such a rebellion? Had he ever cared for her for her own sake?

But with Caillean, from the first moment she had met her, Eilan was above all and only a priestess. When she was with her, Eilan felt that the Goddess might still have some use for her. As deeply as she had loved Gaius she could not help remembering that he had not stood by her. But Caillean had always been there.

She looked at her sister-priestess helplessly, and thought suddenly, *We have been through this before, and I watched her die in pain.*

Suddenly Eilan was angry. If she could do nothing about it, why did Caillean want to harrow her feelings by telling her? She looked at the other woman almost with hostility, and saw a flicker of emotion in Caillean's dark eyes, like a hidden current in a pool. Knowledge came to her suddenly. *She too is afraid.*

She took a deep breath, and the power of the Goddess that Caillean could awaken in her stirred suddenly.

"As High Priestess of Vernemeton, I command you – tell me your dream!"

Caillean's eyes widened, but in a few moments the tale was spilling out of her. Eilan listened with eyes closed, seeing the images as Caillean described them. And soon it seemed to her as if she could see them before the other woman spoke, as if it were her own dream that Caillean was telling, and when Caillean fell silent, she herself continued with the story of her own dream of the swans.

"We will be parted," she said finally, opening her eyes. "Whether by death or some other force I do not know, but it is like death to think of losing you, Caillean."

"But if not by death, what then?" the older woman asked.

Eilan frowned, remembering the gleam of silver waters beneath the clouds. "The Summer Country," she said suddenly. "Surely that is the place we both saw in our dreams. You must go there, Caillean, and take a dozen of the maidens with you. I do not know if this is to fulfill the purpose of the Goddess or to defy it, but surely it is better to do *something* than to sit here waiting for death to take you, even if what we do is wrong!"

Caillean still looked dubious, but the life had returned to her eyes. "Ardanos will never allow it. He is the Arch-Druid, and he wants all the priestesses here at Vernemeton, under his eye!"

Eilan looked at her and smiled. "But I am Priestess of the Oracle. Leave Ardanos to me!"

On Midsummer Morning, the maidens of the Forest House went at dawn to gather dew from the summer flowers. The dew had many powers, both in increasing beauty and bestowing magic. It was said that on that day any maiden who washed her face with the morning dew and then looked into a clear stream could see the face of him who loved her best.

Eilan found herself wondering why the priestesses, who after all were all under vows of chastity or intending to be so, should wish to know such things. Did most of them cherish memories of sweethearts in the lives they had left? She had done worse than dream about her lover. But she hoped that the others who served the Goddess could be more single-minded than she.

Eilan heard the girls laughing as they returned from the forest, but she did not go out to see them. As time went on, she was increasingly aware of the need for ritual seclusion before the great festivals. She had thought it would grow easier with time, but it seemed to her that keeping the balance between all the forces that sought the Power of the Goddess grew harder each year.

Each time Ardanos came to whisper his instructions into her ear, she remembered that by keeping the peace she, no less than the Arch-Druid, was serving the Romans; and she wondered if the fact that they both worked for what they considered to be the good of Britain could ever justify that alliance.

The door opened and Caillean came in. Even she had a wreath of red poppies to celebrate the day. Her cheeks were flushed from the sun and she looked healthier than she had for some time. "You are alone?"

"Who would be with me today? All of the girls in the house have gone out to pick the midsummer flowers and Lia has taken Gawen to visit Mairi." Eilan answered.

"That is well." Caillean sat down on a three-legged stool. "We must speak of tonight's Oracle."

"I have been thinking of little else since I awakened!" Eilan said bitterly. "I wish it was you who must sit here in the dark, preparing. You would have made so much better a High Priestess than I!"

"Gods forbid; I am not such a one as could obediently do Ardanos's will."

Suddenly furious, Eilan said wrathfully, "If I am no more than a creature of the priests, you know best who made me so."

Caillean sighed. "I thought not to criticize you, *mo chridhe*." The endearment defused Eilan's anger. Caillean went on, "We are all in Her hands and do Her will as best we can, I no less than you. You should not be angry with me."

348

"I am not angry," Eilan said, not altogether truthfully, but unwilling to quarrel with the woman to whom she owed so much. Sometimes she felt that the weight of her debt to Caillean should crush her. "I am afraid," she went on, "but I will tell you a thing that no one else knows. The sacred drink that is intended to drug me is not the same as it was in Lhiannon's day. I have altered it so that the trance is not total. I know what Ardanos is telling me to say —"

"But he always seems quite content with your words," Caillean said frowning. "Are you still so in love with your Gaius that you intentionally serve Rome?"

"I serve peace!" Eilan exclaimed. "It has never occurred to Ardanos that I would disobey him, and when my answers are somewhat different from the words I was given he thinks only that I am an imperfect vessel. But the words of peace are not my decision. When I offered myself to the Goddess I was not lying! Do you think the rites we do here at the Forest House are a lie?"

Caillean shook her head. "I have felt the Goddess too strongly — but —"

"Do you remember Midsummer seven years ago, when Cynric came?"

"How could I forget?" Caillean said ruefully. "I was terrified!" For a few moments she was silent. "That was not you, I know it, but a face of the Goddess I hope never to see again. Is it that way always?"

Eilan shrugged. "Sometimes She comes, sometimes not, and I must use my own judgment. But every time I sit in the high seat I make the offering, and each time I wait like this I wonder if this will be the time She will strike me down!"

"I see," said Caillean carefully. "Forgive me if I misunderstood you when you said you would compel Ardanos to send me south. But what will you do about me?"

"This is the testing —" Eilan leaned forward. "For both of us. If all we have built here is not to be a lie I must now risk both myself and you. Tonight I shall make up the potion according to the old recipe. When the Goddess takes me, you must ask about your dream. Everyone will hear the answer, and we all — you, Ardanos, and I — will be bound by it, whatever it may be."

The quality of the light had altered considerably towards sunset when the outer door opened and one of Ardanos's apprentices came in; he was so young that he had as yet only the thinnest straggle of beard.

The young Druid said deferentially, "We are ready for you, my lady." Eilan, who was already beginning to slip into the detached meditative state that preceded trance, rose from her chair. Eilidh and Senara lowered the heavy ritual cloak over her shoulders and fastened it at her throat with a massive gold chain.

The night was cool despite the season, and even in her thick cloak, Eilan shivered as she got into her litter. From out of the darkness came two white-robed priests, pale figures moving with measured step at her side. She knew that they were there to guard her against even accidental injury or pressure from the crowds, but somehow she had never been able to dismiss the thought that they were her guards.

The thought flashed across her mind like a rabbit scuttling into the bushes: *Every priestess is a prisoner of her gods . . .*

She was vaguely aware of passing through the long avenue of trees that led to the hill. Before the mound a great fire was burning, one of many fires on this night. Its red gleam played on the leaves of the ancient oak that grew next to the mound. A sound of anticipation went through the crowd like a soft sigh. She could not help remembering the first time she had heard it greet Lhiannon. Now she stood in Lhiannon's place, and the people who watched had as little understanding of what was really happening here as she had had then.

Two small boys about eight or nine years old, white-robed novices of the bards chosen for their innocence and beauty, brought forward the great golden bowl. They had golden torques about their throats, and belts embroidered with gold cinctured their white robes. As a ray of moonlight lanced through the leaves of the oak tree, a twiglet of mistletoe – cut by a priest hidden in the branches – fluttered downwards. Eilan caught it and dropped it into the bowl.

She murmured the words of blessing, and bracing herself against the bitterness, drank the liquid down. The voices of the Druids rose in invocation; the pressure of expectation from the people beat against her awareness. The liquid burned in her belly; she wondered if she had got the dosage wrong, then remembered that she had felt this way before. It came to her then that each time poisoned her a little, and that she would die as Lhiannon had died, though perhaps not as soon.

But the world was already dimming around her; she was scarcely aware of falling backward into the seeress's chair, or the jolting as they carried it to the top of the mound.

Caillean eyed the figure slumped in the high seat above her with more than usual concern. As always, the intensity of the chanting was pushing her towards trance as well. But there was a tension in the pulsing energies around her that she did not understand. She turned and saw Eilan's father among the white-robed Druids in the circle. Ardanos had said nothing. Had he even known that Bendeigid was going to be there?

Eilan twitched in the high seat and Caillean reached for the back to steady it. It was forbidden to touch the High Priestess when she was entranced, but they must be prepared to catch her if she fell.

"*Goddess!*" she prayed, "*take care of her – I do not care what happens to me!*" It seemed to her then that Eilan stilled; from the corner of her eye she could see one white hand dangling over the edge of the chair, slender as a child's. How could it wield such power?

"Lady of the Cauldron!" cried the people. "Silver Wheel! Great Queen! Come to us! Great Goddess, speak to us now!"

Caillean felt the wood of the chair quiver beneath her hand. Eilan's fingers were curling, and to Caillean's fascinated gaze the pale flesh seemed to glow. *It is true*, she thought then, *the Goddess is here*. Slowly, the figure in the high seat straightened, stretching as if to accommodate a mass greater than the slight figure of the woman sitting there. Caillean felt a little chill run down her spine.

"Behold, oh ye people, the Lady of Life has come. Let the Oracle speak! Let the Goddess declare forth the will of the Immortals!" Ardanos cried.

"Goddess! Deliver us from those who would enslave us!" came another voice. Bendeigid stepped forward. "Lead us to victory!"

They sounded like ravens, crying for blood and death. Eilan alone stood between the Forest House and a people shrieking for war. Did they even know what would happen to this country, between the Romans and their foreign auxiliaries, if it should come to open fighting? Despite her hatred for the Romans, Caillean wondered how any sane man or woman – or even a Goddess – could loose war on this countryside. Had Bendeigid so soon forgotten their home in flames, forgotten the deaths of his wife and little daughter?

Goddess, she thought, *You have given the peace of this*

countryside into Eilan's hands; let her do Your will even if it may
seem it is the will of the Romans as well . . .

The figure in the chair quivered, and thrust the veil back suddenly, surveying the throng with a face as cold and dispassionate as one of the statues the Romans made.

"This is the shortest night," she said softly, and the murmuring people stilled to hear. "But from this moment onward, the forces of light will be declining. Oh ye whose pride it is to learn all secrets of earth and heaven" – she indicated the circle of Druids with a disdainful hand – "can you not read the signs in the world around you? The tribes have seen their day and now grow ever weaker; thus it will be one day with the Empire of the Romans as well. All things reach their peak and thereafter must decline."

"But is there no hope then?" asked Bendeigid. "In time, even the sun is reborn!"

"That is true," said the still, calm voice from above him. "But not until the darkest day has passed. Put away your swords and hang up your shields, children of Don. Let the Roman eagles tear at each other while you till your fields, and be patient, for Time will surely avenge your wrongs! I have read in the mystic scrolls of the Heavens; and I tell you, the name of Rome is not written there."

A sigh of mingled relief and disappointment swept through the crowd.

Ardanos and one of the other priests were whispering. Caillean realized this was the only chance she might have to do what Eilan had asked.

"What then of the old wisdom? How shall Your worship be preserved in a changing world?"

Ardanos and Bendeigid both glared at her, but the question had been asked, and already the Goddess was turning, and Caillean trembled, utterly certain at that moment that what looked down at her was not Eilan at all.

"Is it you, daughter of the elder race, who would truly question Me?" came the soft answer. There was a pause, as the attention of the Goddess appeared to go inward; then She laughed. "Ah, it is this one also who asks. She could ask more than that of Me, but she is afraid. Such a silly child not to understand that My will is for you all to be free." She shrugged Her shoulders gently. "But you are children, all of you." Her gaze lifted to fix Ardanos, who flushed and looked away, "and I will not destroy your illusions now. You are not strong enough to bear too much reality . . ."

She extended one arm, turning the hand and flexing its fingers as if to enjoy the movement. "The flesh is sweet." She laughed softly. "I do not wonder that you cling to it. But as for Me, what do you suppose your puny efforts can do to help or harm? I have been here from the beginning and so long as the sun shines or the waters flow, I will remain. I *am* . . ." There was a terrible truth in that simple statement of being, and Caillean trembled.

"But our lives flow away like the waters and are gone –" Caillean said then. "How shall we pass what You have taught us to those who come after?"

The Goddess looked from her to Ardanos and back again.

"You already know the answer. In ages past your soul has sworn the oath, and so has hers. Let one of you go forth," She cried. "Let one go forth to the Summer Country, there on the shores of the lake to establish a House of Maidens. There shall I be served, side by side with the priests of the Nazarene. So shall My wisdom survive the days that are coming!"

Almost at once the body of the priestess, which had been tight as a strung bow, was released; the arrow had flown, the message had been given. Eilan slumped back in the chair, and Caillean and Miellyn moved quickly to steady her. She was twitching and muttering, coming out of the trance.

Ardanos stood with head bowed, pondering the meaning of this Oracle and how he could use it. Countermand it he could not – nor would he, a pious man, wish to gainsay the direct word of the Goddess – but it was his privilege to interpret it. After a moment his head came up. He looked directly at Caillean, and it seemed to her that he smiled.

"The Goddess has spoken. Now let it be so. And this house shall be founded by the servant of the Goddess; it is you, Caillean, who will go forth to found the House of Maidens on the Tor."

Caillean stared back at him. There was triumph in his pale eyes. To Ardanos, this decision of the Goddess was a fortuitous opportunity to achieve something he had long desired, to part her from Eilan.

He picked up the sprig of mistletoe and shook water over the limp body of the priestess, and all other sound was lost in a mocking jangle of silver bells.

"For someone who has been out of harness for a few years, you seem to be keeping busy!" Gaius grinned at his father across the rolled parchments and stacked wax tablets that littered the table. Outside, a cold, February wind was rattling branches that were just beginning to swell with sap. Indoors, the hypocaust warmed the tiled floors and charcoal burning in iron braziers fought the drafts. "I hope young Brutus appreciates all you are doing for him."

"He appreciates my experience," said Macellius, "and I appreciate his news. He's very well connected, you know, related to half the ancient families of Rome. His father is an old friend of your patron Malleus, by the way."

"Ah." Gaius took another drink of hot spiced wine, beginning to understand. "And what does our Legate think of the Emperor's current policies?"

"Frankly, his letters from Rome have him terrified. His term as Commander finishes at the end of this year, and he's wondering how to get out of going home again! As members of the equestrian order, you and I have one advantage: we're not required by law to reside in Rome. The Eternal City has been extremely unhealthy for senators this year, I am told."

"Like Flavius Clemens?" Gaius asked grimly. No wonder the senators were uneasy. If Domitian's own cousin had been executed, what were the rest of them going to do? "Did you ever hear anything more about what he was charged with?"

"The official accusation was atheism. But according to the rumors, the man was a Christian who refused to burn incense to the Emperor."

"I'm sure our *Dominus et Deus* was highly insulted!"

Macellius smiled sourly. "The gods know those Christians are an exasperating lot, and when the Government isn't persecuting them they persecute each other. If Nero had only tried setting their different factions against each other in the arena he could have saved a fortune in lions – but the kind of adoration Domitian is demanding goes beyond all propriety!"

Gaius nodded. He had heard enough about Father Petros's preaching from Julia to be aware of the Christian fascination with martyrdom, and of their sectarian strife, though Julia referred to it as purging the Church of the ungodly. But in the larger scheme of things the Christians were a minor problem. Far more serious was the megalomania of the Emperor.

"Is he going the way of Nero, or Caligula?" he asked.

"He hasn't tried to deify his horse yet, if that's what you mean," his father replied. "In many ways he has been a very effective

Emperor; that's why he's so dangerous. What will Rome have to fall back on when the next crazy Emperor comes along if Domitian is allowed to destroy what remains of the senatorial class?"

Gaius looked at his father carefully. "You're really worried about this, aren't you?"

"It doesn't matter so much about me," said Macellius, turning his equestrian ring back and forth on his hand. "But most of your career is still ahead of you. With this Emperor, what chance is there for you?"

"Father . . . something's going on, isn't it? What have they asked you to do?"

Macellius sighed and looked around the room with its painted walls and racks of scrolls as if he were afraid it might be about to vanish. "There is a . . . plan . . ." he said carefully, "to end the Flavian dynasty. When Domitian has been dealt with, the senators will elect a new Emperor. For the plan to work, the Provinces must support it. The new Governor is Domitian's man, but most of the legionary legates are from the same kinds of families as Brutus –"

"And so they want us to support them," Gaius said baldly. "What do they imagine the tribes will be doing while we are engaged in this Imperial housecleaning?"

"If we promise them some concessions, they will support us . . . Queen Brigitta's daughters will be coming to us soon, and Valerius is helping me to find appropriate foster parents to raise them. Romans and Britons are bound to become allies in the end. This way it may come a little sooner, that is all."

Gaius whistled soundlessly. This was sedition on a grand scale! He gulped down the last of his wine. When he looked up again, his father was watching him.

"Stranger things have happened," Macellius said quietly. "Depending on how things go, there might be quite an interesting future for a Roman of the Silure royal line!"

Gaius rode home with his head reeling from more than the mulled wine. He had humored Julia long enough. It was now perfectly clear to him that he must adopt his son by Eilan formally. But when he arrived home, he found Julia could speak of nothing but her latest visit to the hermit, Father Petros.

"And he says that it is certain from Holy Writ – and from all the other prophecies – that the world will end with the passing away of this generation," she told him, her eyes glowing. "With the coming of every dawn we should think that it may not be the sun, but the world beginning to burn. And then we shall be reunited with our loved ones. Did you know that?"

He shook his head, amazed that she, who had received a good Roman education, could believe such stuff. But then, women were credulous, which was probably why they could not serve in public office. He wondered if the Christians were trading on the current anxieties about the Emperor.

"Are you going to become a follower of the Nazarene – that prophet of slaves and renegade Jews?" he asked sharply.

"I do not see how any thinking person can possibly do anything else," Julia replied coolly.

Well, Gaius thought, *I am obviously not a thinking person – at least not of her kind.* He only said, "And what will Licinius say?"

"He will not like it," Julia said sadly. "But this is the only thing I have been sure of since . . . since the children died." Her eyes filled with tears.

That makes no sense, he thought, but did not say it aloud; making sense did not seem to have comforted her very much. And indeed she looked happier than he had seen her since Secunda's death. The image of his daughter drowned was still behind his eyes night and day. Logical or not, he almost envied her.

"Well, do as you will," he said resignedly. "I will not try to stop you."

She looked at him with something almost like disappointment, then brightened. "If you had any sense of what was right, you would become a Nazarene as well."

"My dear Julia, you have told me many times I have no sense of what is right," he said sharply. She stared at the floor and he knew there was something else. "What is it?"

"I do not want to say this before the children," she stammered. Gaius laughed, took her arm and led her into another room.

"Well, what is it that you cannot say before our children, Julia?"

Again she cast her eyes on the ground. "Father Petros says that . . . as the end of the world is so near . . ." she stammered, "it is better if all married women – and men – take an oath of chastity."

At this, Gaius threw back his head and did laugh. "You do realize that, as the law now stands, refusing to sleep with your husband is grounds for divorce?"

Julia, although obviously troubled, was ready for the question.

"*In the Kingdom of Heaven*," she quoted, "*there is neither marriage nor giving in marriage.*"

"That settles it," said Gaius, laughing again, "I do not care for your Heaven, at least not that portion of it over which Father Petros rules."

He added, knowing it would hurt her, "Take all the oaths you like, my dear. Considering that for the past year or so you have been about as much use in bed as a stick of wood, I can't imagine how you think it would make any difference to me."

Her eyes were wide with surprise. "Then you will make no difficulty?"

"None, Julia; but it is only fair to tell you that if you are no longer bound by our wedding vows, I will not hold myself bound by them either."

He realized that he was spoiling the scene she had resolved to play; he should, he supposed, have raged or pleaded.

"I would never consider asking you to take such a vow," she said, and then, spitefully, added, "I doubt if you would be able to keep it if you did. Do you think I do not know why you bought that pretty slave girl last year? God knows she is little enough use in the kitchen! With so many sins already upon your soul –"

But Gaius had had enough. He would not discuss the state of his soul – whatever she might mean by that – with her.

"For my own soul I will be myself responsible," he told her and went into his office where he found a bed already made up for him. So she had counted on his willingness to sleep alone, whatever else he might say.

Gaius thought briefly of celebrating his freedom by summoning the slave girl, but he discovered he had no wish to do so. He wanted something more than the compliance of a woman who had no choice in the matter. His mind went to Eilan. Now at least Julia could make no objection if he wished to adopt Gawen. How would he break the news to her?

Finally he was free to seek Eilan out once more. But the face of the Fury he had seen at the Midsummer festival came between him and his memories, and it was the face of the girl he had met at the hermit's the year before that went with him into sleep at last.

twenty-seven

———~~~———

I n the middle of February the storms gave way to a period of
fair, clear weather, brisk but sunny. In sheltered spots early fruit
trees began to put forth buds and the branches grew red with
returning sap. The hills were melodious with the bleating of new
lambs, and the marshes resounded with the calls of returning
swans.

Eilan looked at the blue sky and realized that the time had come
to keep her word to Macellius. She was waiting in the garden when
Senara answered her summons.

"It is a fair day," Senara said, clearly wondering why Eilan had
called her away from her duties.

"It is that," Eilan agreed, "a fair bright day for performing an
unwelcome duty. But you are the only one I can ask."

"And what is that?"

"Brigitta's daughters have been here for a year now, and it is
time to send them to the Romans as I promised. They have kept
their word regarding Brigitta, and I trust them to deal kindly with
the children. But it must be done quietly, lest all the old enmity be
awakened again. You are old enough to take them to Deva, and
you know the Latin tongue enough to ask your way to the house of
Macellius Severus. Will you take them there?"

"Severus?" Senara frowned. "I think I remember that name. My
mother told me once that her brother served him, and that he was a
hard man, but fair."

"That is my understanding." Eilan nodded. "The sooner the
girls are in his care, the sooner he can settle them in their new
home."

"But they will grow up Romans," Senara protested then.

"Would that be so bad a thing?" Eilan smiled at her. "Your own
mother was a Roman, after all."

"That is true . . ." the girl said thoughtfully. "Sometimes I wonder about her family, and what it was like growing up in that world. Very well," she said at last. "I will go."

It took some time to make the children ready, for Eilan wished to make sure that no one in the Roman town should have cause to say that the girls had been neglected while they were among the Druids; but at last even Eilan was satisfied, and Senara, holding a little girl by either hand, was ready to set out for Deva.

The day was crisp but clear, and even with one child in her arms and the other trotting at her side, Senara made good time. The children babbled merrily, excited by the outing. When they grew tired, she tied the younger girl in her shawl, where she soon fell asleep, and picked up the older one in her arms. By this time she could see the straggle of houses at the edge of the city and the stout log walls of the fortress beyond. When she reached the central Forum, she sat down on a bench beside a fountain to rearrange her burdens before asking her way to the house of Macellius.

Suddenly the sunlight was blotted out. Senara looked up to behold the Roman she had met at the house of the hermit the year before. Later it seemed altogether symbolic to her that he should stand between her and the sun; but she did not think of that then.

"I have seen you before, haven't I?" he asked.

"At Father Petros's hut," she said, blushing. One of the children awakened and stared at him with owlish eyes. She had not seen him at any gathering of the small group of local Nazarenes; but then, living as she did actually within the Forest House, she was not able to go there very often. She had gone the first time from curiosity, and later because the Roman tongue seemed somehow a link with her dead mother, and finally, because she found comfort there.

The handsome Roman was still regarding her. He was younger than she had thought at first, and she liked his smile. "Where are you bound, maiden?"

"To the house of Macellius Severus, sir; these girls are to be given into his care —"

"Ah, so these are the children." For a moment he frowned, then the quick smile once more lit his eyes. "We are well met, then. I am myself bound there; may I be your guide?"

He reached out one hand, and the older girl placed her small one within it, smiling up at him.

She looked at him a little dubiously, but he swung the child up to his shoulder, and hearing the little girl's laughter, Senara decided that he must be of a kindly nature after all.

"You hold her as one well used to children, sir," she said, and though she asked no further, he replied, "I have three daughters of my own; I am well accustomed to little ones."

So, she thought, *he is married. Is he one of us?* After a moment she said, "Tell me, sir, are you then a member of Father Petros's flock?"

"I am not," he replied, "but my wife is."

"Then, sir, your wife is my sister in Jesus, and thus kin to me."

His lips twisted rather sardonically at this, and she thought, *He is too young to smile so bitterly. Who has hurt him so?*

"You are very kind to escort me," she said aloud.

"It is no trouble. Macellius is my father, you see —"

They were approaching a fine-looking house near the walls of the fortress, white-washed and tiled in the Roman style. The Roman knocked on the gate, and after a moment a slave pulled it open and they passed through a long hallway into an enclosed garden.

The Roman asked, "Is my father within?"

"He is with the Legate," the man replied. "Go in and wait for him, if you will; he should be getting back just about now."

It was in actual fact only four or five minutes till Macellius arrived. Senara was not sorry to see him, for the younger of the children had wakened and begun to fret. Macellius turned them both over to a buxom and kindly slave woman who would look after them until the foster parents he had chosen for them came. He thanked Senara, and asked her politely if she needed an escort to return.

Senara shook her head quickly. At the Forest House they thought she had taken the girls to relatives of their mother in the town. Returning with an escort of Roman soldiers would have put the fat in the fire for certain. It would have been nice, though, if the younger Severus could have escorted her home — she thrust the thought away.

"Will I see you again?" he asked, and a little tremor of excitement ran through her.

"Perhaps at one of the services." Then, before she could make a fool of herself entirely, she slipped away through the door.

*

Julia Licinia never did anything by halves. One night in April she asked Gaius to accompany her to an evening service in the Nazarene temple in Deva. Though their marriage had become a polite fiction, she was still the mistress of his household, and Gaius felt bound to support her. He had considered divorce, but could see no point in hurting Licinius and his children in order to marry some other Roman girl.

He was not in sufficient favor with the Emperor to make an alliance with a family of his party, and to ally himself with the opposition could have been dangerous. Though the elder Macellius said little, Gaius knew that the conspiracy was growing. If the Emperor fell, all would be changed. It seemed to Gaius better to put off worrying about his personal future until he knew whether he had one.

Since the Nazarene temple had been, in part, purchased with the proceeds of the jewels Julia no longer seemed to wear, Gaius was curious to see what sort of value she had got for her money. By the time they set out they were quite a large party; not only Gaius and Julia, but the little girls and their nurses, and what seemed like half the household. "Why do we have to have all these people with us?" Gaius demanded, not altogether good-naturedly. He and his family would sleep that night at the house of Macellius, but his father did not have room for their whole staff.

"Because they are all members of the congregation," Julia said more pleasantly. Gaius blinked. It would never have occurred to him to question how she managed her household, but he had not realized that her zeal had led her quite so far. She added, "They will return to the villa when this is over. I cannot deny them the chance to worship."

Gaius thought it was, rather, that she would not, but he thought it wiser to say no more. The new Christian church was a largish old building near the river that had belonged originally to an importer of wine. The reek of old wine was overlaid by the fragrance of wax candles and early flowers were heaped on the altar. Rather crudely painted pictures – a shepherd carrying a lamb, a fish, some men in a boat, adorned the white-washed walls.

As they entered Julia made a cryptic sign; he was displeased to see that Cella, Tertia and Quartilla all tried to imitate her. Had Julia converted not only her servants but her daughters as well? He wondered if these Christians were in the business of undermining the authority of the home.

Julia found a seat on a hard bench not too far from the door, and sat down, surrounded by her waiting-women and her daughters. Gaius, standing behind her, looked round to see if anyone else in the congregation was known to him. Most of the assembled worshippers seemed to be working people of the poorer kind, and he wondered how the snobbish Julia liked finding herself among such folk. Then he recognized a face: the girl who had brought Brigitta's daughters to the town. She had told him she came to the meetings when she could get away, and he realized now that one reason he had given in to Julia's request that he accompany her was a faint hope of seeing her.

A priest, closely shaven and wearing a long dalmatica, entered with two boys, one of whom carried a large wooden cross and the other a candle, and a couple of older men whom Julia had told him were deacons, one of whom carried a heavy leather-bound book in his hand. This one was a rather sober-looking man of middle years. As he laid the book on the immense lectern, he stumbled over a four-year-old child in the aisle; but rather than fleeing in terror, the child laughed up at him, and the deacon bent down and hugged the toddler with a smile that transformed his face, then handed it back to its father, a rough-handed grimy man with a blacksmith's brawny arms.

There were prayers and invocations; the congregation was purified with incense and water, all of it similar enough to a Roman ceremony that Gaius did not feel too uncomfortable, though the Latin was rather less pure. Then the priests and deacons were seated and there was a little stir of excitement as another man came forward.

Gaius was not surprised to recognize Father Petros, looking frowsy and bearded next to the others. He gazed at the collected worshippers with such intensity that Gaius wondered uncharitably if the hermit suffered from poor eyesight.

"Our Master once said, *"Suffer the little children to come to me and forbid them not; for of such is the Kingdom of Heaven."* Many of you here tonight have lost a child and you grieve; but your children, I tell you, are safe with Jesus in Heaven, and you parents who grieve are happier than those parents who have given their children over, living, to the service of idols. I tell you that it would be better for these children to be safely dead, having sinned not, than living to serve false gods!" He paused for breath and the people sighed.

They have come here to be frightened! thought Gaius cynically. *They are enjoying the thought of their own virtuous superiority!*

"For the first of the great commandments is this: thou shalt love the Lord thy God with all thy heart and all thy soul; and the second of the great commandments is this: that thou shalt honor thy father and thy mother," Father Petros boomed. "The question arises, then: how far can a young person be held responsible if his guardians place him in the service of a heathen idol? There are Fathers in our Church who have said that all, even infants in arms, are guilty if they are present during the worship of an idol; but there others who hold that if a child's guardians commit him to serve an idol before he shall have arrived at an age of reason, then he should be held guiltless. My own feeling is –"

But Gaius did not really care what the Father's own feeling was. By this time his gaze had fixed on the far more pleasing spectacle of the girl, Senara, who was leaning forward, absorbed in the hermit's words. He had hopelessly lost the thread of the Father's discourse, but he had already decided that these Christian ceremonies were too dull for his taste; no sacrifices, no roaring exhortations, not even the drama the rites of Isis or Mithras could sometimes provide. In fact these Christian ceremonies, all told, were duller than anything he had ever heard except some of the Druidic philosophies.

Even with the girl's bright face to look at it seemed a long time before Father Petros's discourse finally rambled to its end. Gaius was looking forward to leaving, and it was with consternation that he heard that he and the other unbaptized members of the congregation were now expected to wait outside while the initiates participated in some kind of love-feast. His complaints were so loud that Julia finally agreed to leave, although she promised the nurses and serving women they might remain.

He picked up the sleeping Quartilla, and they set out for Macellius's home. But they had hardly started when Tertia began to complain that she wanted to be carried too. Gaius told her brusquely to behave like a big girl and walk; her mother's health had improved but she was not yet strong enough to carry the child, and Cella was still too small. As Tertia began to whimper, someone moved behind them and he heard a sweet voice saying, "I will carry your little girl."

Gaius would have refused, but the British girl had already picked up the drowsy child, who almost instantly fell asleep in her arms.

"Indeed, she is no weight at all," said the girl, "and I am used to harder work than this!"

"You are a true sister in Christ," exclaimed Julia. Gaius could find nothing to add to this, and so they walked along. The women exchanged a few low-voiced commonplaces, and Gaius found himself obscurely relieved that they clearly did not really know each other that well. The moon, just a few nights after full, gave them just enough light to illuminate their path. They could see the street underfoot clearly, and many of the trees were bright with clouds of misty white blossom.

As they pushed open the gate Macellius's steward came out to meet them with a lamp. When Tertia began to stir, the British girl set her down and they stood staring at one another in the sudden brilliance.

"You must stay and join us for something to eat, since you too missed the agape," Julia declared.

"Oh, no, I cannot," the girl said shyly. "It is most kind of you, lady, but I had not leave to come; I must get home at once, or I will be missed, and then, even if I am not punished, I might not be able to come again."

"I will not keep you, then; that would be a poor return for your kindness," Julia said quickly. "Gaius will go with you. This part of the city is quiet, but before you get out of the gates, there might be some people it would not be safe for an honest and proper young girl to meet."

"That will not be necessary, Domina —" she began but Gaius interrupted, "I'll go gladly; I wanted to walk a while before I go to bed, and I can return you safely to your home."

At least he could ask her what a girl from the Forest House was doing among Christians. The answer, he decided, might be revealing. When she pulled her cloak – a dark plain one such as a servant girl in a respectable home would wear – about her closely he wondered if it was because under it she wore the dress of a priestess. Gaius took a torch; even with a moon, he knew better than to brave the streets without one, and he felt that a good light might reassure the girl. She kissed all of the little girls, including the drowsy toddler in Julia's arms, and went down the steps at his side. They passed through the silent streets without attracting any notice, but even when the last houses were behind them his companion made no attempt to put back her hood, even though the night was warm.

The silence seemed oppressive. "How long have you been coming to services at the new temple?" Gaius asked finally.

"Since it was built."

"And before that?"

"When I was a little girl, my mother used to take me to meetings in the servants' quarters in the house of one of the city fathers whose steward was a Christian."

"But you dwell in the Forest House," he said, frowning.

"It is true," she replied quietly. "Their Priestess has given me shelter there – I am an orphan. But no oaths bind me. My father is British, exiled now, but my mother was a Roman. She had me baptized, and when I found that Father Petros was living near I wanted to learn more of her faith."

Gaius smiled. "And your name is Valeria!"

She blinked. It had been a long time since she had heard that name.

"That is the name my mother called me, but I have been Senara so long I had almost forgotten it. Father Petros says it is my duty to obey my guardians, even if they are pagans. At least in the Forest House no harm will come to me. He says that the Druids are among the good pagans who will some day be offered salvation; but I must not take oath to them. And the Apostle Paul commanded slaves to obey their masters. Freedom is of the soul, but the legal status of the body cannot be set aside, and neither can lawful oaths."

"At least they have that much sense," he muttered. "A pity they cannot extend that reasoning to cover their duty to the Emperor!"

Senara chattered on as if she had not heard, and he wondered if her babbling covered fear, but he was too charmed by the music of her voice to care much about the words. She had such innocence, like Eilan's when she was young.

"Of course they do not ask me to sin in the Forest House, and they are good people there, but I want to be a real believer and go to Heaven. I would be afraid to be a martyr though, and I used to be afraid they would think it was my duty to die for my faith like one of the saints Mother told me about; I was only a baby but I can remember – just.

"But the Government is not persecuting Christians now . . ." She hesitated. As Gaius was searching for something to say, she went on. "Of course, tonight, the Father was really talking about me. A few of the people in the congregation know that I am in one of the pagan temples and they despise me because I remain there – but Father Petros says I do not need to leave them until I am of age."

"And then what?" he asked. "Will Valerius arrange a suitable marriage for you?"

"Oh no. It is most likely I will enter a holy sisterhood. In Heaven, the priests say, there is neither marrying nor giving in marriage."

"What a waste," Gaius declared. He had heard that one before. "I truly think the priests must be mistaken."

"Oh no; for when the world ends you do not wish to be found with any sin upon your soul."

Gaius said with absolute truthfulness, "It never occurred to me to be concerned about my soul, nor even to ask myself whether or not I had one."

She stopped short and turned to him in the dark. "But how terrible," she said very earnestly. "You do not want to be cast into the pit of hell, do you?"

"I find it a strange religion that would condemn folk for breeding children, or for the act that begets them! And as for your pit of hell, surely it is as much as a fable as Tartarus or Hades. Nothing to frighten a rational man. Do you mean to tell me that you truly believe that is where those who offend against Father Petros's rules will go?"

She stopped again and raised her face to him, white as a lily in the moonlight. "But of course I do," she said. "You must think about your soul now, before it is too late."

If anyone except a girl as pretty as this one had brought up such a subject to Gaius, he probably would have laughed in her face. Julia's talk of such things bored him almost to tears. Instead he answered more gently, "If you have a care for my soul you will simply have to help me save it."

She said doubtfully, "I think Father Petros could help you a good deal better than I can." They had reached the entrance to the avenue of oaks that led to the Forest House, and she stopped, frowning. "I can find my way from here; and you should certainly not come any closer. You might be seen, and then I too would be caught and punished."

He seized her shoulders and said, half jocularly, half pleading, "Will you let me go with my soul unsaved, then? We must meet again."

She looked troubled. "I should not say this," she said abruptly.

"But I take food to Father Petros's hermitage at noon of every day. If you happened to be there ... I suppose ... we could talk then."

"Then you shall certainly save my soul, if it can be saved," Gaius replied. He did not care a pin about his suppositious soul; but he knew he wanted to see Senara again.

"I will never see you again –" Eilan turned abruptly away from Caillean and stared into the garden.

"That is foolish!" exclaimed Caillean, the stab of fear those words gave her turning to anger. "Now it is you who are having the foolish premonitions. It was you yourself who wanted me to go!"

Eilan's thin shoulders quivered. "Not I, not I. It was the Goddess speaking through me, and I know we must do Her will. But oh, Caillean, now that the time comes, it is hard!"

"Hard indeed!" Caillean spat back at her. "But it is I who must leave you and everything that I have loved. Are you sure it was the Goddess speaking and not Ardanos whispering in your ear? He has wanted to separate us ever since I made him let you keep your son!"

"I suppose this does please him," whispered Eilan, "but do you truly believe it was his doing? Is everything I have tried to do here a lie?"

Caillean heard her pain and could maintain her own anger no longer. "My dear one – my little one." She laid a hand on Eilan's shoulder and the other woman turned into her arms. She made no sound, but her cheeks were streaked with tears. "We must not fight like children when there is so little time! There are moments when the power of the gods burns like the sun, and then it grows dark and the light seems only a dream. It has always been so. But I believe in you, my love."

"Your belief has sustained me," Eilan murmured.

"Listen," said Caillean. "This is not for ever. One day, when we are old women together, we will laugh at our fears."

"I know that we will be together," said Eilan slowly, "but whether it is in this life or another, that I cannot see."

"My Lady," Huw spoke from the gate, "the bearers are waiting."

"Now you must go." Eilan straightened, becoming the High Priestess again. "We must both serve the Lady in the places where She has called us, no matter what we feel."

"It is all right. I will return, you'll see," Caillean said gruffly, giving her a last, swift hug and releasing her.

She went away then, knowing that if she looked back at Eilan she would weep herself, and she must not, not before the young priestesses and the men. It was not until the curtains of the litter closed around her that she gave way to her tears.

She spent most of the rainy, dismal journey to the Summer Country brooding. Her mood was not improved by the fact that they had to travel by litter, a form of transportation that she detested.

She was accompanied by the priestesses chosen for the new establishment. They were mostly young, and all virtual newcomers to the Forest House who were too awed even to address her in anything but the barest commonplaces. Caillean had little to do except to nurse her rage.

It was nearing dusk when the little procession wound through the gap in the hills and transferred to barges to cross the shallow marshes that surrounded the Tor. It stood stark against the fading sky, crowned with a circle of stones, and even from here she could feel its power. The roundhouses of the Druids clustered on its lower slopes. In the hollow beyond, she could just make out a scattering of smaller, beehive huts that must belong to the Christians Ardanos had allowed to settle here. A fragrance of some scented wood, perhaps apple, hung in the air.

They were met at the foot of the hill by the young priests set to watch there, who greeted her with many expressions of deference and good will, although they appeared somewhat uncertain about why she had come. Despite her anger she found herself amused by their confusion, and began reluctantly to come to terms with the inevitable. For better or worse, the Druid priesthood had sent her here, and even they were only instruments of the Goddess, who had commanded her presence here in no uncertain terms.

When they reached the shrine itself, it was full dark. The priests greeted them politely, if not cordially – but then, Caillean had hardly expected to be welcomed. If this was exile, at least it was an honorable exile, and since she could not alter it, she might as well make the best of it.

After the ceremonial greetings, she found her women huddled in wide-eyed confusion by the bonfire. One of the young priests conducted them to a low, thatched-roof dwelling that, as they said apologetically, was not in any way suitable for the housing of a priestess, let alone one of her status. Still, where to put women was not a problem they had had to deal with until now. Since the Arch-Druid had commanded it, however, they were swift to assure her that a suitable house would be built for their use as soon as she made their requirements known, and such attendance as she and her women desired should be secured for them.

By the time Caillean had made sure that all the young women were safely bestowed in the hastily vacated dormitory which had housed the youngest novices, and was able to seek her own bed at last, she was ready to drop from fatigue. Though the bed and the place were strange to her, to her surprise she slept through the night peacefully and woke while dawn was still reddening the sky. She dressed herself without waking her women, and went out alone into the early morning. Streaks of rosy light were just beginning to flush the sky. The path before her led up the hill.

As the light grew, Caillean studied her surroundings carefully. To what, in this remote country, had her destiny led her?

As the sun rose, she could see that the Tor looked out over a vast expanse of wild country entirely surrounded by heavy mists that drifted from the great sheet of water; they had arrived so late the night before, that she hardly noticed, in her fatigue and exhaustion, that the final stage of the journey had been made by barge. The wooded slopes of other islands poked their blackish-green and forested summits through the mist. It was very silent, but as the sun rose and Caillean studied this strange country, she heard the faint murmur of chanting, from somewhere not very far away.

She turned; the sound came from a small structure at the very top of the hill. She moved higher to hear it more clearly. The music was soft and slow, the deep resonance of men's voices strange to her ears after so many years among women. After a time she made out words in the flow of sound; it seemed to her that they were singing in Greek.

Kyrie eleison, Criste eleison. She had heard that this was how the Christians addressed their lord; this must be the community of refugees the Arch-Druid had given leave to settle here. These days all sorts of strange religions were breaking out all over the Empire.

Presently the sound faded, and she saw a little old man, stooped as if with great old age, regarding her. She blinked, for she had not seen him approach, and that was unusual for a priestess of her training. As she looked at him, he dropped his eyes. He must be one of the Christian priests indeed; she had heard that many of their priests would not look upon a strange woman.

But apparently he was allowed to talk to her. He said, in the market-Latin that served as a dialect all over the Empire, "A good day to you, my sister. May I ask your name? I know that you surely are not one of our catechumens, for we have not for many years had any women among us except the venerable ladies who came with us long ago, and you are young."

Caillean smiled a little at the thought that anyone could consider her young, but the priest was white-haired and frail as a fallen leaf. At least in years, he might have been her grandsire.

"I am not," she said. "I am one of those who worship the forest god. I am called Caillean."

"Is it so?" he asked her politely. "I know something of the brothers among the Druids, and I knew not they had women among them."

"Those who dwell here have not," she replied, "or at least not until now. I was sent here from the Forest House in the North, to establish a House of Maidens. I came up the hill to see to what place the gods had led me."

"You speak as one who holds some acquaintance with the truth, my sister. Surely then you know that all the gods are one God . . ." He paused, and Caillean completed, ". . . and all the goddesses one Goddess."

His ancient face was altogether kindly. "It is so. Those to whom our Lord came as God's Divine Son would not see the Godhead in anything female, so to them we speak not of the Goddess, but of Sophia, the Holy Wisdom. But we understand that the Truth is One. So, my sister, to me it seems very fitting that you should establish here, a shrine to the Holy Wisdom after the manner of your people."

Caillean bowed. His face was very deeply wrinkled, but it no longer seemed ugly, for it positively glowed with benevolence.

"What a splendid work to which to devote the remainder of this incarnation, my sister." He smiled, then his gaze went inward. "It feels right for you to be here, for it seems to me that we have served at the same altars before . . ."

Not for the first time in this strange encounter, Caillean was amazed. "I had heard that the brothers of your faith denied the truth of incarnations," she volunteered. But what he had said was true. She did recognize him, with the kind of certainty she had felt when she met Eilan.

"It is written that the Master himself believed," said the ancient priest, "for He said of the Way-shower, whom men called Jochanan, that he was Elijah reborn. It is written as well that he said there was milk for babes and meat for strong men. Many of the babes among us, new in faith, are given such food as is right for spiritual infants, lest they neglect to amend their lives, in the belief that indeed the Earth shall abide for ever. Yet the Master said that this generation shall not pass away before the Son of Man cometh; therefore am I here, that even the folk at the end of the world shall hear and know the Truth."

Caillean said quietly, "May the truth prevail."

"Success to your mission, sister," the old man replied. "There are many here who would welcome a pious sisterhood." He turned as if to go.

"Is it permitted to ask your name, my brother?"

"I am called Joseph, and I was a merchant of Arimathea. There are holy ladies still living among us who looked upon the Master's face in life. They will welcome the company of enlightened women among us."

Caillean bowed once more. She found it a strange but good omen that she should find among these Christians who did not readily embrace women, a better welcome than her Druid brethren had offered. *Servant of the Light* . . . The title rang in her awareness from some place before memory. As the ancient priest moved down the hill, her hands moved in a gesture of reverence more ancient even than the Druids. If such a soul could ally himself to the Christians, there must be some hope for them after all.

As he disappeared inside the little beehive church, Caillean found herself smiling. She knew now that the Goddess would favor her work and that she had indeed been sent here with good reason. She would begin this very day.

As Caillean breakfasted with the other women it occurred to her that in this new home, where they were all far from every familiar thing, she could not quite maintain the aloofness that Lhiannon and then Eilan had observed within the Forest House. She made her first decision: they were not to be served by outsiders. It was the first step in determining just how much contact they would have with the male priesthood. An easier decision was to appoint one of the tallest and strongest of the young novices to locate a site suitable for a garden and to sow it as quickly as might be with as many vegetables as practicable. Some food would, of course, be provided by the local population, but she wished it clear from the very beginning that they would not be in any way dependent upon the Druid priests. The priests would have not the shadow of an excuse for claiming control over the lives of the women there.

She chose another young woman – probably the least intelligent of her subordinates – to be in charge of the cooking and serving of the food, promising her as much assistance as she desired. Later that day she spoke with one of the priests, and established that a building should be completed before the winter snow grew deep that could house four or five times their original number. Politely, but adamantly she discarded the old priest's suggestion that their present accommodations might suffice at least through the present winter.

When she finally dismissed him he looked rather stunned. She suspected that he was probably feeling like someone who had been rolled over by a team of big horses, and felt that for the first time she could have her own will done. It was not at all an unwelcome feeling. The Goddess was at work here indeed, for the Lady could now make use of her talents to their fullest, and that had never been true before.

She missed Dieda; she could have used the younger woman's help with the maidens and in teaching them singing. But, she thought, she was better off without hostility among her associates, especially since they would have been thrown into such close contact. Here there was no one to protest whatever rules she might make. She resolved to choose the woman most experienced in singing or chanting to learn to play upon her own harp, and perhaps even teach her the art of fashioning such instruments.

When she finally laid herself down to sleep, after an evening spent grouping the women together for their first lesson in memorizing the unwritten lore of the Goddess, she could hear the sweet sound of chanting coming once more from the distant church. It was to the renewed chant of "Kyrie eleison," that she fell into sleep, more content with the spot to which the Goddess had led her than she had ever imagined she could be. That night she dreamed of a shrine served by maidens, of courts and halls upon the holy Tor, which might one day rise here. It might not be in her own lifetime; but it would come.

twenty-eight

~~~

The days waxed longer after Beltane; the cattle were driven to the hill pastures, and in the fields men tended the grain. Midsummer came, and for the first time Ardanos did not try to instruct Eilan before the ritual regarding the Oracle. When she saw him at the ritual, he seemed very frail. They told her afterward that the Goddess had foretold a time of disasters and changes, but promised peace to follow. Indeed, the whole land was full of rumors, but no one could say from what direction the danger might come.

Eilan had meant to visit the Arch-Druid after recovering from her own part in the ritual, but at this time of year there was much to do in the Forest House. The days went by and still she did not find the time. In high summer, even the maidens of the Forest House went into the fields of Vernemeton to help with the haying. Eilan supervised those who wove linen for the priests, and worked over the dye pots, preparing fabric for new robes, but it was Caillean who was missed most sorely, for she had always been the most skillful of the women at dying cloth. No law required Eilan to take her turn at this menial work but it seemed to her that as long as she had a responsibility for their little community, it was up to her to participate in it.

She was in the dye sheds, her sleeves rolled above the elbow and her forearms splattered with blue dye, when a shadow fell across the doorway. A ripple of scandalized excitement ran through the women as they realized it was one of the young Druids, flushed and perspiring in his white robe. For though the shed was not within the sacred precinct inside the walls, where only the highest of the priests might enter, they were not used to seeing men.

"The High Priestess," he gasped. "Is the Lady Eilan here?" All the women turned to look at Eilan and as the boy's flush deepened she realized that he had never seen her without her veil. He swallowed. "Please, Lady – the Arch-Druid has been taken ill. You must come!"

Eilan stopped in the doorway of Ardanos's chamber, shocked in spite of having been warned. She heard a little gasp from Miellyn, who was attending her, and motioned her to stand with Huw at the door. Then she sat down beside the bed of the dying man. And indeed there could be no doubt that he was dying. At each breath air rattled and sucked in Ardanos's chest, and she could see the skull beneath the sallow skin. With a pang she remembered how he had sat with Lhiannon during her illness. Even though at times she had hated him, she hoped that his passage would be an easy one.

"He collapsed at dinner and lay unconscious until a little while ago," said Garic, one of the older priests. "We have sent for Bendeigid."

She put back her veil and reached out to take his hand. "Ardanos," she said softly. "Ardanos, can you hear me?"

The papery eyelids fluttered and after a moment of confusion, he focused on her face. "Dieda," he whispered.

"Grandfather, do you not know me even now? Dieda is in the South, testing maidens who wish to join us as priestesses. I am Eilan." She was bitterly amused that he should still be confusing them after all these years.

His gaze focused on the ornaments she had taken the time to put on and he sighed. "You were the right one . . . after all."

"Ardanos," she said firmly, "as High Priestess it is my duty to tell you that you are dying. You must not depart without naming your successor. Tell us, Arch-Druid, who shall bear the golden sickle when you are gone?"

His eyes fixed on her face. "Goddess, I did the best . . . I could," he whispered. "The Merlin knows . . ."

"But *we* must know!" said the Druid who was attending him. "Who will you choose?"

"Peace!" Ardanos said with sudden strength, as if he were ordering them to be silent. "Peace . . ." The word whispered away on a dying gasp; the breath rattled in the old man's throat, and then he was still.

For a moment no one moved. Then Garic reached down to take Ardanos's pulse, waited, counting, and let the limp hand fall.

"He is gone!" he said accusingly.

"I am sorry," said Eilan. "What will you do?"

"We must summon the other members of our order," said one of the others, already taking charge. "Go now, Lady. Your part is done. We will inform you when the gods have led us to a decision, since they did not see fit to inspire Ardanos with their word."

As the fifteenth summer of the Emperor Domitian's reign passed, the weather stayed close and still, as if a storm were brewing somewhere just over the horizon. Gaius, riding through the streets of Deva, found himself constantly listening, waiting for thunder. And he was not the only one. The voices of the vendors in the town grew shrill and angry; there were more fights in the barracks and wine shops, and rumors of risings or mutinies abounded. Even his horse seemed to have picked up the tension, prancing and sidling nervously.

The ides of September . . . the ides of September . . . The words beat at his awareness every time his mount's hoofs struck the hard ground. Since Macellius had told him the date set for the rising, sleep had eluded him. His father believed that the tribes would support them, but Gaius was not so sure. If the Eagles of Rome fought each other, the only victor might be the Ravens. Was it worth the risk of a general insurrection even to unseat Domitian?

When this is over I will be happy to spend the rest of my life running my farm, he thought as he rubbed his eyes. *I was not cut out to be a conspirator.*

And this was the moment that the Arch-Druid, who in his way had been a force for stability, had chosen to die. If Gaius had believed in the Christian hell of which Julia spoke, he would have cursed the old man to its flames for his timing. Mithras alone knew who the Druids would choose to succeed him, but even if his successor was friendly, it would take time to establish the kind of understanding Ardanos had had with Macellius. But at least the news had brought Gaius to a decision. The question of adoption no longer mattered. If the country was about to explode in revolution he had to make sure that his son was safe. His father's informants had confirmed that the current High Priestess was still Eilan. Armed with an official message of condolence from the Legate, he was going to see her.

He had dressed carefully for the occasion, in the Roman style but with a Celtic sense of display, in a tunic of saffron linen embroidered with acanthus leaves at the hem over dark red doeskin breeches, and a mantle of light-weight maroon wool held by a golden brooch. At least no one could expect him to wear a toga when he was riding. But despite his fine clothes, as he turned his mount up the avenue of trees leading to the Forest House Gaius realized that he was nervous. He had just pulled out the first grey hairs at his temples. Would Eilan still find him handsome?

They led him into a garden where someone shrouded in a blue veil waited beneath a shady arbor covered with eglantine. He knew she must be the High Priestess because the same dolt of a bodyguard who had fainted when the cattle stampeded at Beltane all those years ago was standing near by, glaring at him. But he found it hard to believe that this erect, veiled figure was Eilan.

"My Lady . . ." He paused, and compelled by something he did not understand, bowed. "I have come to offer the condolences of the Legate at Deva on the death of the Arch-Druid, your grandfather. He will be greatly missed. He was . . ." he thought for a moment, "a remarkable man."

"Our loss is great indeed," she answered, and though her tone was colorless, his pulse quickened. "Will you take some refreshment?"

In a few moments a maiden in the drab garb of a novice was setting down a tray with honey cakes and a flagon of some drink made with herbs and berries and water, he supposed, from the Sacred Well. He drank, trying to think of something else to say and, looking down, saw that the fabric of her veil was trembling.

"Eilan," he said in a low voice, "let me see your face. It has been too long."

She gave a little laugh. "I was a fool. I thought it would be safe to see you again." She shrugged then and pulled back the veil, and he saw that her eyes were wet with tears.

Gaius blinked, for Eilan looked not older so much as more like herself, as if the girl he had known had been only a blurred sketch of the woman she was to become. Despite the tears and the neck that seemed too slender for the weight of the golden torque, she looked strong. *And why not?* he thought then. *In her own sphere she has wielded as much power as any legionary commander, these past years.* This woman could not be the Fury who had so frightened him. His vision blurred with old memories. He wanted to throw himself at her feet and declare his love for her, but that lout with the spear would be on him in a minute if he moved.

"Listen, for I do not know how long I can stay here," he said quickly. "War is coming – not because of your grandfather's death, but because of events in Rome. I can tell you no more, except that there will be a rising against the Emperor. Macellius hopes the British will support us, but there is no telling which way things will go. I must get you to a place of safety, Eilan, you and the boy."

Eilan looked at him, and her changeable eyes went flat and hard. "Let me be sure I understand you. Now, when the Imperium is about to tear itself apart, you want to offer me Roman protection. After all these years! Isn't it rather more likely that if there should be trouble during the coming weeks I will be safer here" – she indicated the walls and the hulking figure of Huw with a graceful wave of her hand – "than you and yours are likely to be?"

Gaius flushed. "Are you so sure your own people will never turn on you? Your oracles have been a force for peace with Rome – and now that your grandfather is not here, whom do you think people like Cynric will blame if things go wrong? Can't you see that you must come with me?"

"I *must* . . . ?" her eyes flashed. "And what does your Roman wife say to this fine plan? Has she tired of you after twelve years?"

"Julia has become a Christian and sworn an oath of chastity. That is grounds enough for divorce in Roman law. I could marry you, Eilan, and we could be together. If you will not, I can formally adopt our son!"

"So kind of you!" Eilan's face was now as red as it had been pale. She rose to her feet suddenly and started down the path, her skirts sweeping the gravel behind her. Gaius and Huw jumped up, both of them, it seemed to him, equally taken aback, and followed.

At the end of the garden was a hedge, just low enough for Gaius to see over it to a flat space between the buildings and the outer walls where several children were playing with a sewn leather ball. After a few moments it became clear to Gaius that one boy was the leader, a lad as leggy as a young colt who was just beginning to grow into his bones. His curls were tawny on top from a summer in the sun, but underneath they were dark, and as he turned to shout to one of his team-mates, there was something so like Macellius in his expression that it stopped Gaius's breath.

Eilan had begun to speak again, but Gaius's gaze was on the boy. His heart was hammering so hard he thought they must hear it in Deva, but the child, intent on his game, never looked around.

"When I bore him in that hut in the forest where were you?" Her voice, low and furious, was pitched for his ears. "And when I fought to keep him with me, and all these years when I watched over him in secret, never daring to admit he was my own? He does not know I am his mother, but I have kept him safely. Now, when he is almost come to manhood, you would step in and take him away? I think not, Gaius Macellius Severus Siluricus!" she hissed. "Gawen knows nothing of Rome!"

"Eilan!" he whispered. Gaius had thought what he felt for this child the one time he had held him had been some fancy; but he could feel it again, a longing that shook his bones. "Please!"

She turned her back and began to move back down the path. "My thanks to you, Roman, for your sympathy," she said loudly and clearly. "It was kind of you to come. As you say, the death of Ardanos has been a great loss. Do take our respectful greetings back to the Legate and to your father."

Gaius saw Huw looming towards him and, still looking over his shoulder, started to follow her. For a moment Gawen turned towards him, head tipped back, watching the ball. Then he dashed away. Gaius let the big man shepherd him back down the path, feeling as if all the light had gone out of the world.

Eilan had pulled her veil back down. His last sight of her was a shadow disappearing into a dark doorway. As Gaius let his horse choose its own way back down to the road he wondered how it could all have gone so wrong. He had been so relieved to find Eilan was unchanged, and he had meant to tell her he still loved her; but he realized now that she was something worse than a Fury: a woman like the old Empresses, or Boudicca, a woman warped by pride and power.

Abruptly a vision of Senara as he had last seen her gazing up at him overlaid his memory of Eilan's rage. She was so good, and so innocent – as Eilan had been when first he knew her. Eilan had never truly understood him, but Senara was half Roman, as he was, and torn by the same conflicts and uncertainties. If he could win her, it seemed to Gaius he would be whole once more.

He was not yet beaten. One way or another, he would have Senara, and he would have the boy, though all the Legions of Rome and warriors of the tribes stood between.

Eilan spent the days after Gaius's visit in seclusion. The priestesses thought that she was grieving for her grandfather, but although his death had left her shocked and startled, relief rather had predominated. Her reaction to Gaius, however, was another matter entirely. She herself had been as surprised by her own fury as he was. She had not realized how much she had resented his abandonment all these years. It was true that she had agreed to it, but surely he could have tried to contact her before now! How dared he think that he could walk in without a word of love and take her child away . . .

When her thoughts reached this point she would have to stop herself, walk a little or spend some time in the disciplined meditation Caillean had taught her, and try to recover her serenity. It was several days before she began seriously to consider what he had said to her. Who, indeed, would now feel himself privileged to instruct her in what she was to say in the name of the Goddess? The last she had heard, the Druids were still arguing. By now it had become clear that a new Arch-Druid would not be chosen until after Lughnasad, so she need not worry about preparing for the festival. But by Samaine, the new leader would be firmly seated in his power. And if it were someone like her father, he would demand that the Goddess call the tribes to war.

When Dieda returned to the Forest House and came to see her, Eilan found her own offers of sympathy quickly shrugged off.

"Ardanos is no loss," said her kinswoman callously. "My father was always in the hands of the Romans. I wonder who will give the orders to the Oracle now?"

Ever since Gawen's birth, Eilan had felt constrained in Dieda's presence. Still, it seemed impossible she should have no feeling whatever for her own father. Eilan missed Caillean, who might have been able to make some sense out of all this, more with every passing day.

Dieda was still with her when one of the girls came in to tell them that Cynric had come. *So, the Ravens are gathering,* Eilan thought grimly, but she greeted Cynric kindly as a kinsman when Huw brought him in. He looked older than his years, she thought painfully, shaggy as a mountain pony, his fine skin marred by old scars.

"What are you doing in this part of the country? I thought you safely away to the North after things went wrong with Brigitta and the Demetae."

"Oh, I can come and go as I please," he said, "even under the Commander's nose. I am too clever for them." He spoke with a kind of brittle gaiety she found disturbing.

"The proudest beast is soonest taken in the snare of the hunter," murmured Dieda sardonically. She pretended to care nothing for Cynric, but Eilan thought she was not so indifferent as she seemed.

Cynric shrugged. "I might well think some god favors me more than common; it is true that I seem to bear a charmed life. I think I could go into Londinium and pull the Governor's beard."

"I would not try it, if I were you," Dieda said, and he returned her laughter.

"I do not intend to try it at this moment; in another month or two it may be a very different matter. I do not grieve at Ardanos's death; nor should you, Eilan. He was all too eager to have all things ordered as he chose."

"He was indeed," she said honestly, though her blood ran cold as she connected what Gaius had told her with Cynric's words.

"Good; you are honest so far," he said. "I wonder, foster sister, how far your honesty goes."

She said warily, "I, at least, know what I want."

"Do you? And what is that, Eilan?"

"Peace!" *So that my son can grow to be a man,* she thought grimly. But there was no way she could say that to Cynric. Ardanos had blighted her own happiness, and that of Cynric and Dieda as well, but at least in the West, the tribes had been at peace for a dozen years.

Cynric grimaced. "Peace – women think too much of it," he snorted. "You sound like Macellius's mouthpiece; as I sometimes thought old Ardanos was. But he is gone. Now we may have a chance to drive out these Romans. Brigitta waits, knowing what we want of her."

"I should think Brigitta had seen enough of war," Eilan said.

"Say rather that she has seen enough of Roman justice," Cynric said bitterly. "But there are strange rumors going about these days. If the Romans do fight each other, perhaps we can free ourselves of what they call justice. Then every Roman home shall be laid waste as was the home of Bendeigid!"

Eilan interrupted. "Have you forgotten it was not the Romans who leveled the home of my father and killed my mother, but the Hibernians and the wild tribesmen of the North? The Romans themselves punished them."

"For our own homes, who but we should be responsible?" asked Cynric. "It is for us to punish or to spare as we see fit. Are we to accept all this like tame dogs, and let the Romans determine whom we should fight and where?" An angry flush was building beneath the weathered skin.

Eilan said stubbornly, "However it comes, peace is a good thing."

"So you will still speak the traitorous words of Ardanos? Or are they the words of Macellius, or perhaps of his handsome son?" he asked, sneering.

Behind him the giant bodyguard shifted weight uneasily. Eilan hardly noticed, she was so distressed. "At least Macellius has the good of both our peoples at heart."

"And I do not?" Cynric demanded, his eyes flashing.

"I did not say that, or anything like to it."

"But that is what you meant," he threw back at her. "I know Macellius's cub came here. What did he say to you? With you in the high seat, it seems we hardly need the Romans. But we shall hear such traitorous counsels no longer. Bendeigid has been chosen as Arch-Druid – that is what I came to tell you – and he will give you a very different set of instructions at the next festival!"

Dieda was looking from one to the other, her face flaming. Eilan strove for calm, knowing that Cynric was simply trying to hurt her.

"It is true that Ardanos told me what he wanted and interpreted the Oracle's answers. But what the Goddess says while I am in trance is not my doing. I do not declare my own will, Cynric," she said quietly.

"Are you trying to tell me the Goddess wishes for this treason?"

"Why should She not?" shouted Eilan. "She is a mother." *As I am.* Eilan swallowed the words, and added angrily, "You have no right to speak so to me!"

"I am the vengeance of the Goddess," snapped Cynric, "and I speak as I will – and punish –"

Before Eilan could react, his lifted hand had connected with her cheek. She cried out, and Dieda exclaimed in shock, "How dare you?"

"Cathubodva knows I dare deal this way with all Romanized traitors!"

A shadow loomed behind him. Still glaring, Cynric started to turn, Huw's cudgel caught him in motion and his head exploded in a shower of blood and brains. Dieda screamed, and Eilan lifted her hand but it was too late.

For a moment Cynric's body stood swaying, a surprised look on what was left of his face. Then his body understood its death at last and he crumpled to the floor.

Shaking, Eilan touched his wrist, knowing already, as the gush of blood from his head slowed, that she would find no pulse. She looked up at her guard, who was beginning to turn a little green as he stared at the blood.

"Huw – why did you do it? Why?"

"Lady . . . he *hit* you!"

Eilan bowed her head. Even if the offender had been Ardanos himself Huw would have struck him. He had been taught that the Priestess was inviolable. But Cynric's death would have to be concealed. His followers were not many, but they were desperate. If they decide to avenge him, the precarious unity she had built among her people would be shattered. Cynric dead might be more dangerous than he had ever been alive.

Dieda turned away, weeping. Eilan felt that she herself was beyond tears. "Go away, Huw," she said tiredly. "Go tell Miellyn what has happened and ask her to send a message to the new Arch-Druid." *My father* . . . she thought numbly, but she had no time now to consider the implications. "Speak to no others," she instructed, "and when you have carried this message, forget what has happened here today."

She got to her feet, feeling suddenly a hundred years old. "Dieda, come to the garden. There is nothing you can do for him now." She went to comfort the weeping woman, but Dieda jerked away.

"Is it so you reward faithfulness to our people? Then have your tame bear kill me too."

Eilan winced. "I tried to save him. I would have willingly given my own life –"

"Oh indeed, that's easy enough to say –" Dieda turned on her. "But you take lives, not give them. You fed on Caillean's wisdom, and sent her into exile when you had drained her dry. You stole my reputation, and walked away with your honor as bright as a new-born babe's. And now you have taken the life of the only man I ever loved! Your Roman was lucky to be rid of you! Eilan the inviolate! Lady High and Mighty! If only they knew!"

Eilan said wearily, "None of us held a sword to your throat to bid you take vows here, Dieda. When it was clear they had chosen me, you could have been released, and when you went to Eriu, no force was used to bid you return. I have said this before, but I suppose you could not hear." She tried to speak calmly, but the other woman's words struck harder than Cynric's blow.

"I told you once to beware if ever you betrayed our people. Was Cynric right, Eilan? Have you been working for Rome all along?"

Eilan lifted her head and, trembling, stared into that other face, so like her own. "I swear . . . that I have served the Goddess as well as I could," she said hoarsely, "and may the sky fall and cover me, the earth rise up to swallow me, if I lie." She took a deep breath. "I am still High Priestess of Vernemeton. But you may go to Caillean, or wherever else you will, if you feel that you can no longer serve the Goddess in my company!"

Slowly Dieda began to shake her head, a sly expression that Eilan liked even less than her rage creeping into her eyes.

"I won't leave you," she whispered. "I wouldn't leave now for the world. I want to be here when the Goddess strikes you down!"

Senara was already waiting outside the hut in the forest when Gaius arrived, her bright hair like a flame against the dark trees. "I see you have come," he said softly.

Senara turned and, although she had expected him, gave a small startled cry. "Is it you?"

"No other," he said, almost gaily, "in spite of the evil weather. I dare say we shall have rain, and that speedily." He looked at the sky. "What, think you, would Father Petros say to lending the shelter of his roof to a couple of wayfarers?"

"For converts I think he would be delighted. I do not think he would do so to pagans," she said reprovingly.

They moved inside together. The hermit's furnishings consisted of some dilapidated benches and, against the wall, a clumsy box bed. But where, this evening, was Father Petros? Outside the storm broke with a rattle of wind and a slam of rain. Gaius winced, listening to the thunder.

"You see, we made it here just in time," he said. "*Bellissima!*"

"You must not call me so," she said timidly.

"No?" he queried, watching her carefully. "But I thought truth was one of your Christian virtues. The Stoics say so, and even among the Druids, I have heard, truth-telling is valued. Would you have me lie to you, then?"

"You know how to best me with words," she said crossly. "We came here to speak of the state of your soul."

"Ah, yes; a thing that I am not yet convinced I possess."

She said, "I am no philosopher. But do not even the Stoics whom you have mentioned, speak of that part of a man which deals with the evidence of that which you can neither see nor feel?"

"They do; it is that which convinces me that of all women you are the most desirable."

He knew that he was pushing the girl, but the storm, rather than relieving the tension, seemed to have filled him with its own intensity. He had spent the days since his meeting with Eilan in turmoil, alternately raging and in despair. He would have taken her away and done his duty by her, but she had denied him. Julia too had forfeited her claim to him. Surely he was free now to seek comfort elsewhere! And when he told Senara she was beautiful, he had not lied.

She blushed and said timidly, "It is not well done of you to speak so to me."

"On the contrary, I think it is very well done, and you would have me speak the truth. And for what else were you created as a woman?"

Now she was on familiar ground, having listened to many catechumens. "Scripture tells us," she replied, "that we were created for the purpose of giving worship to the Creator."

"How dull for him," Gaius answered. "If I were a god, I would ask more of men than that they should spend their leisure in worshipping me."

"But it is not for the Created to question the ways of the Creator."

"Why not?" Gaius pursued.

"Is there anything better to do than worship God?" she demanded, raising her eyes to his. Flushed, like this, she looked still more beautiful.

Certainly there is, Gaius thought, *and I would rather be doing it with you.* If there was a god, he had created women's beauty, and Gaius could not believe he would condemn any man for appreciating it. But it was not yet time to say so.

"Tell me, then about this Creator."

"Almost every faith – except perhaps that of Rome who worship only their Emperor who is all evil – speaks of a Creator. It was He who made all things that were made, and He placed us here to worship Him."

"Properly speaking, it is the *genius* of the Emperor that we honor, the divine spark that guides him, and through him, the Empire, not the man. That is why those who will not burn incense are prosecuted as traitors."

"There may have been good Emperors, though some of the priests would not believe it," Senara conceded. "But even you will own that Nero, who burned so many Christians in his arena, was an evil one."

"I will grant you Nero," Gaius said, "and Caligula. And there are those in Rome who feel that Domitian in his *hubris* has gone too far. When that happens, those who made a man Emperor have the right to replace him." *And soon*, he thought, shivering. September was passing quickly.

"You are very proud of being a Roman," she said then. "I do not know very much about my mother's family and have always wondered what it would have been like to be raised that way. Were you born in Rome?"

He grinned at her. "Indeed not; I am half British, just as you are. My mother was a royal woman of the Silures. She died when I was very young, bearing my little sister."

"Ah, how sad for you." Her eyes suddenly overflowed; he had not noticed that they were so blue. "What did you do then?"

"I stayed with my father," Gaius told her. "I was his only son, so he had me well educated by tutors, and taught to read Latin and Greek; then I went into the Legions. There is really nothing more to tell."

"And were there no women in your life?"

He could see her fighting this purely worldly curiosity; but he thought it a good sign that she wanted to know.

"My father arranged my marriage with Julia when I was very young," he said carefully. One day she would have to know about Eilan and their son, but not yet. "And as you may know, my wife has taken a vow of chastity, which means I am alone," he said sadly. Outside, the thunder crashed.

She said, "I should not say this, and I am certain Father Petros would not approve, but that seems not fair dealing. I know that a vow of chastity is supposed to be the best of all ways to live, but when she has pledged herself to you –"

"If you were married to me, would you take such a vow?"

She flushed again, but said seriously, "I would not. The learned Paulus wrote that those who were married should continue in that state, and those who were not married should not marry."

"If I had married you, you would have taken your vows more seriously than Julia," he said softly.

"I could never be untrue to a vow to you."

"And you have not taken vows in the Forest House?" She was still looking at the floor, but Gaius moved a little closer, feeling the blood run faster beneath his skin.

"I have not," she said. "They have all been very kind to me, and asked very little, but I cannot serve their Goddess without giving up my Roman heritage. I will have to decide soon."

"There is another alternative." His voice grew hoarse as he took in the sweet scent of her hair, but he kept it low. "Julia has forfeited her rights as my wife by her vow of chastity, and we were married by Roman, not by Christian rites. I would marry you, Senara – or Valeria, as your mother called you. Your uncle Valerius is a good man; he would be happy if I were to take you away from here."

He heard her breath catch. She was like some bright bird hovering almost within reach of his hand, like Eilan when she came to him at Beltane so many years ago. But Eilan and Julia had rejected him; they were shadows, banished by the living reality of this girl who stood so close to him now.

"If only it could be," she whispered. "Where would we go?"

"To Londinium, or even to Rome. Great changes are coming. I can tell you no more, but there is nothing we might not do, together, if you would come with me!"

Not to touch her then seemed the hardest thing he had ever done, for he was mad now with uncertainty and need. But he knew that if he did he would lose her. Senara looked up and he faced her, letting the ardor that filled him glow in his eyes.

She did not flee. Trembling, she said softly, "I wish I knew what to do."

Be mine, he said silently. *Help me to raise my son!* Surely, she would accept Gawen. That was why he needed her, after all, and not some wealthy Roman maiden who would despise Gawen's British blood. It was for the sake of the boy . . .

Now, at last, Gaius dared caress her; she did not pull away, but he felt her tremble at his touch. Afraid to frighten her, he lifted his hands.

"Oh, what shall I do? God help me," she whispered, turning her head so that her cheek lay against his hand.

"I think," he whispered into her ear, "that it must be your God who has brought us together."

"God grant you are right."

"I will go to your uncle and get his authority to take you from the Forest House. Be ready to leave when I come for you," he said. "By the time the next moon has waned you will be on your way to Londinium with me."

Once again, with a great effort, he did not touch her. He had his reward when she shyly stood on tiptoe and whispered, "My brother, let us exchange the kiss of peace."

"Ah, Valeria, it is not the kiss of peace I want from you," he whispered into her fine-spun hair. "And some day you will know it."

She broke away from him; and with a new wisdom – or guile – he let her go. Just in time, for in the next moment a step sounded, and the hermit, Father Petros entered. Senara, he was surprised to see, greeted the hermit without a blush. Had all women that trick of hiding their feelings on the instant? He remembered with what swiftness Eilan, too, had been able to conceal her emotions.

She said, "Rejoice, Father. Gaius Macellius has promised to take me from the Druid temple and find me a new home, perhaps even in Rome."

Father Petros looked sharply at Gaius; he was not as naive as the girl. Gaius said, "Senara has been trying to show me, Good Father, why I ought to become one of your congregation."

"And will you do so?" The priest regarded him suspiciously.

Gaius said quietly, "She has certainly been most persuasive."

Father Petros positively glowed. "I will welcome you to my flock as a son," he said fulsomely. "You will set a fine example for the others of your class."

Indeed, thought Gaius, *a Roman nobleman with my connections would be a good catch for this fisher of men*. So much for the idea that Christians were no respecters of persons. But there must be some good in it, to have attracted a girl like Senara.

twenty-nine

———— ‿‿‿ ————

"**E**ilan! Eilan! The Emperor is dead!" Senara burst through the door, then stopped short, trying to assume the dignity with which the High Priestess of Vernemeton should be approached.

Smiling, Eilan set her spindle on the little table beside her and invited the girl to sit down. With Caillean gone, Miellyn suffering from one of her periodic bouts of depression, and Eilidh busy supervising the maidens, she found herself depending more and more on Senara for company. Dieda had not spoken to her since Cynric died. At least they had managed to bury him without arousing comment. Two of the Druids had come by night and taken the body to the ancient mound on the Hill of the Maidens. Perhaps Cynric's death had been without honor, but he had a hero's burial.

"The man that brings us fresh eggs heard the news in Deva," said Senara, her eyes wide with excitement. "He was assassinated a week ago, just before the Equinox, and the world from Caledonia to Parthia is buzzing like an overturned hive! Some say that a senator will be the next Emperor, and others think one of the Legions will elevate their Commander to the purple. More likely still, several will claim it and there will be civil war!"

"What is happening in Deva?" Eilan asked when she could get a word in.

"The men of the Twentieth are uneasy, but so far they have stayed quiet. The Commander has ordered a great feast for them, with unlimited wine and beer. Lady Eilan, what do you think will happen now?"

Eilan sighed. "No doubt the Roman Commander is hoping that they will all get very drunk, and awaken too sick to make trouble for anyone." If they were lucky that was how it would go. If the drink sent the legionaries fighting mad instead, there was no knowing what they might do.

Senara giggled and shook her head. "I meant about the Emperor. Do you think the senators will take power and Rome will go back to being a Republic again?"

Eilan stared at her, wondering why the child was worrying about events in Rome. Of course she was half Roman, *like Gaius*, but she had never seemed much concerned about that side of her heritage.

"I am a great deal more concerned about what is going to happen in Britannia," she said grimly. "Cynric was not the only one who would see this as a golden opportunity to raise the tribes, and then we could have a civil war here, too!"

My father, for instance, she thought with an inner shudder. What in the name of the Goddess was she to do when he began making demands on her with both the power of the Arch-Druid and a father's authority? Once more she wished desperately that she could discuss this with Caillean.

Senara's eyes widened. "What should we do?"

"There is something *you* can do," Eilan said thoughtfully. "Take the new lengths of linen over to the house of the Druids – you are not under vows yet, and they will not think it odd. Ask, in all innocence, if they have heard the news, and let me know what they say."

Senara gave her a conspiratorial grin and jumped to her feet. In another moment she was gone, leaving Eilan to envy her energy.

What indeed should I do? she wondered then. Perhaps she ought to have taken Gaius up on his offer, but from the sound of it, he must have problems of his own by now. The existence of Gawen had been Ardanos's weapon against her. She had thought that with her grandfather dead, she would be free, but though her father did not know her secret, Dieda did. How long, she wondered, before Dieda's hatred gave the new Arch-Druid a power over her he would not hesitate to use? Unless, of course, he killed her out of hand?

She rested her head in her hands, feeling the beginnings of the headache that had troubled her increasingly during the past few days. *How can I deal with this? Goddess help me now!*

One day, when they all knew why she had done what she had – when all this land was at peace and there was neither Roman nor Briton – ah, then she might be forgiven! She shook her head in anguish, seeing nowhere to turn.

And at that moment, pain like a bolt from heaven lanced through her temple. From what seemed a very great distance, the thought came, *But I shall be long dead by then* . . . Then consciousness fled.

When Eilan came to herself she was slumped over her table. She felt curiously drained and at peace, but with an inner certainty she knew that something had changed. She had always been aware that some of the herbs in the sacred drink she used before giving the Oracle could dangerously thin the blood, and sometimes cause a weakness in the brain. Perhaps that was what was happening now.

"*When it comes to you,*" Caillean had told her once, "*you will know.*" A lingering death like Lhiannon's was unusual. Old Latis had said once that most of the High Priestesses died suddenly. But not, Eilan suspected now, without warning.

Is this my warning? she wondered. *But my work will not be finished.*

"*It is finished.*" Awareness came once more, as in trance when the Goddess spoke to her.

But who should succeed her at her work, declare the Oracles in her stead? She must not leave matters in confusion as Ardanos had done.

"*It does not matter.*" With the words came calm. The Goddess had spoken. What was to come was in Her hands, and not Eilan's concern any more. If she died, it would be a bolt of mercy, not of vengeance, that would strike her down. Caillean had been correct. The Druids had no right to declare how the priestesses should live. What mattered was that she try her best to do the Lady's will.

In autumn the mists rose thick above the marshes of the Summer Country and wreathed around the Tor. On such mornings, when Caillean made the climb to the standing stones that crowned it for her morning meditation, it seemed as if the Tor were an island indeed and she was gazing out over a rolling grey sea. But as the year drew on toward Samaine, she found herself thinking quite obsessively of Eilan.

At first, she dismissed these thoughts, knowing it was not good for Eilan to cling to her; nor for herself to be distracted. But as the days darkened, the other woman's face appeared in her visions with a frequency she could not dismiss. Eilan had grave need of her, and it was perilous to ignore such messages.

At last came a morning when she woke with words ringing in her ears:

"*Here where we stand in darkness and under the shadow of death we call on Thee, O Mother, Sisters and more than Sisters . . .*"

And she knew that by oaths which she and Eilan had sworn together, not only as priestesses of the Sacred Grove, but from life to life before that, she was bound to go to her.

But it was not until two weeks before Samaine that she was able to arrange matters so that she could go back to the Forest House. One advantage of her position in the new temple, she thought, was that it was taken for granted that whatever she chose to do was well done; her every act was assumed to be directly inspired by the will of the Goddess, as Eilan's was at Vernemeton. The drawback, of course, was that she was responsible for seeing that all her duties would be taken care of while she was gone.

A scant three days would bring her to Vernemeton. She would much rather have travelled in the simplicity of men's clothing and afoot, but the temple was not yet ready for that; not this year at least. So she resigned herself to travelling with her formal litter and all the regalia of a priestess. An escort of two young priests went with her. They treated her with as much deference as if they had been her grandsons; which was not particularly surprising, Caillean thought, for both were young enough.

As they wound through the marshes below the Tor, it began to rain; Caillean knew that this would slow her progress, and fretted, but there was nothing to be done. It had been raining off and on since the Equinox, as if the heavens were weeping for the dead Emperor, and no one, however gifted with magic, had ever been able to control the British weather.

Two days' journey brought them to Aquae Sulis, and from there a Roman road led northward to Glevum. To her surprise, it was in considerable disrepair; the recent rains had left it pitted and the stones all awry. There were great ruts in the gravel and she was glad they did not have to drive a chariot or even a farm cart with oxen over such a road.

She had almost fallen asleep when, from the depths of the forest which edged the road, a number of men came running; dirty and rough-looking, in tattered and filthy garments. *Bacaudae*, thought Caillean, a rabble of runaway slaves and criminals who plagued many parts of the Empire. She had heard of them, but never encountered any before. The unrest following the death of the Emperor must have encouraged them.

"Stand aside, fellows," demanded one of her escort. "We bear a great priestess."

"That ain't nothing to us," said one of the bandits, jeering. "What can she do? Throw fire at us, maybe? There's a stall at every market with a juggler who can do that same trick."

Caillean had indeed been regretting that there was no fire within the litter, but these fellows were clearly more sophisticated than the Irish raiders she had once frightened that way. She climbed out of the litter and said to the young priest, "What is the delay?"

He was still sputtering with indignation. "These – these fellows –" he began. Caillean regarded them calmly; then reached into the little pouch at her waist. She still – she realized it only afterwards – had not completely taken in what was happening. For so many years the Romans had kept the roads quiet, the danger did not seem real.

She took out the little purse tied at her waist and said with distant courtesy, "Charity is a duty to the gods. Here, fellow," and she handed him a denarius. He gazed at it for a moment, then guffawed.

"We don't want your charity, lady," he remarked, with an odd, exaggerated courtesy. "But you can start by giving us that little purse –"

Then, finally, Caillean realized what they dared to want from her. Amazement gave way to outrage. With suddenly heightened senses, she felt the energy in the clouds above her and its resonance within her. In that moment she knew she had some power over the weather after all. She lifted her hands and saw a blur as the bandit, who had sensed his danger, struck out with his cudgel. Lightning flared, blanking out vision, and as the thunder boomed, the sky fell on her head and the world disappeared.

It was many hours before she became conscious again.

In the days that followed that first pain, Eilan tried to accept the will of the gods. But although she could believe that the Goddess would watch over Vernemeton and her people, she still feared for her child. She could have trusted Gawen to Caillean. But Caillean – at her work at the far end of the country – was not there. Dieda was kin to the boy, but since the death of Cynric she was the last person to whom Eilan could entrust him. Lia, she knew, would die for her nursling, but she was only a poor woman with no place to go. Perhaps Mairi might be willing to take the child, but Gawen would not be safe even with her if their father should learn his identity.

If she only knew how long she had . . . But no matter how Eilan framed the question, the forces that had warned of her own death remained so obstinately silent that if it had not been for the occasional throb of pain in her brow, the whole thing might have been some morbid product of her own imagination. All she could do was to spend as much time as she dared with the boy.

Gawen had just gone off to his dinner when Senara came in to light the lamps. As usual, Huw was a silent presence by the door. For so many years she had thought him about as much protection as an unhatched chicken, but he had been lethal enough. Seeing him reminded her of the unhealed pain of Cynric's death.

"You go too, and get yourself some dinner," she ordered. "Senara will remain with me until you return."

Senara moved slowly around the room with flint and steel, and the clay lamps – of Roman make even here – flared into life one by one. It was only when the girl had stood for several minutes staring at the last of them that Eilan asked, "What is it, child. Are you unwell?"

"Oh, Eilan!" Senara caught her breath on a sob.

Eilan took a seat on one of the benches. "Come here, child," she said gently. As Senara approached, she saw the girl's face was wet. "Why, my love, what is it? You know me well enough to know that whatever it is, you needn't be afraid to tell me."

Bright drops shone on Senara's cheeks. "You're so good to me, you've always been so good . . . and I'm not worth it," she said, choking, and fell at Eilan's feet, crying helplessly.

"Oh, my dear," Eilan soothed, "you mustn't cry; I'm not strong enough for this. Whatever it is, it can't be that bad." She reached out and gently pulled the girl to her feet. "Come, sit here beside me."

Senara's weeping diminished a little, but instead of taking a place at Eilan's side she began to pace the room. At last she said, her voice half choked with weeping, "I hardly know how to tell you."

And all at once, Eilan knew what ailed the girl. She said "You've come to tell me you don't wish to be sworn as a priestess in the Forest House."

Senara looked up, the bright drops still making glistening tracks down her cheeks in the lamplight. "That's part of it," she whispered, "the least part." She struggled for words. "I'm not worthy to be here at all; I'm not fit; if you knew, you'd cast me out of here –"

You aren't worthy! Eilan thought. *Oh, if you only knew!* And then, aloud, she repeated what Caillean had once said to her. "Perhaps in the sight of the Goddess, none of us is truly worthy. Try to stop crying, my dear, and tell me what ails you."

Senara calmed a little, though she still could not meet Eilan's eyes. Eilan recalled standing like this before Lhiannon, so many years ago. But surely she wronged the girl; Senara had been spending her time with the Christians, and they were even more concerned with chastity than the women of Vernemeton.

"I . . . I have met a man . . . and he wants me to go away with him," she said baldly at last.

Eilan caught Senara in her arms. "Ah, my poor child," she whispered. "But you are still free to leave us and even to marry if you wish. You were brought here so young. It was never really intended that you should take vows among us; but that was so long ago now that most of us had forgotten. Tell me about it. Where did you meet this man? Who is he? I have no objection if you want to marry, but I care for you as much as any mother, and I would like to be sure you are choosing well."

Senara stared at her, hardly understanding that not only was Eilan not angry, but that the older woman would set her free. "I met him at Father Petros's hermitage. He is a Roman, a friend of my uncle Valerius –"

She stopped at the sound of a man's voice. "Senara?" answered one of the newer girls from the other side of the door, "I think you will find her in there."

I will have to speak to that child, thought Eilan. *That is no way to announce visitors, especially a man.* Senara, recalling that with Huw gone, it was her business to protect the High Priestess, took up position between her and the door. A man came through it and, as he closed it behind him, Eilan saw all the color drain out of Senara's face and then flood into it again.

"*This* man . . ." she faltered. "He has come for me . . ."

She moved aside, and in the flickering, deceptive lamplight Eilan saw his face.

"Gaius . . ." she whispered. Surely this was some nightmare born of a fevered imagination. She shut her eyes, but when she opened them he was still there, staring in stupefaction from her to Senara.

Senara took a step towards him. "Gaius!" she cried. "I did not expect you so soon! Has my uncle given his permission for you to marry me?"

Gaius stared wildly around him. "You foolish girl, what are you doing here?"

Eilan felt as if the flame of the lamps had ignited in her breast. Slowly she rose to her feet. "What are *you* doing here?" She turned to Senara. "Are you trying to tell me that Gaius Macellius Severus is the man you love?"

"He is. Why, what is wrong?" Senara stared at Eilan in confusion.

Eilan turned on Gaius. "You tell her what is wrong," she commanded. "Tell her all the truth – if you are still capable of it."

"What truth?" demanded Senara, her voice cracking. "I know that he has a Roman wife who has refused to honor her marriage vows. Of course he will divorce her before he marries me . . ."

"Of course he will," Eilan said in a terrible voice. "So, Gaius, she knows about the little daughters that you will be abandoning. Does she know about our son as well?"

"*Your* son?" Stricken, Senara looked back and forth between Gaius and Eilan. "Tell me this is not true," she said to Gaius, pleading. Her voice caught in her throat.

"You do not understand," Gaius muttered.

"Understand," Senara repeated brokenly. "I wanted to save you, and you have nearly ruined me! I understand that I have been a fool!"

As she turned from him, the door swung wide and the giant Huw thrust into the room, cudgel upraised. But after the death of Cynric he had been severely chastised, and he did not want to make the same mistake again. "Lady," he mumbled, "they said a man was here. I heard shouting. What shall I do?"

Eilan stared at Gaius, thinking that if the danger were not so real he would have looked ridiculous standing there. But perhaps to be caught in this situation was the worst punishment a proud Roman could have endured. After a long moment Eilan lifted her hand to signal Huw to stand still. "Go," she said fiercely to Gaius. "Go, or he will knock out your brains. To Senara she added, "Go with him, if you wish – while I can still protect you."

Senara stared at Gaius for a moment and then flung her arms around Eilan. "Oh, I would not," she cried, "not for the world and everything in it would I go with him now!"

Eilan, startled, tightened her arms around the girl, then she turned upon Gaius.

"Get out of here," she said in a low voice. "Get out or I will let Huw do his worst." Then, losing her control, she cried, "Get out of here, or I will kill you myself!"

Gaius did not stay to argue. He pushed through the door curtain, and it flapped shut behind him.

Gaius sat in the Blue Eagle taverna and called out to the proprietor to bring him a new flagon of sour Gaullish wine. He had been drinking for most of the past three days, moving from one wine shop to another as he outwore his welcome. The tavern keepers knew who he was, and his father. Eventually, they would be paid.

At times Gaius wondered if he had been missed, but he supposed Macellius must think he had gone home to the villa, and Julia would think he was still with his father in the town. Mostly, he wondered how much wine he would have to drink before the pain went away.

He had stayed in Deva at first because of the political situation, and then because he did not want to confront Licinius and inform him that he was about to abandon Julia and the useless daughters she had borne him. In tardy fairness, he supposed that Licinius, doting father though he was, might be willing to remonstrate with Julia. Sonless himself, he would not want Julia divorced for the same reason. But if Licinius had persuaded his daughter to honor her conjugal obligations, Gaius would not be able to marry Senara, and the thought of her had been a warmth that could keep his fears about the future at bay.

Not that it mattered any more, he thought, feeling the cool fire of the wine going down. Senara didn't love him. Julia didn't love him. And Eilan – especially Eilan – didn't love him at all. He shuddered, remembering the face of the Fury once more when she had ordered him away.

The door to the taverna was flung open and another bunch of legionaries crashed in. The Commander must be wondering by now if he had miscalculated, thought Gaius sourly. The feast he had offered had done no more than weaken military discipline. If this had been Rome, the Emperor would have been emptying the treasury to give the men circuses, but a little bear-baiting was all this godforsaken province could provide. It wasn't nearly enough to distract them, and the soldiers seemed to be getting wilder with every day.

But nobody paid any attention to the lone man getting quietly drunk in the corner, and that was all that mattered to Gaius right now. He sighed, and reached for the flagon again.

A hand closed around his wrist. He looked up blearily, and blinked to see Valerius standing there. "By Mercury, man, you've led me a chase!" Valerius stood back to look at him and made a face. "Thank the gods your father can't see you now!"

"Does he know – ?" Gaius began.

"Are you crazy? I care about his feelings, even if you do not. One of the men told me he'd seen you. What possessed you to get drunk now? Never mind that," he said as Gaius started to protest. "First, my lad, we've got to get you out of here!"

Gaius was still protesting when Valerius hauled him into the street and across the town to the bathhouse. But it was not until he had been shoved into the cold pool that Gaius began to sober up enough to understand what was said to him.

"Tell me," Valerius said as he came up, sputtering, "is my niece Valeria still in the Forest House?"

Gaius nodded. "I went there, but she ... changed her mind, wouldn't come with me." Events were coming back to him. He had given Valerius an expurgated version of the situation and gained his permission to marry Senara – that gave the man some rights – but why was he so upset about it now?

"Listen," said Valerius quickly. "You're not the only one who's been drinking. Last night I was with some of the legionaries attached to the Quaestor's office – their names don't matter – who were speculating about the priestesses at Vernemeton. And one of them said, "It's not as if the women there were anything like real Vestals; they're just barbarian women like any others." I protested, but it finally came to a wager that they could carry off one of the sacred virgins there, and it wouldn't be sacrilege."

Gaius picked up a towel and began to rub himself furiously, trying to understand.

"Come into the hot room," said Valerius, offering his arm. "You'll sweat the poisons out faster." When they were settled, gasping as the hot steam hit them, the secretary continued. "I thought it was the sort of silly bet that drunken men make – no more than words born of wine, and nothing to worry about – till this morning, when three of the men turned up missing at muster. One of my drinking companions of the night before told me that they had left Deva this morning to try and win the bet."

"The centurion . . ." Gaius's head was pounding, but he was becoming able to think once more.

". . . has more than enough on his hands without this, and so do the tribunes. Discipline has gone to hell since the assassination. You and your father know the British better than anyone. What do you think will happen if some of our men are discovered raping a native priestess? Boudicca's rebellion will be nothing to it, and we're in no condition to respond!"

"Yes . . . of course," said Gaius. "I will go. Do you know exactly when they left? Have you any idea which way they took?"

"None whatever, I'm sorry to say," Valerius replied. "I suppose I could ask around."

"No, there's not enough time. I'll have to go home for clothes." He rubbed his eyes.

"I have them," said Valerius. "I had an idea you might need a change."

"My father was right," muttered Gaius, "you do think of everything."

He let the slaves dry and shave him, and forced himself to eat something. He had been a fool, he thought bitterly, trying to drown his sorrows in wine when the world was falling to pieces around him. Somewhere during the process of returning to sanity he had realized that tomorrow must be Samaine. Half the tribesmen in the West would be converging on Vernemeton for the festival. It didn't matter what Eilan and Senara thought of him. His blood ran cold at the thought of their danger if a war started there.

"I'll get your niece to safety," he told Valerius as he prepared to ride out of Deva. *And Eilan, and the boy . . . and if they still hate me they can tell me about it on the way home.* He folded back his cloak to free his arms, and patted the last thing he had borrowed from Valerius – a sword.

Not all the years since the coming of the Romans – not all the years since the building of the great Temple of the Sun on the plain, could have been longer to Eilan than the next two days. The night before the Samaine festival seemed to last a thousand years. She had sent Senara away hours ago. As the lights burned down, it seemed to her that the growing shadows were engulfing her own spirit as well.

This must have been what was meant when the warning had come to her; death had waited within her heart and spirit like a seed; it seemed now to expand through her body like an unfolding flower. Her heart pounded as if it would break through walls of bone. Even when her child was born she had felt no such pain. But whether the pain was of the body or of the mind and spirit she could not tell.

When she dozed, her dreams were chaotic; she saw Caillean surrounded by evil men. Then the priestess raised her arms to heaven, lightning flared, and when Eilan could see again, her attackers were stretched lifeless on the ground. But Caillean was lying still as well, and Eilan could not tell if she lived.

She came to herself, shaking, her cheeks wet with tears. Had that been a true seeing? Caillean ought to be safe on the holy Tor with her priestesses. But if she was not, then what hope was there in the world?

Toward morning, Eilan crept into the room where Lia had put Gawen to bed. Huw, barefoot, padded softly at her heels. For almost the first time since she had taken up her duties as High Priestess, she found herself resenting the big man, as if Huw was taking up air which she needed for her own breath.

She remembered a horror story she had heard in the House of Maidens; how a Priestess of the past had been attacked by her own guard, and given him over to the priests to be put to death. For the first time, she could understand how that woman, desperate for a little human warmth, could have reached out to the only thing human within her reach, and how her appeal might have been misunderstood. Shuddering, she turned to Huw and told him to wait at the door.

Ah, gods, she thought, *if only Caillean were here – or Lhiannon – or even my mother – or anyone so that I were not so desperately alone.* But there was no one. In her mind even Senara, for all her weeping and denial, was a foe. And her father? He was the greatest of her enemies.

She looked long on Gawen's sleeping face. It seemed impossible that the pounding of her heart should not be loud enough to awaken him. Had this big boy actually been so small that he could lie in his father's two hands? He had grown from something smaller than the seed of a flower, engendered in that moment in the forest when her last defenses had gone down before Gaius's need. And yet at the time she had been triumphant, certain that this was a sacred thing.

And Gawen was beautiful. How, out of such sorrow could such

beauty be born? She scanned again the childish features, and the long body with hands and feet just a bit too big, discerning within them the promise of the man he could become. She could not see that he resembled Gaius all that much. Once, that had disappointed her, but at least now she would not have to suppress a flicker of hatred whenever she glimpsed his father in his eyes.

But he was Gaius's son; and because of him, she had been willing to let Gaius marry the daughter of a Roman official. Only now, it seemed, he was going to divorce Julia and renounce all his promises for the sake of Senara, who might as well have been her own little sister. Senara, who was younger, and apparently to Gaius, more beautiful.

At Eilan's waist hung the curved dagger she had been given when she became a priestess. She fingered it for a moment. So often, at the rites, she had used it to draw the ritual drop of blood for the cauldron of prophecy. There, at the wrist where she could see the pounding of the blood, one stroke, hard and deep, would end all her troubles, at least for this lifetime. Why should she wait for the fate that the Goddess had promised her? But if she took her life, what would become of Gawen?

Deliberately Eilan took the sickle and returned it to the small sheath at her waist. In the faltering light of the lamp her face must have shown something she had not intended, for Huw rushed forward.

"Lady?"

"We will go back to my rooms now, and then you must bring Senara to me."

It was not long before he returned with the girl in tow. Senara's dress was wrinkled; her eyes were hot and her cheeks smeared as if she had been crying. She saw Eilan and cried out, "Lady, forgive me; not for the world —"

"Be quiet," Eilan said. "I haven't the strength for any more of this. I have had a warning of death; it is a gift of the Goddess that the High Priestess shall know her time." She drew breath, and Senara, seeing the little dagger loose in its sheath at her waist, went white beneath her tears.

"That cannot be true," she said desperately. "It is written in the holy books that no man knows what a day may bring forth —"

"Silence," Eilan said tiredly. "There is something very important that I must say to you. If I am wrong, it will not matter whether you believe me, but if I am right, there is something I must ask."

"Of me? Anything," Senara said submissively.

Eilan drew a long breath. "You heard me say that Gaius and I had a son. Gawen is that child. I want you to marry Gaius and take his son away with you. Promise me" – her voice, which had been perfectly steady when she spoke of her own death, broke – "promise me only that you will be good to him."

"Oh no," Senara cried out. "I would not now marry Gaius Severus if he were the only man on the face of the earth."

"You promised to do as I asked," Eilan said quietly. "Is this how you keep your word?"

Senara looked up, and again her eyes spilled over. She said, "I want only to do what is right. If you think –" She stopped, breathing hard. "If God has chosen to take you, I suppose it is His business, but you must not lay hands on your own life, Eilan!"

Eilan drew all her dignity about her like a cloak as she said, "It does not really matter to me whether you believe it or not. But if you will not help me, Senara, then you may go."

Senara trembled. "I will not leave you alone in this state."

"Then for Gaius's sake, take care of his boy."

"It is for the boy's sake I tell you that you must live," Senara entreated. "You have a child, however that came about, and your life is not your own. Gawen is a beautiful boy. You must live to see him grown. And Gaius –"

"Ah, don't speak of him, I beg you –"

"My Lady," said Senara, shaking, "I tell you, Gaius still cares for you and for his son."

"He has forgotten me."

"I am sure he has not," Senara insisted. "Let me remind him of what is due to the mother of his son. Let me speak to him of his duty as a father, and as a Roman. I am sure that would reach his better nature even if nothing else could do so."

Was it possible? Could Senara actually do that? And would she?

"I believe the warning that the Goddess sent me," she said finally, "but if I live through Samaine, you may try. But before you do, you must get Gawen to safety. I am afraid of what may happen at the festival. Tomorrow – no, tonight," she corrected herself, for it was nearly dawn, "leave the Forest House. Take Gawen to your Father Petros in the forest. No one will think to look for you there!"

thirty

~~~

When Caillean recovered her senses, she knew that she must have been unconscious for some time, for her gown was soaked through. What had wakened her was the sound of a farm cart jolting over the ruts and pits of the road. In the cart were four or five men well armed with cudgels, and a couple of hefty guards walked a few paces ahead with torches. Had they frightened her attackers away? Something must have, for she had not been violated after her assailant struck her down.

Caillean managed to pull herself upright, though the effort made her feel as if the top of her head would fall off. Sprawled around her she could see bodies, and a stink of burnt flesh reached her even through the rain.

One of the men with the torches saw her and quavered, "Be you a ghost, lady? Don't hurt us . . ."

"I give you my word I am no ghost," Caillean said as steadily as she could, "but a priestess from the temple in the Summer Country, left here after an attack by bandits."

Now she could see her litter, turned on its side, the two young priests lying beside it, their throats cut, their golden torques plundered, staring up emptily at the sky. Caillean regarded them with dismay.

And then she looked at the blackened corpses around her and realized that where she had been powerless the gods at least had not. She would rather have saved the young men, but at least they had been avenged.

"Where were you a-going, lady?" asked the farmer from his perch in the driver's seat of the cart.

She controlled her voice with an effort, turning away from the dead men. "To the Forest House near Deva."

"Ah, that explains it then; I understand there's still one of the

Legions left there, and the roads are patrolled. These days, no one puts his nose outside his own door around here without a couple of bodyguards. It will be a good thing when we have a new Emperor, and can get some protection again."

Caillean blinked, for the man spoke the British tongue like a native. It was a measure of the degree to which Britain had become Roman that the native folk should regret the lack of an Emperor.

"I see they killed your bodyguard, lady," said the man driving the cart. "Did you have slaves to carry your litter? You don't any more – no doubt they've taken to their heels." He drew up in the road beside her and stopped, staring at the bodies of the Bacaudae. He looked at her again and made an ancient sign of reverence.

"My Lady – I see that the gods watch over you. We're bound the other way, but we'll take you to the next village, where you can get litter bearers and guards."

He helped her up into the cart and wrapped her in a dry blanket. Some of his men lifted the bodies of the young priests into the wagon. Caillean, huddled in her cloak and the farmer's rough blanket, reflected miserably that from now on she would be getting the best of whatever these folk could offer her, but no power on earth could bring her to the Forest House before Samaine.

Gaius was surprised to find the road south from Deva crowded with other travelers. It took him a moment to remember that they must be going down to the festival. But the glances he got as he rode by were not friendly, and after a time he felt it wiser to turn off the road and take a path through the hills so that he could come at the Forest House from the direction of Father Petros's hermitage.

A cold wind was rattling the bare branches like bones, though for the moment it had ceased to rain. Samaine was the feast of the dead; the Romans considered it a day of ill omen. Well, he thought, it was certainly that for him. But he did not consider turning back. He had fallen into a fatalistic mood he remembered from his days with the Legions; the grim acceptance men find sometimes before battle, when survival is less important than honor. He was not sure he had any left, after the last few days, but he would redeem what he could, no matter what it cost.

As he rode, the beauty in the autumn woods moved him despite, or perhaps because of his grim mood. Gaius realized then that in the past year or so he had learned to love this land. Whoever triumphed in the current conflict, he would not go back to Rome.

Hard as he tried to fulfill Macellius's ambitions, he had never completely belonged in his father's world, yet he was far too Roman to feel anything but an impostor among the tribes. But the trees did not despise him as a barbarian or the stones hate him as a conqueror. In the peace of the forest, Gaius was at home.

He saw smoke rising from Father Petros's hut, and thought for a moment of going in. But the place made him remember Senara. Gaius did not think he could bear that memory, and he was certain he would not be able to keep his temper if the priest came out with any of his holy platitudes.

He supposed that his errant legionaries would be hiding somewhere until nightfall. He tethered his mount loosely enough so that it could pull free if he did not return soon and began to make his way carefully around the building, keeping to the woods that edged the cleared land.

Dusk was falling before he saw movement in the bushes ahead of him. Cautious as a cat, he moved forward. Two soldiers were crouched in the lee of some hazels. They had been dicing to pass the time, and now they were arguing about whether or not to light a fire.

"Flavius Macro!" Gaius snapped in his best tone of command. Automatically, the man came to attention, then looked wildly around him.

"Who is it —" the second soldier had his hand on his sword. Gaius trod loudly on a branch to warn him and moved into the last of the light.

"It's, why it's Gaius Macellius," said Macro. "Sir, what are you doing here?"

"I should think it is rather my place to ask that of you," said Gaius, releasing his breath. "They know in Deva that you are gone. What do you think will happen if they find out you came here?"

The man's face turned gray-white. "You wouldn't tell them, would you, sir?"

Gaius pretended to hesitate long enough for the men to shudder, then shrugged. "Well, I'm not your officer. If you head back now you shouldn't get into too much trouble, not with all that's going on in the town."

"Sir, we can't do that," said the other man. "Longus is still in there."

Gaius felt his heart sink. "You can't help him by staying here," he said evenly. "Go on, that's an order. I'll do what I can for your friend."

His tension eased a little as he heard them crashing off through the trees, but even one legionary was too many if found where he had no business to be.

Moving as if he were leading a patrol back on the border, Gaius slipped across the open space to the wall. There should be a back gate somewhere – the wall was intended more as a symbol of separation than an actual defense. His hand touched the latch, and then he was easing into the open space where he had seen his son playing ball. Senara had chattered a great deal about her life here. The big building in front of him must be the House of Maidens. There was a dark patch behind the kitchen that looked like a good place to watch from. He crept towards it.

Someone else had thought so too. As he knelt, he touched bare skin. Someone yelped and there was a brief struggle before Gaius got the fellow pinned with a hand over his mouth.

"Longus?" he whispered. His captive nodded vigorously. "Your wager is off. Your companions have gone home, and if you know what's good for you you'll follow them." Longus sighed, then nodded again, and Gaius let him go. But as the man crossed the yard, a door opened and lamplight spilled across the ground. Longus froze like a trapped hare. "Run, you fool!" Gaius hissed from the shadows.

Longus scrambled over the gate, but suddenly the place was alive with men in white robes. Druid priests! thought Gaius. What were they doing here? His hiding place would be revealed in a moment, for they were bringing torches. He began to edge around the building. Somebody swore in British behind him and he whirled, instinctively drawing his sword.

The man screamed as the blade went in and the others came pelting towards him. Gaius fought as well as he could, and he supposed he must have done some damage, from the brutality with which they clubbed and kicked him after superior numbers had finally brought him down.

"Well, Daughter, are you ready for the festival?" Bendeigid, arrayed in the ceremonial bull-hide cloak and the golden ornaments of the Arch-Druid over his white woolen gown, looked magnificent, but Eilan's heart sank as she returned his salutation.

"I am ready," she said quietly. The maidens had come as they did before every festival to prepare her. *For the last time*, her heart cried as they bathed her and set the sacred wreath of vervain on her brow. At least she would go the Goddess cleansed and sanctified.

For a moment he leaned on his staff, looking at her. Then he gestured to the priests and her women to leave them.

"Listen, child, there is no longer any need to dissemble. They have told me how Ardanos used to come to you, and the tricks he used to bind your will. I am sorry I accused you of betraying us before."

Eilan kept her gaze lowered, afraid he would see the anger in her eyes. For thirteen years she had been High Priestess, mistress of the Forest House, the most respected woman in the land. Why was he talking as if she were still a child? But this was the loving father who had once said he would rather see her drowned than a Roman's bride. She could not afford to antagonize him; in the confusion, it had been afternoon before Senara and Lia had been able to leave the Forest House with Gawen. She had to buy time for them to get well away.

In the same neutral tone, she asked, "What do you want of me?"

"The Romans are tearing each other to pieces." He grinned wolfishly. "There will never be a better time for us to rise against them. This is the season of slaughter, when the doors open between the worlds. Let us call on Cathubodva, let us raise the spirits of our dead against them. Raise the tribes against Rome, Daughter, summon them to war!"

Eilan repressed a shiver. Much as she had resented Ardanos, her grandfather had been a subtle man, never so blinded by his own dreams that he could not be talked round if he saw something else that would serve. Her father was far more dangerous, because he would sacrifice all else to his inflexible ideals. Yet all she had to do to stay safe was to agree with him. Then she felt the familiar throbbing in her temple, and remembered that whatever she did would not be for long.

"Father," she began, "Ardanos interpreted my answers as it pleased him, and I suppose that you will do the same, but you do not understand about the sacred trance and how the Goddess comes."

She heard a tumult outside and realized that he was no longer listening. The door crashed open, and priests with tangled hair and blood on their robes pushed through the crowd, dragging something that had been a man.

"What is this?" Eilan put all the hauteur a dozen years had taught her into her tone and the babble stilled.

"An intruder, Lady," said one of the priests. "We found him

outside the House of Maidens. There was another man, but he got away."

"He killed Dinan!"

"He must have been after one of the priestesses!"

"But which one?"

This time it was the Arch-Druid who brought silence by striking the floor with his staff. "Who are you, fellow, and what were you doing here?"

Eilan shut her eyes, hoping no one would notice that the man's ripped tunic was made from good Roman cloth. Even grimed with blood and dust she knew Gaius, but perhaps no one else would, if she made no sign. *Did he come here for Senara*, she wondered, *or for his son?*

"Don't you recognize him, Lord Druid?" Dieda pushed her way forward. Eilan winced at the edge in her laughter. "Well, perhaps he is not so handsome now. Your men have netted a fine pig for our feasting. If you look, you will see the scar of the boar pit on his shoulder there."

Bendeigid should have been your father, thought Eilan hysterically, *and Ardanos mine!* They pulled the prisoner's head up and for a moment he met her appalled gaze, then the sense left his eyes once more.

"You!" Bendeigid's voice held mingled astonishment and fury. "Have you not done enough damage to me and mine that you should trouble us now?" Suddenly his expression changed. "Well, you shall do so no longer. Dieda, show my men where they can bathe him and tend his wounds, but by no means unbind him. Garic and Vedras" – he pointed to the two most senior Druids – "we must talk. The rest of you, leave us alone!"

The priests dragged Gaius away and the room emptied. Eilan sat back in her chair, wondering whether the pain in her belly was an echo of the throbbing in her head, or fear.

"I see that you know the man," said Vedras, the elder of the two Druids who had remained, "Who is he?"

"His name is Gaius Macellius Severus the younger," snarled Bendeigid.

"The Prefect's son!" exclaimed Garic. "Do you think he came for one of the priestesses as they say?"

"It does not matter why he came," said Vedras. "We must get him out of here. The Red-cloaks would deny our right to punish even an ordinary legionary. The gods alone know what they will do to us for laying hands on a chieftain's son!"

"Indeed," Bendeigid smiled craftily. "But I do not believe his own people know where he has gone. And no one here knows his name or even that he is a Roman but Dieda and ourselves."

"Then you mean to kill him secretly?"

"Not secretly." Bendeigid's gaze burned like a flame. "Do not you understand? For such a man as this to deliver himself into our hands is a sign from the gods. Let his death at least serve some purpose. We will never find a more noble offering!"

He turned to Garic. "Go tell the men who are guarding the prisoner to dress him in the finest robe you can find."

Eilan felt a chill lift the hair on her arms. An image of the Year-King walking through the Beltane fair came to her, garlanded and clad in an embroidered tunic.

"And if the Romans learn of it?" asked Vedras.

"It is true, their wrath will be terrible," said the Arch-Druid triumphantly. "So terrible that even those who call for peace now will have no choice but to follow us to war!"

For a long moment the other Druid looked at him. Then he nodded, and followed Garic out the door.

"Did Gaius come with your knowledge, Eilan?" Bendeigid asked when they were alone. "Have you been seeing this monster all along?"

"I have not," she whispered, "by the Goddess I swear it!"

"I suppose it does not matter whether I believe you," the Arch-Druid muttered. "All truth will be tested at the Samaine fire."

"*Behold, the holy priestess comes, the sacred herbs are in her crown,*" the priests were singing, but tonight there were more verses to their hymn, with different words.

> "*War! War! Let British woods*
> *A warrior bear for every tree;*
> *As ravening wolves attack the sheep*
> *So shall we make the Romans flee!*"

Gaius groaned, but the prick of a spear kept him moving. If only that bitch Dieda had not identified him! Macellius would grieve when he heard of the death of his son; but he would be shamed when the manner of it was known. How could he have blundered so badly, provoking the very incident he had hoped to prevent? He had not even succeeded in saving those he loved. The only ray of hope in all this was that he had not seen Senara anywhere, or the boy.

The road up the Hill of the Maidens had never seemed so steep before. He much preferred the last time he had come up here, he thought grimly, with a weapon in his hand and a detachment of cavalry behind him! The embroidered robe rasped his abrasions, and the sacred garland pricked his brow. They had cleaned him up and given him a drink that cleared his head, but Gaius had no illusions about what was in store for him.

From the top of the hill he could see the glow of a great bonfire. Memories of a time before he had entered his father's world were returning with frightening clarity. The Silures had sacrificed one of their own princes in those last days before the Romans crushed them utterly. The man had been one of his uncles, with the royal dragons tattooed on his arms. Gaius's mother had tried to hide her half-Roman child, but he had seen them take the Year-King away. He had been smiling, believing his death would help his people.

And what is it, he wondered then, *that I will be dying for?*

Then they were on the hilltop. A ring of priests surrounded them; beyond, Gaius saw a sea of faces, grim or gleeful as they listened to the Druids' song. Was Eilan glad or sorry to see him here? He wished he could see her face behind the veil.

Eilan stood beside her father with Dieda and two other priestesses behind her. For the first time he wondered if she also was a prisoner. She had rejected him. It seemed to him that he should be glad of her downfall, but even his own danger had not filled him with such fear as the thought of hers.

> *"Destroy them all! Avenge our shame!*
> *Now let the slaughter be begun!*
> *In ranks the Roman troops shall fall*
> *As by the scythe the corn is mown!"*

The singing ended and the drums grew silent, but a murmur swept through the people and Gaius knew this was only a pause in the storm.

"Children of Don!" the Arch-Druid cried. "It is Samaine Eve! This is a time of changes! The new year is beginning, and a new era for this land! Let the changing of the seasons sweep away the Romans who have blighted Britannia! Tonight we shall gladden the gods of war with a sacrifice. But we must purge our ranks of all offenders. Traitor," he turned to Gaius, "we can make your death hard or easy. Tell us what you came to Vernemeton to do!"

"Kill me, if you will, but ask no foolish questions!" Gaius said hoarsely. "I will say only that I meant no harm to any here." Perhaps he had not lived well, but at least he could die with dignity.

"You were in the sacred precinct, where no men but the Druids may come. Have you seduced one of our maidens? Which of them did you come to carry away?"

Gaius shook his head and gasped as a spearpoint pressed into his side. There was a sensation of warmth and he felt blood trickling down.

"Was it Rhian, Tanais, Bethoc?" the litany went on. For each name they cut him again. Once he tried to drive himself upon the spearpoint, but his captors knew their business and held him still. Loss of blood and the ill-treatment he had already endured were making him dizzy. *Soon,* he thought, *I will pass out and it will not matter what they do to me.*

"Senara . . ."

At the name, Gaius jerked involuntarily. In the next moment he tried to conceal his reaction, but no one was watching him. Eilan had stepped forward and thrown back her veil.

"Stop!" she said clearly. "I can tell you who the Roman came for. It was I!"

What is she saying? Gaius stared at her in horror. Then he understood that she must be trying to protect Senara, and perhaps the child. In that moment she had an unearthly beauty. In comparison, Senara's unformed prettiness was a star paled by the full moon's majesty. As had happened sometimes in the moment before battle, Gaius saw his own heart with a terrible clarity. He cared about Senara, but his desire for her had not been love. In the younger woman he had only been trying to recover Eilan as she had been when he first knew her, the maiden that time and his own mistakes had put forever beyond his grasp.

In the shocked silence, the only sound was the crackling of the fire. For a moment some powerful emotion contorted the Arch-Druid's features, then he mastered it and turned from Eilan to Gaius.

"For your sake and hers, on your honor I ask you to tell me if this is true."

True . . . For a moment the word had no meaning. Torn between

Rome and Britannia, he did not even know who he was himself. How could he know whom he loved? Slowly Gaius straightened and met Eilan's clear gaze. Her eyes seemed to be asking him a question. At that, all the tension went out of him in a long sigh.

"It is true," he said softly. "I have always loved Eilan."

For a moment Eilan closed her eyes, dizzied by a tide of joy. Gaius had understood her, but he had not spoken only for the sake of Senara. She had seen such a look – such an expression of wonder – on his face once only, when he held her in his arms on that Beltane so long ago.

"Have you betrayed us all along then?" Bendeigid hissed, bending close to her ear. "Were you lying when you swore to me that he had not touched you? Or did it begin later, when you were a sworn virgin of the temple? Has he been teaching you Roman lies along with his love-talk, and treason with his caresses? Did you lie with him in the sacred precincts, or in the Sacred Grove?"

She could feel her father's fury, but she seemed to see him through a wall of Roman glass. In the end it had all become so simple. She was living under sentence of death already, and had faced its terrors. Now that the time was come, she was not afraid at all.

"I lay with the Sacred King once only," she said calmly, "as was my right, at the Beltane fires . . ."

"What do you mean?" Miellyn exclaimed behind her. "It was Dieda who had to be sent away – it was Dieda who had a child!"

"It was not!" The shocked echo of speculation ceased as Dieda hurried to the Arch-Druid's side. "They made me agree to the deception. I took her place while she went away to have the baby, and when she returned, they exiled *me*! She has queened it over the Forest House ever since as if she were as chaste as the moon, but it was all a lie!"

"But I always served the Goddess, not the Romans!" Eilan cried, her composure cracking at the threat to her child. She saw fury replacing the questions in Bendeigid's eyes as he turned on her. The people crowed closer, trying to hear; voices rose in query or condemnation. Rumors of trouble among the Romans had made them like tinder that any spark could set aflame. If she appealed to them, would she set in motion the very catastrophe she had suffered so to avoid?

"Why should I believe you, bitch?" snarled her father. "Your whole life has been a lie!"

411

He lifted his hand to strike her. A bulky form burst through the line of Druids; Huw, with his cudgel upraised to defend her one last time. But more priests were running between them. Before Huw could reach Bendeigid, bronze blades flared in the firelight, came away a deeper crimson and stabbed once more. Again the Druids struck, and again, and Huw, still struggling towards her, fell without a cry.

Huw would have attacked the Arch-Druid himself, if he had threatened me . . . Eilan thought numbly, and in the end, he had.

"Take him away," Bendeigid was breathing hard. "He was a fool." Abruptly he turned, and grasped Eilan by the arm. "If you had been true, I would have asked you to invoke the Goddess to bless us. But instead, you shall be Her sacrifice!"

Why should that frighten me? My life has been one long offering, thought Eilan as her father dragged her across the circle to stand at Gaius's side. There was a mutter from the people at that. Some of those who had heard the accusations wanted her blood immediately, others thought it sacrilege to lay hands on the High Priestess, whatever her crime.

"Eilan, can you forgive me?" Gaius said in a low voice. "I was never worthy of your love. You wanted me to be your Sacred King, but I am only an ordinary man . . ."

She turned to look at him, and found a nobility in his bruised face that had never been there before. She wished that she could take him in her arms, but the priests were holding her and she realized that he did not need it; she no longer saw the lost child that before had always waited in his eyes. He met her gaze without flinching, at peace with himself at last.

"I see a god in you," Eilan answered fiercely. "I see a spirit that will never die. We did what was required of us, and if we did not do as well as we would have wished, the Lady's purpose was accomplished all the same. Surely it will be given to us to walk together in the Summerland for a time before we come back again."

"You have called him a Sacred King," said Bendeigid hoarsely, "and as such he shall die."

Slowly she saw the stern acceptance that had upheld Gaius deepen to a kind of wonder. He continued to gaze at her as they slipped the noose around his neck and began to tighten it. But before the sword went in beneath his ribs, his eyes had lost focus, fixed for ever on something beyond the world. The blood was still pumping from his breast when they carried him to the fire.

"Tell me, Priestess, what omens do you read in this sacrifice?" Eilan turned her gaze from the flames to her father, and something in her face made him take a step backwards, though she had not moved.

"I see royal blood that sanctifies the ground," she said in a still voice. "In this man the seed of Rome and Britannia was mingled, and you have bound it for ever to the land by giving him to the sacred fire."

Eilan took a deep breath. Her head was pounding so that she could hardly see, but it no longer mattered. The final thing she had desired to see in this world was the glory in Gaius's eyes. There was a roaring in her ears. She felt the surge of trance taking her though she had not tasted the sacred herbs, and heard a voice that was not her own ring out.

"Hear me, ye men of the Cornovii and the Ordovices and all you others of the tribes, for this is the last time a priestess shall prophesy from this sacred hill. Hide your swords, oh warriors, and put away your spears, for not until the ninth generation has been born and died shall the Roman Eagles depart. And when they have flown, those who bear your blood and theirs together shall be left to defend the land!"

"You are lying! You must be lying!" Bendeigid's voice cracked. "You betrayed your oaths!"

Eilan felt herself falling back into her body; pain stabbed her temple, but she shook her head. "I did not, for Gaius was the Year-King. You yourself have made it so, and thus my love for him was no sin!"

Bendeigid swayed, his face contorting with the agony of a man who sees all his certainties crumbling. "If what you say is truth," he cried, "let the Goddess show us a sign before I give you living to the fire!"

Even as he spoke, it seemed to Eilan that a great thunder crashed through her head; startled by the weight of it, she felt herself slip to her knees. Her father reached out, but she was sliding down a long tunnel away from him. Her heartbeat was a fading drum; then it ceased suddenly, and she was free.

So the Goddess struck me down after all, Eilan thought with an odd clarity. *But it was Her mercy, not Her wrath!*

Far below she could see people bending over her motionless body. This was the ending that had awaited her since she had lain in Gaius's arms, but she had delayed it long enough to build a bridge between her people and his. Two of the Druids were holding her father upright; he was still shouting, but the people were turning from him with frightened faces, beginning to stream away down the hill.

She saw the priests lifting the flesh she had abandoned and carrying it to the pyre on which Gaius was already burning. Then she turned away from that lesser light to the radiance that was opening before her, brighter than the fire, more lovely than the moon.

epilogue

CAILLEAN SPEAKS

When I arrived at the Forest House the following evening, all the Samaine fires had burned out and only ashes remained. It took some time to find anyone who could give me a coherent account of what had happened. Miellyn had not been seen; some people thought she had died trying to shield Eilan. Eilidh had been killed in the fighting that followed the sacrifice. Dieda was dead also; she lay in the sanctuary, and it was clear that she had fallen by her own hand.

There was certainly no sense to be got from Bendeigid and, except for those Druids who had stayed to tend him, the priesthood had scattered. So, thank the gods, had the warriors who had gathered for the festival. But I found that the folk who remained were eager to obey me, for I was the closest thing they had to a High Priestess now.

I moved through the tumult, giving orders with a calm that astonished me, for I dared not give way to a grief that might prove measureless. Yet there had to be some meaning to all this; a life – or a death – must not be wasted.

The following day I was awakened by the news that a party of Romans had requested an interview with the High Priestess. I went out and saw Macellius Severus with his secretary behind him and another man whom they said was the father of Gaius's Roman wife, sitting their horses under a weeping autumn sky. I was impressed by the fact that he had come here without a detachment of soldiers to back him. But then his son had been brave enough too, at the end.

It was hard to face Macellius, knowing the answer to the question he did not quite dare to ask me, and realizing that I could never tell him how his boy had died. By now the most amazing rumors were flying about the countryside. Gaius had died as a

British Year-King, and though some thought he was a Roman, the only people who knew his name had a powerful reason for keeping silence.

Disorganized the Romans might be, but they still had the force to drown the countryside in blood if they found proof that a Roman officer had been sacrificed on that hill. But of course there was no body, only a pile of ashes mingled with the embers of the Samaine fire.

As they were leaving, Macellius turned to me, and I saw that hope was not quite dead in his eyes. "There was a boy living in the Forest House," he said. "They called him Gawen. I believe he is . . . my grandson. Can you tell me where he is now?"

This time, at least, I could answer truthfully that I did not know, for Gawen had not been seen since Samaine Eve, the day that his nurse and Senara had also disappeared.

For it was not until the third day afterward that Senara came creeping back, her young face haggard with tears, followed by a lanky lad who looked about him with troubled eyes.

"She died for my sake," Senara sobbed when we told her what had happened to Eilan. "She condemned herself to save me – and her child."

My throat was aching, but I forced myself to speak calmly. "Then her sacrifice must not be wasted. Will you take the vows and serve the Goddess in her place, now that she is gone?"

"I cannot, I cannot," wailed Senara. "It would be a sin, for I am a Nazarene. Father Petros is moving into Deva. He will let me stay in his hermitage, and I will spend the rest of my days in prayer!"

I blinked, for suddenly it seemed to me that I could see that small house in the forest surrounded by many others. In time, I thought, more female hermits would gather around her. And what I saw then has indeed come to pass, for this was one of the first of the pious sisterhoods that now serve the people as the Forest House did then; but that was many years in the future. Did Eilan foresee it? Either way, the younger woman had played her part. Senara might refuse to become High Priestess of Vernemeton, but in a sense she was still Eilan's heir.

"Will you take Gawen to his grandfather?" Senara asked. "I cannot keep him with me once I have taken Christian vows."

Which one? I wondered wryly, and then I realized that I was unwilling to surrender the boy to either of those old men, both still prisoned by the hatred of a dying past.

"Gawen . . ." I looked at him, and saw a creature neither Roman nor Briton, neither boy nor man, standing on the threshold of possibility. In the end, Eilan had died so that this child might live in a new world. "I am going back to the Summer Country, where the mists roll around the vale that they call Afallon. Will you come with me?"

"Is that the Summerland?" he asked. "They tell me my mother has gone there."

"Not quite." My eyes filled. "But close to it, some would say."

He looked around him and shivered, and I thought how hard it must be for him, not yet really knowing what he had lost. Almost as hard as it was for me, who understood all too well.

Then he looked up at me, and I saw a spirit that resembled neither grandfather, nor his parents either, looking out of his eyes.

"Very well. I will come with you to Afallon."

Here at the heart of the Summer Country I sometimes wonder why of all who played such a part in this story, I alone have been spared. I know that I am only beginning to see the great design in all of this. Can it be that Eilan's child, who represents two great strains which have gone into the making of our people, will be the founder of a line from which their savior shall one day spring?

I have not been told. I have not even the counsel of the Merlin, although Eilan said once that he had spoken to her of her destiny. There must be some pattern. I know only that it is from the Eagle and the Dragon, not the Raven of vengeance, that a defender shall come for our land, and perhaps the Merlin will take flesh to aid that hero in his day . . .

Here in the Summer Country, where the ringstones shadow the mighty Tor and the promise of power remains, I await the outcome of the tale.

LADY OF AVALON

MARION ZIMMER BRADLEY
Bestselling author of *The Mists of Avalon*

This enchanting story of the holy isle spans the creation of Avalon itself and foreshadows the birth of King Arthur. Conjuring myth, magic, romance, and history, it tells of three powerful priestesses who steer the fortunes of legendary Britain as they struggle with their own destinies. Caillean, reclaiming the old magic, founds a sisterhood to serve the Great Goddess, fosters the orphan Gawen—heir to the mystic royal line—and veils Avalon from the hostile world in its everlasting mists. The tribal princess Teleri, schooled in the ways of Avalon, seeks in vain to save it by her marriage to a Roman general. And Viviane, high priestess of Avalon and Lady of the Lake, must safeguard the Grail and prepare the way for the King to come.

Spellbinding, dynamically plotted, rich in ritual, character, and the turbulence of Roman Britain, *Lady of Avalon* is brimming with lush epic grandeur and fantastic mystical power.

Available from VIKING

Prices slightly higher in Canada   (857831—$24.95)